Ex Terra Expeditions

Westley Stark

ISBN: 978-1-956150-10-0 (7x10 paperback)
       978-1-956150-11-7 (EPUB)

Library of Congress Control Number (LCCN): 2021907516

Published with the assistance of
    Turner Publishing, a service of
    TurnerEditing.com

Dedication

This story is dedicated to my children…*all* of them, and *their* children as well. It started off as yet another bedtime tale intended to entertain, but it grew to have a life of its own. I have struggled over this epic for waay too many years, but like all good things, it takes time to come to full realization.

Acknowledgements

This book could not have been possible without the support of the members of the local writers community, especially Sacramento Suburban Writers Club. Specifically, I would like to thank the critique groups who helped teach me the ways of writing:

- The Third Wednesday Critique Group (We could have come up with a better name for our group, but it never became a priority.) members including Tom Hessler, Mort Rumberg, Mary Lou Anderson, Ron Smith
- The Book Lover's Critique Group members including Brad Simkins, Myrl Pardee, and Mort Rumberg (again)

Thanks also to my beta readers: Jeannie Turner and Phyllistean Hamilton, who gave numerous points of feedback, edits, grammar corrections, etc. (Though all remaining errors are mine alone.)

Biggest thanks to my wife, Kim, who allowed me the time to write (as opposed to mowing the front yard or something else useful) and kept me fed while I was so focused on writing that I never even noticed the passing of time.

Origin of the *Stark* Name

From Sir John Mackenzie's History of Scotland

Crest: Stark (Killermont, Scotland, 1642) beareth azur a chevron argent between three acorns in chief or. and a bulls head erased of ye 2nd. in base. A Dexter hand holding by the horns a bull's head erased or distilling drops of blood.
Motto: Fortiorum fortia facta. "Strong Deeds of Strong (or Brave) Men"
These of ye name are descended of one John Muirhead, 2nd. son of ye Laird of Lachop, who at hunting one day in ye forest of Cumbernauld seeing King James ye 4 in hazard of his life by a bull hottly w'th ye hounds, stept in betwixt ye King and ye bull and griping ye bull by ye horns, and by his strenth almost wrung ye head from him, for which he was called Stark and his posteritie after him, and bears ye rugged Bull's Head in theire armes.
Ye old sword of ye family has on it Stark alias Muirhead.

A bit of history concerning the Stark Family

The family of Stark is derived from that of Muirhead of Lachop, who are derived from Muirhead of that ilk of Bothwell and can be authenticated to the 6th century. As now prepared and authenticated, the pedigree begins in Muirhead of that ilk of Bothwell 1100 descending by Primogeniture until in the reign of Robert 2nd. of Scotland 1347 Muirhead etc. was created Laird of Lachop. Following the same rule in 1480 John Muirhead 3rd. son of the then Laird of Lachop by reason of his bravery was named John Stark, Stark in ancient Gallic meaning strength, and was given the estate of Killermont, which was on the banks of the River Kelvin just before it enters the Clyde, near Dumbarton Castle, and the last Stark to occupy it sold it in the 1700s.

The name then appears as John Stark of Killermont. Following down by primogeniture we find John Stark of Killermont in 1635 noted as a zealous Covenanter. His grandson John Stark of Killermont was the first one to depart from the custom by calling his eldest son Archibald. Said Archibald married Eleanor Nichols of Londonderry, Ireland, and moved to America in 1720.

Archibald Stark and Eleanor Nichols were the parents of John Stark who later became a general in the American Revolution. Early in his military career, Indian warriors captured him and forced him to run a gauntlet of warriors armed with sticks, but he grabbed the stick from the first warrior's hands and proceeded to attack him, taking the rest of the warriors by surprise. Impressed by his actions, the chief adopted him into the tribe. Years later, as second in command of Rogers' Rangers, he was directed to attack those same Indians, but he refused to accompany the troops.

He was also known for his ability to anticipate enemy action. When the French attacked Fort William Henry, the regular enlisted were in no condition to fight because they had been celebrating St. Patrick's Day the previous day, but Stark had refused to let his Rangers carouse with the rest, so they were ready to defend the entire Fort, driving off the French. On the occasion of the Battle of Bunker Hill, he correctly identified the route the British would take and defended it against at least three waves of troops, causing massive losses to the attackers.

He is well known for his closing comment in a letter to fellow military leaders: "Live free or die: Death is not the worst of evils."

Another military man in the family tree (though with a variant spelling of the name) was William Edwin Starke, who served as a brigadier general in the Confederate States Army during the American Civil War. Said of him upon his death:

> "I cannot forbear doing but scant justice to a gallant soldier now no more. It was my fortune during the two days of battle, during which he commanded the division, to be thrown constantly in contact with Brigadier-General Starke. The buoyant dash with which he led his brigade into the most withering fire on Friday, though then in command of the division; the force he showed in the handling of this command; the coolness and judgment which distinguished him in action, made him to me a marked man, and I regretted his early death as a great loss to the army and the cause."

—Col. Bradley T. Johnson, in his official report on Second Manassas, concerning the death of Starke.

(As a bearer of bad news, I have to tell you that there is no one named Tony or Howard or Rickard in this branch of the family tree.)

Table of Contents

C HAPTER Z ERO
I T B EGINS

Ben and his friends sat at the big table in the corner of their favorite café. He smiled as the waitress set a steaming bowl of grits in front of him. Glancing at the others, he saw that they were already digging into breakfast, so he didn't wait.

He was just enjoying the first creamy bite when Eric finally showed up, racing across the room. "Slow down there, Eric. Nothing can be so important that you need to kill yourself on the way."

Eric plopped across from Ben as Patrick scooted out of the way, pulling his plate of scrambled eggs with him. Eric huffed and puffed and tried to catch his breath, shaking a piece of paper in the air.

Ben reached across the table and said, "Whoa, slow down. We're all here." He gestured at the half-dozen guys waiting. "Relax, will ya? We've waited this long. We can wait longer." He smiled at Eric. "It's not like we expected you to be on time."

Trahern snorted. "He wouldn't be on time to his own funeral."

Patrick laughed under his breath. "Yeah, and with that uniform, it'd have to be a closed casket affair."

Ben frowned at Trey and Patrick. "Guys, give him a moment. Can't you see that he has something important to tell us?"

Eric's head bobbed as he gasped and held the paper aloft one last time, slapped it on the table, and squeaked out one word: "Campout!"

"A campout? We haven't been on a campout since we graduated from scouts. That was three years ago, and now you want to go on another campout?"

Eric's head bobbed up and down. "One last campout."

Ben shrugged. "That could be fun, but the timing…" He frowned. "I'm close to being done with college, one more semester to go." He listed off everyone sitting at the table. "Trey has the best place in town for a proper tune-up, Robb is hoping to be picked up by a professional ball team, Patrick is cooking at the finest restaurant in the county, and Joe has his life in the army. Ready to ship out, aren't you?"

"Yeah," Joe said. "Orders are to head out with the next deployment, should be by early next month. I'm on leave until then."

"Where will you be going?" Ben asked.

Joe shrugged. "Don't know, don't care. Anything'd be better than killing time sitting in the barracks doing nothing. We spent a lot of time in training, but now I want to *use* what they taught us."

Ben stared at Joe. "You mean you want to kill something?"

"Not exactly—" Joe started.

Eric butted in, "You can!"

Everyone stared as Ben asked, "He can what? Kill something?"

"Yeah," Eric said. "It's well beyond a mere campout. Beyond a simple hunting trip. Think bigger, an expedition, a walk-about, a safari."

"Safari? Where're we going?" Robb asked. "Africa?"

Patrick poked Trey with his elbow, snickered, and asked, "Got your shots?"

Trey ignored Patrick and studied the flyer. "Says here that it's someplace never before explored."

"Yup." Eric grinned. "Remember my uncle? The crackpot professor?"

Patrick commented to Trey. "Is there any other kind?"

Trey continued to read the flyer. "It says this stuff is from Area 51 and is based on alien labor. Is this one of those of holodeck things?"

Patrick nudged Trey again and muttered, "A pleasure planet?"

Joe leaned back and stared at Eric. "What kind of joke are you pulling now?"

"It's no joke. My uncle's friends out in New Mexico hit pay dirt. They secured access to some stuff the military dumped, some interesting stuff."

Joe perked up. "What'd the military do?"

"They gave up on technology that they'd been working on for years, kept hidden, naturally. After they tossed it out, my uncle found a use for it. His team discovered that it opens a door to a parallel world."

Robb dropped the lighter he'd been idly flicking and stared. "A door?" he asked. "Modern Science had an article on a teleport door last month."

"You've heard of it before?" Trey asked. "It's legit?"

"Could be. It was a wormhole device, but only theoretical at this point…" Robb gawked at Eric. "…because they couldn't figure out how to build the key hardware…the heart of the system."

"I'd say *someone* figured it out," Trey said tipping his head at Eric.

Robb frowned. "How could *you* have done that? Entire investigative teams have been hard at work on it for years, even backed by Elon Musk. They know the math works out, so it's assumed the rest will work, but no one is even *close* to a real-world application." He stared at Eric. "So what is this thing you've claim to have?"

"My uncle, and his friends, managed to acquire a device being tested at Edwards Air Base. Once the Air Force was done with it, my uncle snagged it up and figured out what it could do."

"And it works?" Robb asked.

"It not only works," Eric said, stretching towards the paper in Trey's hand. "They even founded this company to use it."

"Use it to do what?"

"To send people on trips, journeys, treks."

"Speaking of treks, you gonna wear that uniform on the campout?" Joe eyeballed Eric and his long-sleeved, red shirt with an insignia on the chest over black, bell-bottomed, tight pants over tall, shiny black boots.

"Certainly not my intention. I wouldn't want it to become soiled."

Joe reached up and straightened the black beret sitting on his head, smiling. "I know that they say women like men in uniform, but I don't think standard issue trekkie counts."

Trey gawked. "Doesn't it ever bother you to wear that out in public?"

Patrick set his fork down. "Hey, where's your communicator? And phaser?"

Eric pulled out a cell phone, flipped it open, and beamed as it chirped. "Though I don't carry my phaser all the time. It tends to excite the local constabularies."

Ben stifled a laugh. "Did Officer Romero bust you for carrying a phaser?"

"Well, I…"

"You'll never get a woman doing that!" Trey said.

Eric sat up. "You'd be surprised at the women who find this uniform appealing."

Patrick snorted. "Yeah, you're right. I *would* be surprised by them."

"How about back to the question at hand?" Robb wondered aloud.

"Ouch!" Trey grunted. "Have you seen the prices on this thing?" He flipped the flyer to the back and smashed his finger on it.

"Oh, you can ignore those prices," Eric boasted. "My uncle wants to send a bunch of us on the trip, gratis, as part of a test run."

"Test run? They want *us* to test it?" Ben asked.

"Yeah," Eric said. "They're mostly testing their marketing. They've already had big groups go out, but they want to see how it would work with common folks, not professional hunters and scientists."

"Common folks? Now we're common?" Ben laughed. "Not us."

"And we all can go?" Joe asked.

"Of course," Eric said. "They want a dozen to go on this trip."

"A dozen?" Joe counted heads. "You only have half that many now. Who else is going?"

"I asked all the old scouts to go with us," Eric said.

Joe frowned. "You didn't invite *all* the scouts from the old troop, did you?"

Eric sat there with a blank look on his face. "Yes, I did. I used the spreadsheet I had with all their contact information and sent invites to the ones not still here in town. Mostly John and his buddies."

Trey flopped into a chair. "Oh, great. That'll be just dandy."

Eric stared. "What's wrong? Wouldn't you have invited them?"

"Well," Ben said, "if you remember, they were the ones who never followed instructions, were always in trouble, or were just a pain to deal with." He paused. "Remember Melvin? We don't need anyone like that, especially on a Model-T trip like this."

"Oh, I'm certain they've grown up. Take a gander at those around you," Eric said, still proudly wearing his trekkie uniform.

Patrick stared at Eric, then said, "I saw John's name in the paper last week…in the police blotter. He's still up to his old tricks, and still getting caught, too. If he comes along, there'll be trouble. I can see it now."

Trey leaned and said *sotto voce*, "No trouble. We can handle them."

Joe patted Trey on the shoulder. "I'm with you."

"Oh, well." Eric shrugged. "Anyway, if there's anyone else you'd like to invite, you'd best tell them soon."

"Hey, Ben, do you think your sister could join us?" Trey glanced at Patrick. "She can keep us all fed."

Patrick started, "Hey, I'm a wonderful cook ask anyone—"

"I'll ask her," Ben said. "But I'm certain she'll have serious doubts. She's not as brave, or should I say as foolhardy, as all of us seem to be."

Robb frowned. "I wouldn't say 'foolhardy,' but wouldn't it be nice to have a bit of an adventure before we're forced into a boring life?"

"Good point," Ben said. "So, Eric, when is this trip going to be?"

"They want the trip to head out by late next week."

"Next week?" Joe asked. "Short notice." He glanced at Trey and crossed his fingers. "Maybe the others won't make it."

"Oh, no," Eric said. "They all replied that they'll be here, short notice or not."

"Did you invite YB?" Ben asked.

"Yeah," Patrick said. "As our old scoutmaster, he'd probably enjoy going on a campout, too."

"I'm certain he'd *like* to go," Eric said. "But when I asked Melvin, he said his dad was in the middle of a big project at work. Most of the old scout leaders can't manage to enjoy a couple weeks off."

"And you think *we* can?" Patrick asked. "We have to work, too."

"Oh! I hadn't thought of that," Eric said. "Will you all make it?"

Robb leaned back. "If Eric truly has a connection to this stuff, I'm all for it! I won't miss out on that opportunity…no matter how dangerous."

"Dangerous?" Joe raised his eyebrows. "Well, in that case, it may be worth my time…as long as we're back before I have to report."

Patrick put his elbows on the table. "I wouldn't want to miss out either. Count me in."

"Me, too," Ben said. "But I have a question: do we *want* to be their guinea pigs?" He frowned.

"Why not?" Trey asked. "If we're going to go out, I'd prefer to go in a blaze of glory!"

Eric gasped. "It's not going to be *that* dangerous. It's just a campout."

Robb laughed. "Yeah, *just* a campout…to a different planet!"

Patrick said, "How dangerous can it be? Eric already told us that we won't be the first."

Robb agreed. "As long as we aren't the last, I'm all for it."

"Then it's decided. We're going." Ben shrugged. "Eric, do you have the permission forms for our parents to sign?"

"No need," Eric said. "Uncle Eugene says that we're all adults, so we can sign for ourselves. They'll have waiver forms ready for us."

"No permission forms?" Robb asked. "So, we tell our folks nothing?"

"Well…" Eric started. "He did ask that we keep it under our hats. He doesn't want word leaked to the press for the time being, not yet. Still working on the marketing aspect, he said."

"Trying to keep it away from interested parties," Robb said.

Ben frowned. "I'm not certain that we should keep quiet. Our parents should know. It doesn't need to be kept a secret from them, does it?"

Robb shrugged. "If the government found out that he managed to get this thing working, they'd snap it right back. We don't want to spoil it for them. Do we?" Robb asked.

"Yeah," Trey said fixing his gaze on everyone meaningfully. "We'll tell our families that we're going on a campout…out of cell range. They won't be able to contact us until we get back to civilization." He raised an eyebrow at Ben. "That's not a lie, is it?"

Ben hesitated. "Not a blatant lie, but—"

"Does that work for you, Eric?" Trey asked.

"Yes," Eric said. "That should suffice."

"But what if they ask more?" Ben asked.

Robb laughed. "Can you imagine trying to explain to them that went to another planet?" he asked. "They aren't as open minded as we are."

"That was his concern," Eric said. "He wasn't certain that he could trust them to keep quiet if they knew what was in fact going on."

"They'd probably keep it to themselves better than we would. They don't post half their life on the Internet," Ben said quietly.

"Good point," Joe said. "And we'll be back in a week, right?"

With the flyer still in hand, Trey frowned. "Over a week. It says here that the trip will last ten days. Why ten days? Why not exactly a week? That would make more sense."

"They can't charge the flux capacitors enough in a week. They need a full ten days to build up the required power. Any faster and the electric company might notice the extra drain. It's not like they can tap into a nuclear power plant or anything."

Trey tried not to laugh. "Flux capacitors?"

Robb ignored Trey and asked, "It draws that much power? I didn't see anything about that in the article."

Eric smiled. "Do you think they told the reporter everything?"

Robb laughed. "Touché."

"You're all convinced?" Ben waited for nods. "So what's next?"

Trey read from the flyer. "It says that all we'll need is standard camping equipment. Meals and lodging will be provided by the natives."

Ben raised his eyebrows. "There're natives?"

Eric responded, "Definitely, we're not going to a desert."

Trey read more. "It says here that hunting is available, too, but if we plan on doing any, then we'll need to bring our own firearms…and all the ammo we'll need for the entire trip—no resupply along the way."

Joe perked up. "Firearms? Ammo? And no resupply? Then we'll need to bring lots. Too much is better than not enough. We don't want to run out. Remember, as scouts we need to 'Be Prepared.' Bring all you need."

Ben shrugged. "Well, Eric, you may tell your uncle that he has himself some white mice for his experiment." Ben checked with the others. "Hooked like a fish."

Eric chuckled. "I already told him. I knew you'd be happy to go."

"One more question," Trey said. "This place has never been explored, so what if we get lost?"

"Oh, we won't get lost," Eric said. "We'll have a guide along with us."

"Sounds more and more like a safari," Robb said.

"The guide has been there before? And knows his way around?" Ben asked.

"I would assume that he's been there more than once," Eric said. "Maybe even made contact with the people there. We'll find out when we get there."

"Where *is* there?" Patrick asked.

"We'll meet at the vacant Wal-Mart at 8:00 AM next Thursday, five days from today."

Trey laughed. "We're going to Wally-World?"

Eric stared at Trey. "No. That was where they set up their equipment. It was left vacant after the Super Wal-Mart moved in on the other side of town, so it worked out for them. Right next to the railroad tracks, so they could bring in their equipment without arousing suspicion, and close enough to the electric sub-station to tap into the extra power needed to run the thing."

"They tapped into the power?" Ben asked.

"Yeah. They're on the upstream side, so if there's a power outage anywhere in town, they still have juice."

"They thought of everything," Patrick said.

"Does that fit everyone's schedule? We can all make it, right?" Ben raised his eyebrows. Everyone agreed.

"As long as we're back in time," Joe said. "I wouldn't want to go AWOL."

"That shouldn't be a problem. We leave next Thursday and return ten days later, Sunday after next." Eric said.

"Thursday?" Patrick asked. "Well, I'd better get my gear ready. I can't remember the last time I went on a camping trip. This'll be fun!"

"Be certain to say 'Hi' to the others when you see them," Eric added.

Trey caught Joe's eye and muttered, "Yeah, *if* we see them."

Chapter One
The Door Out

Benjamin's eyelids practically clicked as they snapped open. *Awake in an instant*, he thought. *Feels like Christmas morning. I don't want to oversleep today.* Today he and his old scout buddies would be heading out on one last big trip. A week off, avoid all the hustle and bustle of life, and have an adventure…the adventure of their lives. That's what the Ex Terra Expeditions flyer said—"Experience an out-of-this-world vacation." He had hoped for a well-deserved break from his studies, and now that the opportunity presented itself, Ben planned to make the most of it. A week off wouldn't affect his graduation— and a couple weeks off wouldn't be bad either. He'd still be done with school in a year. He was caught up enough that he didn't even need any classes this summer, so why not enjoy himself in his last summer as a student?

They'd already told everyone that they'd be out of touch for a couple weeks, so now all they had to do was show up at the right time and right place with all the equipment they'd need. No chance for more supplies once there, but that didn't bother him because he knew that he could survive in the wilds for a week, more if needed—he'd done it as a scout. Although, back then there had always been an adult standing by in case a problem came up. This time they'd be all on their own—they were their own adult. *How things change*, he thought.

Ben gently thumped the wall and whispered loudly, "Hey, Annie. Up and at 'em. Time to be on the way." He grabbed the old M-14 off the rack above his bed and wiped off a thin layer of dust. What used to be a decent military rifle certainly made a good hunting rifle. This rifle had once saved his grandfather's life on a hunting trip, and now he'd carry it with pride on another, hoping to return with a trophy good enough to hang over the mantelpiece.

He still didn't hear any movement from his sister's room, so he pounded on her wall as he pulled on pants and shirt. *Slowpoke.* He'd packed most of his gear the night before, so that wouldn't delay him, but he didn't know how ready she was. He grabbed his backpack and thumped on her door as he stumbled along the hallway. As he rounded the corner in the front room, he saw light under the kitchen door. *Who could be up already this time of the morning?* he wondered. He burst into the kitchen, running into Annie as she put a plate of bacon and eggs on the table.

"Here's breakfast, sleepyhead!" she said.

"Annie! How'd you get up before me?"

She smirked at him. "Simply one step ahead of you…again. Always up and ready to go when needed."

Ben's face reddened as he sat. "Thanks for breakfast. I would have realized I was hungry soon enough. Honestly, I'm not much of a morning person."

"Yeah, so I've noticed," Annie said. "I've seen you go for hours before you realize your stomach is finally awake…and empty." He smiled at her through a mouthful of eggs. She continued, "I've always said, it's better to have a decent breakfast before setting out on any adventure, especially one like this, than to run around on an empty stomach." She sat next to him and ate her breakfast.

He agreed. "You'll be glad you decided to join us, besides if we didn't have a girl along, who would cook for us?" He avoided her playful fist as she swung at his head.

"You know I can cook well enough, but Patrick will be there, and he can cook up a feast with anything…with practically nothing, too!"

"Yeah," he said. "With him coming along, we won't starve!" He ducked again and tried to block her blow, but this time she aimed lower and caught him in the ribs. "Ouch! You are one dangerous girl. Remember that technique in case we need it on the campout."

She laughed. "With all the practice I've had beating you up, I won't have any problems in the wild for a week."

"You're my older sister, but that doesn't mean that I can't beat you up. It's that I'm not allowed to hit a lady. *That's* what saves your hide every time."

Annie laughed as she put away the breakfast dishes. "Yeah, right. We'll see. Come on, you'd best haul your equipment out to your jeep. We need to be to the old Wal-Mart in less than an hour."

Ben grabbed his backpack, stepped out the back door, and tossed his gear into his Jeep. Then he went back and forth a couple times getting all of his sister's accessories, wondering if he should ask her if all of it was necessary, but he knew what she'd likely say, so he decided to keep his mouth shut. He snugged up the ropes on the last of the gear and glanced up to see Annie come out in a parka with the hood up. He stared at her, unable to hold his tongue. "A fur coat? You expect it to be that cold?"

She shrugged. "Better safe than sorry, I always say."

Ben hopped into the Jeep. "Well, don't get too warm in that thing."

"If I do, then I can simply carry it, right?"

He kept silent. *She always has to be right.* As he pulled out of the driveway and headed down the street, he checked the rearview mirror. Still dark, the house faded into the distance—they'd managed to leave without waking anyone else.

Light traffic at that time of the morning made the trip easy. First light appeared as they pulled into the car park in front of the old Wal-Mart building. A sign for Ex Terra Expeditions hung above the front door, painted by a fifth-grader. *I hope their engineers are better than their marketing folks.*

Most of the guys had already arrived, standing next to an old trash barrel roasting hot-dogs in flames that leaped six feet into the air. *Robb was here early,* he thought. Some of them must have spent the night, partying and carousing. He hoped that they took advantage of the bed in the back of Patrick's old VW bus. Ben knew that van well. The dings and dents didn't matter—it was a Godsend when the snow caves and igloos collapsed in on half of the scouts. *I'd say we needed more practice,* he thought to himself. *Those party animals better not waste too much time. I'd hate to miss out on something simply because they 'forgot' to sleep at night.*

With no hinge strap, the door of the Jeep swung all the way open and bounced off the fender as Ben bailed out. "Hey! You guys ready to leave? It's close to time for our group to check in."

"Yo, Ben," Patrick said. "How's it going?" He glanced at the guys behind him and yelled to Ben, "We're getting ready now." Patrick made a beeline towards the van, shouting orders, and getting everyone moving. All the hotdogs packed away and the rest of the food cleaned up, they even managed to extinguish the fire in the trash barrel without catching anyone on fire.

Amazed at the action, Ben thought, He'd make a good sergeant the way everyone follows his commands. He smiled as he watched each person grab a pack and line up. Yup, these guys'll work together just fine.

John was grabbing his pack when he saw Annie. "Hey, Ben, is your sister coming?"

Annie stepped closer. "You have a problem with that, John?"

John backpedaled and held his hands up. "No, no, not at all." He quickly stepped away. "Hey, Eric, is *your* sister coming, too?"

Eric blinked. "Liz? No, though she tried. I talked her out of it."

"Oh, shoot. That would have been fun if she'd made it."

Eric shrugged. "Maybe next time."

"Yeah, that would be good," John said.

Ben noticed that most of the group equipment, cooking supplies, tents, etc. were already packed into a couple of duffel bags, but no one had offered to carry them, so Ben yelled up towards the group already heading in, "Trey, grab that last bit of stuff, will ya?"

Trahern stopped his meandering and saw the pile. "On it," he said, then spoke to the person next to him. "Hey, Eric. Give me a hand with that stuff." Most suited to carrying the extra load, the strongest one in their group, Trey was used to carrying a greater share of the load, and Eric, well, he was Eric, the one and only. A hanger-on, a social misfit, an outcast of society (as Eric himself would say), Eric belonged to the group, and everyone tolerated, instead of pitying, him, mostly because he simply didn't seem to understand.

The two of them managed to load the duffel bags onto Trey's back, but in the process had had to transfer equipment from Trey's backpack to Eric's. Sharing like that, they would have to be close friends on this trip. They hurried to catch up and found everyone else already checking in.

The guard at the front gate said, "These are the last two?"

"Yup, that's the last of 'em." Ben noticed all the equipment Trey had carried and said, "We wouldn't have gotten far without the two of you." He grabbed his pack and said to the guard, "Now we're ready to go."

The guard made one or two notations on his list, checked his watch, and smiled. "Not even a bit late. May you have a good trip, and may you bring back some interesting trophies, but before you go, I need everyone to fill out a waiver. Everyone *is* over 21, right?"

"Yup," Eric said. "We're all adults."

The guard smiled. "Forms and pens are on that table." He directed his gaze across the room. "We can't be held liable for anything you do out on the trip. Also, please remove any watches, phones, radios, CD players, or any other electronic equipment. They can go on the table with the forms."

Ben said, "We read the brochure. No one brought anything like that." He slowly eyed everyone, folded his arms, and said, "Right?"

Everyone nodded except Eric. He raised his hand, holding aloft an old pocket watch. He asked, "Not even this watch from my grandfather? It's an old one, a wind-up, not electronic at all."

The guard showed a thumbs down. "*Especially* not that. It may not be electronic, but it would freeze up solid with all the magnetic fields and would never work again."

Eric slowly handed his watch to the guard who put it into an envelope, wrote something on it, then put it under his clipboard. "It'll be safe here until you return. Now then, on to the more technical part. I'll need each of you to step up on the scale, one at a time. Please keep your gear with you." The guard noted the weight and a number for each of the travelers on his clipboard, did a cursory glance into everyone's pack, then ushered them into the antechamber. "Please have a seat." He tipped his head towards a couple rows of chairs by the wall. "One of the techies will be with you in a moment." He stepped through a door next to a silvered window on the side of the room.

Seconds later, a young man in a white lab coat stuck his head in through the same door. "Are you guys the oh-eight-thirty party?" The way he said it, it sounded like an insult.

"That would be us," Ben said. "But I thought we had to be here by 8:00."

The technician smirked. "That's what we tell you, so you aren't late. We need time to do the introduction, as well as inspect your equipment."

"Then that *is* us," Ben said. "All ready and waiting to leave." He glanced over the tech's head. "Are there other groups ready to head out, too?"

The technician frowned. "Once trip every two weeks is all we can handle."

Ben frowned. "Then why do we have to be here at a particular time?"

Blinking in confusion, the technician said, "Eugene's instructions."

"Whatever." Ben shrugged. "Then we're ready to go."

"But you can't leave quite yet." The technician held up his hand. "I still have to give you the introduction." He stepped into the center of the room, dimmed the lights, and launched into his spiel, "If you'll watch the demonstration, I'll explain how this works." A 3D image coalesced in the middle of the room and drew everyone's attention, but few paid attention to the technician as he continued to spew forth irrelevant trivialities. "The Gauss-Jacobi Door is based on a theorem proved by Karl Friedrich Gauss [1777-1855] when he studied electrostatics and magnetism." The red ball in the image stretched larger, and light green lines surrounded it like the magnetic field of the Earth. "Simply stated it says that if E is a simple solid region and S is the boundary surface of E, with positive orientation, then there is a vector field called F whose component functions have continuous partial derivatives on an open region that contains E." Little blue plusses appeared on the surface of the ball opposite yellow minuses right under the surface, then they spread across the now immense ball, as the middle two-thirds faded away and leaving thin slices on the top and bottom.

The techie inhaled and continued, "When combined with the matrix transformation of partial derivatives developed by Carl Gustav Jacob Jacobi [1804-1851]," the top of the ball twisted, and the plusses and minuses moved in little circles, distorting the magnetic lines, "and applied to the delta-epsilon definition of a limit refined by Augustin-Louis Cauchy [1789-1857]," the magnetic lines twisted far enough that they touched each other in the middle, and became a small, white, glowing ball, "they discovered that there is a way to manipulate a magnetic field to bypass the limits set by the speed of light." The white ball blossomed open and showed a picture of a small planet circling a far-away sun. "Understandably it wasn't possible to proceed beyond theoretical until the advancement of electronics and computers fast enough to complete the calculations in real-time, but now…" He continued for what felt like hours droning on and on, but the pretty pictures kept the group's undivided attention until he at last paused to take a breath. "So, are there any questions?" He finally stopped talking.

Annie raised her hand. "I'll bet you love giving that speech, don't you?"

"Well, it *is* fairly interesting how it all happened when you consider it." He launched off into yet another mind-numbing speech. "Most of the theory had been quite completely developed back in the mid-1800s, yet it required technology that hadn't been perfected until the late 20th Century to make it even possible, and now it is…possible, that is…and profitable. That's why you're here," he declared as he smirked.

She poked Trey in the ribs and muttered, "He doesn't understand sarcasm, does he?" Trey snickered.

Ben stood up. "If that's all, then are we ready to head out now?"

The technician stepped towards the silvered window, then, as though he'd been given a signal, he said, "Yes, everything checked out fine. None of your equipment is on our banned list, and the group didn't exceed the Gaussian count, so if you'll follow me to the Gauss-Jacobi Door."

"The *what* count?" Eric asked.

The technician repeated, "The Gaussian count. It's a measure of the way magnetic fields interact with you and your equipment. If we exceed a certain amount, there's an exponential increase for required energy. Now *that* discovery caught us all by surprise when it happened."

"It? What happened?" Eric expressed sincere curiosity.

The technician glanced at the silvered window like a kid with his hand in the cookie jar and quickly waked towards what appeared to be a bank vault without answering. The door swung open as he approached, revealing a large room that had wires and cables strewn across the floor. People in white lab coats scurried back and forth.

"In here," the technician said, walking in.

Everyone followed, staring around. The top slice of a sphere floated high on a set of transparent plastic catwalks directly above a circular platform, which looked like the bottom slice from the demonstration.

"If you'll stay out of the way for a moment, I'll go see where your guide is," he said as he scampered off.

Ben shrugged. "Come on, guys. It's time to hurry up and wait again."

Joe leaned back. "Used to that already."

The group wove their way through all the mess to the side of the room, trying to stay out of the way and not trip over anything. "Somehow this doesn't seem as professional as I'd've expected," criticized Annie. "For the price listed on the flyer they should have most of the bugs worked out."

"Oh, they tried," Eric said, "But with the opposition from tree-huggers, they had to have it up and running before some someone passed legislation against it."

"I can see that," Annie said. "That could have caused quite a delay."

Swinging shut, the massive wall-doors created a gust of wind that flapped lab coats left and right, much to the irritation of the techies. At last, the ponderous doors slammed shut with an impact that vibrated through the floor and sealed off the room with a hiss, which implied an airtight seal.

A techie stepped up to the group (they couldn't tell if was the same techie or if a new one had swapped in—they were virtually identical in those lab coats). He ushered along a man that was more dressed for the occasion: long tan coat with well-worn dungarees, tall black boots, a leather backpack hanging across his shoulder, all topped off by a dirty, brown hat. The techie checked his clipboard hesitated, then stuttered, "Uh, 8:30 group, this is Thomas Campbell, your guide." Seeming to be embarrassed by his 'public' speech, the techie quickly handed off the clipboard then vanished into the crowd of other white-lab-coated techies.

"Hello. Call me Tom. Who's in charge of your group?"

Ben stepped up. "I suppose you could say that I am. After all, I was patrol leader of most of these guys…a long time ago. I'm Ben."

Tom offered his hand. "Hello, Ben," then he perused the rest of the group, his eyes settling on Annie. "You led the *guys*? This one doesn't look like a guy. She's a lady!"

Ben laughed as Annie blushed. "She's my sister. That doesn't count!"

Tom winked. "Yeah, right, whatever you say." He held up the clipboard the techie had left behind. "Let me check you off. As I call your name, go stand by that railing." He stepped across the room. "Find a spot where you can hang on. Understand?" He verified that everyone knew where to go, then went back to the list. "Ben…you're checked off already. Head to the waiting area."

Ben grabbed his pack, snaked his way through the equipment, and stepped up to the front of the small waiting area, feeling as if he were waiting in line for one of the rides at a carnival.

Tom read off the rest of the names as everyone fell in line behind Ben: "Annie, Carl, Douglas, Eric." He paused. "Are you Eugene's Eric?"

"That I am," Eric said as he walked past.

"I thought so. I've heard him talk of you. Have fun out there," Tom said, then continued, "Joe, John, Melvin, Patrick, Robert, and last of all, Trahern." He checked off each one, then joined them. "Close to a full dozen. This should be a good trip. I look forward to yet another foray out into that other world."

The scouts lined up next to the railing, staring at all the commotion going on around them.

As everyone settled in, Tom gave one last set of instructions. "When they start applying power, the platform will start moving. It might be noisy, but just wait for it. We want to stay out of the way as much as possible, and don't forget to hang on. The breeze can be quite stiff when the air pressure equalizes."

The brash buzz of a klaxon startled them, and the platform started moving. Tom spun. "This is it. The Door is opening. Quick! Everyone grab the rail. If you have anything loose, hold onto it!" He dropped one knee onto his own pack, then opened his mouth as if yawning.

Everyone else hesitated for an instant, long enough to be caught off guard. The floor of the platform spun up, slowly picking up speed. Sparks snapped and crackled from all the metal surfaces, the smell of ozone filled the room, and a flash of light and loud pop startled them all. Then they could see it: a ball of cold, white fire floating high in the middle of the sphere. A hissing sound followed the pop and grew into a howl as the ball grew larger. Loose papers flew, circling the room as if in a tornado, and plastered themselves to any flat surface.

Ben felt a pressure in his ears, then felt a pop, akin to the feeling when a plane cabin pressurizes. He winced and stared. "What was that?" He thought he had yelled, but he couldn't even hear himself.

Tom laughed. "That's the Door. The pressure difference between the worlds causes that wind when it equalizes from this side to the other." He apologized, "I didn't have a chance to tell you what was going to happen." He held his hand by his ears. "Give it a minute. You'll recover. Next time try yawning or swallowing. It'll ease the pressure."

The platform drew everyone's gaze. Where, at first, there had been nothing, and then the ball of fire, now a large round window appeared, or what could be a window, if a window could be a ball. It reached from the upper slice to the lower. Through it, a yellow-brown field stretched out before them. Scattered tree clumps stood nearby, and beyond those, a mountain range glowed through the distortion of the Door, but more than all that, the flare of bright sunlight filled the room.

Tom hefted his backpack and stepped up the small ramp that led to the Door. "Is this team heading out? Or shall we stand here all day and gawk?" He yelled at the near deaf group, "Come on!"

Ben and his buddies hesitated for a mere moment, then snapped out of it, grabbed their gear, and passed Tom as they ran out through the Door. One moment the cold, dark, stale, technology-based room surrounded them, the next a deep blue sky lit up the wide-open space before them. The sun warmed the landscape, a cool breeze wafted the scent of vitality to encircle them, and they spread out like marbles spilled on the floor, blinking at the brightness, amazed at the pure essence of nature.

Tom scowled. "Hello?" They ignored him as he stood in the darkness, still waiting on the platform. He held out his hand. "So, Annie, was it? Need help with that pack?"

She smiled. "Yes, thank you." Gazing out through the Door, she chuckled. "They're sorta focused, aren't they? Typical guys." Then noticing Tom's frown, she hastily added, "Present company excepted."

Tom lifted her pack and helped her secure it, ignoring the flirtatious sideways glances. Fastening the waist belt he said, "There, how's that? Is it snug enough? You don't want it to shift as we're hiking."

Annie said, "Yes, that's fine," but she thought to herself, *And* he's *pretty fine, too.* She hid her face before he could see her blush, changing the subject by yelling out to Ben, "Hey guys, we're right behind you!" then hurried through the Door into the broad daylight.

Ben stared at the Door, a dark ball the size of a small house perched in the middle of the field, and he could still see the techies inside working frantically in the semi-dark. The moment Tom and Annie came out, the edges started to shimmer, then the whole thing began to shrink.

Tom faced the Door and laughed. "Last chance, everyone! It's closing!" It continued to contract, going through a reverse of the opening process, becoming smaller and smaller, then changing from a floating hole to a white flaming ball, then with a slight pop, nothing. "That's it! In exactly ten days we need to be right here." He shot a marker post into the ground, then fastened a small flag to it. "That should make it easy to find."

Eric wandered across the empty field. "That's so we know where the Door will open…right here?"

"Not necessarily *right* here, but close enough. The techies haven't figured out how to eliminate all the drifting." He paused. "It's still pretty much experimental, you know."

Ben asked, "How far does it drift?"

"It's never been far, at the most a short walk away. The farthest I've ever had to go was a couple hundred meters, but that was on one of the early expeditions, on a month long trip, too."

"A month long trip?" Annie asked. "That must have been exciting."

Tom smiled. "This trip is only a week long, so it'll be much closer. I'll bet it'll be right here." He stomped his foot next to the flag, then said, "You've noticed that it's easy to spot, too, tends to stand out."

"What if it's night over here?" Eric asked.

"Ah, if they see it's dark when the Door opens, they turn on big spotlights, so there's no need to fret that you'll get stuck here." He raised an eyebrow. "But then there was this *one* time…" He trailed off.

Eric gasped. "And?"

Ben winced. Eric would be the only one to not get a joke.

Tom patted Eric on the shoulder and confessed, "I was kidding!"

Ben watched Eric's face relax, much too slowly. *This might be a long trip.*

"Seriously, if you guys are done sightseeing, we can be off now," Tom said.

Ben noticed that half the guys were skipping stones across a creek. "Patrick, can you get those guys back up here? We need to move out."

Tom consulted a small hand-drawn map, pivoting to line up the symbols on the map with their landmarks. Straightening up he said, "Our course is mostly southwest, so following that creek is the right direction. It's the guys on that hill that need to be pulled in."

Ben noticed a group of scouts using the higher ground of a small rise to get a better view. Squinting into the still rising sun all he could see were silhouettes, but he could tell that the tall one was Trahern, and standing too close next to him had to be Annie. Ben frowned, *I don't want to spend too much time keeping an eye on those two.* Cupping his hands around his mouth, he called out, "Hey! Trey! Bring everyone back here. We're going that-a-way," swinging his arm in the direction of the creek. Trey herded the group towards Ben.

Tom sighted on his map, then said, "If we keep following this creek downstream, it will connect to the river. We'll spend the night there and get to the village late morning tomorrow, and I want us to be well rested before we head out for a hunt."

Ben glanced at the sun. "How much time would you say we have?"

"Plenty," Tom said. "As long as we don't have to keep gathering up strays." He noted the group still playing by the water's edge.

"I was afraid that we'd end up with a delay," Ben said. "But I didn't expect it to happen so soon." He mumbled something about walkie-talkies, then hollered back, "Hurry up! We have a lot of ground to cover!"

Patrick rounded up the scouts near him. The sound of clamor carried faintly across the field as the guys picked up their gear and hoofed along the sandy shore. Someone was calling out a cadence as they ran beside the creek. Getting closer, Patrick whooped and hollered, "We'll be there in a moment!"

Yelling back he shouted, "Keep moving! Take your time, but hurry!" Satisfied with their progress, Ben checked that Trey's group was catching up as well. "Give them a moment. We'll all be here in a bit."

"Good, then let's get cracking." Facing downstream, Tom stepped off at a slow pace. "If we stay on top of this ridgeline next to the stream, we'll be able to see farther ahead, to anticipate anything that we might encounter."

"Will we run into anyone?" Ben wondered hopefully.

"Probably not, at least not for a while yet. The Door doesn't open close to *Roadranusis*," Tom said. "That's the name of the nearest town, so there's not much chance of running across anyone, but we might scare up an animal or two."

"That would make Patrick happy," Ben said. "He wanted to test out new cooking ideas."

"Sounds good. I'd like to see what he can do," Tom said. "Anyway, once the techies figured out how to generally aim the Door, management insisted that they aim for uninhabited places. Less chance of us running into someone right as we come out, or letting *them* in."

"That makes sense," Ben said. "So the whole trip isn't as desolate as this?"

"Oh, no, not at all. The techies were glad that we happened to get dumped as far from anything as possible." He raised an eyebrow at Ben. "Can you imagine what the locals would do if a bunch of folks popped out of a big hole in the clear blue sky?"

Ben laughed. "Yeah, I can see that could be a problem."

"So now we get to walk the rest of the way in."

"How far is that?" Ben asked.

"Half a day to the camp site, then in the morning, it's only two or three hours into town. We'd continue straight into town, but we'll be using that site as our base to go hunting, so we might as well set it up first," Tom said.

"And it's easy enough to find?" Ben asked.

"Oh, yes. The path from camp into town is well worn from all the traipsing back and forth, but getting *to* the camp site can be a bit elusive. It would be easier if they dropped us off at the same spot each time, but with the way the techies aim, they never hit the same place twice."

"Like lightning?" Ben asked.

Tom snickered. "Yeah, except the techies aren't as bright!"

They continued laughing as Trey caught up to them barely out of breath even though he'd run the last part. "Wow, Ben, we could see that mountain range much better from up on that crest. It's bigger than I thought because it's a lot farther off."

"Yeah, it is," Tom said. "We haven't mapped much in that direction yet. We know there's a big desert to the west, and on the other side of that are the mountains, but no one wants to cross through all that when there's so much out this way that's easier to cover. The plan is to follow along the waterways and spread out later as we have time."

Ben craned his neck to stare at the mountains behind them as he walked beside Tom. "So, how long has this world been open?"

"The first contacts were as much as a year ago, but we didn't know if we were even in the same place each time it opened, and the power required to keep it open dictated that all the trips were short. Open the Door, run outside, check what we could, drop a marker, run back in, and close. No time to do any sightseeing."

"How many trips have you been on?" Trey asked.

"Oh, lots. The first were exploratory, but once they were confident that they could open it to the same place later, we were able to map it out."

"So you know your way around here pretty much?" Ben asked.

"Well, I've gone out on the most trips, so I have the most experience here."

"And you've mapped it all out?" Trey asked.

"As much as we can. We can't use any GPS surveying equipment because there aren't any satellites to lock onto—besides, we've never been able to get stuff like that to operate properly here. Not simply getting messed up in the magnetic fields as they pass through the Door. There's something in the air, nothing electronic works, so we ended up having to rely on the old tried-and-true historical methods." He shrugged.

Ben leaned closer to look at the map. "But you can get a compass to work?" Ben asked.

"Nope. That's one of the big problems. When we started mapping, we just decided that where the sun rises is east, and where it sets west." He grinned. "After that, north and south were easy."

"But no compass," Trey said.

"Nothing with a magnetic field works here. In fact, magnetic fields cause a real drain on the Door's power. That's one of the reasons we check your packs: to check for stray magnetic fields."

"One reason?" Trey stared suspiciously at Tom. "And the other reason?"

Tom laughed. "Contraband! We can't have you out here getting wasted." Then he leaned to Ben. "But what they don't know is that the locals here can cook up a pretty potent brew."

Trey smiled widely. "Well, we'll have to check into that."

Ben narrowed his eyes at them. "Hey, can you keep it under control?"

Trey snickered. "Yes, sir!" he said as he continued to conspire with Tom. "You'll have to lead the way when we get to town."

"I will," Tom said. "That's my job. That and baby-sitting, so you all make it back safely."

Annie piped up from right behind them. "Well, good that *someone* has that in mind."

Tom stepped aside to let Annie lead. "Welcome to the front," he said.

"We were just chatting about, uh…" Trey started, "…a trip to the mountains!"

Annie glared at him. "Oh, you were?"

Ben jumped in. "Yeah, Trey was telling us what he could see. Right, Trey?"

Trey stuttered. "Uh…oh, yeah. Right," then blurted, "They're far away."

Tom broke in covering for Trey. "True, and if you can see them at them at night, they seem to glow. The techies don't know what causes it, but they plan to find out." He paused. "But, as you know, *they* won't be going out anywhere—they'll send someone *else* to do all the exploring, but then *they* will claim all the credit for any discoveries."

Ben missed Tom's complaint. "They glow? That would be worth checking out."

Tom agreed. "But not until we can manage to get a vehicle through the Door. Those mountains are way too far for even a month-long outing."

Satisfied for the moment Annie asked, "So if all the leaders are up here, who's keeping an eye on the stragglers?"

Tom and Ben spun at the same time, finding that the group had indeed spread out quite a ways, meandering along the ridge, puddle hopping at the creek's side, and drifting into the brush off to the side. Eric was the farthest off, wandering away from the creek, getting himself lost, again.

Ben sent Trey up the hill. "Head that way, and pull Eric and those guys back to the ridgeline. I'll see what the delay is with Patrick and the guys by the creek."

Trey threw a half-assed salute and jogged off. "Yes, sir!"

Tom approved Ben's supervision of the group. "Get things under control and join us when you can."

"I'll stay at the back and lead from behind. How's that?"

"That'll be fine for today, but tomorrow I'd prefer to have you up front with me."

"I'll see if I can get the others to act more responsibly, put them in charge of smaller groups and have them report to us."

"I can live with that. Out here, you'd be too busy unless you delegate. If you try to constantly micromanage, you'll be stretched so thin that you'll never get anything done. Make them acting sergeants."

"I know a couple that would fit right in."

Tom checked out the path ahead as Ben fell back. "We'll keep going, but slowly."

"Annie," Ben called out as he trotted off, "you stay up here with Tom. He can keep an eye on you."

Annie smiled to herself, *And I can keep an eye on him. This is a good chance to get to know him better.*

She and Tom walked along the ridgeline quietly discussing their respective backgrounds for a while. Annie mentioned that Ben had always enjoyed outdoor activities like scouting, so when Eric told them of this opportunity, this Ex Terra camp out, she knew that he'd enjoy it. She was glad that he'd asked her to come, along with all his scout buddies. She listed her siblings, with Ben being the youngest. She had been chatting on for quite a while when she realized that she was doing all the talking. Without thinking, she blurted out, "So, Tom, enough about me, tell me about you." She blushed at such a lame line. *He's going to think I'm a half-wit.*

Not missing a step Tom responded brightly, "That's a long story, but I can't use 'we don't have time' as an excuse."

"You can say that again!"

They walked on, the banter going through whatever topic happened to come up. Tom told of his background and upbringing, and Annie told of her goals in life. They checked back occasionally, keeping an eye on the rest. At one point Tom had to call back for the group to stick together.

Annie smiled. "They aren't too bad, but some of them tend to get into trouble…a lot." She was quiet for a moment, then asked, "So how did you get involved with all this Ex Terra stuff?"

"Pretty much right out of high school, I joined the Army. After I did my time, I used the training they had given me and worked in a wilderness camp for a while, taking city folks for adventures in bush country, like a dude ranch, but without horses."

"That sounds fun," Annie said, putting her hand on his arm.

Tom was aware of her hand and could swear he felt a gentle warmth emanating from her touch. Trying to ignore the strange feeling, he continued, "During the winter months, when they shut everything down, I started doing hunting excursions across the world. Apparently I was kinda well known, because when this Ex Terra thing started up, they contacted me, so here I am."

"Sounds to me like you have plenty of experience for this job, so all we have to do is have fun and enjoy the trip." She smiled.

"That's my goal. Get you out here, have fun, and get you back, all in one piece, in less than two weeks' time. That's doable. There might be a couple places where we'll have to muddle through, but I have yet to lose anyone."

"Well, that's good to know." They both laughed.

Trey followed a ways behind, keeping an eye on his group, an eye on Eric, and yet still managing to keep an eye on the two leaders. He wasn't jealous, because Annie wasn't his girl, but she was a friend, a close friend, and he didn't want to see her getting involved with someone who might hurt her, even inadvertently.

Ben worked with Patrick to keep that group moving, and they all kept plodding on, following Tom's lead.

Dry yellow grass soon yielded to a carpet of deep green, lush clover as they left behind the desert that Trey had spotted earlier. The hike was pleasant, and the day was warm with a cool breeze coming across the creek. The bright sun was working its way past zenith when Tom finally called for a break. They gathered by the creek for a brief lunch, and Tom showed everyone how to use the water pump filters that he'd brought. They wanted to make camp before dark, so he encouraged them to finish their lunch quickly and get on the way.

The sun drifted across the sky, slowly descending before Tom spotted the line of trees that marked the river they were seeking. Following it downstream, southeast a little ways, he located the familiar campsite he had used on his prior visits. A lot of preparation had already been done: spots for the tents were levelled, a gentle path to the river for fresh water had been marked, and a well-built fire circle was ready for cooking. Gathering firewood was an easy task as the river tended to encourage the growth of trees, lending a calm, quiet, forest-like feel to their first night's bivouac.

Settling into camp was straightforward because most of the guys had been together as scouts since they were young. Everyone knew his job and went right to it. Trey and Eric had already pitched the larger tents and were now in the process of setting up a smaller one for Annie. Robb had a roaring fire going. He was so good, he could even get soggy wood to burn. Along the way, Joe had bagged a couple of critters with his .22 pistol. Patrick treated them like squirrels, making them into a stew. By the time Ben brought up the rear, chasing the laggards in front of him, the feast was ready.

"We can't be as spread out tomorrow," Ben said as they all sat to eat.

"That's true," Tom said. "If we are going to get anywhere, we need to keep bunched together. There are beasts out here that you certainly don't want to tangle with if you're in a small group, much less alone. We haven't had enough time to categories everything we've come across, but there has been evidence of much larger animals that we haven't seen, carnivorous animals."

Eric shuddered. "Do we need to have someone keep watch tonight?"

"Yes," Tom said. "We'll do that every night, even in town. We can't be too careful. We'll have two-hour shifts. That should give everyone plenty of time to sleep. I've used porters before, but this trip, Eugene said you guys are on your own. I don't understand it, but he didn't want anyone else to come along."

Ben frowned. "That's strange. I wonder why."

Tom shrugged. "Anyway, you know your troops best, so I'll leave it up to you to make the assignments. This far out, all they'll have to do is keep the fire going. I have yet to hear of any animals that aren't afraid of fire."

Remembering his grandfather's watch Eric asked, "How will we know when to change shifts?"

"I have an hourglass, made of wood, glass, and sand. Nothing there that will be affected by magnetic fields." Tom smiled. "Remember that for your next trip. Any non-metallic technology is acceptable."

Ben picked up his M-14. "Is this good?"

Tom admired the weapon. "Nice choice. Excellent at a distance, yet still useful up close. The sights might have been tweaked by passing through the magnetic fields, but it's good that lead isn't affected much by magnetism. How many rounds did you bring?"

"Not as many as I wanted to. They weigh too much. I have them in a bag in my backpack."

"Well, they won't do much good there," Tom walked around the fire circle, reviewing the equipment. "If you're feeling brave, now would be a good time for everyone to load up a couple magazines. Keep one in your gun and the other close at hand, in a shirt pocket if you don't have loops on your belt. Carry your gun holstered, *without* a round in the chamber. It's easier to lock and load in a hurry than it is to patch up an idiot who shoots himself in the foot."

Everyone went through their packs pulling out ammo and loading up, everyone except Eric. He sat off to the side, fretting. "Do I need a gun, too?"

Ben walked over. "No, Eric. You don't *have* to have a gun."

"Yeah," Doug suggested teasingly, "You can be our cannon fodder."

Eric relaxed. "Good, I can manage that." A moment later he blurted out, "Wait! What's a cannon fodder?"

Tom surreptitiously watched to see how Ben was going to handle this.

Ben frowned at Doug. "Cool it, will ya?" He patted Eric on the back. "Never mind. We'll find something for you to do."

Eric wandered off into the darkness muttering about cannon fodder and what it meant for him.

Everyone else finished loading their magazines, oiling and wiping down their guns, checking to make certain the actions worked smoothly. Tom meandered through the motley band of adventurers. "Interesting collection of guns you guys have here. Quite a wide range of firepower, too, all the way from the Saturday Night Special that Robb has, to the .50 caliber muzzle loader that Trey has."

"How's this?" John held his .30-'06 in the air. "Small clip, bolt action, used for *hunting*," he said as he glared at all the unusual guns everyone else had.

"Yeah, that's more what I would have expected," Tom said. "But don't load it until we have prey in sight." He smiled. "I expect you'll have the best chance of hitting your target, but I look forward to seeing how useful these others will be."

John sneered at Robb, then sat near Melvin and the other serious hunters, ignoring the rest.

With the meal cleaned up and the dishes done by lantern light at the river's edge, the tents slowly filled, with Carl getting the first shift. He sat in a folding camp chair halfway between the tents and the fire facing off to one side, *I don't want to blind myself by staring into the fire*. The first watch was as monotonous as the second. It wasn't until the third that the excitement picked up.

Joe grabbed the lantern and circled the campsite, checking that everything was as it should be. At the half-way point, he stopped to look across the river where he could see the moon sinking towards the treetops. Finishing his circuit, he heard Patrick crawl into his sleeping bag. All was quiet as he sat to wait out his turn. He shivered as a cold breeze whistled up from the river, and a wall of fog drifted in off the cold water. Tendrils of mist curled high, obscuring the roughly full moon.

Joe squinted to see as far as he could out into the forest. *Not much light from the fire. Maybe I'd better put on more wood.* Making certain the safety was on, he set his rifle across the arms of the camp chair and headed to the woodpile. As he reached for a log, he froze, *What's that noise? Something doesn't sound right.* He swiveled, carefully perusing each and every tree, *I don't see anything moving, nothing making noise, so what did I hear?* He picked up an armful of wood and stepped towards the fire—that's when they hit.

Joe snapped around, startled by a half a dozen men coming right at him. They were dressed in dirty, torn clothing, brandishing tree branches and charging at him from all directions. Throwing a log he was carrying at the closest one, Joe let loose with a blood curdling bellow and dove for his rifle—he never made it. The first one swung his branch, hitting Joe full in the back, dropping him instantly. The next one swung his branch hard at Joe's head, but Joe rolled to his back, grabbing for his Bowie knife. He had intended to block with it, but somehow he managed to flip it, and holding it by the blade, he tossed it—it embedded itself in the middle of the guy's chest. Joe rolled away as the body toppled to the ground, and he grabbed for his pistol.

Two, startled sleepy heads pushed out through tent flaps in time to see Joe shoot three more, firing from the ground, rolling between double taps. He grimaced in pain, pulled himself to one knee, and fired at the last couple of marauders sprinting for the woods. He did a quick scan for movement and, seeing none, collapsed.

The noise woke everyone, and Tom was at his side in a flash. "What happened?!"

Joe moaned, held his side, and tried to answer, "They…"

"Never mind. Relax." Tom put his hand on Joe's shoulder. "Ben! Where's the first aid kit?"

Annie stepped up. "I have mine. Let me see what I can do."

"Ben, get a couple of your guys," Tom said. "I want to see what's out there."

Ben grabbed Trey and Robb. "Let's check it out."

Following Tom's lead, they crept off in the direction the last attackers had fled. Annie put her first aid kit on the ground next to Joe and kneeled.

Patrick unhooked the lantern from the post it was hanging on and held it above Annie, trying to give her as much light as possible.

Eric wandered through the campsite, gagging as he stepped over the bodies. He stopped at the corpse with the knife in it and stood there staring at it. "He's dead, passed away, breathed his last…"

Annie stared. "Eric, sit down. Joe's hurt and you're talking about *those* guys?"

Eric muttered, "…departed this life, been called by his Maker, winged into Eternity…"

Annie suppressed her incredulity at Eric and tried to pay attention to Joe. She palpated his ribs and thought, *A couple cracked. All that rolling around could have punctured a lung.* Aloud she said, "You're going to be fine, Joe. We have things under control."

His eyes, wide with fright, locked onto Annie's. He tried to speak but choked on his spittle. A drizzle of foamy blood leaked out of the corner of his mouth.

Eric stood motionless, still mumbling, "…paid his debt to nature, taken his last sleep, joined the choir invisible…"

Annie tried to suppress a gasp, *Foamy blood! He* had *punctured a lung. We aren't prepared to handle an emergency like* this. Trying to smile, she put her hand on his forehead and said, "You'll be fine. Hang in there. Ben will be back in shortly." She searched through the shadows beyond the fire but didn't see the search party. They were still out in the darkness, investigating. Waggling her head at Patrick, she quietly said, "Do me a favor: get Eric out of here. He's not doing *anyone* any good."

Patrick grabbed Eric and dragged him off. As they left, Annie could still hear Eric muttering under his breath, "…awakened to life immortal, shuffled off his mortal coil, crossed to the Great Beyond…"

With that distraction gone, she was better able to focus on Joe. She ran her hands along his sides but didn't find any external wounds. Not knowing anything else to do, she closed her eyes, concentrated on his pain, and swore that she could feel his broken ribs inside her own chest.

Joe gasped for air twice, then relaxed, and regained his composure. He surrendered to Annie's ministrations and let her hands calm him. Everything slowed down, everything quieted, everything faded away, except her hands, her warm hands. He closed his eyes, and yet he could still see them: her hands, full of fire, on his ribs. Her hands *were* fire, burning deep into him. The heat radiated throughout his entire body, melting away the pain but leaving the fever. Then gradually the fever abated as well. He drew in a deep, cool breath and opened his eyes.

Everyone stepped back. Annie had been leaning over Joe, but when he opened his eyes, she dropped her hands and slumped off to the side. Patrick caught her as she fell. "Annie! What happened?"

She leaned back into his arms. "I don't know. Did I faint?"

"Maybe, but Joe's certainly better."

Annie's eyes flew open. "Joe! How is he?"

Joe grinned. "There's no need to fear, Underdog—" He coughed and grimaced, then caught his breath. "It only hurts when I laugh."

"But, Joe, how could you be fine? I mean…I saw…you were…"

Patrick stared at the two of them. "Annie, is Joe hurt or not?"

Joe laughed, then groaned. "Yeah, I'm not hurt, not at all. It doesn't hurt to get whacked with a tree by a raving lunatic in the middle of the night." He grimaced again and laid back down. "Well it doesn't hurt *too* much. If you guys don't mind, I'll sit out the next one."

"You do that," Patrick said. "We'll keep an eye on you while you rest."

Annie's head snapped up. "Patrick! You're here, but…what did you do with Eric?"

"Oh! I gave him a simple task: keep the fire going."

She almost laughed. "Will *somebody* go get him before he catches something on fire, like himself?" She sighed. "Patrick, you know you can't leave Eric alone near a fire. Ben told me what happened at scout camp that one time."

Joe snickered. "You mean when he caught his sleeping bag on fire?" He tried not to groan as he laughed again. "That was so funny."

Annie frowned. "It wouldn't have been funny if he'd been hurt!"

Patrick agreed. "Yeah, but he didn't, though he did have to sleep in a half-burnt sleeping bag that night. He might have frozen…all because he was trying too hard to keep warm!"

Carl came back from the fire pit with Eric in tow. "He was trying to keep the fire going…by putting on *all* the wood. He could have smothered it."

"Leave it alone," Annie said. "Robb can fix it when he gets back."

"I wonder where they are." Patrick peered into the darkness. "And what they've found."

Joe tried to twist his head to see but couldn't get that far. "Did anyone hear any shots out there?" He waited for an answer, but only saw negative responses. "Well, *that's* good," he said. "No one's been shot." Then he thought for a moment, and said, "On the other hand it could be bad. Those weirdoes weren't using guns, so it also means none of *our* guys shot."

Annie was starting to get anxious when she heard the sharp snap of a branch breaking. The group stared as one into the darkness. Movement off to one side caught their attention as Tom stepped out into the light of the campfire, followed closely by Ben and Robb. "Well?"

Ben paused. "Nothing. Whatever they were, they move fast and quietly. We may have scared them off for the night."

Robb headed to the fire. "Hey! Who's trying to kill my fire?"

Everyone ignored him as he stirred the fire.

Tom checked up to see how Joe was doing.

Annie paused half way up. "Wait, where's Trey?"

Ben's head popped up. "He stopped behind that thirsty tree."

A moment later Trey stepped into the light adjusting his belt. "Ah, much better." He paused, realizing that everyone was watching him. "What's up? Why is everyone staring at me?"

"Oh, nothing," Annie said. "You were slow coming back. That's all. We were wondering…"

Patrick quietly said, "What do you mean 'We,' Annie?"

Annie's face reddened. "Shh!"

Tom dropped to the ground beside Joe. "You did an excellent job of shooting, but you were hit pretty good. How are you feeling now?"

"A bit beat up at first, but after Annie did her first aid on me, it's better." Joe tried to smile. "I'll live."

Tom smiled. "I'm amazed you weren't hurt as much as I'd have assumed." He knew Joe had taken a solid blow to the back and hadn't expected to find him conscious, much less chatting. He raised an eyebrow at Annie. *She certainly knows her stuff. I'm glad the guys brought her along.* Giving her a slow, careful look, he thought, *Yup, I'm* really *glad she came.*

Trey joined the group. "That was some impressive shooting! Did you learn that in the army?"

"Not really." Joe tried to downplay his shooting. "The Ranger training must have sunk in. I've never been that good on the range, but when it's real, well, I didn't even have time to think. It just happened."

Ben strolled to the body with the knife in it. "And whose might this be?" He pulled at the knife, but it didn't move.

Joe rolled towards Ben. "Well, it might be Eric's…but it isn't!" He tried to laugh, but grimaced in pain instead.

Eric, who had been sitting there morosely staring off into the distance, flinched at the mention of his name. "What?"

Joe sat up. "Never mind. Hey, Eric, why don't you head back to bed?"

Eric stood and silently headed for his tent.

Carl followed him saying, "I'll see to it he gets there."

Tom agreed with Joe. "We all need to hit the sack. Morning comes early out here. Ben, hang on for a minute. Help me stash these bodies."

Ben continued to struggle with the knife. "Yeah. I'll be right there, let me get this knife out first."

Trey ambled up and said, "Let me try." Ben stepped back as Trey planted a foot on the body's chest, grabbed the knife firmly, and pulled. It stuck for a moment, but as he wiggled it, it finally came loose with a sucking sound. "Yuck! You stuck it right in his sternum. I'll go wash it off in the river."

"Thanks," Joe said. "I don't know if I'd make it that far right now. Anyone want to help me get into a sleeping bag?"

Everyone surged forward, all offering to carry the hero of the day single-handedly. Ben assigned two guys to buddy-carry Joe gently to his tent as two more went ahead to get his bag ready. Patrick held the lantern as he walked Annie to her tent, and the rest of the group gradually broke up, several going in search of more thirsty trees, but soon enough the camp was quiet again.

Tom and Ben moved all the bodies into one heap, then used the branches from the attack and stacked them to cover the bodies, piling on larger branches to secure it until morning. The plan was to check them out later, when they had more light than the lanterns put out. Carl put Eric to bed, then came back out to cover what was left of Joe's shift. The rest of the night passed quietly. The morning, however, gave them a new problem to consider.

Sunrise brought new hope for the adventuresome party: Joe was recovering nicely. They even managed to cook, eat, clean up an early breakfast, and strike the tents, all without paying attention to the pile of dead bodies. As everyone packed up, ready to head out, Tom called Ben, Trey, and Patrick off to the side for a strategy session.

"Now I know this wasn't the type of adventure you guys imagined, but this is where we are now. We can either go on and work through this or head back to the pickup point and wait out the rest of the time there. It's up to you."

Ben searched the other faces, then said what they were all thinking, "Joe reacted in self-defense, pure self-defense. He had no choice. *We* had no choice." He frowned. "We should clean up now, at least clean up what we can, then head on."

Everyone mumbled their approval.

Trey snickered and said, "No use crying over spilled blood."

Ben shuddered. "That's sick, Trey."

Ignoring his comment, Tom suggested, "As long as they're dead, they don't need anything they have, right? And if we search the bodies, it might give us an idea of who they are and where they come from. I've never heard of anything like this on other outings, so I'll need to bring back as much info as I can, to let the others know what's going on out here."

The four of them went to the pile and unstacked the branches, revealing the bodies, even more gruesome in the daylight. Tom grimaced, then said, "Joe certainly knows how to use a pistol. Two shots each, but both centered in the chest." He heard a couple of grunts as an answer. *Trying to hold their breath, too,* he thought, *I don't blame them.*

Beyond the blood, Ben could see that these guys had been living out in the wild for quite a while. They were filthy, had matted hair, and wore skimpy rags held on by vine ropes.

Other than the branches they'd been wielding, each had a short, stone knife blade tied into a stick handle. One of them, the leader they assumed, wore a tight leather cap and a strangely carved wooden amulet on a leather cord around his neck. He had a small cloth sack tied to his waist that contained several copper rings linked together and three animal skin scrolls with writing on them. One might have been a map, but they couldn't make heads nor tails of the other two. They came across an animal bladder filled with liquid, and not wanting to risk opening it, they set it aside to continue searching.

Two of the other bodies wore necklaces that appeared to be made out of garlic or something that stinks like garlic. The third had a necklace of vines covered with small purple flowers. Lastly, they found another container of liquid lying nearby where it had landed in the skirmish. It could be a wine skin made from an animal's stomach.

Focusing on the booty, Tom said, "Well, I recognize money when I see it, so we'll keep that in case we need to buy something in town."

"Money? Ben asked. "Where's there any money?"

Tom picked up the linked rings and jingled them. "This is what they use for money here. Small rings linked on bigger rings. Copper, silver, gold, and other local metals. The more rings linked, the more it's worth. I've seen people who have a bunch of smaller rings looped onto a bigger ring that still manages to fit onto a finger like a normal ring, so they can show off how rich they are."

"Keeping money is good, but you can stick it in *your* pocket," Ben said. "I don't know where it's been before," he said.

Tom poked through the rest of the pile. "Joe might like that amulet thing as a trophy, but I don't think anyone would want to wear that helmet."

Trey peeled the helmet off and cringed. "Yeah, you should see all the crawlies under it! I'll grab the wine skins, or whatever they are. We can check them out when we don't have to fight off a gag reflex."

Patrick snagged the scrolls. "I'd like to try to figure out where this map leads. As far as the others, it would be interesting to see if anyone in town can read 'em. What's the name of the town again?"

"*Roadranusis*." Tom shrugged. "You want the map? Keep it."

Tossing the rest of their findings aside, they dug shallow graves on a small knoll overlooking the river, placed rocks to cover the mounds, and put the necklaces reverently on top to act as a monument. They hung the leather cap on a stick posted at the leader's grave.

Finally, they tackled the question of the bladder and wine skin. Holding the bladder at arm's length, Ben pulled the cork gingerly, expecting a pop or hiss, but nothing happened. Pulling the   it closer, he stared into the depths and shrugged. Taking a hesitant sniff he said, "No smell either. I wonder what it is."

Patrick asked, "What's it look like? Pour it out."

Ben shrugged and poured a little out. "Water? Why such a small container, especially when there's a river full of it right here?"

No one had an answer, so he dumped the rest of it on the nearest grave and tossed the bladder on top.

"What should we do with the wine?" Trey asked.

"Is that what it is?" Ben asked.

Trey shrugged as he pulled the cork and sniffed. He shuddered. "Whatever it is, it's gone rancid. Smells like vinegar."

"A vinegar smell is caused by oxidation of alcohol. Rancid is when an oil is oxidized."

Ben spun to see Eric standing nearby. "Hey, why are you here?"

Eric shrugged. "Wanted to see what you guys were up to."

Ben glanced back at the hastily dug graves. "Nothing that needs to trouble you." He grabbed Trey and Patrick. "Let's skedaddle."

No one argued with that idea, so they re-joined the rest of the group, who were getting ready to head out. Annie had Joe sitting on a rock with his shirt pulled up examining him. The extensive bruising across his back was ugly, but he could still move in spite of the pain, so he wouldn't hamper the group's progress. As they packed up the equipment, they shifted things to lighten his load. Plenty of volunteers offered to help carry his stuff.

Tom walked up to Joe and ceremoniously kneeled in front of him. "In recognition of your valiant effort in protecting our party, I hereby bestow upon you the amulet of bravery." With that, he solemnly looped the cord over Joe's head, the wooden carving hanging in front, and everyone cheered. Trey reached to pat him on the back but then, remembered his injuries and quickly held off.

Joe sat there uncomfortable at the attention. "Why, thanks. I don't deserve it." He stood up, tucked in his shirt, and stared at his new medal, a wooden disk with three circles carved into the front. The cord passed through one of the circles, leaving the other two to form the base of a triangle. "Shucks, folks, I'm speechless." He glanced conspiratorially at Ben as he grabbed his now-lightened pack.

Following Joe's lead, Ben linked arms and launched into an entirely irrelevant song, "We're off to see the Wizard…"

Trey hooked into Joe's other arm and joined in, "…The Wonderful Wizard of Oz…"

Tom stepped back, staring at these discordant singers not knowing what to make of them.

Annie stepped up to Tom. "That's my brother for you. When *those* scouts go hiking, the whole countryside hears it. Come on. Don't get left behind." She linked arms with him and stepped out, adding her voice to the fray, "…We hear he is a whiz of a wiz, if ever a wiz there was…"

All the others picked up their packs and joined in on the distinctly non-military cadence as Patrick brought up the rear.

Tom thought, That's not the kind of song I would have expected as they march…show tunes…but it keeps them together. We won't get spread out at this pace.

The path was easy to follow as long as they kept by the river, so Tom let Ben and his chorus lead. The song changed often, but Ben kept the group together and moving at a good clip. They followed the river downstream, heading generally southeast, as the sun slowly climbed. After they'd been hiking a while, the gentle slope they'd been following suddenly steepened and the river became a torrent, rushing through closely spaced rocks. Then the path plunged as the river went over a cliff, becoming a waterfall. The cliffs on both sides had animal trails worn into them, but as tight and narrow as they were, it would be nigh to impossible to carry any kind of boat up or down.

Tom knew this was the boundary at the edge of civilization. He considered the area and thought, *The techies certainly picked a good spot for the drop off point. It'd be unlikely that any locals would wander up this far,* but then thinking back to what happened last night he wondered, *So then where did those wild men come from?*

They stopped for a short rest and a quick brunch at the bottom of the rapids where the river once again slowed and spread out. A small pool had formed on the near side of the river where a circle of rocks isolated part of the water. Cool and deep, the pool tempted a couple of the guys to jump in for "a quick dip," but Tom persuaded the group to stick together and keep moving.

The tall grass they moved through so easily soon gave way to a well-used animal trail, which then became a real path through old-growth trees. As the sparse trees of the plains became a serious forest alongside the river, the footpath widened and was more worn, easily big enough for a couple of horses side by side, a trail undoubtedly used by local hunters who patrolled this forest. The canopy of leaves blocking the sun gave the travelers a slight chill as a light breeze came up, but after the scouts had walked a couple more hours, the trees thinned, and light was visible ahead of them.

The forest opened out into green fields that appeared to be well tended and watered. Small hillocks separated the fields into sections, and the group soon passed by a human-powered pump consisting of small buckets on a rope that dipped into the river and emptied into a basin that had actual clay pipes leading to small, damp depressions in the fields.

It struck Ben as strange that they had developed such an involved irrigation system. "I thought this was more of a primitive, old-fashioned kind of a place."

"This society is interesting," Tom said. "In some things, they're still in the dark ages, yet in others, they're closer to modern society. Almost as if they leaped from the shoulders of a previous, much more advanced, civilization."

"*Is* there a previous civilization?" Annie asked.

Tom shrugged. "Not that we've found anywhere, but then again, we haven't had the time to map out much territory, much less go digging up old burial grounds."

"So, with all this technology," Trey said, "where *is* everyone?"

Frowning, Tom checked out the fields. "I don't know. That's strange. Usually by time we get this far, there's a dozen kids deserting their field duties to check us out, but I don't even see anyone working out there."

"The locals don't mind you bringing all these strangers through?" Ben asked.

"Not at all. They know that good times are in store when travelers come through. They look forward to the business we bring, and often they'll follow along to help out with the hunt."

Annie smiled. "It's nice to be on such good terms with the locals."

"Oh, I'm on good terms with most of the ones I've met. The kids in town can even say my name close enough that I recognize it."

Ben glanced back. "Is language much of a problem? I'm certain Patrick would love to interview the locals."

"He's into languages? That's good. We could use the expertise. Not many of the folks here speak English well enough to get things across. There's the mayor and a couple of his buddies, but we usually just wave and point, what we have in one hand, what we want in the other."

Ben could go along with that. "You do what's necessary." He thought of the loot they'd plundered from the bodies. "How much do you think those copper rings are worth?"

Tom shrugged. "Never gave much thought to costs. No need to be bothered by the monetary exchange for such a short stay. Barter works well enough."

"So…how much farther to town?" Trey asked.

Glancing at the mid-day sun, he said, "Shouldn't be much farther. Just past the next ridge, I think."

"Good, 'cause this pack is getting heavy. I'm carrying all the kitchen goods, the main tent, my own stuff, and half of Joe's."

Tom stared at Trey. "And *now* you're complaining? With half the camp in your pack?"

"Not so much that it's heavy." Trey shrugged. "It's been a long morning."

"Well, you can look forward to dropping your pack soon." Tom led the way up the slope they were climbing. "There's *Roadranusis* now."

Ben yelled, "The end is in sight. The town's right ahead."

Patrick answered from the back. "Last one to the tavern buys!"

Ben could barely hear his reply, but everyone else must have heard it because the pace of the entire column picked up. They descended the hill at a quick trot, but the closer they approached the town, the slower they went. The town was empty, deserted. Cooking fires were still burning, but no one was visible.

Tom called a halt. "Hang on guys. This isn't right." He frowned as he scrutinized the buildings. "Something's going on."

The group closed in naturally, everyone at the ready.

Abruptly, a man stepped out from behind the building in front of them, an older man, but what caught everyone's attention was the six-foot long, two-handed broadsword in his hand, glinting in the sun. A peasant farmer ready for war, he scrutinized the group carefully, then, keeping his sword at the ready, he called out, "Tomss?"

"Shess? What's happening?" Tom could feel tension behind him. He glanced over his shoulder. "Stay put. I'll see what's up." He faced the sword, half stepped, bowed slightly with his wrists together, and in a calm voice said, "Shess, peace, *mi pismi gu*. We speak, *mu tahknah?*"

Shess looked Tom up and down slowly, finally saying, "*aa-eh, mu dislu lo pahlnah*. Yes, we talk of trouble." Then he leaned back and yelled out in that strange, flowing language. In response, more men stepped out from behind buildings all around them. Armed with no weapons other than swords and spears, the locals stood their ground. The threat was unmistakable, so the scouts stayed put as well.

Glancing at all the weaponry, Tom bowed again to the group's leader. "Peace, Shessicheros. We hunt, *zhahnto*, we trade, *bahtmi*."

"Yes, Tomss. We know you." He called out again and archers rose up from nearby rooftops.

Ben whispered to Tom, "Ouch! Not the kind of reception I'd expected."

"Me neither," Tom said. "I have no idea what's wrong, Ben." To the rest of them he said, "Everyone sit tight. I'll go talk with the mayor and see if I can figure it out."

Trey plopped on a wooden bench next to a small cook fire. "I'm dropping my pack here. If something goes wrong, I want to be able to move quickly."

Shess frowned at Trey and walked towards one of the larger buildings. "We sit there, *mu skitu vaa*."

The armed men moved up behind them, closing off any chance of retreat or escape.

Trey shrugged. "We follow them?"

Slowly walking through a gauntlet of warriors, they filed into the meeting hall. As Joe stepped inside, one of the young men jumped out and grabbed him, yelling, "*vahlnimlimre!*" He threw Joe against the side of the door holding a quickly drawn knife to his throat.

Joe's eyes went wide with fear. He held out his empty hands in front as a token of surrender. Shess pushed through the crowd as he hurried back to see what was going on. He spoke harshly, and the young man replied excitedly but didn't move his knife, instead he used his free hand to pull at the 'medal' that Joe was wearing.

Shess frowned. "*ti zahvlo*." He reached for the medal. "This bad. We fight, *miyi kahmdah*."

"Yes, we fight, too," Tom said fervently. He grabbed Joe's shoulder and held up four fingers. "He kill four!"

Shess stepped back and blinked. "He kill four, *di mormah zi daa?*"

Joe tried to nod without running into the blade at his throat. "I kill them," he said holding up the medal.

All of the townsfolk spoke at once, gesturing at Joe and his medal, trying to decide whether to believe the story or not. The decision finally made, the young man pulled the knife away from Joe's throat, slipped it into his sheath, then offered to help Joe inside.

Tom breathed with relief. "Close call. A few run-ins with those wild men would tend to make anyone touchy, but it sounds to me like they've had *more* than a *few* run-ins."

Now accepted, the adventurers and the townsfolk bypassed the language barrier by using a lot of pantomime, though both sides were quickly learning the speech of the other. They muddled through the story of Joe's squabble, and Trey practically ripped Joe's shirt off in his haste to show the wounds Joe had received. Some of the natives called him "*vebri*, hero," but others didn't think he was so tough. They had their own tales to tell, and, trying to outdo each other, they alternately launched into tales of derring-do and argued the details in others' stories. Although Trey, Joe, and the others couldn't keep up with the details of the conversation, they were certainly able to follow the emotions of the controversy.

Annie found a small stool nearby and sat, leaning back on the wall with her feet up on a bench, trying to keep out of the testosterone-slinging match by watching from a safe distance.

Meanwhile, across the room, a discussion of a different sort took place as the leaders studied a map working through the details of the problem.

Shess drew his finger along a blue line on the map and explained why they had greeted Tom's group at sword point, "Here *vahlnimlimre* pass river south."

Ben squinted. "Valnirie?"

Shess appreciated Ben's futile attempt at the native language. He said it again, more slowly, "*vahl-neem-LEE-mre*, wild-animal-like men." Seeing confusion, he tried again. "Say short NEE-mre, animal men."

Ben tried, "*nimre, nimre*. Hmm…It flows nicely."

"You say good," the mayor said.

"And you speak English reasonably well, too."

Tom interrupted the language lesson, "And you thought we were more of the same, more *nimre*?"

"Yes, hunters see men moving into forest from north. They warn us someone coming from outside. We worry because the *vahlnimlimre*," he acknowledged Ben, "the *nimre*, they not good. They burn fields, raid stores, take food, kill workers. We hear someone pass waterfall, we bring all from fields into town, get ready."

Ben leaned in to see the map. "The waterfall is there?"

Tom put his finger on the map. "Yes, that's where it should be."

"It is our land edge," Shess said. "Farther is animal land. Animals live there, we live here."

"But the *nimre* came from up there, from the animal land?"

"They animal men, live in animal land. They same as animal, stay there, not come here long times."

"Well, considering the one time we encountered them, I don't blame you for being jumpy. If it weren't for Joe's quick action…and good shooting, we'd be in a world of hurt, too."

Shess smiled at the raucous group, still exchanging stories. "Your people and mine, they friends now, *gui fremi miaa*."

Tom stood slightly, put his hands on the table, and studied the map. "So how do we handle these *nimre*?"

Ben interrupted, "Wait a minute. Who said *we're* doing anything? It's *their* problem, not ours. We're here to hunt, and anything we do besides hunt will cut into what little time we have, and we have barely over *one* week. I can't see that we'd even have *time* to do anything more."

"Relax, Ben. I was thinking," Tom said, "as long as we're here, we could be useful and help. After all, check out what Joe did, and he was by himself. Can you imagine our whole group going after them? We have enough firepower that it'd be a slaughter. We could wipe out the whole band of them and still have time to do some hunting."

"I don't know." Ben stopped to think. "We weren't planning to do anything like that. When they attacked Joe, he *had* to fight back, in self-defense. What you're suggesting would be a pre-emptive attack against unarmed people…not the same at all. It wouldn't be fair. And can you imagine trying to bring back a trophy of one of *them*? We'd get arrested for murder!"

"So, no trophies, but we'd have established some good friends here," Tom said tipping his head towards Shess.

"That sounds nice, but I don't think so…I mean…I can't see how it would affect *us* much. We're going to be here a short time, but I can see why *you'd* like to help 'em out. You'll be coming back here again with the next group to visit Ex Terra, but this is the *only* time *we're* going to be here."

"So how would you feel, being the guests of these people, abandoning them in their time of need? If you ever did want to come back, they might not be as welcoming…if they were even still here at all."

"I'll tell you what. I like these people, and I like the mayor here." Shess smiled as Ben continued, "I'll go talk to the guys and see what they think."

Tom stood up. "That's all I can ask. Talk to them, and let us know."

Shess stood up to follow Ben as he headed towards the noisy group. He took Ben by the arm. "We first eat. You later talk. They need time, relax and know us. Then they good decide."

Ben smiled weakly. "Yeah, they 'good decide.' For us as well as you." Ben considered leading his buddies to war…because that's what it would be. They would be killing *people*, not the animals they'd planned on hunting. No trophies, just terror. He shuddered at the idea.

The mayor stepped up to the group of braggarts, and, with one look, they all fell silent. He signaled his men to move off to one side and the adventurers to the other. He was surveying the room when suddenly, at an inaudible command, a horde of children burst out of a side door and spread out through the room. They showed that they knew their role well as the older children shuffled tables and benches, forming a large 'U' with one table at the head of the room and two tables along each side, as if they were in the great room of a castle. As the group continued to watch, the younger children placed plates and mugs spread out on each table, then ran to stand against the walls.

Shess observed, approving their actions, though he frowned once, when a young boy tried to go out the wrong door and ran into a girl coming in with a platter. She paused to direct him to the right door, then hurried back to her task. Shess smiled.

Ben glanced at Tom. "This is neat to watch. As if they're doing a dance."

"Yeah," Tom said. "It's kinda exciting to watch…the first few times. It gets boring after that. I've seen them do this every time I bring through a hunting party, but you're the first group to watch with me. Usually the soldiers are too busy guarding everything, and the scientists are too busy doing whatever they do to even notice."

"They treat you like this because of all the technology you guys bring?"

"It has nothing to do with us or our technology. They do the same thing when they have visitors from anywhere, even the next town just downriver. And the other towns do the same, too, when Shess visits them. Everyone here does it."

"I don't think I've ever heard of an entire society with such a level of self-sacrificing service."

"Get used to it." Tom said. "It happens all the time here."

Once things were set and the children had left the room, Shessicheros walked towards the head table followed by a couple of his higher-ups. He called Ben and Tom to join them, then answering Ben's unasked question, he allowed Annie to join them as well. The rest of the group wandered, then slowly divided up and found spots along the side tables. Ben was happy to see that his friends weren't at all uncomfortable mixing in with the townsfolk, and he could see camaraderie starting to form between the two groups. Then he realized that it might be difficult to *not* help these generous people.

As they were getting settled, young women came in carrying clay pitchers, filling all the mugs with a dark liquid. Following them were women carrying bowls full of what could be small potatoes mixed with bright green leafy vegetables. After filling all the mugs, the servers stood at attention along the inside edge of the tables and waited.

The door leading from the kitchen flew open as an imposing lady came through carrying a huge, deep dish filled with sliced meat that had broth sloshing up to the edge. She stopped in front of Shess, and he made quite a show of picking through the slices with his knife, finally proclaiming it good. The servers all started ladling the veggies onto plates as the large lady carried the platter of meat to each person, letting them reach across with their knives to slice their own portion.

Ben hesitated, glancing at Tom with a question in his eyes.

"It's good stuff," Tom said. "We've eaten it before, and no one has gotten sick. I don't know how they cook it, but the flavor is decent."

Ben watched as the guys dug in without a moment's hesitation. "Well, you'd better be right, because we're into it now." He stuck his tongue out at Annie, knowing how much of a food fussy she was, but she had already followed suit, trying to fit a green leaf dripping with juice into her mouth without making too much of a mess. He shrugged and dove in, taking cautious bites at first, finding that the tart concoction made his mouth water not quite to the point of pain. Swallowing gingerly, he decided it was quite good. Grabbing his mug for a quick swig, he noticed Tom staring at him.

"Go ahead," Tom said. "It's fine."

Ben sipped cautiously, and the sudden sharpness of the beverage caused him to wince.

Tom chuckled. "Yes, they have something here like a lemon. Close enough to be a citrusy fruit. This certainly isn't lemonade, but it is brewed with a touch of lemon in it."

Ben choked out, "A touch? It's way sour."

Eric spoke up, "Essentially the acerbic flavor serves to enhance the modicum of alcohol."

Ignoring the rest, Trey reacted to the words 'brewed' and 'alcohol.' He swallowed quickly and said, "Yeah, this stuff is kinda light. When do we get the good stuff?"

"They won't serve that until later," Tom said. "Much later, after the kids are in bed."

"Can't wait," Trey said, then went back to his food as if he hadn't eaten for a week.

"Quite a workout, carrying all that weight," Ben said. "Built up his appetite."

"I can see that," Tom said. "He carried all that gear? He's stronger than I expected."

Ben thought for a moment. "Yeah, much stronger."

Everyone continued stuffing their faces, but not so much so that they couldn't talk, as the noise level in the room continued at a muted roar. As they finished the meal, everyone used the dark brown bread to sop up the last of the drippings. Pulling small a piece from the loaf set near him, Ben could feel its warmth, still fresh from the oven. As dark on the inside as it was on the outside, the bread had such a soft crust that it made an excellent sponge to catch the last of the juice on his plate, so good that he thought about 'accidentally' dropping one or two loves in his pack when he went home.

Wiping up the last of the tasty broth from his plate, Ben considered how he was going to address the issue of helping these people. He knew that most of the guys were here to have fun, and some had their hearts set on bringing back something unique to show off. *No time for hunting, certainly not for trophies, if we go on a campaign to rid the area of those wild invaders*, he thought. *Having the northernmost town in the area isn't doing Shess any good. I truly wish that we could do something to help, but I don't think war is it.*

Startled from his musings, Ben suddenly realized that Shess had spoken, softly but firmly, and the room had instantly become quiet. Shess addressed Ben saying, "We now leave. You talk." He stood and headed for the door, followed by all the townsfolk.

Tom stood to head out, too, heading for the door. He stopped as he stepped out to say, "I don't want to inhibit your discussion, so I'll hang with the locals for a while."

Ben stepped back in surprise. He's leaving me to bring up the subject?

"You have all the time you need." He paused. "Remember, if you aren't done by this eve, you'll have to continue the discussion in the morning. No missing out on our first night on the town." He stepped out and closed the door with finality.

An expectant silence filled the room. Ben stood at the doorway as everyone else waited. An eternally long awkward moment later, Robb said, "What did he mean by that? Why are we going to 'talk'?"

Ben walked to the table and stood at the front. "You know those wild men that attacked last night?" He heard a murmured assent, and the guys twisted around to find Joe. "Well, Shess says that they've been coming past the waterfall, as far as this town, too. They've been attacking villagers and causing all kinds of problems for Shess and his people."

Ben thought he heard someone say something about kicking butt.

He continued, "When we were talking with Shess, Tom suggested that something be done. He had an idea that *we* might want to get involved."

This time he heard it distinctly: Someone said, "Yeah, let's get 'em!"

Ben quieted the crowd. "It isn't that easy. If we spend too much time chasing off these *nimre*, animal men as the mayor calls them, we won't have time to do any real hunting."

He saw a couple heads pop up and stare his direction, but no one said anything.

"So, any comments? Should we help out or stick to our plan?"

Voices exploded as everyone argued, some wanting to help, others wanting to focus on camping and staying out of local affairs, and a small faction remaining quiet. Ben sat at the head of the room, trying to listen in on all the conversations going on.

Patrick wanted to trade recipes, so he wanted to help out the town, but Trey was focused on hunting. Joe was gung-ho for paying back the *nimre*, but then again, no one could blame him for wanting to go after the ones who'd escaped after last night's attack, so his choice was to help the town. Robb didn't mind either way, as long as they were out camping, but he thought it would be safer and more fun to hunt animals, instead of trying to track someone who could shoot back.

Ben felt the room was pretty close to evenly split until Annie spoke up. With her pushing to help out the town, he could see the group quickly coming to a decision, but he wondered if the quiet ones would go along with the consensus. He'd have to exert some pressure if they dissented.

Suddenly it all came to a head as Eric stood up. "We must not interfere with the society here." The room silenced. Everyone was stunned, the first time Eric had ever shown any backbone. He had an opinion and stood up to express it loudly and clearly. Regrettably, the appearance of intelligence was a brief event as he then continued, "Remember the Prime Directive: We are not to interfere with the natural development of any other culture."

The room relaxed, the scouts letting out loud guffaws. Someone yelled from the back, "There's no Prime Directive here. We're not in that dumb TV show of yours!"

Eric countered with, "May I point out that my connection with 'that dumb TV show' is what got us here in the first place?"

John stood up. "No, you may not. *How* we got here isn't important. We're here now, and we came here to *hunt*."

Eric ignored John, instead focusing next to him, "You've been noticeably quiet, Mel." He deliberately asked, "What's your opinion?"

Ben could feel the tension in the room tighten as Eric pulled a stupid move. All the scouts knew that Melvin detested nicknames.

Melvin stood up, bristling in anger, and glared at Eric. "The name's Melvin, you twit, and you and all your star geeky friends can sit here and rot if that's what you want."

John laughed out loud. "You tell 'em!"

Melvin slapped John on the back, then continued, "We came here to hunt, to bring back trophies, and that's what we're going to do, even if it has to be your head on a stick!"

Eric sat abruptly as John expressed his agreement. "Yeah, and we're tired of all this talk, so we're leaving right now." He walked to the door, grabbing his pack on the way. "Anyone else here to *hunt*?"

Melvin was right behind him, quickly followed by Carl, who paused in the doorway and said, "See you in a week or so…at the Door." The three of them were outside before anyone could react. By the time Ben stood, cleared the table, and made it out of the building, they were double-timing it out of town to the north, heading back on the road that they had followed into town.

Annie followed Ben outside. "What're we going to do now?"

Ben shrugged. "I don't know, but we should wait here until we figure it out." He paused. "Anyone want to find Tom and let him know what's happened?"

Patrick volunteered. "I'll find someone who knows where he is." He spoke to a group of natives for a moment, then the group ran off, heading through the middle of town.

"Good," Ben said. "The message has been sent." He slumped on the steps outside of the meeting hall and waited. Annie sat beside him, and the other scouts hung around nearby.

"I'm certain they'll come back," she said.

"Yeah?" Ben said. "But in one piece?"

"Hey, if they don't, it's their own fault. You're not responsible for them."

"That may be true, but I still feel responsible. Back when we were in the scout troop, they all expected me to handle any problems, and now I feel obligated to keep them safe on this trip, too."

Annie put her hand on Ben's shoulder. "Give them a chance to explore their limits. Soon enough they'll realize that all you're trying to do is protect them."

Ben felt a warmth from Annie's hand, and he relaxed. "What else can I do?"

"Not much." Annie smiled as she sensed his relaxation. "That's better."

Ben jumped as he heard a shout from across the grassy area in the middle of town. Patrick was heading their way at a quick jog, followed by Tom. They slowed as they approached.

Tom walked up to stand in front of Ben. "Here I am trying to relax with the mayor and get information on this situation with the wild men when someone runs up and tells me that part of your group has left?" He stared at Ben. "Well?"

Ben tried to explain what happened in the meeting hall, but Tom stopped him. "I don't care that you guys have petty squabbles. I want to know where they went!"

Ben dropped his head and indicated across the fields. "They went north, back into the animal land."

Tom struggled to keep his temper under control. "How could you let them walk away like that?" he asked.

"What could I have done? They stood up and left. They didn't even give us a chance to talk."

"So how many left?" Tom demanded.

"Three of them. Carl, John, and Melvin. They've always hung out together."

"Well, that's just fine and dandy." Tom stepped past Ben heading into the meeting hall. "No need to stand out here." He stood in the doorway waiting for the others. As soon as they were all inside, he pulled the door shut and glared. "This is the first time I've ever had a group break up and wander off. I don't know what Eugene had in mind, leaving me to tend to this trip all on my own." He stared at Ben. "I thought you had these guys under control."

"I can't control them," Ben said. "We could go find them."

"Yeah, we could." Tom frowned. "And get lost ourselves."

Ben's head sank.

Tom continued, "They don't know their way around here, so what worries me is whether they'll get back to the Door on time." He stopped to stare at Ben. "Make that get back at all."

"Should we go get them?" Ben asked.

"I don't think so," Tom said. "The only options I see are to either continue with the hunting, hoping to stumble across them, or completely skip the hunting and spend the entire time searching the area between here and the Door. That's assuming that they're heading in that direction. All I can say is hopefully we'll come across them before we leave. Until then, I suggest that no one head anywhere."

Trey slumped into a seat. "So there's no party tonight?"

"You're darn'd right there's no party. I am *not* having anyone *else* go wandering off. I can't believe it." He fumed. "I've never had problems *in* town before…it's been work enough to keep the hunting parties from shooting each other." He glared around the room. "You're hitting the sack *early* and *staying* there." He gave Trey a dirty look as he emphasized, "No partying, no wandering the town, no one else getting lost."

Ben started to answer, but before he could say anything, Tom continued, "An early start in the morning, and straight for the hunting area. We'll head north and cross the river before we get to the waterfall. Should be there in a couple hours."

Glumly picking up their packs, the group followed the townsfolk across the village to a building that extended out above the river on piers. Tom ran after them yelling, "And another thing: everyone *unload all* weapons. I don't want to have to *carry* anyone back."

Morning came way too early for the annoyed travelers. Well before dawn, Tom trolled the hallways, pounding on all the lodge doors. "Up and at 'em. We need to get moving quickly."

Ben and the others moaned at the noise. "What time is it, anyway?"

Tom kept pounding and answered, "Oh-dark-thirty. Move it, now!"

Gathering in the main room, they found the innkeeper serving a cold breakfast—stew with congealed grease on top. Patrick shuddered when he saw it and immediately tried to find something else to eat.

The innkeeper continued to push the stew on everyone. "What you want at butt crack of dawn?" he asked.

The scouts snickered, and Patrick raised an eyebrow asking, "Where'd you get that line?"

Shrugging, the innkeeper glanced at Tom who did a poor job of trying to hide as he quickly shoved food in his mouth to avoid answering the question.

Patrick almost smiled. "Isn't it interesting how the cuss words and gutter talk are always the first to make it across the language barrier?"

"The stew might be cold," Ben said, "but we still have that bread to sop up the last of it. Too bad it's not fresh and soft like yesterday."

"Yeah, that was excellent bread," Patrick said. "I wish I had the time to chat with the cook and get a decent recipe." He sat and ate the stew in silence.

Everyone jumped as the outer door flew open, and a gust of cold air followed Annie in. She glared. "No flush toilets? Come on, Tom, *you* don't have any kind of Prime Directive, so *give* these folks sanitation!"

Tom didn't look up. "We have more important things in front of us right now."

Annie pouted. "Like running water? Hot would be nice, but even cold would be good, then I wouldn't have to crack through ice to wash up."

Tom frowned. "It's not cold enough for ice."

"It certainly felt like it when I was brushing my teeth!"

Eric piped up, "Did you know that the toothbrush was invented in 1498? On June 26th…a Friday, according to most scholars."

A voice from the back asked, "What time?"

Eric frowned. "Hmm…Good question. I'll have to check on that."

Eyes rolled, but no one answered, though some stared at him rather coldly, blaming him for the unexpected change of plans.

Eric shut up and quickly went back to eating.

Tom called to the innkeeper. "Done or not, we're leaving now. Collect the bowls." Then standing up, he addressed the group, "Breakfast is done. Drop it now, grab your gear, and meet out on the green."

Outside, the brisk, cold air assaulted everyone's lungs, certainly not as cold as Annie had implied, but definitely cold enough that they could see their breath. Not many grumbles later, they stood in not quite straight lines, ready to go.

Tom called to Ben, "Put yourself midway, and let Patrick bring up the rear. I want everyone to stick close together. What do you say about not getting separated?" Everyone nodded, though none answered. Tom gave the group a once over, then headed north, his head slumping. *What a trip,* he thought. *I better not hear any complaints if these guys never make it back.*

Trying to keep warm, Tom moved quickly. Colder than he'd expected, he didn't want to admit it to the others. Unlike the trip into town, the scouts didn't sing as they marched—instead, the hike was silent and moody. He kept checking the line to make certain no one lagged behind, but in the dim pre-dawn grayness, all he could see were the lanterns swinging. He'd have to trust that Patrick, carrying the last one, was able to keep the group together.

The sky was barely starting to get light as they passed through the tilled and irrigated fields, still empty at this time of morning, but now covered in a thick fog. As they exited the fields and approached the forest, the sun glowed across the horizon, its first rays starting to burn off the tule fog and warm the day, but as the scouts entered the dank, gloomy forest, the dense branches filtered the light, making it seem as if the sun hadn't even risen at all today. Sadly, the dismal lighting fit everyone's frame of mind.

They were in the darkest part of the forest when a gunshot startled them. The column froze, and everyone spun around, trying to find the source. The sound came from the direction of the rising sun, a ways off, much farther from the river than the path. The fact that it wasn't a single shot caught their attention—three distinct shots followed by a pause, then three more: someone was signaling for help!

A couple of the guys ran towards the sound. Tom yelled, "Ben! Stop those guys!"

Ben yelled, "Sit tight! Are you guys thinking or not thinking at all?" Glancing up to the front, he hollered, "Tom, someone needs help."

"I know, I know. Everyone stay put." He squinted into the woods. "A couple of us will head out there and see what we can find."

Dropping to his knee and unslinging his pack, Ben pulled out a fully loaded magazine. *He didn't tell us to unload the magazines.* He slid the clip into his pistol, chambered a round, and flipped the safety on. At the front of the line, Robb and Joe were getting ready to follow Tom off the trail. He called out, "Patrick, Trey, on me!" He paused. "Annie, can you control the rest?"

"I'll keep them here," she said. "You go see what's up out there. We'll be ready when you get back."

"Keep everyone here. We don't want to search for the search parties." Ben didn't smile.

Patrick and Trey, already locked and loaded as well, were ready to follow, so Ben signaled to Tom then stepped into the tangle of trees. Locking his sight on a pair of trees in the distance, he glanced to see Patrick and Trey right on his tail. "Keep within sight and keep up." They both grunted a reply.

Tom yelled from the side, "Ben, go, but stop every so often to listen."

"That's the plan!" Ben yelled back.

Suddenly another group of three shots rang out. Ben called out to Tom, "I'm going to answer!"

"Go ahead!" was the reply.

Ben released the safety on his pistol, verified Patrick and Trey's position, aimed up and off to the side away from Tom, and fired off a slow double shot. A single shot replied, followed by the unmistakable click of a hammer falling on an empty chamber. They were that close.

Behind him, Trey said, "There!" Ben saw both Patrick and Trey, arms stretched out, aiming ahead and to the left slightly. *Good, they both locked in on the sound.* He could hear Tom crashing through the trees running through the thick brush. "Hey, Tom! Not so far! He's right here." Ben ducked a branch, stepped across a downed tree, skirted a bush, and entered a small gap in the trees. Trey was right behind, and Patrick a little farther back.

Tom came crashing through the lower branches of a small tree, barely missing stepping on Carl. Ben saw Joe standing in the trees a ways beyond Tom, searching the forest. *Good. He's keeping an eye out for anything.* Robb approached, first aid kit in hand. He kneeled next to Carl as Ben checked the area carefully. *I don't see anything, so we might be good here.*

Tom glanced up. "Trey, circle out and look for the others! Joe, hang tight and watch for anything moving. Patrick, help Robb with the first aid."

As Ben took stock of the situation, Patrick and Robb worked to staunch the bleeding from multiple stab wounds, mostly on Carl's arms and legs, but a couple in the gut. His left arm was broken, and his left ankle so swollen that Ben knew he couldn't have made it far before collapsing. Then he noticed all the empty magazines and empty shell casings littering the place. Carl had spent the night here, shooting triplets every so often, but now he was out of ammo, right as they happened along. Had they been delayed by even minutes, he wouldn't have had any shots left—they would have passed right by, never knowing he was here.

"Where's Trey?" Tom asked.

"He's out in the woods somewhere," Joe said. "Checking it out."

Even though Tom could hear Trey crashing around through the brush, he wanted him in sight, so he snapped to Joe, "He's checked enough. I don't want him too far out. Get him back before he gets lost!"

Joe bellowed as he stepped into the trees, then went deeper. "Hey! Trey! Enough! Head back."

Grabbing some small branched, Tom trimmed them down, making a smooth surface. "These'll work for a splint for that arm."

Ben pulled out a couple long strips of cloth from the first aid kit and wrapped the swollen foot, mumbling the first aid litany to himself, "Keep the pressure on, don't remove the boot, or it'll swell even more."

Joe and Trey came bursting out of the trees and stopped dead. Joe said, "No one out there."

Trey caught Ben's eye and mouthed, "He's alone."

Ben raised an eyebrow, then asked, "Can you guys clean up this mess?" indicating the gear spread across the forest floor.

They grabbed Carl's pack, and picked up the things that were lying around: Carl's supplies, all the magazines and, being good scouts, as much of the spent brass as they could.

Tom grabbed Carl's arm to set the bone. Bracing himself, he said to Robb, "Hold him." He pulled, gently at first, but then with more force. Finally, the bone slipped into place. Carl screamed, his face went pale, his eyes rolled back, and he passed out. Tom snarled, "We need some serious pain relief. The town's medic should have something she can use." Tying the makeshift splint as tightly as he could, he stepped back. "We're ready to move him."

Trey handed Carl's backpack to Joe. "Here." He stepped forward and squatted, his back to them. "Go ahead and load him up. I'm ready."

Patrick and Robb picked up Carl and laid him across Trey's shoulders, then helped lift as he stood up. Hefting the load, Trey said, "Don't get left behind," and stepped off at a quick but smooth pace, high stepping through the rough terrain. Amazed at his unrelenting pace, the rest of them quickly followed.

Trey met the pathway half a click north of where the group waited.

Annie saw him first and joined him as he approached. "What can I do to help?" she asked.

With his hands busy holding Carl's legs, Trey waggled his head at the gear on the side of the road. "Could you grab my backpack? I don't want to drop him until we get to a doctor."

"I'll see that it gets brought," Ben said. "You go ahead and head to town. We'll be right there."

Tom popped out of the trees. "Keep going, Trey. I'll be right behind you." Then he grabbed his pack. "Ben, I'll head in with him. You get the rest of the crew moving and join us as soon as possible."

"We'll get Trey's pack divvied up, then move out," Ben said.

Tom ran to catch up with Trey, yelling back, "When you exit the forest, cut left through the fields, follow the path to the east side of *Roadranusis*. We're heading directly to the medic's hut!"

Ben shouted assent as he started going through Trey's pack, splitting up the gear among the others. When all the equipment he had been carrying had been sorted out, he thought, *Wow, he* was *carrying half the camp.*

Giving up on being neat, Ben dumped Trey's pack out, calling for everyone to come grab something. They stuffed as much as they could into all the other packs, barely managing to pack it all away. Ben listened to all the complaining, but no one commented on the fact that Trey had been carrying *all* that extra gear by himself…without a word of complaint.

Getting everything packed up took longer than Ben had expected, so by the time they were ready to head out, he had no hope that they could catch up with Tom and Trey, even with the load Trey now carried.

Getting as quick a start as possible, they soon came to the edge of the forest. Coming out of the shade into the full brilliance of the rising sun, Ben squinted and finally located the turnoff Tom had mentioned. He shouted, "Everyone, turn here!" He headed off again, but this time slower than before to keep the group squeezed together.

He watched until he saw Patrick come out of the forest, then he shouted. He heard a shout back but couldn't tell what Patrick said. He waited for Patrick to start up the side path, then he strode off knowing that the group wouldn't get separated.

The path went curved through the fields, aiming southward, towards some small hills well to the east of the town. As they crossed a stone bridge over a small creek, Ben could see a crowd of people. *Is the whole town here? Has word of our calamity spread that fast?* He urged the group onward, to a ramshackle hut surrounded by herb gardens. *Must be the medic's hut.*

When the crowd spotted Ben and his group approaching, they moved to the side, opening up a passageway, allowing them to get to the hut. Tom's pack was on the ground outside the fenced gardens, abandoned on the side of the road. Ben yelled, "Drop your packs there…and wait with them. I'm going to go see what's going on." Everyone dropped their packs, but no one waited. They all followed him up the steps right to the door.

When they burst through the door, they ran into Tom standing inside the small one-room hut now holding up his hands. "Whoa! There's barely enough room for the medic and her crew. No need to get in the way. She'll tell us if she needs any help from us."

Annie pushed to the front. "Well, *I* can help," she said as she held up her first aid kit. "Let me in there."

Tom backed out of the way as she went in. "Wow, I certainly wouldn't want to get on her bad side."

"Yeah, but better yet," Ben said. "Don't get in her *way*. When she knows what she wants, you can't dissuade her. She goes for it in spite of anything…or anyone." He raised an eyebrow at Tom.

"I understand," Tom said, holding up a hand. "Hey, if you stand here in the doorway, you can see what's going on without getting in the way."

Ben stepped to the doorway, then leaned. "Yeah, good view. Thanks."

"I know you want to see what's going on," Tom said.

Ben opened his mouth to answer but was suddenly transfixed by what was going on inside.

Annie had positioned herself in the middle of the action. Taking a fleeting glance at Carl lying on a high bed in the middle of the room, she plopped her first aid kit on a small table to the side and gave orders, directing the medics. "You, in the blue, put direct pressure on that cut on his head. You there, leave that leg alone. Hold this arm out straight. We need to clean out this cut first."

Ben stared as she ignored the deep gash on Carl's leg and instead focused on a much smaller cut on his arm. She grabbed a handful of gauze, pulled the cut open, and scrubbed hard. If Carl hadn't already been out of it, Ben was certain that the pain of that treatment would have put him over the edge.

The older lady sitting at a nearby table glanced up from what she was doing and watched from across the room, then stood to watch Annie. "*gu kishmu*? You doctor?"

"Yeah, *kishmu*, whatever," Annie said not taking her eyes off Carl. "This cut is bad."

The medic stared at Annie with interest. "I Deezhlahmahs. I make healthy." She lifted Carl's arm and peered at the cut. "Why you think that bad?"

Annie gaped at her. "Can't you see it? The color is wrong. Those other cuts are yellow, bright yellow perhaps, but this one is a dark green, almost blue." She pulled the cut open more and said, "And look there. At the bottom, see the violet streak? That's not right."

Ben couldn't stay back any more. He stepped in and saw blood, lots of it. "Annie, you see colors? All I see is red, blood red. Nothing else."

She glared at him. "You don't see the violet? Deep in the cut. Look past the blood."

He stared at her. "*Past* the blood? Like I said, all I see is blood, lots of it."

"You don't see the violet, practically glowing?" She sounded alarmed.

Ben stared at Annie and started to answer, but Deezhlahmahs held up a hand, breathed slowly, then stepped towards Ben and Tom, still standing in the doorway. "Out." One word, but the way she said it, you could tell she meant it. Ben backed zombie-like out of the room. Tom had already stepped backwards off the porch. The door closed firmly, seemingly of its own accord.

All was quiet for a moment.

Tom slowly refocused his eyes and blinked. "Wow! What was that?"

Ben snapped out of it. "Huh? I don't know, but whatever she did, she now has the privacy she wanted!"

Frowning, Tom eyed the door. "Should we see what's going on in there?"

Ben raised an eyebrow. "*I* wouldn't, but if you're foolish enough to risk the ire of both Deezhlahmahs *and* Annie, be my guest."

"Point taken," Tom said. "Let's just sit out here and wait. I hope Annie's safe in there."

Ben plopped on the step beside him. "Annie? I'm thinking of Deezhlahmahs." He slapped Tom on the back.

Annie dragged her gaze from the door to Deezhlahmahs. *What did I say? Did I offend her…or worse?*

Deezhlahmahs stepped in front of Annie. "*gu kahnvi tah-oo*? You see violet? *zahfko*? Bad color?"

Annie nodded nervously. She hadn't thought, simply reacted to what she could see: Carl was in need of help, and she knew what was needed.

Deezhlahmahs stepped next to Carl lying on the table, then pulled Annie along. "True you see other color there?" she asked, leaning closer.

Annie examined Carl. "Yes. Besides the violet in this arm, there's a bright spot of yellow on his head, a darker yellow on this leg, and a kinda dark orangey fuzzy area near that foot." Moving on to Carl's left arm, she said, "That arm is deep blue, and…" She paused as she realized what she was saying. "…and his face is a pale blue." She dropped her head, wondering if she was seeing things, if she was going crazy.

Deezhlahmahs spun and spoke to her helpers in the room, then asked Annie, "You see them what color?"

Lifting her eyes slowly, Annie noticed that the helpers had lined up along the wall…and they had color on them as well. Her finger trembled as she called them off, left to right, "Red, orange, kind of a pink, yellow, and…" She gasped when she looked at Deezhlahmahs, "…and red, bright red, like the setting sun!"

Deezhlahmahs frowned at her helpers. "Who yellow?"

Annie checked them again, as one stepped forward and spoke. She didn't understand, but Deezhlahmahs replied, and the man left. "He have sick, not good now. Make better later, then he more help."

Annie stared. "He was sick? How did I know that?"

Deezhlahmahs leaned in close, staring into Annie's eyes. "You have sight."

She laughed then stopped and frowned. "Of course I have sight. Everyone has sight. What's so special about it?"

Deezhlahmahs smiled and continued, "You see health."

"Wait a minute. You're saying that I can see how healthy someone is? I've heard of folks claiming to see an aura, but that's a bunch of bunk. There's no such thing."

"Maybe you not notice before, but when need, you see." She paused. "Now you need." She held on to Carl's right arm. "Why you first here clean?"

Annie stuttered, "Well, I…it needed to be cleaned." She hesitated, not wanting to admit that she *had* seen something different in that cut. "Didn't it?"

Deezhlahmahs reached to a collection of tools and picked up a long skinny one. It had a spoon-like bowl, a couple millimeters across. She used one hand to spread open the cut, then scooped through from end to end, scraping close to the bone. Lifting the spoon to eye level, she perused it for a moment, then said, "Yes, it need." Showing Annie what she'd scraped out of the cut, she explained, "*vendu*, poison."

The spoon glowed with a bright purple, as if it were a black light, shining in Annie's eyes, making them water. She shuddered. "He was poisoned?"

"The *vahlnimlimre* sometimes use," Deezhlahmahs said. "But not like this." She frowned. "This not used by them. Must get from others. Shessicheros need know." She resumed working on Carl. "Make healthy now, tell later." She glanced at one of her aides, spoke curtly at him, then went back to work.

Annie watched Deezhlahmahs close the cut on Carl's arm. "Do you see the colors as well?" she asked.

Deezhlahmahs smiled. "Yes. As you, I have sight, so I make better. Some have, some not. If have and learn, can much make better." Then she frowned. "If have and not learn, can much make bad." She went mute after that comment, letting her aides finish the work. They continued silently as Deezhlahmahs directed them, monitoring their efforts. They cleaned and closed the wounds one after another, sometimes stitching, sometimes wrapping with a wide, tape-like bandage.

When they started working on Carl's left arm, Deezhlahmahs pushed them aside and did the work herself. She gently undid the wrapping Tom had put on the arm and removed the splint, then pulled the now relaxed muscles to set the bone. Annie watched in amazement as the colors slowly changed from deep blue, back through green, then finally into a dull yellow as the bone shifted into place. The color continued to change to a burnt orange as the aides finished wrapping it up tightly.

Deep in thought, Annie realized that this sight thing could be useful. It'd certainly be easier to work with patients if you could see their pain. Even better than an x-ray, but how did it work? Was this related to that thing with Joe last night? She tried to clear her head. She needed to stay focused—Carl needed her help. She couldn't let it bother her right now. She'd have to try to figure it out later when she had the time.

She did what she could to help, using supplies from her first aid kit. They finished, and Annie packed away her things.

Deezhlahmahs finally spoke again. "You good work. You learn make better soon, you then be same me, *foh-ah gu shenzha kishmu*."

Shuffling the supplies in the first aid kit back and forth, and keeping her eyes on the task, she asked over her shoulder, "Will you teach me?"

"*aa-eh, mi ditchah gu kishmu*. I first teach use plants, then use self."

Wondering how to use herself to heal, she smiled. "Can you tell me how to say 'thank you'?"

"*garshoo. mi garshoo gu*. From garti shootseh, grateful say, but if friend, say, gah-oo. mi gah-oo gu."

Annie faced her and said, "Deezhlahmahs, *mi garshoo gu*, thank you for offering to teach me. One day, may I say *mi gah-oo gu*."

Deezhlahmahs made a slight bow to Annie. "*mi tow-oo gu*, you welcome…as friend."

Annie blushed. "I will earn that friendship soon, Deezhlahmahs."

"You will, I certain. We friends, you call me Deezh." Without giving Annie a chance to react, she spoke briefly to one of her aides. The young man stepped to the door, and as he exited, Annie could see Tom and Ben sitting on the porch. Both jumped to their feet as the man rushed by, but they didn't have time to say anything before the door swung closed.

A moment later, the door flew open again as the man came back. He stepped in and pulled the door shut, intentionally closing it before either Tom or Ben could react. He handed Deezhlahmahs a small handful of leaves, then pulled a mortar and pestle from a shelf. He placed them on the table along with a small brown, earthenware jar. Sitting, Deezhlahmahs picked through the leaves, keeping certain ones and setting others to the side. Then she placed the selected ones into the mortar and gestured for the others to be removed.

She picked up the small jar, removed the lid, sniffed gently, and smiled. Shaking a few grains of powder from the jar into the mortar, she replaced the lid and set the jar back on the table. An aide immediately picked it up and put it back on the shelf.

Deezhlahmahs took the pestle and ground the mixture with a twist of her wrist. Responding to Annie's studious gaze, she said, "Plant let him sleep. Make better faster if not move."

Annie understood. She'd seen many folks sedated in the hospital, so they wouldn't have to endure the pain of the healing process. She was glad that Deezhlahmahs had the knowledge to help Carl. She certainly didn't have any drugs powerful enough for that in her first aid kit.

Pouring a bit of water into the mortar, Deezhlahmahs swirled it cautiously, then poured it into a thick bowl that one of the aides had set on the table. A fine cloth covered the top of the bowl to catch the larger pieces, allowing the juice to collect in the depression below. Deezhlahmahs raised the cloth, gently folding the corners together covering the crushed leaves, then lifted it off gingerly, holding it by the dry corners. She dropped it onto a small tray next to the discarded leaves, then dipped a small stick with a short strip of cloth wrapped around its end into the bowl and wiped the juice across Carl's lips.

She put the stick on the tray and handed both the bowl and the tray to a waiting aide. He apprehensively carried the tray to the back of the room and slowly tipped it, letting the rejected leaves and the stick slide into a large vat, then he poured out any liquid left in the bowl into the vat as well. Annie thought she could see a small flash and a slight puff of smoke as it all vanished into the depths, though she didn't hear even the slightest sound of a splash.

Deezhlahmahs broke her concentration when she said, "Now sleep, check later, when time dark."

Annie stared. *A slight wipe across his lips, and he sleeps all day? That must be one strong narcotic. I'll need to be careful with that plant.*

Deezhlahmahs pulled out a thick, heavy blanket and spread it across Carl. She spoke to the aide sitting next to the bed, then explained to Annie, "He stay, watch, if problem, he get me." Then she stepped towards the door, pulled a long dark cloak from a peg, and waited for Annie, who quickly picked up her first aid kit and joined her at the door.

The door swung open revealing a waiting crowd. Deezhlahmahs stood with Annie at her side, who was still holding the first aid kit. Tom and Ben were sitting on the porch steps but stood quietly as Deezhlahmahs addressed the crowd in her native tongue. The townsfolk slowly dispersed, most of them heading back into town. Then in her broken English, she said to Ben and the others, "I send home. Not need now." She motioned towards the room and said, "Now sleep and make better."

Annie agreed. "They've given him something to help him sleep. He'll be out for a while," she checked with Deezhlahmahs, "'Til this evening?"

"Return, look more, after eat," Deezhlahmahs said.

Annie continued, "Anyway Deezhlahmahs knows her craft fully well. The medicine here is as good as, if not better than, what we're used to."

Ben raised an eyebrow. "Better? How can that be?"

Annie glared at him. "We can talk more later…" she paused, "…when I figure it out."

Ben raised both eyebrows. "Whatever."

Tom stared at the two of them, wondering what silent messages passed between siblings, then shrugged and announced to the group, "Well, we aren't heading out hunting right now, and we still have two missing guys, so no wandering off. We'll stay here in the town until Carl is good enough to move, then head out *as a group* and see if we can get back unscathed."

Ben stepped up onto the porch, faced everyone, and continued the instructions, "We'll use the lodge as a base. Leave most of your gear there. They'll watch our stuff." He frowned. "Oh, and stay in pairs."

Tom agreed. "Yeah, that's a good way to keep anyone from getting lost." He faced the group. "Ben and I are heading to talk to Shess. Missing guys is serious, but this is *more* serious, and I want his advice."

Annie spoke up from behind them. "Well, I'm going to spend time with Deezhlahmahs. She has a different attitude on medicine, and I'd like to check into it."

"Go ahead, but who are you taking with you? No one goes anyplace alone," Ben reminded her.

She walked towards Trey, who was sitting on a big rock in the middle of the garden, and smiled. "I pick the biggest, strongest guy in the group to protect me."

Trey glanced up as Annie sauntered up. He'd been listening in, so he smiled back and said in a sing-songy, hillbilly accent, "Sounds good t'me. I could use me some larning in doctoring. All ah know is what they learned us in scouts: basic first aid."

She frowned. "Then again, someone else could go if you're going to keep up with that silly talk."

He flushed slightly. "Consider it gone." He stood, and she linked arms with him.

While they were talking, Deezhlahmahs had stepped into the garden and picked some leaves, then, without a word, spun, her cloak swirling, and headed around the corner of the hut.

Annie flipped her hair out of her face and said, "We'll be back later."

"See ya," Ben said.

Annie hurried to catch up with Deezhlahmahs, dragging Trey along with her, but Trey slowed enough to look back at Ben and give a quick Cheshire cat grin before Annie dragged him off, following Deezhlahmahs.

Deezhlahmahs had disappeared from view. No one was in sight behind the hut, but the path she had taken was obvious, so they hurried, trying to catch up, following a small trail through the woods.

A moment later, Trey caught sight of a cloak fluttering past the bend ahead, so he lengthened his stride, now pulling Annie along, trying to keep an eye on the dark cloak, it vanished again as he watched.

Annie had to run to keep up with Trey's long legs. Watching her step, trying not to trip, she didn't see Deezhlahmahs disappear. Trey stumbled, then came to an abrupt stop right where he'd last seen the cloak, and Annie ran into him. "What's wrong? Where's Deezhlahmahs?"

Trey shrugged. "She was here. I saw her standing right here," he said, "but then she wasn't."

"She wasn't what?" Annie asked.

"She just…wasn't. I saw her one moment, then she wasn't…anything. Just gone."

"Well, she didn't blink out of existence. She's somewhere." Annie leaned around the thick trees on both sides of the path. "Maybe she stepped into the forest along here."

Trey tipped his head. "She might have, but it didn't look like it to me."

She cupped her hands around her mouth and shouted, first to one side, then to the other, "Deezhlahmahs! Where'd you go? We were following you, but then…" she frowned at Trey, "…*we* lost you."

Deezhlahmahs' voice floated on the breeze. "You want learn, use sight."

Frustrated, she said, "I *am* looking, but I can't see you."

"Not look. See, use sight."

Taking up the challenge, she closed her eyes, bowed her head, and focused. Taking a deep breath, she lifted her head and studied the trees. The colors she saw ranged from a reddish orange to bright orange, though one was a deep yellow, fading into green. *Must be dying,* she absently thought. Then she noticed one brilliantly red. Stepping forward she leaned to look past the tree and said, "Deezhlahmahs?"

The tree faded, and Deezhlahmahs was standing there facing them.

Trey gasped. "Hey! How'd you do that?"

Ignoring Trey, Deezhlahmahs spoke to Annie, "You good see. You have *shlikanmo*, ability." She thought for a moment, then made up her mind. *"mi ditchah gu moh-oo kishmu.* I teach you more healing, then you make better." She stepped away. *"gu prigo mi,* you follow me."

"And Trey?" she asked.

Trey blinked at Deezhlahmahs. "Yeah, what am I, chopped liver?"

Still ignoring Trey, Deezhlahmahs said, *"di prigo ino tirku mu,* he follow, but not hear us."

Trey waved his hands in Annie's face. "Hello? Am I here?"

Annie tried to reassure him as Deezhlahmahs walked away. "She says you can come watch, but if she doesn't want to talk to you, don't let it bother you. She did the same thing when we worked on Carl, too. It's probably the way she is, overly fixated on her work."

Trey shrugged. "Yeah, right, well as long as she doesn't get nasty, I can handle being ignored."

Annie held his arm, and they followed Deezhlahmahs as she walked much more sedately this time. A cool breeze filtered through the trees, birds could be heard flitting from branch to branch, singing gently, and Trey relaxed, lulled by the peaceful melody of nature surrounding him.

Deezhlahmahs walked slowly, but deliberately, going down a side path, and Trey stepped quickly, *I don't want to lose sight of her again,* but this time she had paused at the corner, waiting.

The path opened into a small opening. The trees surrounding them were tall and straight and reached high overhead. The upper branches closed above creating a green canopy, backlit by the sun.

Trey stopped and stared. Wow, he thought. Feels like a church or something. I wonder if this is a druid cathedral.

Deezhlahmahs stood in front of a small stone altar on the far side. Annie left Trey staring up and went to see what Deezhlahmahs was doing.

On the altar was a small pile of twigs, with leaves still attached. Without preface, Deezhlahmahs commenced the lesson by picking one up. She explained what the plant could do and how to identify it. She set it aside and continued by selecting another twig and repeating the process.

Deezhlahmahs went through the entire pile, then began again, this time asking Annie, instead of telling her. At first, Annie hesitated often, but by using her sight, she was soon able to associate the color she saw with what each plant did. They cycled through the pile, changing the order each time, until Annie could reel off all the pertinent information every time.

After going through the stack almost a dozen times, Deezhlahmahs finished with the last leaf she held and ended Annie's training. "Good study. You fast learn."

"Once I understood how the colors worked, it all made more sense. Red is healthy, and the more yellow means sicker, and a plain green means infected, and the violet I saw in Carl's arm was the poison. It's like a full color wheel."

"Yes," Deezhlahmahs said. "You good see, and use sight, understand. You also have good feel."

"I have good feel?"

Deezhlahmahs put her hand on her chest. "You know others feel, important to make better them."

"You mean empathy? With me, that's natural. I tend to feel first, and think later," she said, a little embarrassed.

Deezhlahmahs picked up the pile of leaves on the altar. "Good medicine here, remember and use, but," reaching down to pick up Annie's first aid kit and handing it to her, "You also good medicine here. Careful use. Not get more."

"True. I need to conserve. I won't be able to refill until we get home." She hefted the case. "Hopefully, I won't need it."

With the lesson done, she found Trey still sitting under a tree, just as he had been when they started the training, carving on a small piece of wood. She had seen him look up every now and then, but he never paid attention to what they were saying—exactly as Deezhlahmahs had predicted.

Meanwhile, back at the medic's hut, Tom stood and watched Annie walk off with Trey. *Well, so much for* that *idea. She already has a boyfriend.*

Ben scowled. "Oh, great! There they go. Now someone *else* will have to haul their packs to the lodge."

"Trey didn't have a pack. He was carrying Carl," Tom reminded Ben. "We already divvied up his stuff."

"Oh, yeah. In that case I'm stuck carrying Annie's to the lodge."

"Ha! Hers won't be as heavy as *his* would have been. She's not as strong as that gorilla is." Tom picked up a couple packs.

"True, so what else are brothers for?" Ben cleared his throat and spoke to the group. "So, anyway, as I was saying before *they* trotted off…Leave your gear at the lodge, don't wander off, and keep in pairs."

Tom started to comment when Patrick interrupted, "Does that mean we have free rein of *Roadranusis*?"

"That would depend on what you have in mind." Tom glared.

"Joe and I want to see if we can get those scrolls translated…the ones we salvaged from the wildmen."

Tom raised his eyebrows. "Hey, that could be useful. If you come up with anything, hightail it to Shess' cottage. Both of you. Any of the locals can direct you to his house."

Joe stepped up. "Easy enough to keep an eye on him."

"If you could get a translation done, it would help," Tom said. "The techies have yet to get a real grip on the language here, but if you're as good with languages as Ben thinks, you might be able to show them up."

Patrick reddened slightly. "I'll try to live up to his bragging."

"Oh, watch out when you talk to the townsfolk," Tom said. "They can be kinda set in their ways and might not want to talk. When they're busy working, it's as if you aren't even there, so don't get offended if they ignore you. You can always find someone else to talk to. They can get uppity, so don't expect much."

Patrick shrugged. "Well, they seem fine to me, so we'll give it a shot."

"I wish you well!" Ben shouted.

Joe followed Patrick to town. "Thanks! See ya!"

"Well, Ben," Tom said. "It'll be interesting if those guys manage to accomplish something."

"That would be unexpected," Ben said. "Most of them just want to kick back and have a bit of fun."

Tom laughed. "That's the plan for all of us." He stepped towards the pile of packs, hurriedly dropped by the scouts. "Let's get this stuff moved. I want to talk to Shess." He grabbed his own and slung it on one shoulder, then reached to grab one strap of Annie's pack as Ben grabbed the other. Letting Annie's pack swing between them, they headed along the now deserted road. The group hadn't taken long to get going after having been cooped up so much yesterday.

Back in town, they went to the lodge and added all three backpacks to the pile, then followed the road to the upper part of town, well away from the fields and river.

Ben was impressed with the houses. "We've certainly moved up into the posh neighborhood. The size of these houses proves it."

"I'd say good ol' Shess is doing quite well for himself. That's his cottage there." Tom walked towards a house on the edge of a hill.

"Cottage? That's big enough to be a mansion, and up on that hill he has an excellent view of the whole village. I'll bet he can see all the way to the next town. It has to be the biggest house in the area."

"What do you expect?" Tom said. "He *is* the mayor. That's what you get for being the boss."

Following the path to the gate, they were met by a doorman who welcomed them then ran on ahead to announce them. Before they even arrived at the house itself, the entire household staff scrambled to make the guests feel welcome: A maid put out a vase of fresh flowers, the steward tapped a keg of last year's finest hops, the chef grilled up a warm snack, and the housekeeper prepared chairs on the back porch for the guests.

At the top of the steps, the same man who had greeted them at the outer gate held the door open for them. He led them down a long hallway that extended from one end of the house to the other. As the servant led them through a door on the right, Tom nudged Ben and tipped his head at a partially open door to the left.

Ben glanced in and saw Shess in deep conversation. He didn't have time to say anything as they were hustled past the room and onto the west porch. They walked to the railing and checked out the view, then strolled to the table and gazed at the piles of food: fresh cheese, warm bread, still steaming roast something, and a jug of what must be cold ale.

Tom poured a cold one as he glanced at Ben. "Now *this* is the way to treat guests."

"Yeah, much better than at the lodge," Ben said. "Privileges of the upper crust. This guy has it good." He glanced back inside. "Did you see that guy in there talking to Shess? Wasn't he in the medic's hut working on Carl?"

Tom craned his neck to stare. "It could be one of the guys who was helping out there. I doubt that he has bad news."

Reaching for a slice of bread, Ben watched Shess enter the inside room, pull a large book from the shelves behind the desk, and the two men consulted momentarily, then the aide quickly left.

Carrying the book with him, Shess joined them, taking a slow look across the river, inspecting the fields to the edge of the forest, before taking a seat. He motioned back at the man who had just left. "*di zhi ditchah Dijlahmahs kishmu*, he learn from Deezhlahmahs medicine. He help her."

"How is Carl doing?" Ben asked.

"Your friend not problem, he better soon. News not of him, news of *nimre*. They not alone, have help."

"Help? Help doing what?" Tom asked.

"Carl…" Shess thoughtfully wrapped his tongue around the strange name, "Carl have *vendu*, poison."

Ben stood up suddenly. "He was poisoned?"

Tom put his hand on Ben's arm as Shess set the book on the table and opened it.

Ben leaned in to try to read the book. "Is that an encyclopedia?"

"Yes, book of knowledge." Shess flipped the pages to an entry and said, "Most times *nimre* use *firvendu*, weak poison, to get food. Easy to heal." He turned the page and read more. "But now they use *folvendu*, much stronger poison. Not for get food, use for kill enemy."

"Why would they use something like that?" Ben asked.

"They not use, not before, not have. They not know make *folvendu*, must get from others, can get in *grosi*, big city, south on river, to coast."

"We've *heard* of the bigger cities to the south," Tom said. "But we haven't managed to get that far in our explorations…not yet."

Ben's face darkened and he asked, "So who'd be supplying poison to these wildmen?"

"Poison and weapons," Shess said. "They have weapons for get food, but now more, not normal."

"I agree," Tom said. "That certainly doesn't sound normal to me, not based on what we've seen so far."

"They not like this any time before," Shess said.

Ben stood there listening, his anger growing. "Someone is supplying them poison *and* weapons?"

"Hmm, so they aren't spreading south randomly," Tom said. "Someone is helping them, pushing them. Their movement from animal land to civilization is intentional." He spoke to the city father. "Shess, they're trying to get your land." Glancing at Ben he said, "That may explain why they attacked us that first night. They probably thought that we were from *Roadranusis*. No one will be safe out there with them running loose."

Ben slowly searched across the landscape, then stared at Tom. "When you wanted us to get involved with the locals and those wildmen, I didn't like it." He frowned. "I still don't." He paused, then went on, "I don't like playing politics, but if it means getting back at them for what they did to Carl, and possibly finding John and Melvin, I'm all for it."

Shess frowned and put his hand on Ben's shoulder. "You visit, not know this people, not need help, you hunt, get food, not see *nimre*."

Tom agreed, "Yeah, you guys came here to hunt and have fun, so do that. We can send in some troops later to clean up this problem."

"No." Ben stood his ground. "If all they did was attack us that one time, I could assume they needed food or supplies or something and leave it, walking away, but then they tried to kill Carl, and who knows what they've done with the others."

"You need us help, we go help," Shess offered.

"Thank you, Shess. We certainly could use your help. We don't know the countryside as well as *any* of you, and I'm certain you have a couple of guys who know it *much* better. Any advice you have to help us with the *nimre* would be greatly appreciated." He stepped back. "Tom, we need to have a war council."

"If you're ready for it, then I'll do what I can to help." Tom paused then asked Shess. "Will you have your best fighters meet us at the tavern?"

"*aa-eh*, I send message." He checked the sky. "They there when sun high."

"Thanks." Tom glanced at the food, then gazed longingly at the ale. "Ben, we'd best be getting back into town. I don't know how long before we round up all your guys, and with Annie off in the woods with Deezhlahmahs, we might not be able to get *all* of them back."

"We'll do what we can." Ben said.

Shess stood slowly and closed the book, leaving it on the table, then started to leave. "*kahmlah*. We send word." He stepped through the office into the hallway. Tom tossed down one last swig of the ale, then hurried to catch up with Ben. Shess was talking to a young boy, and as they followed Shess to the front door, the boy ran back through the house to the back door. As they circled the wall surrounding Shess' house, they could hear the clanging of a bell.

Shess answered their curious stares, "Alarm. Call together all, then send fighters *saarstoku*, for talk."

"Quite effective system you have," Ben said. "Tom, these people certainly aren't the backwater peasant farmers we were led to believe."

Tom agreed, "I'm surprised at how advanced they are every time I come back. They live closer to the earth than we do, but they don't lack in the finer points of civilization either."

As they were walking across the town green, Ben noticed some kids playing. Shess glanced at them and yelled, "*kahmlah uh ri gu kahmlah*." The kids stopped playing and ran to Shess. He grabbed one by the shoulder then leaned down and said, "*dootrah ri zhahnto uhshi shootseh li ben ehnd tomss seh-ee go lah-juh loo zhahnto*." They shrugged at each other. Shess glared and said, "*genshu ti mi*"

In unison, the kids repeated in what barely sounded like English, "*ben ehnd tomss seh-ee go lah-juh*."

Shess approved, then sent the kids throughout the town, "*gotso! doo-rzoh!*"

The kids spread out and ran off in every direction.

Shess explained, "I send them, find all hunters, tell them go to lodge."

As they approached, they saw a bunch of folks crowded in the doorway, trying to see inside. Something was going on. Tom tried to push through, but couldn't make it—then Shess growled, and the whole crowd moved out of the way.

They stepped through the doorway but still couldn't see into the darkness of the room. The crowd at the doorway may have blocked *some* of the light, but dozens of folks were peering in through the windows, blocking the rest. The little bit of light there was came from the fire Robb was manning.

They waited, silhouetted in the doorway, for a moment or two, and as their eyes adjusted, they saw a circle of people to one side, watching something on the floor.

Ben stepped in and asked, "What's going on?"

Doug shrugged and answered, "Nothing much. The guys here wanted to learn how to play craps."

"And *why* would they want to know that?" Ben frowned. "Wait. How would they even *know* about craps?"

Doug shrugged and said, "Well, I brought along these dice…in case we had any free time, and we do. We have plenty of time waiting for Carl to heal up."

Ben crossed his arms. "Well, I can't blame you for that, but keep it down to a dull roar, will ya? And be ready to quit at a moment's notice. We have issues, but they'll wait 'til everyone else arrives."

"Gotcha," Doug said and went back to the game.

As Ben followed Shess to a table, he stopped and looked closer at the game. "Doug, are you guys betting real money? Any of you bring cash?"

Eric laughed. "Nope, no money. I don't think our money would be any good here, so we're using bullets instead."

"Bullets?" Ben tried to see past the crowd.

"Yeah," Eric said. "A .45 is worth three .22 rounds, a .30-'06 bullet is worth five 5.56mm rounds, and so on. I don't have any bullets, so they're letting me bet whatever I have."

Tom frowned. "Huh? How's that work?" Then he stopped. "Never mind. I don't want to know, and I don't want to hear any squabbling over the rules."

"Doug, keep things under control. I don't want anyone," Ben tipped his head towards Eric, "losing his shirt here."

"It's not losing his shirt that worries us. We don't want him losing his pants!" Doug laughed.

"Yeah, right, but keep things under control."

"I plan to." All eyes focused on the dice in Doug's hand as the game reconvened.

Ben stood there and watched one or two tosses of the dice. He noticed that Doug was winning more often than he was losing, an expected outcome, as Doug had brought the dice, and the house tends to win in the long run. He hoped that it wouldn't cause any problems. He had barely settled into his seat next to Tom and Shess, when the innkeeper brought out a round of pale ale.

Tom sipped the ale. "Not as good as that stuff at your place, Shess, but not bad."

Shess set his mug down. "Wets lips, but not *smiso*, mind asleep."

"Drunk. The word is drunk." Tom thought what kind of problem a drunk with dice would be. "Yeah, it wouldn't do to have drunks running amuck in the lodge. I don't blame the innkeeper for watering it down."

"Drunkuh. I remember word." Shess practiced, "Drunkuh, drunkuh."

Tom smiled. "Close enough. We'll know what you mean."

Shess leaned closer to watch the game. "*shahpli*? Chance game?"

"Yeah, it's called gambling," Tom said. "That game is craps. I don't know why it's called that, unless it's because that's what you say when you lose." He shrugged.

As they sat and waited, Ben kept an eye on the game. Suddenly a crowd of kids burst in through the door, following a tall, young man. The young man stopped for a moment, waiting for everyone to notice his arrival, then went straight for the game, still followed by his entourage, trailing after him as if he were a rock star. He pushed his way to the front, definitely wanting to play. The game stopped, and the room went silent as everyone wanted to see what he'd brought to bet. He slowly opened a small cloth sack hanging on a cord around his neck and pulled out an old .50 caliber cartridge. Even from across the room Ben could see that he handled it with reverence and awe.

Ben asked Tom, "Who brought a gun that size?"

Tom shrugged and asked Shess, "Where'd he get that?"

Shess said, "That Shankaktos. He good *kahmdah*. He have metal guard since birth. It keep him safe. His father give him for *po shoormah*, protection."

Ben stared at the bullet, then realized something. "Tom, when was the first time you guys opened that Door to this place?"

"I had the same thought," Tom said. "We hadn't managed to get the Door open until a couple years ago, and that was barely big enough to send anyone through. It had existed in a lab as a curiosity for five years or so, but that's it."

They stared at each other as Ben asked the looming question, "So where'd he get that bullet?"

"And when?" Tom asked.

The game drew their attention again as Shankaktos bartered for the worth of his prize. He held the large bullet in one hand, scooped up a pile of .30-'06 bullets, and counted out four.

Fascinated with the size of the bullet, Doug agreed to the exchange rate, even though he didn't have a gun big enough to use it.

Shankaktos set the huge bullet in front of the pile of other bets, then picked up the dice. Ben held his breath. He couldn't see the dice land, but the reaction of the crowd told him all he needed to know: it wasn't a win. Now he had to make that point. Someone grabbed the dice, handing them back to Shankaktos, and all the players leaned in closer to watch.

In fact, Ben noticed that everyone had stopped to watch. All was quiet as Shankaktos shook the dice, then let them fly. Everyone breathed again as he missed his point but didn't crap out…yet. One more roll, and this time everyone in the room was straining to see. The players were packed shoulder to shoulder, the dice were hidden, but it didn't take seeing to know the result—a bad throw.

The room froze as Doug reached for the ammo, one eye on Shankaktos. As Doug swept the ammo from the floor, Shankaktos stared, unmoving, then grabbed Doug's wrist and tried to twist it. Before Ben, Tom, or even Shess, could get close, the fight had escalated. Not quite a free-for-all, the townsfolk were all backing Shankaktos as he struggled with Doug and the others. Everyone yelled, but no one paid any attention to anyone else.

Ben grabbed at bodies, pulling them off the pile, noticing that Tom and Shess were doing the same, but when Shess pulled someone off, they went flying across the room, smashing into tables and chairs, not getting back up.

There were so many people still fighting that it was going to be quite a while before things were back in hand.

Suddenly the door flew open, and Joe came running in, a sword held high over his head, with Patrick right behind him. Joe slammed to a halt as he saw the mess. He sagged, his sword falling to his side, then he yelled at Patrick, "Do your thing! Use what you learned!"

Patrick stepped forward as Joe backed to the wall bracing himself. Patrick glanced at the crowd, then stood still, slowly sweeping his arms above his head, taking a deep breath. Holding his hands high in the air, he stared at a spot near the ceiling above the struggling mass, mumbling to himself. Abruptly he drove his fists down with a guttural yell.

A sonic boom filled the room, stunning everyone, knocking most of the fighters to the floor, some out cold.

It bowled Ben over as well, and he slowly picked himself up and stared. "Patrick?"

Patrick rushed to help Ben to his feet. "Oops. Didn't mean for it to get you. I had to act fast, so I just did the quickest thing to stop the fighting."

"Yeah," Ben said. "But what *was* it?"

Back outside the medic's hut again, Patrick jumped as the door flew open and Annie came out. She and the healer lady stood, staring at the crowd, then the healer announced something, and as the crowd dispersed, Patrick whispered to Joe, "What'd she say?"

Joe shrugged. "I don't speak that stuff. You're the language expert."

"Well, I haven't had much chance to study the language…not yet." Patrick smirked at Joe slyly. "But I certainly plan to, if we can get past Ben's hunting binge."

Joe shushed Patrick. "I heard Annie say that Carl was going to sleep 'til this eve. They must have fixed him up well enough."

Pulling the tattered scroll from his pocket, Patrick nudged Joe and held it up.

"For the last time, I haven't a clue what it means, and asking me again won't help." Joe started to leave, then said, "Maybe Ben will let you go find a translator for it."

"My thoughts exactly. Now's a good time to try. Hey, if Carl's going to be on R&R for hours, they can't keep us cooped up like yesterday."

They watched Annie head off arm-in-arm with Trey. Patrick snickered at them. "What a pair! Those two make me sick."

Joe snorted. "Really? I heard that she doesn't hang out with Trey because they *like* each other, not *that* way. He's just another brother to her. She's even said so."

Patrick raised his eyebrows. "Oh? Well, she puts on a good show. I'd be convinced."

"You're too easy. Always busy with your books to know how real life works. I think she's trying to make someone jealous," Joe said nodding towards Tom.

Patrick didn't pay attention to what Joe said. He was too busy listening to Ben say something exploring the area, but not wandering off. Jumping at the opportunity, he spoke up and asked, "Does that mean we have free rein of *Roadranusis*?"

Tom glared at him. "Depends on what you have in mind."

Patrick grabbed Joe and pulled him up to the front. "Joe and I want to get these scrolls translated."

Joe pulled his arm away from Patrick and whispered, "*We* do?"

"That could help," Tom said. "Let us know what you find."

Joe accepted his fate and grabbed his gear. "We will," he said out loud, then he spoke quietly to Patrick, "So, it's my job to escort the egghead? Nobody's safe wandering alone."

Tom explained that the natives were not being quite as friendly as might be expected, but Patrick was oblivious to the warning—he was already on the way, quickly heading off towards town without hesitation.

Ben shouted, "Wish you well!"

Joe grinned. "Thanks, I'll need it!" He caught up quickly as Patrick made a beeline for the center of town. Joe walked alongside for a moment, then asked, "Do you know where you're going, or do you always rush off like that?"

"Yesterday I noticed a bunch of kids coming out of school or what might have been a school. They were carrying books and talking excitedly. If not a school, then it might be a library. Either way, they had books, so that's where I want to go."

"How can you see things like that?"

"I just do," Patrick said. "How can you see animals and things like that when you're out hunting?"

Joe shrugged. "It's what I focus on, what stands out to me." He paused. "So you're saying that a bookworm would notice books."

Patrick beamed. "Exactly!"

When they reached the town center, Patrick went to one side of the square and stopped. "There it is."

"Yeah, yeah, so let's go have a look."

As they approached the small building, Joe had to admit that it did look like a school. A group of younger children were around the side of the building kicking a ball back and forth, and older ones were hanging out on the front steps, studying a book together. Joe glanced at Patrick and thought, *How does he find his way around in every new town we visit, even when we're out camping?*

Patrick stepped to the front porch and said, "*kee-oo, mi nahmshi pahtrik.*"

Joe stared. *He speaks that stuff?*

Surprised at Patrick's attempt at their language, they all answered at once, but Patrick couldn't follow what they were all saying, so he held up his hands to stop them and said, "*vi yuh gu ditchah?*" The kids homed in on the door right behind them. Patrick questioned them, "*o-ah?*"

The kids all nodded, and a couple said, "*aa-eh.*"

Patrick stepped towards the door and said, "*gah-oo.*" He grabbed Joe's arm. "Come on."

"Nah, you go on in. I don't need to spend my vacation in school."

Patrick replied but the clamor of the kids drowned him out. They had followed the conversation enough to know what was going on. Indicating Patrick, their books, and the door, they made frowny faces, then grabbing Joe, they smiled and started pulling him towards the side of the school where the youngsters were playing.

Joe shrugged. "You go see the teacher. You can see that they want me to play out here with them."

Shrugging, Patrick said, "Whatever, play nicely, don't hurt anyone."

"Yeah, yeah. I know how to be careful." He stepped towards the corner of the building, but the kids literally dragged him around the side of the school.

Patrick laughed and knocked on the door as the kids shanghaied Joe. *I hope they survive…No, I hope* he *survives.*

The door swung open, and an older gentleman stuck his head out. Giving Patrick the once over, he said. "I help?" with disdain in his voice.

"I hope so," Patrick said. *"eh-oh gu ditchah mi?"*

The old man blinked, leaned out to look past Patrick, then stepped out onto the porch. "You trick? Where others?"

"It's just me." Patrick stepped closer. "I want to learn. Will you teach me? *ah-o mi shirna lengu gu.*"

"You want learn language?" The man frowned. "You speak already."

"Not well. I can speak it a bit, but I want to learn it better, to be able to read these." Patrick held up the scrolls.

The old man squinted at the scrolls, then frowned. "Can read, but not understand."

"Why not?"

"gu nrileh poordah ee jahno poordah ino kahnmo plizo sahdjah, you read word and know word, but not can use knowledge."

"I'm not certain I understand that, but I'm willing to give it a try. If I can manage to read the words, it'll help."

"Not stand here. Come in. We learn." The old man brought Patrick in and closed the door. Putting the scrolls aside, he said, "Later. Need more to read those. Now do *naarooshkela,* first school. You child here."

Patrick sat at one of the small tables, and the teacher sat on the other side. He introduced himself, *"mi nahmshi Zhahmonichas.* You say, Zhahmonichas."

Dutifully, Patrick echoed, "Zhahmonichas."

"Good," Zhahmonichas said. "Now hear. Children stay with family. Have books there. In cold time, *solvetkah,* not work in field, learn with parents. In warm time, *solvedgo,* work fields in day, learn when dark. Everyone read and write, is good for all."

Patrick raised his eyebrows. "Everyone is literate?" When Zhahmonichas frowned, he tried to explain, "All the people can read and write, even in this agrarian society?"

Frowning even more, Zhahmonichas spoke as if telling a little child something basic, "I say good all read and write. Is so. Everyone."

Feeling like an idiot in class, Patrick apologized, "Yes, it is good."

Zhahmonichas continued, "Older children, not to be farmers, need learn more. Here." He put his hand on the table. "After here, some go to *grositchi,* big town, south, some stay in *Roadranusis.* All work."

"That's a good way to do it. We have something similar where I'm from."

"You good student. Might learn things." A smile tried to crack through the teacher's face, but he managed to keep his scholarly frown.

Patrick pulled out one of the scrolls and smoothed it on the table.

Zhahmonichas glanced at it, then said, "We try now?"

"Yes, if we could." Patrick beamed.

Zhahmonichas squinted at the writing on the scroll. "Not know this now. Need more. Come." He stood and crossed to a door at the back of the room. Patrick followed him into a large supply cupboard. Shelves lined every wall, and most of them held books. Some of the books were quite large and old, but Zhahmonichas didn't stop there. He continued to a small table at the back of the room. On the table was a lantern and some dryer lint. He pulled out a flint and steel and started striking them, trying to light the fluff.

Patrick pulled out his lighter and flicked it on. "Do you want to use this?"

Zhahmonichas stepped back. "Hmm. Fire in pocket?"

"That's a good word for it. Here." Patrick released the lever and handed the now dark lighter to Zhahmonichas. "Hold it like this." Patrick showed him where to put his fingers. "Then slide here quickly and hold this." Zhahmonichas lit the flame. "Release when you're done."

"This good. Easy." Zhahmonichas lit the lantern, then handed the lighter back to Patrick.

Shaking his head, Patrick refused, as he reached into his pocket and pulled out another one, saying, "Just in case. Always be prepared. You can keep that one."

Zhahmonichas leaned back. "Prepare is good." He put the lighter into a pouch hanging from his belt, picked up the lantern, and grabbed a large brass ring built into the floor. Opening a trap door, he stepped down into the darkness. "Come."

A musty smell drifted up as Patrick descended the rickety staircase. At the bottom was a much larger room with more books. Zhahmonichas put the lantern on the edge of a small reading desk, angling the light to shine on the top. He rummaged through an adjacent shelf. "Ah, here." He pulled out an old-looking tome and set it gently on the desk. The light from the lantern glinted off woven metallic bands looped around the book, one from top to bottom, one from side to side, both held shut by a small lock. From inside his shirt, Zhahmonichas pulled a chain with a handful of keys on it. Selecting the right one, he released the bands and opened the book. Casually flipping the pages, he held his hand out to Patrick, waiting. Finally catching on, Patrick pulled one of the scrolls from his pocket and gingerly placed it into Zhahmonichas's hand. Flattening it out on the book, he compared symbols.

After a moment, he said, "As thought, this *dirtrahjahno*, lost nature knowledge. You read, but not say right, so not good. Must say exact to be of use."

"Can you say it right?"

"Yes, I say right." Zhahmonichas sat on a tall stool next to the desk. "I have *lahlzhi* but not *zhoonpah*, so not use either."

Patrick didn't quite follow what the teacher said but was ready to learn. "That's fine. You say it, slowly, and I'll take notes." He pulled out a small pad and pencil, ready to transcribe.

Slowly reading the scroll out loud, Zhahmonichas watched as Patrick scribbled on his paper. After a couple of phrases, Zhahmonichas asked Patrick to read it back. Stutteringly at first, but then smoother, Patrick read back from his jottings. Zhahmonichas frowned. "You say good. What you write?"

Patrick showed him, but as neither knew the other's written language, it meant nothing. He tried to explain. "I didn't write *what* you said, but instead the *sounds* you made when you said it. I'm using symbols from a phonetic alphabet. Each sound has a symbol, and each symbol represents exactly one sound." He flipped a page in his notebook and quickly wrote something down. "Here, this is your name. See?" He handed the notebook over:

Zhahmonichas sat back and stared. "That good. What you say sound right." He picked up the scroll and flattened it out. "Not all sounds in old language still in language now. Some removed to make easier, some not used and lost for many years."

"Well, this alphabet isn't based on any one language. It's designed to be as universal as it can be. It even covers sounds I can barely make."

"Say again this part." Zhahmonichas circled the symbols near the middle of the scroll with his finger.

Patrick studied his notes, the scroll, and the big book, rewriting his strange letters for that one part. Reading it once or twice, he breathed once and said the phrase aloud.

They heard a loud pop, and the lantern went dark.

"Hey! What happened?"

Zhahmonichas fumbled with the lighter finally getting the lantern relit. "You look at light when you said?"

Patrick shrugged. "I wasn't paying attention. Why do you ask?"

"What you write, what you say, is right, exactly. Can use."

"Use? For what?"

"Use to change, control nature."

"Control nature? How am I going to do that?"

Zhahmonichas settled back into his scholarly demeanor. "Sound change things. You say, it do."

"The sounds I make affect things physically? How is that possible?"

"Not know *how*, but know *does*. Do again. Look at light and say."

Patrick glanced at his paper, looked at the light, and said the phrase again.

The pop was louder, more explosive, and the lantern went out, but, in the sudden darkness, the noise of shattering glass filled the now dark room.

Using the dim light filtering in from the open trapdoor above, Zhahmonichas picked up what remained of the lantern. The frame bent out of shape, the glass chimney in shards, the reservoir at the bottom split and leaking—no one would be using that lantern again.

Patrick gasped. "Oh! I didn't mean to do that."

Zhahmonichas smiled, his first real smile. "Is good, can fix. Not see control of words for long time. Last one good with words left for *garsi* when I young."

"So you're saying that I'm able to do that whenever I want? By saying the right words, or sounds?"

"*aa-eh*, you control sound, you control all. Now you *rahrgendu*, practice, study more, make easy. Then you make proud your family."

Patrick focused on his notepad. He carefully closed the cover with new respect for the spoken word. *I don't know if the pen is mightier than the sword, but in this case words are definitely louder than actions.* He gawked at the debris. *And messier.*

Zhahmonichas headed towards the steep steps. "We go up now. Too dark for study." He smiled again.

As he climbed up, Patrick heard an audible click as Zhahmonichas locked the metal bands, sealing the book. *Now I understand why that book was sealed. A little knowledge could certainly be a dangerous thing here.*

Back upstairs in the classroom, they heard the clamor of cheering and chanting out back. Stepping out the back door, they found Joe in the middle of a circle of noisy children. In the circle with Joe were young men, maybe half a dozen or so. They could have all been in their late teens, or even early twenties, but what caught Patrick's eyes were the swords that they all carried, even Joe.

A closer look revealed that they were merely wooden swords, not lethal but could certainly do some damage.

Patrick noticed two of the young men advancing on Joe, swords at the ready. He yelled a warning, but before he could get a word out, Joe spun under the sword swinging at his head, rolled on the ground and twisted, hitting the young man in the back of the thigh. The crack of the hit made the kids cheer even more. The young man's knee buckled as he grimaced in pain, and his sword flew out of his hand, rolling away.

Joe was barely getting to his feet when the next sword came at him. He blocked it and kicked high, hitting the wielder full in the chest, knocking him to the ground. Joe swung his sword hard and fast, aiming at the side of the now sitting man's neck, but it never hit. Though seated, he still managed to block Joe's attempt.

The cheer of the kids watching drowned out the noise of sword hitting sword.

Three more young men jumped into the fray at the same time, all swinging for Joe's exposed back. He let the impact of sword on sword bounce his blade up and behind, blocking all three hits without even looking. Now spinning, he made a wide sweep, and all three swordsmen had to leap back to avoid being hit. One of them tripped and fell. Joe ignored him, going after the other two. With a jab and a thrust to their middle, he got inside their guard. Smacking the hilt of his sword on a hand, he disarmed one, then confronted the last one. Face to face, they circled once or twice, then charged at each other. The swords clashed, and one went flying. When the combatants released each other and stepped apart, Joe still had his sword in hand.

The kids cheered again.

Joe raised his sword to his opponents and bowed formally. When he came up, he glanced to the porch, finally noticing Zhahmonichas and Patrick standing there watching. Flushing with chagrin, he tried to explain, but before he could get much out, Zhahmonichas stopped him.

The schoolmaster smiled. "Good fight. Those trained men, yet you bested."

Joe helped his opponents get back to their feet, uncomfortable at his victory. "They showed me how."

"They show good. You learn good." Zhahmonichas put his hand on Patrick's shoulder. "You both learn good, have good family. Be proud, not embarrass. If I teach you from child, you both go to *garsi*, help govern. Be good men."

Now Patrick felt embarrassed, too.

By this time, the kids had surrounded Joe, chanting. Zhahmonichas quieted the kids. Once they settled down somewhat, he told Joe, "They think you *blahtahmre*, sword man, already. They want see your sword."

Joe shrugged and held his hands up, still holding the practice sword he'd been using. Expressing their dissatisfaction quite vocally, the kids clamored at Zhahmonichas. He tried to explain to Joe, "They want you have sword. I tell them no sword until earned. Have to properly show control, then can award."

"I can see that," Joe said, offering to return his practice sword to Zhahmonichas. "When I'm ready, I'll return."

"You keep *bivdi* sword, *rahrgendu*, use often. Become easy with it, then return and show learning."

Joe bowed. "Thank you. I will practice often."

Zhahmonichas stepped off the porch and scattered the children with a wave of his hand. Turning to Joe, he said, "Practice often is good, you have time, so do now."

"Yes, sir." Joe walked to the middle of the open area, checked to the sides and behind, then faced front, relaxed, and bowed to an imaginary opponent. Taking a half step forward, he drew his sword and commenced his moves. Slow at first, yet firm, the actions progressed, his sword whistling. Two steps and a turn, the sword spun before him, above his head, up one side and down the other, a front thrust, followed by one to each side.

His momentum increased, his sword a blur. He circled one way, then the other. The crowd stood in awestruck silence as he leaped, spun, and rolled. They'd never seen anything like that before.

Joe completed one circuit, then did it all over again, completing the same moves in mirror image. Coming back to the beginning, he slowed, swung his sword high, then acknowledged his invisible but now defeated opponents. Sheathing his sword, he breathed evenly and bowed.

The young men he'd been sparring with murmured among themselves, in admiration of his abilities. Zhahmonichas approved of Joe's display. "You do study sword before."

Joe replied, "Not exactly. When I was in Korea, I kept in shape with Tae Kwan-do, but we never used any weapons or anything, certainly not a sword, but the moves I learned then seem to work well here, too, and it felt good with the sword to counterbalance me. The flow was right."

"*nirbo* true. You need have sword." Zhahmonichas stared at Joe. "You not have already?"

Joe stood there, wide eyed. "No, sir. I've never had a sword."

Zhahmonichas spoke to one of the older boys, a short, curt phrase. The boy stood and stared for a moment, then at a glance from the schoolmaster, ran into the schoolhouse. Everyone waited patiently in silence, awaiting the boy's return. Finally, the door slowly opened, and the boy stepped out carrying a long, flat box. He stopped in front of Zhahmonichas, holding the box high. At the sight of the box, the kids muttered to each other, but Zhahmonichas silenced them with a look, then opened the box. Slowly he drew out a shiny sword.

Joe couldn't help but stare.

Zhahmonichas held the sword in his right hand, the blade resting on the back of his left sleeve. He presented the sword to Joe. "This my sword. I not need, too old to use, but you young, and show ready for true sword."

Continuing to stare, Joe managed to stammer out, "But, sir, *your* sword?"

"I not need, not use. You use, have pride, for good. Make proud all of us." Zhahmonichas indicated his students…*and* the entire town.

Joe was speechless, but with the encouragement of the kids, he let them help him get the belt wrapped on his waist, the scabbard hanging on his left hip. With appropriate reverence, he accepted the beautiful sword from Zhahmonichas. It had the general shape of samurai swords he'd seen in movies, but the color was not quite right. This sword was a coppery color, parts deep red, and incredibly shiny. The intricate engravings on the blade were beautiful. He'd have to find out what they meant later. "Thank you, sir. I am honored to wield your sword."

Zhahmonichas spoke, including Patrick, "You both boys have gain today. Must return and tell what you do with knowledge and skill."

Joe slowly sheathed the sword, then glanced at Patrick. "What'd you learn in there?"

Patrick shrugged. "How to turn off lights, destructively, though."

"Huh? What's that supposed to mean?"

With a wide sweep of his arm, Zhahmonichas said, "Show friend you know."

"Yeah, show me," Joe insisted.

"I need a target," Patrick said.

Zhahmonichas suggested a tree branch overhanging the yard.

Patrick concentrated on a leafless section and tried to recall the phrase from memory. Speaking quietly, he mumbled it as best he remembered. Nothing happened.

Joe watched the branch along with all the kids. "Is that what you expected? A little disappointing."

"Hang on. Let me get this right." Patrick dug out his notes. "Ah, that's it!" Concentrating on the branch, he whispered the phrase. The branch shook, leaves fell from the tree, and some birds hiding took flight.

Joe laughed. "That's it? Well, whoop-dee-do."

Patrick shrugged. "It worked better when we were inside."

Zhahmonichas gripped Patrick's shoulders, staring him in the eyes. "You able do. Say properly, loud. Not work if not sound. Put force in."

"I'll try." He held his breath, tensed up, stared at the branch, and spoke aloud.

A loud pop, then a snap, a crack, and the branch broke off, falling into the yard with a crash.

Joe blinked. "Wow! *You* did that? That's better than a sword. You have range!"

"Range? Yeah, but it takes too much time for me to get ready. It won't do me much good if I'm in a hurry."

"You think so? By the time someone gets close enough to use a sword, you can already be knocking them on their butts."

"As long as I see them coming. It won't do a thing for me if I get jumped in a dark alley."

"So stay out of any alleys." Joe laughed. "It's still pretty useful."

Zhahmonichas suggested, "Practice, you not need paper. Like sword, make easy with study."

"I'll do that." Patrick grinned. "Now that we're outside."

"Then go with *nirbo*, show them word control."

Patrick drifted to a small copse, followed by a group of children. The rest stayed back to admire Joe and his sword. Not wanting to damage it, Joe was careful as he checked the blade's edge but determined it to be solid and well built. He swung the sword back and forth, and the kids scattered, content to watch from a safe distance. On the other side of the yard, under the trees, Patrick used his newly found skill to break up larger branches, telling the kids that he was making firewood for them.

Catching everyone off guard, two small boys came running past the schoolhouse, pushed their way by the other kids, and ran right up to Joe. In unison they shouted, *"ben ehnd tomss seh-ee go lah-juh."*

Joe frowned at them in bewilderment, then realized what they'd said. He shouted to Patrick, "Hey, something's up! We need to get going!"

The boys noticed Patrick, then ran to him and repeated their message, *"ben ehnd tomss seh-ee go lah-juh."*

Patrick scrambled to his feet and followed Joe past the building and across the town green straight to the lodge. As soon as they could see the lodge, Joe noticed a crowd milling around outside, and as he reached the door, he heard a fight in progress. Not knowing why, he drew his sword as he burst through, ready for anything. What he stumbled across appeared to be a typical barroom brawl, well under way. In the pile, he could see both his buddies and the townsfolk all struggling in a mass.

Joe tripped over three guys grappling on the floor and realized that his sword would probably do more damage than good, so he held it out of the way and backed up. As Patrick came through the door, Joe yelled, "Do that thing you learned, now!"

Patrick quickly stepped up, faced the crowd, then focused on an empty spot above the worst of the fight. He raised his hands as he sucked in air. He whispered the phrase that he'd been rehearsing with the kids, tightened his gut, and yelled it, forcing the sound out.

The blast shook the room, knocking dust from the ceiling beams. Windows shattered, and the onlookers outside ran for cover. *A little too much,* Patrick thought, *but better than not enough.*

The room was suddenly quiet in the aftermath of the explosion. Those who were still conscious stared in amazement. In the stunned silence, everyone was trying to figure out what had happened. Patrick noticed Ben trying to get to his feet, so he hurried to help him.

Ben stared up from the floor. "Patrick? Wha…"

"Didn't mean to get *you,* Ben. Just the quickest way to stop the fight."

A confused look on his face, Ben said, "Yeah, but what *was* it?"

"That might be difficult to explain," Patrick said. "Let's get you seated first, then we can talk."

"Shouldn't we look after them, too?" Ben surveyed the remains of the brawl.

Patrick saw Shess, Tom, and Joe, all helping to pull the bodies apart. "They have things under control. Let them handle it."

Patrick led Ben to a table where he plopped and grabbed a pint of the weak ale, mumbling and frowning at the watered down drinks.

After sorting out the slightly injured from the more seriously injured, Tom and Joe were busy trying to treat the ones they could, while Shess kept the combatants from starting anything again, which wasn't difficult as most weren't in the mood for any more roughhousing.

Ben spotted Doug in the middle of the crowd helping with the injured. "Hey, Doug. A moment of your time?"

Doug handed off his patient and trotted to Ben. "What's up?"

"All this ruckus was because of that monster bullet and a bad roll of the dice, wasn't it?"

"Yeah, so?" Doug said.

"You know," Ben started, "It would be good to return it to…" Ben asked Patrick, "What's his name?"

Patrick shrugged. "I didn't get here 'til the fight was going full force."

Doug glanced across the room. "His name is Shawn, or something like that. He was telling us about his bullet."

Ben stared. "So you *knew* it was special? That it was his amulet?"

Doug dropped his head. "Yeah. It's a well-told story in this town."

"So, don't you think you should give it back?"

Doug blinked. "Wait! I won it fair and square. He bet, he lost. There's nothing else to consider, is there?"

"Yes, you won it, but what are you going to do with it?" Ben asked. "You certainly didn't bring a .50 cal rifle, did you?"

Doug shuffled his feet. "No, but I was getting annoyed at Eric. Did you see how much he was winning? I had *one* good throw. It wasn't my fault that it happened to be the one with that big bullet in it."

"I don't see how that makes any difference."

"I was already losing nearly every roll to Eric, and I didn't want to lose to some backwater native, too, not in front of everyone."

"I understand, but it could help cement relations with the townsfolk."

Doug frowned. "Why would I want to do that? We aren't going to be here for long."

"That's one of the things to consider." Ben stood up. "You should hear what we found out when we were talking to Shess. Important stuff that may affect our stay, and it might involve us directly." He paused. "It would be helpful."

Doug slumped. "Whatever you say." He spotted the prior owner of the bullet in the middle of the injured and headed his way. "Hey, Shawn. How're you doing?"

Shankaktos held his head. "*poontosku.*"

"Your head hurts?"

Shankaktos started to nod, then grimaced. "Head hurt."

Doug shrugged. "Probably from the explosion." Shankaktos stared, so he continued, "Well, anyway, Ben thinks I should give this back." He held the bullet in his open hand, offering it to Shankaktos.

Shankaktos started to grab it, then hesitated, staring suspiciously at Doug.

"Go ahead. It's yours," Doug said. "I've heard how much it means to you."

Still uncertain, Shankaktos slowly reached for the bullet. Doug let it roll off his fingers into Shankaktos' hand.

With a big smile, Shankaktos said, "*gartah,* thank you. Should not bet."

Doug had to agree. "Yeah, you did a foolish thing."

"Want to know you, so join game," he said. "Why give back?"

Doug started to point to Ben but then said, "I don't have any use for it, and it's important to you, so you might as well keep it. Is that good for you?"

"Yes," Shankaktos said. "Much good, many thank you." He carefully put the bullet into the cloth pouch, pulled the cords tight, tucked it into his shirt, and put his hand on his head. "I hurt because not protected." Patting the bullet firmly pressed against his chest, he said, "Now safe."

"I've heard that it keeps you safe. Where'd it come from?"

"*mi fardo.* I first boy, so father give me."

"You inherited it? Passed on from father to son?"

"*aa-eh,* inherited."

"Wow, that's neat." Doug offered his hand to help Shankaktos to his feet.

Shankaktos smiled as he stood. He put his fist on his chest and said, "*mi nahmshi Shankaktos.*"

Doug smiled back. "Yeah, so I've heard. Shawn, right? My name is Doug."

"Doe-guss?"

"Close enough. Come on, let's go tell Ben that everything's under control."

They were part way across the room when the door flew open. The bright light caused Shankaktos to wince. Annie rushed into the room followed by Deezhlahmahs. Trey followed, a little behind them.

Hurrying to Ben, she asked, "What's going on? We heard an explosion."

"We have yet to find out all the details, but if your healer friend here wants to help, the injured are mostly gathered over there." He stretched out his arm and watched it quiver.

She glanced at the bruised and battered and said, "We'll handle it." She casually spoke to Deezhlahmahs as they walked across the room.

Ben couldn't understand a word of what they said. He gaped. *Is everyone going native on me?*

As Annie and Deezhlahmahs passed Doug and Shankaktos, Annie stopped. "You guys are good?"

Doug replied, "I am, but Shawn here has a headache."

Annie slowed long enough to use her special sight. "Ah, yes, I see." She reached out and put a hand on the side of Shankaktos' head. Closing her eyes for a moment, she said, "There, that should help."

Doug stared at her, but Shankaktos said, "*gartah.*"

She ignored Doug's stare, responding to Shankaktos instead, "*tow-oo,*" then she joined Deezhlahmahs to help the others.

Using her newly-found ability, Annie did quick assessments, generally agreeing with the triage that someone had already done. As Deezhlahmahs stood and watched, Annie went to each person, performing a less than formal 'laying on of hands' to relieve pain. The injuries were mostly minor bumps, bruises, and bloody lips, but the cracked ribs needed closer attention. She thought to herself, *If I had known then what I know now, I could have* really *helped Joe when we were attacked.*

Ben watched from across the room, and although Annie never touched her first aid kit, she easily handled of all the problems. He leaned to Patrick. "Do you see what she's doing?"

"Yeah," Patrick said. "But considering what *I've* learned in the last couple hours, it makes as much sense as anything else."

Ben wanted to ask what Patrick had learned, but just then, Doug and Shankaktos stepped up.

"Shawn is feeling much better," Doug said, "His headache is gone, and he has his bullet back."

Shankaktos smiled. "Doe-guss friend now."

"That means there's not going to be any more issues between the two of you, right?"

"Right."

Ben asked Shankaktos, "If you don't mind, where did you get that bullet?"

Shankaktos frowned. "Boollet?"

Doug reached for Shankaktos' chest. "Your…whatever."

Shankaktos smiled. "*zvonatri?*" He pulled out the small pouch and dumped the bullet into his hand.

"Yeah, that." Doug smiled proudly. "He inherited it from his father."

"Thank you, Doug." Ben then asked, "Mind if I ask where your father acquired it?"

Shankaktos frowned. "He go fight long time. He get there. He bring home."

Ben raised an eyebrow. "So, we still don't know where it came from." He shrugged. "Oh, well. We'll look into it later. Right now, I'm hoping that the two of you will work well together."

Doug frowned. "How's that?"

Shankaktos smiled.

"We'll get to that later. Can you help Annie and that healer?"

Watching Annie fly from person to person, Doug shrugged. "I'm afraid that we might get in the way."

"Yeah, probably so." Ben tried to find something else for them to do. "Hey, could you help Trey? He's trying to move all the tables back where they belong." He frowned. "They were kinda messed up in the fight."

"Yeah, we can help him with that." Doug and Shankaktos helped Trey fix the tables. Staying out of Annie and Deezhlahmahs's way, the three of them put the lodge back into some semblance of order.

Tom wandered back and sat next to Ben. "Annie has things under control there, so we weren't needed at all." He shrugged. "She basically dismissed us."

"Well, she probably wants to keep you guys from getting in her way," Ben said. "Remember what I said…wanting to her having her own way?"

"Yeah," Tom said. "But does she have to be so short?"

"Yup, she does," Ben said. "That is, when she gets focused."

Before Tom had a chance to reply, Joe plopped next to Patrick. "Hey, you guys have anything to drink here?"

Ben pushed a couple of fresh mugs towards him, followed by the pitcher of ale. "It's not as good as what Shess serves…according to Tom." He glanced at their guide. "Right?"

"Oh, it's not bad stuff, but don't plan to get blind drunk on it. You'll spend most of the night out back watering the bushes."

"That's fine with me. Right now I'm just thirsty." Joe grabbed a mug.

"Tom, have you ever seen anything like that before?"

"Huh? Like what?" Tom scrunched up his eyes.

"The way Annie is…I don't know…healing those guys over there."

Tom shrugged. "She hasn't done that before? I assumed she's always done stuff like that, weird things."

"Not that *I* know of." Ben paused. "Never seen anything like *that* at all."

As they watched the activity across the room, Eric wandered up. "Pretty good idea, wasn't it?"

Ben frowned. "The brawl?"

"No, the concussion grenade that someone brought. It did an excellent job of breaking up the fight."

Ben slowly stared at Patrick. "Is *that* what caused the explosion?"

Patrick tried to look innocent. "No way. I don't have access to stuff like that. Check with Joe."

"Nope, not me," Joe said. "Not this time."

Tom raised an eyebrow. "This time?"

"Yeah, *this* time." Joe shushed Ben.

Ben stared at Eric. "Hey, weren't you right in the middle of the fight?"

Eric shrugged. "Yeah, that's where the game was, why?"

"You don't seem injured at all."

Tom scrutinized Eric. "Hey, Ben's right. You're not touched. How'd you manage that?"

Eric held his arms up, searching for injuries. "In the right place at the right time?" He shrugged.

Patrick frowned. "Hmm…"

"So if that explosion wasn't a grenade," Ben said, "then what was it?"

"It's a thing I learned," Patrick replied. "Want to see it again?"

Joe laughed as everyone else at the table pulled back sharply.

"No, no thank you," Ben said. "We're quite happy sitting here in one piece."

"I didn't mean *just* the same. Smaller, more of a demo."

Ben leaned forward with curiosity. "Can you do that?"

"Yeah. I've been practicing."

Joe grabbed a pitcher and poured a quick slosh into his empty mug, then pushed it in front of Patrick. "Here, try this for a target."

"What kind of trick are you trying to pull?" Ben asked, staring back and forth between the two of them.

Tom hadn't been paying much attention to what these guys were saying, but when they started pushing mugs of ale back and forth, it piqued his interest, and he leaned in to watch.

Patrick explained as he set up his target. "I need to concentrate and say a couple words." He gazed at the base of the mug and whispered the phrase. They heard a small pop, the mug jumped, and the ale splashed.

Ben frowned at Joe, Tom stared at the mug, and Eric studied Patrick's face. "Not bad," Joe said. "Now again, but a little bigger. This time aim at the middle of the ale, not at the mug itself."

"It might make a mess."

"I'm betting on it."

Shrugging, Patrick focused on the mug and mumbled. This time the pop was louder as a bubble at the bottom of the mug burst, spraying ale on all of them.

Ben slowly wiped at the drops of ale running down his face. Tom froze and stared. Eric leaned back and said something about the power of the word. Joe burst out in laughter. "Hey! You pulled a good one!"

Patrick wiped his sleeve across his face. "Next time, I'm going to block better."

"Next time you're going to have to save the ale," Joe said.

Eric shuddered. "As James says, the tongue can no man tame; it is an unruly evil, full of deadly poison."

"You're right, Eric," Joe said. "What a waste of good ale."

Ben dragged his stare from the mug. "Never mind what we saw Annie doing, Tom. Have you ever seen anything like *that* before?"

Tom stared at the mug woodenly and managed to say, "I have to admit, that's a new one on me."

"Can you explain what's going on? How they're doing that stuff?"

"No clue. No one has ever done anything like that before." Tom stared at Ben. "We've never had anyone attack us either. *This* time all kinds of weird stuff is happening."

"Anything else different this time?"

Tom thought for a moment, then said, "Well, this is the first trip with young folks."

Joe piped up. "Who're you calling young?"

"Well, maybe not *young*, but younger than the scientists on the first trips, younger than the military that escorted them, younger than the old fogies that came out here to hunt. That's what I meant."

"Yeah," Joe said. "I can handle that kind of explanation."

"This is also the first time anyone has *had* to defend themselves. On the previous trips, we'd bring along some grunts."

"Grunts can be useful," Joe said.

"Yeah, but we never needed them," Tom said. "The biggest problems I had to deal with were the 'big game hunters'…fetching drinks for them like a bunch of gophers." He leaned back and smiled. "On the other hand, this is the first time I've had a chance to enjoy myself."

Ben shrugged. "I don't see how that could be related."

"Well, I don't see how *any* of it is related."

Ticking off his fingers, Ben summarized, "Annie heals, Patrick makes explosions. Has anyone else had any weird experiences?"

"You should see Joe with that sword," Patrick said.

Ben leaned closer to inspect Joe. "Yeah, I'd noticed it when you came in. How did you come by it?"

"The local school teacher gave it to me, after I'd demonstrated some martial arts moves I'd learned."

Frowning, Ben asked, "He just *gave* it to you?"

"No, not *just*. I'd just been goofing off with the kids. Drilling on some fighting skills, using a practice sword that they let me borrow, and he was watching me. He must have thought that I was good enough, because he told me to keep the wooden sword I'd been using."

Tom stared at the sword hanging from Joe's belt. "That's not wooden. Pretty wicked, too."

"Yeah," Joe said, patting the sword. "When he saw me with the practice sword, he told me to show what I could do with it, so I went through a *kata*." He leaned to the side. "That's a set of moves used for martial arts exercise, to perfect the moves learned at each level." He sat up. "So that's what I did. When I was done, he sent for *his* sword and gave it to me."

"He gave you *his* sword?"

"Yeah," Joe said. Apparently he was impressed, *really* impressed."

Patrick spoke up. "Hey, do a demo for us."

Joe's face flushed. "Nah, I don't need to do that."

"You convinced *me* to demo *my* thing, so now *you* have to demo what *you've* learned."

Tom agreed, "If it's anything I haven't seen in my training, I'll know."

Joe considered the room, checking the ceiling. "I could try that. Last time I was outdoors, so I need to keep the height in mind."

"The ceiling is high enough. You shouldn't have any problem with it."

Joe stepped to the empty area in front of the fireplace, positioned himself, and checked his surroundings, making certain that no one was in range, then slowly drew his sword, bowing to an invisible opponent. The sound of a sword sliding out of its scabbard carried across the general hubbub of the room, and everyone stopped what they were doing to look. The less injured sat up to see what was going on. The whole room went quiet as Joe started his moves, attracting the attention of Annie and Deezhlahmahs as well. Step, swing, block, step, swing, turn. The sword whistled through the air as Joe stabbed, slashed, and parried. He spun to confront all his imaginary opponents, one after another.

At one point, as he retreated from his invisible quarry, he backed up a little too close to the seated spectators, and they tried to lean back out of the way. One of the guys slipped, sending his mug flying across the room right at Joe's unguarded back. Without even turning, Joe slid the sword under his arm and snagged the mug, the sword sliding through the handle—a slight twist and the mug sailed back across the room in a gentle curve, landing in the middle of a table. It stopped without even a roll.

Joe whirled, the sword leading, then suddenly he ended it, bowing to his still unseen opponent. He sheathed his sword as the room broke out into cheers, going wild with approval.

"So, does that look familiar, Tom?" Ben asked. "Have you seen anything like that before?"

"Yeah…in the movies. Impressive. How long has he been training?"

"As far as I know, the only training he had was basic martial arts when he was overseas with his family. His dad was in the military."

"Then where did he learn to do *that* stuff?"

Ben shrugged watching Joe manage to break through the crowd of enthusiastic fans. "Ask him."

Joe pulled up a chair and plopped down, grabbing a mug. "Now I'm *really* thirsty." He guzzled the ale then sat back and hefted the mug. "Not bad stuff."

"Not as good as what Shess has," Ben said.

"Those moves," Tom said. "Where'd you learn them?"

"I didn't," Joe said. "Not in a class or anything. I never even held a sword until today."

"Well, Ben," Tom said. "You're going to *have* to add this to your list of weird experiences."

Joe protested, "It's not weird."

"Who can pick up a sword and move like that without extensive training?" Tom asked. "It's unnatural. There's something funny going on here."

"If you say so, but the moving…it felt right. All I've ever done before were straightforward exercises, but this, this was so smooth. I don't even have to think. It just happens."

Ben stared. "Annie, Patrick, and now Joe." He raised an eyebrow. "Any *others*?"

Before anyone could answer, Annie walked up and put her hand on Joe's shoulder. "Amazing demo." Then she made her report, "Everyone's been attended to. Some might need a couple days to fully heal, but I've eased the pain for everyone, though after that show Joe did, it'll be difficult to keep them contained," she frowned, "with all that adrenaline rushing through their veins."

"I didn't even see you open your first aid kit."

Annie smiled across the room and watched Deezhlahmahs talking with one of her helpers. "I've had some good training."

"How much training can you have in one day?"

"I'd say enough." She shrugged. "It was easy to pick up, so natural. Not difficult at all."

"Maybe not difficult for you, but I don't think I could handle it," Ben said, then thought, If that's what she's learned from that healer lady, I'll have to admit that the local version of medicine is much better than what we had back home.

The conversation suddenly stopped as Deezhlahmahs walked up. "Carl awake."

Deezhlahmahs opened the door to the infirmary and held it as the others went in. Annie was there to see how 'her' patient was doing, Tom to assess the possibility of getting everyone out alive, and Ben because he wanted to see what was going on. In spite of the dim light coming from the lantern, they could all easily see that Carl was sitting up. Deezhlahmahs slowly turned up the flame on a lantern hanging on a hook, and Carl squinted at the group.

Carl stared at them and managed to croak out, "Hey. What's up?" then he stopped to cough.

Ben stepped closer. "That's what we'd like to know. You had a few injuries."

Carl shrugged. "I might have been messed up a bit, but now I feel much better. No need for the body cart yet." Then he snickered and said in a phony Brit accent, "I'm not dead yet."

Tom frowned quizzically, but Annie ignored the film quote. Giving him a quick check, she examined the arm that had had the poison in it. "Doing much better than we'd expected," she said. "Right, Deezh?"

Leaning across the bed, Deezhlahmahs took Carl's arm and squeezed gently. When Carl didn't flinch, she pried Carl's eyelids wider open, squinting closely at the whites. "*aa-eh* not expect him awake yet. He fast heal."

Carl spoke up, "Must be the soup. I was barely awake before they started pouring it in me. It did help, in spite of the taste." He frowned.

"The soup?" Annie asked Deezhlahmahs a quick question in the native tongue and received a terse reply. She thanked the healer, then pried open Carl's eyes as she spoke. "They put medicine in the soup, mostly to relieve pain and let the patient rest, but it includes a variety of herbals specifically meant to speed healing."

Carl shrugged. "The flavor wasn't all that horrible, a bit salty, but they had to practically ladle it into me. I was so exhausted that I couldn't even hold the spoon. What a baby!"

"We could have expected your weakness, probably from the poison."

Carl sat up straighter. "Poison?"

"Evidently they wanted you dead." She held his arm. "We found it deep in that cut."

Carl frowned. "Why would they want *me* dead, when they took Melvin off like that?"

Annie stared. "Took Melvin—?"

Ben interrupted. "Why don't you start at the beginning and tell us the whole thing?"

Annie propped herself on the edge of the bed and using her best bedside voice, said, "Yes, take your time and tell us everything," as she held his wrist to monitor his pulse.

The others found seats. Ben plopped on a tall stool in the corner, Tom stretched out on a bench by the door, and Deezhlahmahs stepped behind her desk, sitting in a regal manner.

Carl inhaled slowly, then opened his story. "Remember when we were trying to decide what to do…right after that feast…and how John got pissed off and stormed out? Well, I do…"

* * *

John had stood up in the middle of the meeting. "This is too much talking. We came here to hunt, and that's what we're going to do." He grabbed his pack, barely slowing as he went to the door, stepping out of the dining hall. "Anyone else here to *hunt*?"

"Yeah," Melvin said. "Way to go, John! Let's leave them here."

"Hey, don't leave without me," Carl said and quickly followed them to the door, then hesitated and said, "See you at the Door, Ben, in a week or so," then stepped outside.

John was already heading up the road. He yelled back, "Come on! Let's get a move on. Don't give him a chance to talk us out of it."

All three broke into a quick trot, heading north, out of town. Taking a quick look, Carl saw Ben, Annie, and others standing right outside the meeting hall, staring at them as they ran off. He quickened his pace and ran, slowing for one last, quick look as he crested a small hill. No one followed, so he relaxed as he caught up with John and Melvin.

"No rush," he said. "We got the jump on them easily."

"Good," John said. "Let's keep going."

Melvin grunted his agreement and quickened his pace.

The path was easy enough to follow as they passed the fields and entered the forest. They kept up their speed, an easy jog, barely slowing until they were well into the forest.

Finally, Melvin broke the silence. "Done. I'm bushed, need a break!" he gasped, out of breath.

Carl agreed, "Yeah, they'll never catch up now. We can relax for a little while."

"Wimps. If you need to, we can stop here. Even if they did try to follow us, we'd be able to hear them in plenty of time to get moving again. They won't catch us napping!"

Melvin slowed to a walk. "Yeah, we could be off and running before they even get close enough to do anything."

Carl wondered what Ben could even *try* to do. After all, Ben hadn't been officially in charge, not of *all* the scouts. He was only *one* of the patrol leaders. John had always had his own patrol, his own clique, that Ben could never influence.

All three let their packs fall where they stood. A quick trip to the side of the path to relieve themselves, a swig of water from their canteens, and they kicked back. Carl dug through his pack, finding a piece of candy, not that he was hungry, certainly not after that sumptuous meal, but he wanted something that tasted normal, like home. He leaned his pack against a tree, then sat in the crevice between a couple of roots, sucking on a lemon drop, watching the birds in the trees, listening to the soft breeze rustling through the leaves. Soon his head sagged as he fell asleep.

If it hadn't been for the large meal, they might have been up and ready to go much sooner, but with their full bellies and the warmth of the afternoon they stayed deep asleep for hours.

At long last, John rolled in his sleep, easing the pressure on his hip, and his head slid off his backpack, hitting the ground. He snapped awake and sat up. "Hey! Wake up! It's getting late."

Groggily they scrambled to their feet, grabbed their gear and followed the road, as the late afternoon sun was setting somewhere beyond the vast branches of the forest.

"If we push it, we can get back to last night's camp site before we have to stop," John hoped. "We can use it as our base. We'll hunt in circles out from there, and we'll be ready to head back to the Door when Ben and his wimps show up."

Melvin spoke softly, "Yeah, right."

A short time later, Carl realized that he was having problems seeing the path. "I hate to say it, guys," he said, "But it's getting too dark to keep going. We'll have to make camp right here where we are."

John kept walking. "You can stop here if you want, but I'm going to cover more ground before bedding down for the night."

"If we wait, the moon will come up," Melvin said, trying to see the skyline in the dark. "Then we'll be able to see what we're stepping in."

"Listen. Hear that?" John asked. "It's the waterfall. We're almost there." He continued walking.

Silently they followed him, though Carl scowled at his back.

They easily found the base of the cliff next to the waterfall and started up it. With minimal light from the slowly rising moon, they did their best, managing to feel their painful way along. Scrabbling up the side of the hill, they scratched their fingers and skinned their knees, and a couple times they slid backwards a dozen feet, but prodded on by John, they kept going.

By the time they made it up to the brink of the cliff, all three were bruised and bleeding, though nothing so bad that they couldn't ignore it and move on.

John urged them on. "We don't want to stop so close to the cliff. Knowing you two, someone'd fall off the edge in the middle of the night."

Grumbling quietly, Carl said, "It *is* the middle of the night."

Melvin snickered but kept going.

Keeping the river to their left, they tried to follow the path, but soon the smooth surface wasn't beneath their feet anymore—it had vanished. Trying to avoid running into trees in the dim moonlight, they thrashed on through the tall grass, making so much noise that they didn't realize the sound of the river was long gone.

"Hey! Wait!" Melvin yelled. "We're lost!"

Carl stopped moving, then called out to John, "We can't keep going!"

Pausing for a moment, John said, "We aren't there yet."

"Aren't where? You have no idea where we are, so how do you know we're not there yet?"

John stopped. "You guys want to spend the night sitting out here in the grass?"

In the moment of silence before anyone answered, the sharp crack of a branch echoed.

Everyone froze, then Melvin's voice quavered, "Did you hear that?"

John shushed him, whispering aloud, "Quiet!"

Carl squatted as silently as he could, trying to sense which way the wind was blowing. *If there's an animal out there, I don't want to be his next meal.*

Melvin spun. "It's this way! I can hear it moving!"

John shouted, "Shut up, will ya? You trying to let it know where we are?"

Dropping to one knee, Carl slowly swung his head from side to side, listening in every direction. He could hear a group of animals moving out there. Two of them were getting close to Melvin, but more of them were circling them. He was annoyed that he'd allowed them to get so spread out. *Should have kept everyone together.*

Melvin suddenly jumped up, dancing and screeching like a banshee. He bellowed, "If we make enough noise, maybe we can scare it off."

John launched himself towards Melvin. "You don't know what it is! It might be attracted to noise!" He suddenly fell, his foot caught in a coil of grass. Thudding to the ground, he cussed up a storm.

The blast of Melvin's pistol rang out as he fired un-aimed potshots. "Did you hear that? I hit it!"

"You barely missed hitting *me!*" John screamed. "If I hadn't ducked, you *would* have!"

Carl cautiously unclipped his pistol and slid it out. Quickly cocking the slide in the middle of the yelling, he tried to time it so that the sound wouldn't reveal his location. He heard the noise near Melvin echo behind him, so he twisted to see what was there. Something ran past him. *That wasn't an animal. It was one of those crazies from last night!* he thought. Not wanting to take any chances, he aimed high and fired—the guy flew sideways and disappeared into the darkness, but Carl could hear him flopping in the grass, screaming in pain. Quickly ducking, Carl tried to remain hidden, but the flash of his .45 drew the attackers. He fired twice more times, and from the sounds of it, he hit some, then he fired off a quick barrage, ducked, and rolled off to the side.

In the momentary stillness, he heard John struggling to get his pistol unholstered as Melvin kept firing, his hammer clicking on empty cartridges—he'd already shot all six rounds in his revolver.

Carl could hear the crazies charge Melvin, knocking him to the ground. John was no help, so he crawled towards the scuffle and peered through the brush quickly. He saw a couple of the crazies dragging Melvin to his feet as others stood with spears centered on him. Continuing to crawl through the grass, Carl made certain that he was close enough, then aimed carefully and dropped the two nearest him.

A mistake he regretted instantly.

Throwing Melvin to the ground, they stormed Carl's position. He continued shooting, but with that many targets, he ran out sooner than expected. Trying to grab for another magazine, he blocked their thrusts with his arms, but that didn't work. Giving up trying to reload, he curled into a ball, letting them stab at his backpack.

Suddenly the crazies abandoned their attack. Carl could see Melvin standing unsteadily, his gun held loosely in his raised hands. *Surrendering? That won't work,* he thought. *He's going to get sliced to ribbons.* Instead, the crazies grabbed Melvin's arms, lifted him off the ground, and ran away.

Melvin yelled, "I don't know what they want, but they aren't hurting me!"

John popped up from a bush right next to them, screaming, "You're not taking one of *my* men!"

Ignoring him, the crazies kept running. John ran off after them, taking an occasional wild shot as he ran.

Carl laid low as he listened to the chase fading off into the distance. The night slowly quieted as he waited for the moon to rise enough to see anything. In the dim light, he checked his injuries and saw that none were as bad as he'd imagined: his legs were sliced up, he wouldn't be running any time soon, and his right arm was burning, but he'd heard of worse, though usually from an animal attack. Pulling bandages from his pack, he tied them as tightly as he could on each wound, succeeding in stopping the worst of the bleeding, but as Murphy would have it, he ran out of dressings before he ran out of cuts.

After taking a short break, he decided to head back towards town. Even if he didn't make it all the way, the closer he was, the better chance he had of finding help, or of being found. Taking a sighting on the moon, he got his bearings and headed in a direction that he hoped was west.

Hearing the water in the creek before he could see it, he adjusted his aim, relieved that he'd managed to head in the right direction. He stopped at the water's edge and carefully loosened the bandages, trying not to reopen the wounds and did his best to clean out the worst of them. Now, he could find the way to town, straight along the river, so he moved out with confidence and soon came to the cliff where the waterfall was.

In the harsh moonlight, it appeared steeper than he remembered. Although the dim light made it a little easier, heading down was always more difficult, and more dangerous, than heading up. He tried sliding by sitting on his pack but lost control and slid off. Tumbling the rest of the way, he smacked into a rock and passed out from the pain.

When he came to, he realized that his cuts had pulled open, one bandage was completely missing, and now it felt as though his arm was broken, but he had to press on.

He walked slowly but then suddenly started shivering. Knowing that he was finally coming off the adrenaline rush, he thought, *I have to find a place to get some sleep before I drop.*

Stopping at a flat spot between scattered trees, he shrugged out of his pack and leaned up against a tree. Not having to force himself to move anymore, he finally became aware of his every pain. He tried to sleep, drifting off for mere moments at a time. Every move, every twitch, every shudder sent waves of pain coursing through him, returning him to consciousness again and again. Giving up on getting any real sleep, and now shivering because of the cold, he decided to call for help.

He drew his gun and checked the magazine, empty, as he expected. He still had a couple spares in his belt, and more in his pack that he didn't think he could get to easily, if at all. Dropping the empty magazine on the ground, he pulled a full one from his belt and slid in, then fired off a shot into the air.

He wasn't ready for the kick of that first shot, and he fumbled for a better grip. Using two hands to hold his gun, he fired twice more, then flipped the safety and tried to rest, succeeding in falling into a light sleep. The next time the shivering woke him, he fired off another three round burst. He kept firing every time he woke up. When the magazine emptied, he pulled another from his belt, swapping it out. He lost track of how long he'd been there or how many rounds he'd fired. At one point, he imagined that he heard an answering shot and someone yelling, but everything was so dream-like that it didn't bother him anymore—he was beyond caring.

Sharp pain hit him one last time as someone lifted him onto their back. The gentle vibration of running was somehow comforting, and he passed out with relief.

* * *

"And then I woke up here. Maybe we shouldn't have run off like that, but we didn't want to lounge around, doing nothing, especially if we could get some hunting time in."

Ben put his hand on Carl's shoulder. "That's fine. We want to have fun, too, but now we have to slow down. Our big problem is first finding John and Melvin."

"I'll do what I can. Even if it's staying here in bed, out of the way."

Annie scowled. "The best rest for you isn't in bed. You'd develop bedsores. We'll work with the other guys and get you moving, slowly at first, but we don't want you to stiffen up."

Carl smiled. "Thanks." He said to Deezhlahmahs, "Thank you, too. I appreciate all the doctoring you did for me."

"Deezhlahmahs wasn't working on you alone." Tom put his hand on Annie's shoulder. "She had quite a hand in the healing process, too."

Annie hesitated, then said, "All I did was what I could."

Trying to sit up, Carl reached for Annie. "I'd give you a hug…if your brother weren't here."

Ben sauntered off towards the door, whistling a tuneless song.

Annie gasped. "Hey!" Then she pushed at Carl. "Besides, you still need to get dressed, though in what, I don't know. *You've* managed to survive, but your clothes are nothing but bloody rags."

Carl eyed the heap of what used to be his clothing, now lying in a pile on the floor. "Yuck."

"Anyone bring extras?" She looked Ben up and down. "Aren't you supposed to be prepared?"

"Not for that, we weren't," he said.

Deezhlahmahs walked to a set of pegs on the wall and selected a tunic and a pair of pants. "You use this."

"That'll have to do." Annie grabbed Ben and Tom by the arms and marched them towards the door. "Come on, you guys. Give him a moment to get dressed." Glancing back as she dragged them out, she said, "Carl, we'll be right outside."

With one arm on Ben's shoulder and one on Tom's, Carl limped across town and into the lodge. As he stepped through the door, everyone turned, and the room went silent. The quiet lasted a fleeting moment, then all were on their feet, mobbing Carl, trying to get the whole story out of him, all talking at once.

Annie tried to keep the crowd back, yelling, "Give him some air!"

Tom asked, "Make a place for him to sit, will ya?"

Carl croaked out, "Anyone have something for me to drink?"

Tables were moved, benches shifted, and mugs offered.

"Now that's more like it!" Carl leaned back. "That's the proper way to welcome the wounded hero." He was certainly enjoying all the attention he was getting.

Getting Carl settled at the nearest table, Ben and Tom stepped away from the crowd.

Ben said, "We'll leave things in your capable hands, Annie."

"Thank you, Ben," Annie said. "I'll do what I can to keep the herd of well-wishers back."

"Yeah," Tom said. "We could do with a little more quiet. We have a few things to discuss."

On their way past the fireplace, Ben noticed that another craps game was going on. Rolling his eyes, he tried to find Patrick, seeing him at a nearby table. "Are we going to have to break up another fight?"

"We'd better not," Tom replied. Frowning at those in the game, he asked, "You guys are keeping things under control, aren't you?"

Shankaktos held the dice. "All good." He punched Doug in the shoulder. "We friends now. We all friends."

Doug sat up and smiled. "We let Shawn run the game for a while. He gave each of us a handful of these ring-rings, funny money, and when someone runs out, he gives us more. No one is betting with anything important. We're just having fun."

Eric picked up a large handful of rings, most copper, but some shiny silver, spilling several on the floor. "Look what I won!"

"Shut up, Eric. You know you can't keep those. You have to give it all back when we leave." Frowning at the game, Doug complained, "No matter how much he bets, he keeps winning!"

Grinning like an idiot, Eric went back to the game.

Satisfied, Ben walked to Patrick's table, mumbling, "As long as everyone's happy."

"Anyone know where Shess is?" Tom asked. "We should update him on what happened to Carl."

"Last I saw," Doug said, "he was heading into the kitchen, rounding up some food."

"Food? Good thinking," Ben said. "I wonder if Carl's hungry. He didn't get any breakfast."

Laughing quietly, Tom said, "If he's hungry, I'm certain he'll get taken care of. They're treating him like he's a king or something!"

"Yeah, they're glad to have him back." Ben frowned. "Too bad we're still short by two more."

"We'll handle that soon enough." Tom said as he sat. "Here comes Shess now."

Coming out of the back room with a couple of platters, Shess stopped by Carl's table first, spoke to him for a moment, then set one of the platters in the middle of the table. He set the other one on the next table where the guys attacked it like flies after fresh droppings. Heading back to get more, he nearly ran into Trey, who was coming out with his own load of platters. Shess relieved him of one, then joined Ben and Tom, commenting as he sat, "Carl doing better."

Ben smiled, "Yeah, he'll survive. The medicine here is certainly different from what we're used to. Different but definitely good."

"Deezhlahmahs teach Annie," Shess said. "Annie have *shlikanmo*. She use good."

"Uh, yeah, whatever," Ben agreed. "She's always been kinda handy to have around, but I never expected her to be *this* handy." Ben watched as Trey delivered the platters of food, bringing the last one to their table.

Trey offered the platter. "I see you already have some food. May I join you?"

Ben offered an empty chair next to Patrick. "Be my guest."

Depositing the platter on the table, Trey parked himself in front of it as if it were his personal plate.

"Watch those elbows, Patrick," Ben said. "He's going to bump into you."

Tom raised an eyebrow at Trey. "Hungry?"

Trey's cheeks reddened as he answered, "Yeah. I built up quite an appetite with all the work."

"Work? What have you been up to?" asked Ben.

"Well, after the innkeeper saw me moving the tables after the fight, he sorta invited me out back to help with moving other stuff. A wagon full of grain arrived this morning, so he had me unload it, carrying the sacks to the storehouse, then we needed to transfer the kegs of ale from the cellar back to the wagon." Trey smiled. "Did you know that he exports the best ale in the whole area, brewed right here?"

"That's good to know," Tom said, smiling at Trey. "Gotta be in the right place at the right time, right?"

Trey continued, "Yeah. The guy that brews it trades with the other towns south of here. He gets the supplies he needs from them, then sells back freshly brewed ale."

"Sounds to me like A profitable venture," Tom said.

Trey continued, "So anyway, I hauled the kegs up from the cellar, loading them into the wagon, but right as we were loading the last one, a spoke cracked."

"Lousy timing," Ben said. "Did you have to unload the whole thing?"

"That would have been the smart thing to do," Trey shrugged, "But instead, I held the back corner of the wagon as they changed out the wheel."

Staring at Trey, Ben asked, "You held it? How long did you hold it?"

"Not too long. The rough roads here often crack the wheels, so they always carry spares. All we had to do was shift the barrels to get the extra wheel out. Once it was unloaded, I held the corner of the wagon as they pulled off the cracked wheel and stuck the new one back on."

"So you held up a wagon full of ale barrels while they changed out a wheel?" Ben wondered.

"It sounds different when you say it," Trey said. "But, yeah, that's what happened."

Tom glanced at Ben. "Has he always been a gorilla, or is that another one to add to your list?"

"He's always been a strong one," Ben said. "But this may be another one for the list."

Trey stared back and forth. "Hey, guys, I'm right here."

"Yeah, I see you," Ben said. "It's been a busy morning."

"Well, Trey, you've certainly been busy," Patrick said. "No wonder you're hungry. Please, dig in."

Not needing a second invitation, Trey tackled the plate of food with gusto.

Tom watched Trey dig in then wondered aloud, "So why aren't you sitting with your girlfriend there?"

Trey slowed, lifted his head, frowned, then swallowed quickly and said, "Me? Girlfriend? You mean Annie? She's more of a little sister. We've been friends since…" He glanced at Ben. "How long has it been?"

Ben shrugged. "Forever. We all grew up in the same neighborhood."

Tom's eyebrows went up. "So you two aren't a thing?"

Trey laughed quietly and replied, "No, we aren't a thing, but if you have any intentions, you might want to check with the *other* big brother." He tipped his head towards Ben.

Tom checked with Ben. "Well? Any issue?"

Ben laughed, "Not from me. I have nothing against you, Tom, but you might have some competition there." He tipped his head. "This healing thing is taking a lot of her time. I don't know if she'll be able to squeeze you in."

Tom shrugged. "Yeah, well it doesn't hurt to try."

Shess had been trying to follow the conversation. "*gu shlizhi di*? You meet for love her?"

Tom hesitated and said, "Well, uh, yeah, but I don't know if I'd put it quite like that."

All the guys at the table laughed at him as Ben said, "Go ahead, Tom. I wouldn't mind having you as a brother-in-law!"

Once all the laughter faded, Shess returned to business and asked, "What Carl say?"

Ben replied, "Well, Carl told us that after they ran off, they hiked for quite a while, in spite of not being able to see where they were going, so they ended up lost. They were well past the waterfall, into what you call the animal land, before they ran into real trouble. Up there somewhere, more of the *nimre* attacked them. They were caught off guard, so the *nimre* whipped their butts."

Shess frowned. "Whip butts?"

Patrick paused, a bite halfway to his mouth, and translated, *"nimre kahmgah di."*

"aa-eh," Shess said. *"viyaa spahsi nimre moi daa kahmgah.* They in animal land, so *nimre* win."

Ben continued, "The problem is that this time the *nimre* captured Melvin. He's always been a pain, but as much as I dislike him, I wouldn't wish any harm on him."

"aa-eh, trouble but friend still. *mi jahno,* this I know." Shess put his hand on Ben's shoulder.

"Thanks," Ben said.

Shess continued, "Some our people taken. We fight, but they *sahnmu,* quiet move. They come from side and take. Most they take food and supplies, some they take people." He frowned, "Why now your people?"

Ben shrugged, "We don't know, but from what we can tell they wanted *just* Melvin. They aimed specifically for him." He asked the group, "Any idea why'd they want him specifically?"

Trey laughed and chimed in, "His big ego?"

Tom shrugged. "I haven't a clue."

"Well," Ben said, "John followed them, so now we have two guys missing: one carried off, one chasing after."

Tom glared. "It would be nice to could get *some* technology to work here. Then I'd give each of you an ankle bracelet to track everywhere you go."

Ben blinked. "Hey, it isn't my fault. I want them back as well."

"I know, I know," Tom said. "So now that we know what happened to them, what's your plan to get them back?"

"Like I said back at Shess' house, *I'm* ready to go after them." Ben paused. "But we should ask the others."

"Put it to a vote?"

Ben breathed deeply, watching the group across the lodge. "Yeah."

Tom stood up and bellowed across the room, "Quiet, everyone!" The room went silent as everyone stared. "Ben, you want to address this gang?"

"I may as well," Ben said. "Thanks for getting everyone's attention."

"I yield the floor to Ben," Tom said loudly, then sat.

Ben stood, slowly and deliberately. Everyone twisted in their seats to face him, and he studied the crowd, taking careful measure of their mood, considered his stratagem, waited a moment, then spoke. "We have a new choice now. No question of hunting, camping, or even merely having fun. The question we have before us now is: do we try to rescue our friends?" he paused, "or abandon them?"

Tom leaned to Trey and Patrick, who had both stopped eating to listen to Ben. "Wow! I never saw this coming. I expected him to use cool, logical arguments to convince them."

"That's what he usually does," Patrick said. "But sometimes, when he knows that logic won't work, he plays with their egos, taking full advantage of any emotional bias."

Trey agreed. "That's why he was always the patrol leader. Everyone always followed his suggestions, even if they were dead set against it to begin with."

Ben stepped up onto his chair. "I won't ask 'Are you with me or against me?' because none of you are truly against me." He paused. "You simply do not yet realize the importance of finding our missing friends."

Tom leaned towards Patrick, practically yelling to be heard, "Listen to him go. He knows how to run a rally!" He half stood up. "I'm ready to follow him into battle, too." He sat back down and watched the crowd.

"Look at the natives, too," Patrick said. "They are all for it, even though I don't think they know half of what he's saying, yet they're willing to follow him anywhere."

Ben continued, "Are we now ready to go? Not quite. We have yet to decide *when* to go." Pausing a moment to identify the loudest ones, Ben monitored the reaction of the crowd, feeling their emotions like a doctor taking a pulse. "I see that some of you are ready to leave this *very* moment, but there are others out there who would still prefer to wait until morning. Starting early in the morning might work, but I ask you this: if you were the ones who were lost, out there in an unknown world, separated from your friends, would you want your rescuers to wait? Would you want *anyone* to wait? Of course not!" He paused to let the noise subside again.

Tom leaned to Shess. "Do you think it'll work?"

"*aa-eh*," Shess said, shouting back, "He good lead. They follow."

Ben went on, "And we *won't* wait, but we also won't foolishly rush out into the strange, the foreign, the unfamiliar, for fear of getting lost ourselves! Who then would search for the searchers? We will *not* repeat the disastrous incidents of our past—we can, and we will, learn from our mistakes."

Someone in the crowd shouted, "We don't know our way around in this world."

Ben took the criticism in stride, replying to the crowd in general, "We *will* succeed in our hard-fought efforts. And how can we be so certain of that?" Ben reached out to Shess. "Because we will look to our newly-found friends here in this world for their advice." With a dramatic wave of his arm, Ben asked, "Shess, who of your well-trained citizens would *you* trust us to? Who would keep us from danger? Who is your best tracker of lost souls?" The crowd held its collective breath as it awaited an answer, Ben stepped off his chair and spoke to Tom quietly, "No offense intended. You're a good guide, but these folks know the land much better."

"No offense taken," Tom whispered back. "I'd prefer to *follow* these guys than be at the front of this mob you've created."

Ben waited for Shess to answer as the crowd grew impatient. "Well?"

Shess thought a moment, then replied, "Fredekas. He best to lead and find way."

Ben stepped back up on his chair and shouted, "Fredekas! Bring him forward."

Soft mumblings filled the room as they all waited to see who Fredekas was.

Shess easily spoke above the noise. "Fredekas! *kahmlah vi, uh miyi shnida gu.*"

A fairly short, young man sitting next to Carl blinked. "*mi eh-ee? aa-ee gui shnida mi? ioo rah-oo?*"

"aa-eh, miyi dahnzah gu frego dohgru," Shess called back.

Ben leaned to Tom. "Does he look old enough to you?"

Tom shrugged. "If Shess says he's good, that's enough for me."

Fredekas jumped to his feet, grabbed Carl, and ran up. "*Kharl selbah!*"

Carl blinked at Fredekas. "I'm going to help with what?"

"We need Fredekas lead war-group," Shess explained.

"War group?" Carl punched Fredekas in the arm then ducked. "Where Fred here leads, I'll follow!"

Fredekas grabbed Carl's wrist and twisted, making Carl wince in fake pain as he said, "Hey! Remember, I'm the wounded war hero!"

Shess stepped in to break it up. "We need you work now, not time for play. Ben want this serious."

Fredekas frowned at Ben and said, "Ben want serious, Ben get. Now we go." He confronted the mass still raring to go and said, "*ri bi getsi legui rahtchi uh gu targeh uh jimi vaa grahsah zvoto.*"

Patrick stepped up to translate. "Everyone, get your gear, arm up, and head outside to the grassy area!"

"Do now!" Fredekas said.

Ben clarified, "Grab the minimum for a search and rescue. Leave anything extra behind. We'll need to move fast."

"The townsfolk will watch our stuff until we get back, right, Shess?" Tom asked.

"They guard," Shess said. "We go."

Fredekas asked Carl, "Where you things? I carry."

Carl glanced at Ben.

"No problem," Ben said, "Your stuff was unloaded with the others. It's mostly piled along that wall."

Fredekas followed Carl to start going through his stuff.

As Ben dug through his pack, he frowned at Shess. "Do we need to think about firepower? We have guns, but all they have is swords and spears."

Shess smiled at the young men from *Roadranusis* and said, "Not problem. You attack when far, we finish when close." The look on his face grew into an evil smile as he drew out his sword, wiped it on his pant leg, and slid it back into its scabbard. "We get any left."

Ben stepped back. "I was referring to the *nimre*. They won't have guns at all." Ben glanced at Tom. "Is this going to work?"

"The *nimre* are going to find out that they've bitten off more than they can chew," Tom said. "It'll be a long time before they come back to bother *this* town. You're doing these folks a favor, Ben."

"Shess thinks *they* can handle it without us."

"We've worked with his men before," Tom said. "But we were hunting wild animals then, not wild *men*." He paused. "Ben, we need to be careful to hold our fire when the townsfolk are in the way. We don't want the wrong people getting shot."

Ben frowned then grabbed his gear. He thought, *I don't want* any *casualties out there*... Then he realized that they might need Annie along with them. "Do you think we should bring Annie, too? That way, if anyone *does* get hurt, she could help."

"Better than leaving her behind," Tom said. "She can bring up the rear, with guys to protect her while she does her thing."

"*di bilkishmu*," Shess said, then headed for the door, yelling at his men.

Ben shrugged. "Yeah, what he said." He followed Shess quickly.

Right behind him, Tom said, "If we push it, we can make it past the waterfall before it gets too dark."

"That would be good," Ben said. "Then we can stop for the night, or, if the moon is bright enough, keep going 'til we *have* to stop. Let's see if this Fredekas is as good as Shess thinks."

"Even if we stop for the night," Tom said. "Following *this* crowd, I'm expecting that we'll be able to find John and Melvin by tomorrow afternoon at the latest."

Ben stepped out the door. "I certainly hope so."

Hiking along in the late afternoon sun, Carl and Fredekas led the way as the rest of the war party trailed behind, with Ben, Tom, Annie and her entourage bringing up the rear. They'd been on the road for less than an hour but had already come to the bottom of the switchbacks at the base of the waterfall.

A little out of breath, Carl stopped to sit. "Fred, you head on up to the top. I'll catch up."

Fredekas said, "Good. Rest. We wait at top."

As each person walked past, they stopped to offer Carl a drink, something quick to eat, well wishes, or just congratulations on his ability to survive. He didn't mind *some* of the attention, but all the interest was quickly getting to be too much, and he even said so when the end of the line arrived. "Ben, can I be done being the wounded hero? They'll drop it if you ask 'em, right?"

"How can they?" Ben asked. "You've had quite an adventure: you survived an attack worse than Joe's, were wounded, yet managed to crawl back through the forest in spite of your wounds, and now you're nearly healed, practically a model soldier! If we were back home, they'd make a movie, and *you* would be the lead."

Carl grimaced. "Oh, come on. It isn't *that* great."

"The rest up there think so," Tom said, pointing ahead. "Besides, with *your* inspiration, we've made terrific time."

"We *did* make good time, didn't we?" Carl snorted. "Better than last night."

"Yeah, but unless we get moving, everyone else will have to sit and wait for *us*," Tom declared.

"That's fine. I'm done resting." Carl stood and headed up the trail. "I'll tell you this, it's certainly a lot easier crawling up this cliff if you can *see* where you're going." He almost laughed.

The three of them headed up, slowly ascending as the trail switched back and forth. Cresting the top, they started to follow the trail but then heard a loud crack. Following the noise, they saw Patrick sitting on a boulder half in the river.

He yelled to them, "Hey, guys! Watch this!"

Joe, standing by the edge of the river, picked up a rock, and flung it in a high arc. Patrick watched it sail, waiting until it reached its peak. He whipped his arm up at the rock and spoke quietly. Another loud crack, and the rock split, the larger pieces dropping into the water, the rest leaving behind a small cloud of dust that slowly drifted across the river.

Ben cheered him on, "Hey! You're getting good at that!"

Patrick bowed. "Like Zhahmonichas told Joe, *rahrgendu*, practice!"

"Well, we don't need it, but you're getting good."

"Let's get going," Tom said. "We don't want to get too spread out."

Patrick jumped off his boulder to join Joe who double-timed it to Ben. "We were waiting here to show you guys the way. Fred didn't want *everyone* to wait for the slow-pokes." He snickered.

Joe led the group towards the bushes, but Tom stopped him and asked, "That way? Why not stay out of the bushes and stick to the trail?"

"If you were here earlier, before we ploughed through," Joe said. "You'd've seen the mess that John left when they came through. We could easily see where they'd gone." He apologized to Carl, "No offense intended, but Fred thinks that when you guys got up here, you didn't see that the trail went off to the side, so you guys continued straight into the brush."

"Yep," Carl said. "That's certainly possible. Climbing up the hill, we weren't certain where we were, so we just kept pushing on." Shaking his head, he continued, "John can be kinda pushy at times. If I'd known we were going to have so much trouble, I'd have convinced him to stop 'til the moon came up."

"If you'd known that," Ben said, "I'd have to add you to my list! Come on, let's get moving."

Heading into the brush, they followed the impromptu trail, finally catching up. Coming to a wide area of flattened grass, they knew that this must have been where the attack on Melvin had taken place. Everyone fell silent, standing there in silence. The whole area was a mess, with blood smears showing where the majority of the combat had been.

They slowly circled the area, assessing the damage. *Nimre* bodies lay spread around, weapons still in hand, already mangled by wild animals.

Ben had a disquieting feeling as he viewed those poor souls.

Finally, Annie broke the silence, "Should we take time to honor their dead?"

Fredekas replied, "They not have time, why we?"

"It would be the proper thing to do," she said. "We could bury them where they lie."

"Proper is get weapons, supplies. We need, not they."

Ben shuddered as he thought, *Like what* we *did when Joe was attacked.* Aloud he said, "Do what you think is right. We'll wait." He sat on a nearby rock and kept an eye on Annie.

Fredekas called his friends to help, and they quickly stripped the bodies of all the usable weapons, armor, and supplies. After separating out the plunder, they dug a single, shallow grave, hastily stacked the bodies, then piled it with sticks and rocks. He asked Ben, "This proper for you?"

"Yes," Ben said. "Close enough. What would you normally do?"

"Hang from trees. This their land, near ours. We warn, they not pass."

Tom stepped up. "Brutal, aren't they, Ben?"

Ben shrugged. "If that's what's normal for their society, it's fine, but it's not what I'd expect considering how well they treated us."

"Friends get the royal treatment. Enemies get the shaft, the royal shaft." Tom shrugged. "Sounds equitable to me."

"A bit harsh," Ben said. "Maybe I'm just not used to it."

"Don't worry. You're only going to be here a few days. Then you're back to your cozy, warm house, so don't fret." Tom sounded sarcastic.

Frowning, Ben swore, "I'm going to do what I can to help ease the burden these people have to bear."

"In that case, let's get moving."

"Which way?" Ben asked. "The grass was already mashed flat when we arrived, and now it's even worse."

Tom frowned. "I don't know. Where's that guide?"

Ben yelled across the mess, "Fred! Which way do we go?"

Before Fredekas could answer, Carl stepped up and headed straight at the trees. "They went this way," he said, the forest closing in behind him.

Ben tried to keep him in sight but kept losing him. Ben shouted, "Don't get too far ahead!"

Carl either didn't hear him or ignored him, so Ben ran after him.

Tom yelled, "You go after him. I'll get the others."

Ben followed Carl, trying to keep half-way between him and the rest of the group. Fredekas herded the natives forward as Tom pushed the scouts. Soon Tom came running up alongside Ben slightly out of breath, with Fredekas right behind.

Tom huffed, "We're all moving fine. Patrick and Joe are bringing up the rear."

"Good," Ben said, quickening his pace, trying to keep an eye on Carl. "Does he know where he's going?"

Tom shrugged. "He thinks so, but in the dark last night he couldn't possibly have seen this far."

"Hey, Fred, is this the right direction?" Ben asked.

"Carl *frego* good," Fredekas said. "He *klikah*, see clear."

Ben squinted at the trees they were passing. "I don't see anything different." He picked up speed, closing the gap. When he finally caught up to Carl, he asked, "Are you certain this is the way they went?"

Without taking his eyes from the ground, Carl said, "See that bush up there ahead of us? See the bent branches? Those leaves don't naturally grow like that. Something rubbed up against them…recently."

Ben stared at the bush Carl indicated, thirty meters ahead of them. He could barely see the branches, much less the individual leaves. "You can see that?"

"Yeah," Carl said dragging his eyes from the ground. "Why?"

"You're not from here, so how would you know that they don't grow that way?"

Carl stopped suddenly and stared at Ben. "Hmm…I don't know." He frowned. "But it still doesn't look right."

Fredekas spoke slower, "The *nimre* finish fight, now give what they get to *zhaarkahgdi*, what they not want to *gahndi*."

Ben was ready to ask what that meant, when suddenly a cloud of gray, greasy smoke billowed up, followed by a chorus of voices echoing up the canyon. It sounded like they were shouting approval. "Whatever they're doing, something big just happened. Can we move closer and get a better look?"

Fredekas checked the ridge they were on. "Move back, go that way, *then* close to edge, and see."

Carl agreed. "Too much movement close to the edge might give us away."

Ben and Tom slunk back from the edge, then followed as Fredekas led the way. They had barely gone a hundred meters when they ran into Joe heading the same direction.

Joe had his group sit tight, then joined Ben. "Someone has a big fire going. A funeral pyre?"

"Fred thinks so," Carl said.

Joe grinned. "Can we keep Robb away? He'd probably try to make it bigger."

"Fred says the *nimre* are celebrating after their battle," Carl explained, "divvying up their ill-gotten gains."

Joe considered the situation. "This is the right time to hit 'em. Catch them unawares."

Ben stared at him. "Is that fair?"

"No way." Joe gawked at Ben. "That's why we hit them now, hard and fast."

Ben wanted to argue but had to agree. "Set up your group on the top of the ridge a ways farther. We'll go back and get the rest. You'll have plenty of time before we're ready. When you hear the first shots, dive in."

Joe saluted as he guided his troops along the ridge.

"How 'bout if Carl and I wait here?" Tom asked. "You go with Fred to get the others, and we'll monitor things from here."

"Works for me," Ben said. "Come on, Fred. You lead. I'll follow."

Fredekas grunted and jogged off. Ben trailed behind, but they were back in a moment with everyone else.

"What's up?" Patrick asked in a low whisper.

Ben crouched. "From what I've been told, we're all set to start a war."

Sitting up straight, Patrick stared. "How's that?"

Fredekas said, "mui tahkmah nimre lew no kahnshe mui."

"A sneak attack? On the *nimre*?" Patrick blinked. "As long as we get our guys back! Let's go."

Ben stood slowly as Patrick signaled to the others. He watched them form up and move out. He wasn't in as much of a hurry and lagged behind. Annie joined him, but didn't say anything. In his mood, he wasn't up to any conversation, and he knew that she sensed it, too, because she kept quiet. They crept up to Tom and Carl and watched Fredekas start directing everyone to a good spot. Then they all crawled towards Patrick.

Joe stared at John. "Nope, we were cleaning up the mess *you* left behind."

"Ah, those guys." John scoffed. "So how many were there?"

"We didn't stop to count. Shess was in charge, but mostly Fred and his buddies did the cleanup. They did a good job of stripping the bodies before giving them a half-way decent burial."

"They stripped them?"

"Not completely," Joe said. "Mostly their weapons and anything else useful. Like what we did when the *nimre* attacked our camp."

"Oh, yeah," John said. "That's all."

Joe commented, "Well, it is a good technique to use in combat. Keep armed and resupplied as much as possible. You never know when you'll need something you just left behind on a dead body. He certainly won't need it anymore."

"If you say so," John said. "Survival *is* important."

"Survival is the *only* important thing," Joe said.

John saw Carl heading across the camp, so he yelled out, "Hey! You were going to tell me how Patrick can speak like a native, and what's with Annie? I've never seen anything like before."

Carl headed their way. "Yeah. Let's go sit by the fire, and I'll see if I can get you up to speed."

John plopped on a log and stretched his legs. "I could use a drink." He paused and when no one answered, he said. "Anybody have anything?"

Someone passed a canteen to John.

"Nothing stronger?" Shrugging, he swigged it and passed it on.

Carl cleared his throat and began, "We weren't attacked by chance that first night. Those guys had been told to go after Melvin specifically."

After a short discussion, John started to understand the situation, and he summed things up, "So, Melvin was snatched by some god-like idiot who thinks he can mess with the JBA patrol with impunity?"

"It's not just us that's involved in this." Carl tipped his head towards Shess and the other natives.

"Yeah, I know, but still we *are* involved," John said. "And now we need to rectify the situation and rescue Melvin."

"Melvin isn't the only problem we have now," Carl said indicating the still comatose Ben.

"Yeah, that's true," John said. "By the way, what's with Annie doing that healing stuff?"

Tom walked up, hearing the discussion. "Haven't you heard of Ben's list? The one he's making…as a joke." He listed the peculiarities they'd noticed.

John stared at the group. "So let me get this straight. Joe can work a sword like a ninja, and Annie can heal by touch?"

"That's pretty much it," Tom said.

Chapter Sixteen
Ben recovers

Ben moaned softly, then opened his eyes. A sudden need woke him, and he sat up in a moment of panic, but before he could wonder where he was, the pressure that had roused him was his priority. He tossed off the smelly animal skin that covered him. In the pre-dawn dimness, he could see a variety of shapes scattered near a dying campfire in various states of repose. *It must have been quite a party,* he thought as he tip-toed over and around the bodies, careful not to step on anyone, heading quickly for the first bush or tree he could spot. Having responded to Nature's request, he stopped to consider the situation, checking out the area more thoroughly and realized that he couldn't remember what had happened last night.

He wandered to the campfire and sat near the wood pile. He pulled a stick from the pile and pushed the dimly glowing coals in circles as he tried to puzzle it out. He let his mind wander back to yesterday evening when they had headed out to locate John and Melvin. He smiled as he pictured arriving at the top of the falls—that's where they had seen Joe tossing rocks for Patrick to crack. Strange that he could do that, but he didn't dwell on that right now. He had more important things to occupy his mind.

He remembered cleaning up the remains of the fight Carl had survived, salvaging the equipment and burying the casualties. The group moved on…and they spotted some sort of campfire…that's where it all went fuzzy. Was it a *nimre* camp? Straining to remember the campfire, he couldn't drag his memories from the depths. He focused on the tip of the stick he held, watching it slowly turn black, a trail of smoke curling up. He pulled it from the fire, blew on the end, and studied the glow, then stared into the design he'd made in the coals. Was this the campfire that he was remembering?

Distracted by his thoughts, he hadn't noticed anyone else up and about yet, but then he glanced up to see a couple of the native women carrying a large pot. They placed it near the campfire, and one of them set up a small tripod in the middle of the embers as the other one worked on the fire, stoking up the coals and adding sticks and logs to it. *Where is Robb when you need him?* Lifting the pot together, they hung it above the fire and quickly left, coming back occasionally to fill the pot with water they had drawn from a nearby creek.

Ben noticed that somehow they had managed to complete the entire operation without once making eye contact with him. He watched them the entire time, but they kept their eyes averted. Though he did catch them glancing at him furtively, when either one did, they both broke out into quiet conversation, twittering to each other. It would be helpful to understand the native language, but he didn't think that even Patrick would have been able to follow their comments. He watched them duck into a supply tent, then noticed more folks stirring. One by one, they would get up and head off, returning moments later. *Taking care of morning business,* he thought.

What bothered him the most was the fact that so far no one, other than the two women, had even approached him. Was he a pariah? What had happened last night? What had he done? He sagged.

"How're you doing?" a voice said right behind him.

Ben twisted to discover Joe standing behind him. "I don't know." He shrugged. "Fine."

"Well, you had us a bit shaken up last night." Joe sat next to Ben.

"Why? What happened last night? I don't remember much after we got here." Ben stopped, then asked, "By the way, where *is* here, anyway?"

"We're at the *nimre* camp. We attacked last night and pretty much wiped them out. In the aftermath, we suddenly realized that you were missing. John organized a search, an effective search, but when we finally came across you, you were in a catatonic state. Annie wasn't able to do a thing for you."

"Whoa. Slow down there. You say John found me? That means *you* found John, right? Did you find Melvin, too?"

"Oh, yeah, I forgot that part. Melvin wasn't here, and John was caged up on the far side of the camp when we attacked, but he wasn't hurt."

"John was caged up?"

"Yeah, they didn't want *him*." Joe looked across the clearing. "They left him in a cage behind those bushes when they ran off with their prize, Melvin, to wherever they were headed."

"So now we have John," Ben said, "but Melvin is still missing. Counting Carl, that makes two out of three—not good enough."

"According to the guys we questioned," Joe said, "Some guy named Mr. Bentnose sent them out to get Melvin. We have no clue how this Bentnose guy even knew we were here, but the nimer guys seem willing to do anything he wants. They are seriously afraid of him."

"So now we're after a guy with a bent nose?" Ben asked.

"Well, we don't know if he *actually* has a bent nose. That's what they call him, but you're not going anywhere. You need to rest. Annie says so."

"I feel fine…well I'm tired…that and the fact that I don't remember anything from last night."

"That's battle amnesia," Joe said. "We studied it in training. In fact we had a second Looie who had been sick for days after his first battle but then later couldn't even remember who they'd been fighting."

"Well I don't need to be loafing off, doing nothing." Ben stood up, then hesitated, wobbled, and collapsed back where he was sitting "On the other hand, I think I'll just sit here for a while. No rush, right?" He hoped to get confirmation from Joe.

"Right," Joe said. "Sit there while we get breakfast going." Joe drooled at the pot. "Whatever they have planned, I'm ready for it."

Ben stared at the pot. "We're having boiled water for breakfast?"

"Is that all that's in there?"

Ben shrugged. "I'm not in charge of breakfast, but I didn't see them put anything in there besides water."

"Well, we'll find out when Shess tells us." Joe sat up. "Hey, there's Annie." He stood up and called her over.

Annie came quickly and peered at Ben. "Are you up already?" She put her hand on his forehead.

Ben could feel the warmth of her hand. The feeling radiated across his face, around his neck, and through his shoulders. He felt a shudder run up his spine. He closed his eyes and leaned back onto Joe. "Wow."

Joe pushed him back up. "Ben?"

"What? It felt so good." He blushed. "I just relaxed too much."

Annie frowned at Joe. "It's fine, Ben. You go ahead and relax if you want to. I'm going to check you over, that's all."

"A minor case of battle amnesia," Joe said. "He'll recover soon enough."

Annie frowned. "Whatever it is, I can't seem to do a thing for him. I wish Deezhlahmahs would hurry up and get here."

"She'll get here soon enough, but as much as I care for Ben, breakfast is at the top of my list right now." Joe patted his stomach.

Annie laughed. "You have your priorities set, don't you?"

"Well, I wouldn't mind having something to eat, either," Ben said, noticing the two native women standing by the supply tent, waiting. He thought that they were watching their conversation. "I'm not certain, but are *we* holding up breakfast?"

Joe stared at him. "How's that?"

"See those women there?" Ben asked. "They stoked the fire and set up the pot but then ran off, like they were afraid to be near me. Not even looking my way, even though I could see that they wanted to, and every time I turned their way, they jumped, as if they're scared of me."

Joe grabbed Ben's arm and pulled him to his feet. "Annie, grab his other arm. We're getting him out of the way. Let them cook, and we'll keep Ben busy."

Annie stared at the women in front of the supply tent and helped lift Ben. "I don't know what their problem is, but if you think moving Ben will help, then let's get him moved."

As soon as Ben was settled back on the pad where he'd spent the night, the women hurried to the pot and dropped things into it. He could tell that a lot of the water had already boiled away because one of the women frowned and went back to the tent, brought a jug, and poured in more water. Whatever they were cooking, the smell was enticing, and they were sitting downwind of the fire, so he couldn't avoid it. Trying to distract himself from his growling stomach, Ben asked, "So, is there any chance of getting more details about what went on last night?"

Joe sat on one side of Ben as Annie sat on the other. As Annie kept a wary eye on Ben, Joe told him about finding John chained up in a crate on the far side of the camp and how it was John who was the first to notice that Ben was missing and then went on to organize the search party that eventually found him. "Leave it to Eric to find you by literally stumbling on you, but that's typical of Eric anyway."

Ben laughed. He was starting to feel much better.

"So then Trey carried you here, and you slept near the big fire," Joe said, "not near the cook fire."

Annie suddenly noticed Deezhlahmahs approaching. "Ah! She's here finally."

Ben sat back and agreed to put up with more inspections, detections, and rejections as Annie and the healer examined him. After an intense discussion, most of which he didn't follow, they decided that whatever had caused him to black out had been temporary, and his loss of memory could be attributed to PTSD as Joe had suggested. Other than that, they declared him hale and hearty.

"I'm fit for duty? If that's the case, then where's breakfast?" Ben located Shess in the rapidly growing crowd and asked, "What's the plan for food this morning? Are those women done yet?"

Everyone waited for Shess to answer, so he went to see how the women were doing. When he drew near, the women launched into a tirade, chattering and flailing their arms, constantly glancing towards the hungry group, Ben in the middle. Ben could see that Shess had to work at shushing them and getting them back to the task at hand. Finally getting them under control, Shess called to everyone: breakfast was served.

Forming a line to one side, the group dutifully picked a wooden bowl from the first woman as the second one scooped a thick gruel from the pot for each person. When Ben got to the front of the line, he noticed that neither woman would look directly at him, so he had to catch his scoop-full of gruel before it landed on his feet.

He headed to join the scouts sitting by the campfire, noticing that most of them were having problems trying to drink the gruel from the bowl, but none of the natives were having any difficulties at all. They had simply pulled small wooden spoons from their pouches and dug in.

"Hey, Shess. Any possibility for silverware here?" Ben asked.

Shess yelled to the cooks, "kahmbe ruh spootah vaa ri kahnkah."

The women stood up and one of them dug through the wooden box they had been sitting on, bringing a handful of well-used wooden spoons to the scouts, large ones that would do for serving, small ones that had seen better days, but not many that might suffice for eating.

When Ben received the handful, he picked the least damaged one and passed the rest on to the other scouts. Slurping down the quickly cooling gruel, he yelled to Tom, "You forgot to tell us to bring spoons."

Tom slapped the hip pack hanging from his belt. "I figured all of you'd bring what you needed."

"We did, but we only brought the bare minimum, leaving most of our group gear at the village, so we could travel light and quick."

Tom held up his aluminum camp spoon and said, "Yeah, well, I should have said something about spoons. I know you all brought knives of various sorts, so with a spoon, you'd have everything you need to eat with because they always supply bowls when we set up out in the field."

Ben grunted as he scooped the last of the gruel from his bowl. Following the example of the natives, he deposited his bowl into a pot full of water hanging above the fire. He noticed that the natives swished their spoons in the water, then wiped them off and put them back into their pouch. He wondered what to do with his spoon, but then Tom came by and chucked his into the water along with all the bowls.

"I'll collect it later," Tom explained. "They know which spoon is mine."

"Thanks," Ben said and tossed his in with all the other dirty dishes.

The arrangement was that the women cleaned up camp, then followed the group later, which made for an efficient travel technique, well suited to moving an army across long distances. Ben casually wondered why these people had developed such a practice. *What have they been forced to endure?*

He didn't have a chance to dwell on it because right then Shess walked to the middle of the camp and called everyone together for a quick rally.

Speaking first to the natives, Shess said, "thee fe-u gotso, sho-oo thee vu uh mu kukrah muvdo moi mu saa zhahnzhu thee."

Shess paused as the scouts waited for Patrick to translate. "He said that the *nimre* have a head start, so we need to move our butts to catch them."

"Duh," Joe said. "We spent time gathering up the prisoners, and the nimer guys kept going, without stopping for all we know. They're probably a dozen clicks away by now, and around here that's far."

"Well, we did have to look after Ben," Annie added.

Joe agreed. "Yeah, we *did* have that problem."

Annie frowned at him.

Joe stuttered, "Ben's not a problem, but we need to follow these guys quickly…if we're going to rescue Melvin. Right, Ben?"

"Right," Ben said. "But you guys could have gone on ahead. Although I'm glad that you waited, Joe. I'd like to be there when we find Melvin."

Everyone fell silent, waiting for Shess to continue.

Shess said, "soondi ri preni preedi Roadranusis uh ruh gu kerzhoo thee."

Patrick leaned in. "He wants to send all the prisoners back to the town under guard."

"Works for me," Tom said. "Any time we spend trying to keep them under control will delay the search, and we don't want to do that, not if we hope to have any chance of finding your friend."

Joe frowned. "Waste of manpower. We should contain them here, or dispatch them quickly."

"Wait a minute." Annie frowned again. "You don't mean that, Joe."

"Well, we can't be splitting the group to keep track of them, and we can't let them wander off. They'd be right at our backs, and we'd end up caught in the middle."

"That may be true, Joe," Tom said, "but this isn't the military, so I don't think we can get away with 'dispatching' them at all."

"We can let a *few* guards control the prisoners," Carl said. "Either here or back at town, it doesn't make any difference."

"You're that certain that we won't need the guards?" Joe asked.

"No, I *don't* know that we *won't* need them," Carl said. "But if we're going to find Melvin, we need to get moving. I'm confident that Fred and I can track the *nimre* easily enough, but we might be able to get there faster if we let the prisoners lead the way: *they* know where to go."

"Does that work for you, Shess?" Ben asked. "Can we trust them?"

Bear stepped up next to Shess. "We control, *if* we pick."

Shess agreed. "We pick not violent. They lead and not fight."

Joe was hesitant. "How can we make certain that they won't lead us the wrong way?"

Carl put his hand on Fredekas' arm. "Fred and I will keep a close watch on them, and if we feel that they're leading us astray, I'll let you know, and then you can explain it to them."

"I can handle that," Joe said as he twisted his fist in his other hand. "I can explain it nice and carefully, and they won't want to hear it again."

Annie put her hand on Joe's arm. "As long as no one gets hurt."

Tom shrugged. "Hey, at this point, it's on them. No one will get hurt as long as we keep moving in the right direction."

"I'll have to settle for that," Annie said.

"Shess, Bear, we'll get ready to head out. We'll grab our things while you pick our guides." He paused. "Carl, do you want to go with Fred and help with the selecting? After all, you two will be working with them directly, so you should be involved in choosing them."

"Thanks. That'd be helpful." He snagged Fredekas by the elbow. "Come on, Bear. We have work to do." The three of them headed to the prisoners as Ben and the others grabbed their packs.

Patrick hesitated and asked, "Do we know what we're getting into?"

Joe leered. "We do—it's called a war."

Following the lead of the suddenly helpful *nimre*, the company headed out at what Joe called a 'quick march,' though everyone else called it a quick jog if not an all-out run. Carl and Fredekas were at the front of the group, keeping an eye on the three *nimre* deemed trustworthy enough to lead the march. Tom and Joe kept the main group together, and the rest followed as Ben encouraged everyone to keep the mood light.

They continued at that pace for less than a half-hour when Ben noticed that the group was spreading out too much. Not used to so much physical exercise, Eric was one of the first to start falling behind—and no one paid any attention. Ben slowed to check on him. That's when he noticed that the camp followers were also having difficulties keeping up—with all the equipment they were carrying, they were falling farther and farther behind. He should have had Trey help with the carrying, but he hadn't thought of it earlier.

Ben yelled towards the front of the group, trying to call for a short rest break, but the message didn't get through. Hating to split up the group, but knowing that these people wouldn't be able to keep up the pace, Ben told the stragglers to stop for a while.

Keeping up an appearance of control, and working on morale, Ben said, "Eric, I need you to supervise Annie and the rest of these folks while I head up to the front and see how they're doing." He smiled. "You can have a break right here."

Huffing and puffing, Eric gladly slumped to the ground, quickly followed by the others. Ben sprinted on ahead to catch up with the main body. The first group he encountered was Trey, Bear, and a group of natives jogging along, talking to each other as if they were out on a Sunday jaunt.

Trey stared. "What's wrong, Ben?"

"We're stretching out too much. I need to talk to Joe or whoever is leading up there, but I don't think I can catch up with them."

Bear understood and said something to the other natives. One of them pulled an animal horn out of his belt and blew into it. The noise echoed through the woods and soon another blast answered back. Moments later Joe ran into sight, followed by Tom.

Barely out of breath, Joe asked, "What's the problem, Ben?"

"We're too spread out, losing half our force."

"Never mind the women," Joe said. "Based on what I've seen, it's normal to leave them behind. They'll catch up later."

Tom wheezed. "Not all of us are in as good a shape as you, Joe, so if we cut the pace, it would make it easier."

"Cut the pace? We'll never catch those nimer guys if we take it easy."

Tom put his hands on his knees, breathing deeply. "Not take it easy, Joe, but yes, take it slower." He stood up, still breathing heavily. "You're right that we can't slow down *too* much." He glanced over his shoulder. "And the women *will* eventually catch up, but that's no reason to leave them so far behind."

"Not just the women. Eric isn't making it, either."

Joe tried not to laugh. "Yeah, like I said: The *women* tend to fall behind."

Frowning, Ben ignored Joe. "At this pace, even if we do manage to catch up with the *nimre*, we'll be in no condition to confront them," he said watching Tom still trying to catch his breath.

Joe thought a moment. "Yeah, that makes good tactical sense. I'll see that we ease the pace for those who aren't in shape." He turned with a snap and ran off before Ben could reply.

One more deep breath and Tom glanced at Ben. "Thanks. We might make it through this after all." He followed Joe at a slow, casual jog.

Ben plopped on a fallen tree. Trey joined him, sitting on one side as the native with the horn sat on the other side. As Trey pulled out his canteen, the native pulled out what Ben figured had to be the local version of a canteen: a large leather pouch, tied shut at the top. It had been hanging from a cord on the native's belt. *Probably an animal bladder,* Ben thought.

When the native offered Ben a drink, he shuddered and shook his head, showing the native his canteen, made of aluminum. The native shrugged, took a long drink, and passed the water sack to Bear who gladly drank some before passing it on to the others. Ben preferred his own canteen, finding the water to be cool and refreshing. He thought, *Parts of this world are so relaxing and enjoyable. Why does the rest have to be so difficult?*

Ben leaned back onto the remains of an adjacent tree trunk, finally starting to relax, when he heard a horn signaling in the distance. The natives all jumped to their feet and ran towards the sound, Trey right with them, but Bear stopped a couple feet away and waited for Ben to join them. Ben clambered to his feet and checked to see if the rest of the group had caught up yet, but he didn't see anyone. Ahead he could see the grass was flattened and underbrush had been trampled flat by the many feet that had run through ahead of them. "The path is so unmistakable that even Eric will be able to find the way," he said to no one in particular as he joined the group of natives.

Ben could tell that they were getting close to the rest of the group because, even before they could see anything, they could hear loud talking, just about shouting. They rounded a bend in the path and found Joe and Carl in the middle of a heated discussion, with Shess and Fredekas staying out of the way, holding back, watching. Tom was nowhere to be seen. Carl was saying, "We're never going to catch up to them if we don't keep moving. We can't wait for the slow ones."

"Yeah, but let's say that we do catch up, all out of breath, then we stop and say, 'Hey, wait a minute. Let me catch my breath, then I'll stomp your face.' I don't think so." Joe sneered. "They won't hold still for that."

Carl was about to answer when he noticed Ben. "Hey, Ben! Where have you been? We could use your help on this." He frowned in Joe's direction. "Well, we could use your opinion."

Joe didn't give Ben a chance to answer. "Opinions don't help. We need facts."

"We don't have facts," Carl growled, gritting his teeth.

"Then we don't need another opinion, do we?" Joe grumbled.

Carl asked again, "Ben, do you have anything to say?"

"Let's sit and see what we can come up with," Ben said, walking to a downed tree.

The two grudgingly sat on either side of Ben.

"It would help," Ben started, "if we knew exactly where we were going, then we could plan ahead. I mean, if we're close, then we should push it and get there fast. On the other hand, if there's a long march ahead of us, then I'm afraid that going fast won't help."

"Either way," Carl said. "We need to hurry. Melvin needs our help."

"True," Ben said, "but if we get there fast and then can't do anything, it won't help Melvin at all."

Carl sat back. "Yeah, that makes sense."

Joe smiled. "Thanks, Ben, for talking him into it."

Carl said, "He didn't talk me into anything. It simply made more sense when he said it."

"Whatever." Joe shrugged. "Ben, you mentioned planning ahead. If we could get intel from those nimer guys that are leading us, we *could* plan what we're going to do. Not having a map puts a real crimp in things." He stared at Ben. "And we don't have one," he raised his eyebrows, "or do we?"

"Do you think we have one?" Ben asked.

"Well, we're not from around here, but *they* are." Joe said, waggling his head at Shess and Fredekas.

Ben frowned. "They're not hiding anything, Joe. Shess has already shown us the maps he has of this area, and in spite of the fact that they have a lot of detail south of the waterfall, they don't have much north of it mapped out. This isn't their land, Joe. It belongs to the *nimre*."

"Frustrating not knowing where they went," Carl said.

"If we had a nimer map, we'd know where we're going," Joe said. "Talking with them instead of shooting them might have worked better."

Ben blinked. "Wait. You're talking about the *nimre* that attacked us that first night?"

"Yeah," Joe said. "Might have been helpful to question them."

"That didn't happen…but the next morning," Ben said slowly, "when we were cleaning up the bodies, we found that amulet you're wearing." He reached for the carved wooden object hanging from Joe's neck.

Joe lifted up his amulet. "This?"

"Yeah, and there were a couple of scrolls," Ben said. "That Patrick kept because they had writing on them."

"Yeah. What about those scrolls?" Carl asked.

Ben slapped himself on the forehead. "One of them was a map!"

Joe sat up. "We *do* have a map of the nimer area?"

Ben spun. "Find Patrick! Bring him here," he shouted.

After a quick search, Patrick trotted up to the group.

When asked, Patrick said, "Scrolls? Yeah. There were three of them. The school teacher helped me translate the first one, but we never had a chance to do anything with the other two."

Joe just about danced as he sat there. "Is one a map?"

Patrick pulled off his backpack, flipped it open, and dug through it. He pulled out a scroll, for all to see. "I thought it was a map, but I didn't know if it even covered this area. I have no idea if it's any good."

"You didn't leave the scrolls in the village with the other gear?" Ben asked.

"I might have because we didn't need them," Patrick said. "But they were light enough, so I grabbed them, just in case."

"Good thinking," Ben said. "Now we need to know what it says."

Carl called to Fredekas, "Fred! Come and read this. Tell us what it says."

Fredekas hesitated at first, then approached slowly. "You mad. You fight. We not want be with."

"Yeah, well it's fine, now," Carl said. "We're done with that." He handed the scroll over to Fredekas. "Can you help us with this? Does it show where the *nimre* went?"

Fredekas lifted the scroll, dropped to one knee, and carefully spread it out across his other knee. He stared at it, consulting the area around them, and rotating it a couple times, then he raised his arm. "Mountain there," he dropped his arm to put a finger on the map, "is here."

Joe jumped up. "Wah-hoo! We have a map!"

"Hang on, Joe," Ben said. "Yes, we have a map. Now let's see if it's a *helpful* map." He stepped over. "Fred, does it show you where the *nimre* camp is? Where Melvin is?"

Fredekas traced out the lines on the map, trying to read the words. "This," he said, "is ugly writing, not easy read."

"I don't care how ugly it is, does it help?" Joe urged.

Fredekas put his finger on the map, then squinted at the forest. "We here." He slid along a line, then stabbed at a spot on the map. "They go there."

"That's all we need to know!" Joe jumped to his feet. "Grab your gear, we're heading out!"

Ben stood up slowly. "Wait a minute. We know where, but we still need to know how far. Give Fred time to make certain."

"We've located them! That's all we need, but go ahead and see what else you can find." Joe danced a moment then waltzed off into the woods. "I'll be right back," he yelled back as he ran.

Carl laughed. "I don't think Joe was dancing because of excitement."

Fredekas watched Joe run off. "He *pishtoo?*"

Before Patrick could translate, Ben laughed at Fredekas. "Yeah, he needed to piss!"

Fredekas laughed loudly as they all had a good time at Joe's expense.

Everyone fell silent when Ben refocused on the map. "Can you tell how long to get there?"

Fredekas used his hand as a ruler, measuring out the distance, and comparing it to what had to be a legend at the bottom of the map. "Not long, *thu fee* day."

Ben waited for Patrick to clarify.

Patrick scratched his head. "What I'm getting is that it'll be less than a couple hours. The way he phrased it was an eighth of a day. Strange way to measure it, but I figure that'd be close to a couple of hours. We'll be there in time to mop up the *nimre* and still have a leisurely lunch."

"Not easy go," Fredekas said dropping his finger on a wide, brown line drawn across their path on the map. "Here is block. We get through if we have guide."

"Block? What kind of block?" Carl asked.

Fredekas read the legend, stopping at a symbol that matched the cross line. "This say mountain door."

"Mountain door? What's that?" Ben asked.

Fredekas shrugged. "It say 'mountain door' not what *is* mountain door."

"We get so close and then this," Ben said. "What kind of guide do we need now? Will the *nimre* we have be able to open it?"

Fredekas shrugged again. "Maybe open, but first have to find. This say need finder, not key." He referred to the legend on the map. "It show need finder."

"First we have to find it, *then* we have to open it? Oh, wonderful! A hidden lock," Carl said.

"We get finder, then easy we find," Fredekas said.

"Usually finding is easy. It's opening a lock that's tough," Ben said.

Joe sauntered up. "Opening a lock? No problem. I have a universal key right here," he said as he patted his holster. "A .45 caliber key. You find me the lock, and I'll open it."

"That may be the problem. The map says that it's a hidden lock," Carl explained.

"We'll deal with that when we get there. Are we ready to move out?" Joe asked.

Ben stood up and checked the group. "Yup." He gave the head-out command right as the last of the scouts and camp followers showed up.

"Ah, you guys waited," Eric said, smiling. "Annie was getting to be an earful. Let her talk *you* to death." He pulled off his pack and dropped next to Fredekas.

Ben noticed how out of breath he was. "We were about to head out, Eric, but we found that Patrick had a map. Based on what it says, we have about an hour's travel, then there's a door, then one more hour, and we'll be there."

"There?" Eric said out of breath. "We'll try to keep up."

Ben noticed Trey and Bear hanging out with a group of natives. "Eric, I'll see if Trey can help out with carrying the equipment. It'll be easier to keep up that way. Sit here for a bit. When you've rested enough, follow along. Someone will be waiting at the door for you."

Eric sighed in relief. "We'll wait here but not too long, then we'll be right behind you."

"That's good, don't rush. We'll wait for you at the mountain door."

"Umm, Ben?" Eric started.

"Yes?"

"Is there anything you can do about Annie? She's talking my ear off."

Ben grinned. "Well, as two of the English speaking folks in the group, I would expect you to stick together…but if it's bothering you…"

Eric visibly sagged.

"Wait," Ben said. "Let me see what I can do." I'll bet Tom would be glad to help with the lagging group…as long as Annie is there, too.

Ben found Tom resting under a tree, and once he explained the problem, Tom was quite willing to help Eric keep the last group intact, so with Trey helping to carry things and Tom keeping Annie busy, Eric wouldn't have to do anything but walk.

Gathering the rest of the company, Ben let Fredekas and Carl use the map to lead, with the three *nimre* verifying the path as they went. Less than an hour later, they could see what had to be the Mountain Door: they were approaching the base of a tall, mountain cliff, hundreds of feet high, straight up, with no visible way to go around it and no way to climb it.

As Ben drew near, he saw Carl and Fredekas moving back and forth across the scree, tripping through the loose rocks at the base of the mountain, running their hands across the face of the cliff. Joe was using the butt of his knife to tap on the rocks. "Yo! What's up?" he called.

"We figure if it's a hidden lock," Carl said, "it might be right here in front of us, but we can't see it. We were hoping to find it by touch."

"Or by sound," Joe said, continuing to tap on the wall.

"And nothing unusual?" Ben asked.

"Nothing. Without that finder, I don't think we'll be able to find it at all."

Ben wondered about the *nimre* sitting to the side, staring off into the forest. "Do they have any idea how to find it?" he asked.

"We thought of that, too," Joe said.

Carl shrugged. "It doesn't seem so. Despite knowing their way through the woods, they say that they've never seen the door being opened. Everyone always turned their backs when it was opened. One of them said that he tried to see once but a watcher knocked him to the ground. They were told that it had to be done that way."

"Can you use that tracking ability of yours, Carl?" Ben asked. "To see where they walked?"

Carl glanced quickly at the ground. "Not much I can do with what's here. The ground is solid stone with inches of loose rock covering it. Nothing to leave a trail." He backtracked their path. "Right before all the rock starts, the path we were following spreads out across the entire face of the mountain. They didn't leave us much to go on. I can't tell where they went."

"So without this finder thing, we're S.O.L?"

"Yeah, that about covers it. Where's Patrick? Maybe that other scroll of his has a clue," Carl said.

Finding Patrick was an oft-repeated activity these days, but he was always easy enough to locate, usually surrounded by natives, conversing as if he were their long lost brother.

Patrick pulled out the other scroll and called Fredekas to help examine it. As they were trying to make it out, the end of the line arrived. Ben was glad to see that Eric wasn't as much out of breath this time—having Trey carry part of Eric's load was helpful, and Tom certainly didn't seem to be minding his walk with Annie.

"Hey, Ben," Tom said as they approached. "Annie told me how she's been doing that healing thing. Did you know that she can *see* someone's pain?"

"She can *see* pain? How does that work?" Ben frowned.

Tom shrugged. "She said different colors show the level of pain."

"Do you think she could see the door?"

Tom shrugged. "We could ask her."

Ben tried to find Annie and found her helping Eric. "Hey, Annie. If you're done there, we could use you here."

She handed Eric the canteen and said, "Keep drinking," then joined them.

As she walked up, Tom asked, "Can you see any colors on the face of the cliff? Can you see any doors?"

She leaned in close, then shook her head. "No. No colors there at all. From what Deezh told me, the kind of aura I see is based on living things. The rocks aren't alive…they don't feel pain, so there's nothing for me to see." She shrugged. "All I see is a flat, gray wall of stone."

Ben shrugged. "Oh, well, it might have worked. Right now I'm open to anything."

Annie bent over, searching the ground. "Hey, Carl, you said the path spreads out? Can you see where they went? It could give us a clue as to where to look."

Carl stepped away from the wall and examined the ground. "From what I can see, they intentionally changed their approach each time, probably to mislead anyone trying to track them."

Annie was amazed. "You think so? Are they that paranoid? That they would expect *anyone* to be tracking them that closely?"

Carl stopped, then walked to Annie and Ben. "You're right. No one can be *that* paranoid. Let me look again." He walked along the edge, occasionally bending to flip a blade of grass. "Good call, Annie. They didn't spread out *every* time they came through. Sometimes they went single file here, and sometimes there." He shrugged. "It's like the door was in a different place each time they went through."

Ben glared. "So the door is invisible *and* it moves?"

Annie put her hand on Ben's shoulder. "We'll figure it out, Ben, and find a way through."

Ben walked over to Patrick and Fredekas, still studying the scroll. "Does that thing help at all?"

Patrick stood up. "Nope. No help here. The second scroll is like the first one, and the parts that Fred can read are about something other than making a bang." He shrugged. "But I don't know what. When we get back, I'll have Zhahmonichas read it for us."

Ben plopped on a pile of gravel. "Still no clue from the map either?"

"No help there," Patrick said. "Fredekas says the relevant symbols on the map imply using a detector." He stuck his thumb over his shoulder at Fredekas. "It tells how to use it, but what that means, I don't know. A compass of some sort, I'd venture."

"Compass? Or finder? That's the word Fred used." Ben said. "That's what you said, right, Fred? We need a finder."

"Not need *a* finder, need *the* finder." Fredekas explained, "Not find anything, find door."

"So there's a specific finder *just* for this door?" Ben asked.

"Finder for other things find them," Fredekas said. "Not door."

"There are other finders? For what? How do they work?" Ben was getting frustrated trying to find this door, but there had to be a way to get through to Melvin, and he was going to keep at it until he found it.

Fredekas thought a moment. "Depend on what find. Made of stick from dry tree, find water. Bone when hunting animal for food. Have heard of one made to find metal for money."

Annie blinked. "A water witch? I've heard of people doing that back home, but here it's more of a science than witchcraft."

"I haven't heard of using a bone compass for finding animals," Ben said. "But it makes as much sense as anything else here."

Tom pulled a bunch of linked rings out of his pocket and jingled them. "Like these? Those *nimre* that attacked Joe had 'em."

Ben considered the descriptions of finders. "So if we're trying to find a door in a rock, the finder would be made of stone?"

Fredekas frowned. "Don't think. Stone no life, is dead. How show things?"

"So what would it be made of?" Ben wanted to know.

"Wood, from nature. Metal, from man. Bone, from animal. Not those."

Ben felt like giving up. "What else did they have? If they had the map to show them the way *to* the door, they must have had the finder to *find* the door *and* to be able to open it, right? It wouldn't do them any good to get this far and not be able to get through." Ben stood in thought, then asked Trey, "You helped us when we stripped those *nimre* bodies, right? What's missing?"

Trey paused his conversation with Bear, shrugged, and threw a thumb over his shoulder at Joe. "His amulet?"

"Joe's amulet?" Ben's mouth gaped open. "*It's* the finder?"

Annie asked Joe, "Can you show us the amulet?"

Joe pulled the amulet out of his shirt. "You want to see it?"

"We want to compare it to the map," Annie said.

"Hey, Carl, what's that map say, again?" Ben asked.

Carl pulled Fredekas with him, holding the map. He pushed it at Fredekas and said, "Read it to us again."

Fredekas held the map and read it aloud. "Hold one circle, balance-make two circle."

"And check it out," Annie said, smiling. "Joe's amulet is three circles in a triangle. Exactly what we need."

Joe grabbed the amulet by the cord, holding it away from his body as far as possible. "It does what?" he said in a panic.

Annie stepped up and put her hand on his shoulder. "I don't think it'll hurt you, Joe. Let me have it, and we'll figure it out from there."

Joe gingerly lifted the amulet, unlooped the cord from around his neck, and handed it to Annie, then dropped onto a pile of rocks, breathing deeply.

"So now we've found the finder?" Ben's mouth gaped open. "We've been trying to figure out what it is, and Joe's had it all this time?"

Annie chided him. "Don't hold it against him. He couldn't have known."

"So now that we have it, how does it work?" Ben asked.

"What did the map say to do with it, Carl?" Annie asked.

Carl shrugged. "Hey, Fred, read it again."

Fredekas held the map and read carefully. "Hold one circle, balance-make two circle. That all, balance-make."

Annie offered the amulet to Fredekas. "Here. Can you figure it out?"

"Why me?" Fredekas asked.

Annie shrugged. "You're a good tracker, you're familiar with the language, *and* you're from around here." She threw up her hands in frustration. "I don't know. Please see if you can make it work."

Fredekas held out his hand, and Annie carefully placed the amulet in it. Fredekas faced the mountain, holding it gently, moving it back and forth. Then he tried up and down. He shrugged and waited for ideas from the group.

Carl suggested, "The map said to balance it, right? Maybe you need to put it on a stick like a compass needle. Is there a hole in the back?"

Fredekas flipped the amulet face down, showing everyone the back, smooth and flat.

"Nope, not that kind of balance. Point it at the mountain again."

Fredekas did, and Carl continued, "Moving it around didn't seem to do much good. See what twisting it does."

Fredekas laid the amulet flat on his open palm, then twisted it back and forth. Then he held it up, flat side towards the mountain and twisted it in the air, as if he were trying to screw it into the rock wall. Then he hunched over it, tipping it side to side, slowly. Squinting at it, he said, "Color change."

"Wait. Where?" Carl asked. "Show me." He leaned in close, putting his hand on Fredekas' arm. "Again, slower."

Fredekas tipped the amulet again, first to one side, then to the other.

"Yeah," Carl said. "There is a bit of a color difference." He squinted at the sky. "I can't tell if it's because the angle of the sun is making shadows or if the amulet itself is changing color."

"You're seeing a color change?" Tom asked. "Annie can see colors where we can't. Let her try it."

Annie was distraught. "Me? I don't know anything about stuff like that." She looked through the group. "Where's Deezhlahmahs? She's better than I am at seeing these things."

Deezhlahmahs strode to the front of the group. She leaned in to look closely at the amulet. Her hands at her side, she frowned and said, "I have *lahlzhi* but not *zhoonpah*, so not able do."

Patrick stepped up and thought a moment. "Old-age wisdom? But not youth power?"

"Yes," Deezhlahmahs said. "I know but not have force to work."

"The knowledge, but not the essence needed to power it." Patrick paused. "You know, as I remember, that's the same thing Zhahmonichas said to me. He could *read* the scroll, but it wouldn't do any good—he wasn't able to make it *do* anything." His mouth dropped open. "That's when I learned to make that bang."

"That bang," Tom said slowly. "And Annie with the medicine, and Carl with the tracking, and…" He asked Patrick, "What is this 'youth power' anyway? What's that even mean?"

Patrick shrugged. "I don't know." He shrugged. "Something about youth having power."

Tom collapsed onto a nearby rock. "Wow. This is strange…but I can't think of anything changed this time…except the age of the group." He wiggled his head to clear it. "The other trips consisted of scientists and soldiers…book smarts, but no 'vitality of youth' as you say." He waggled his fingers in the air to emphasize the phrase. "They were all set in their ways, not open to new ideas." He faced Ben. "In spite of wandering the surface of a new world, they expected everything to be the same as back home."

"But this time?" Ben asked.

"This time, you kids are not only quite willing to accept the strange things going on here," he raised an eyebrow at John, "but you seem to be *expecting* to being strange."

John shrugged. "What can I say?"

142

Joe ignored Tom's comment about kids. "*That* is certainly true."

"So who do you think has the 'power of youth' needed to work this thing, Annie?"

"Oh, all right," Annie said. "I can give it a try." Fredekas gladly handed the amulet back to Annie, and she stood in front of the rock wall. "You say that the color changed when you tipped it, Carl?"

"Yeah," Carl said. "I could see a subtle shading difference between the two circles in front."

She examined the amulet carefully as she tipped it side to side. "Yes, there's definitely a change, but it's slight."

"The map said to balance the two circles," Carl said. "Can you make the colors the same on both of them?"

"I can get close," Annie said. "But even when I hold it as still as I can, the colors keep changing, not quite flickering. They don't stay still, and they're so faint." She exhaled. "I don't know what to do."

"We need to ask the nimer guys," Joe said. "Someone in their group used it every time they came through, right?"

The three *nimre* escorts were standing off to one side, their backs to the entire fiasco. Someone said, "Hey! They aren't even paying attention to what we're trying to do."

Suddenly, Annie shouted, "Wow! The colors just got brighter! I can see them much better."

Ben asked, "Can you see the door?"

"No." Annie blinked. "And the colors are gone again. Well, not quite gone, but not stable, not quite twinkling, too muted, too pastel, to call it that."

"But you *did* see something?"

"Yeah, for a moment," she said. "When Joe asked about the *nimre*."

When she said "*nimre*" again, everyone looked at them again.

"There it is! A flash of color." She pouted. "But then it's gone." She lifted her head. "It happens every time someone talks about the *nimre*."

"When someone *talks* about them them…or when we *look* at them…or actually when we look *away* from you?" Ben asked, staring at the *nimre*, still standing with their backs to the conversation. "Maybe security isn't the only reason the *nimre* turn their backs."

Annie shrugged. "I don't know. Try it. Everyone turn around and look at the forest, the trees, anything but me."

Everyone turned their backs to Annie, even Carl and Ben.

"Yes! That's it. I can see it now. Don't anyone turn around." Annie stepped unsteadily on the gravel as she neared the rock wall. "Green on one side, but blue on the other." More gravel crunching underfoot. "Hang on, the colors seem to shift as I move back and forth here." More shaky steps. "Better, much better. They are about the same." More rocks shifted. "A bit more—"

Sudden silence filled the area, total silence.

Hesitantly Ben looked.

No one was near the rock wall.

Annie was gone.

Ben shouted, "Annie?"

Everyone spun to stare, and they stood there, frozen. Annie wasn't there. The scouts stepped forward, starting to pound on the wall, a couple were hitting it with their fists, Joe pulled out his hunting knife, flipped it, and beat on the wall with the hilt.

Suddenly Tom ploughed through the crowd, grabbed a boulder in each hand, and pummeled the rock prison. "Annie!" he yelled.

Panic set in as everyone grabbed what they could to beat on the wall, using rocks as Tom did or using knives, swords, clubs, anything they could get their hands on. Someone called for Patrick to blast through the rock, in spite of the avalanche that might result. Even the *nimre* had joined in, using branches pulled from nearby trees, but no one pounded harder than Tom. Chips flew, rocks crumbled, but he kept clobbering the wall, and it was starting to give way. He was making headway, digging a depression into the side of the mountain.

In the middle of picking up more rocks Tom suddenly stopped, Annie's hand on his arm.

Everyone else froze, except for Eric. He continued flailing at the wall with the weed stem he'd picked up until Ben grabbed his arm. "You can stop now. She's back."

Eric sagged. "Thanks."

Annie stood next to Tom. "Thank you, Tom, for trying to rescue me. I'm fine."

Tom let the rocks fall and hugged her. "Where *were* you?" he demanded.

"Right there, inside the mountain, through the door," she said.

"But we couldn't see you."

"I didn't know." She noticed his hands. "Oh! You're bleeding. Let me fix that for you." She held his hands in hers and closed her eyes.

Tom closed his eyes as well and leaned back slightly. They stood there together, hand in hand, for a bit as everyone else paused to catch their breath.

Annie opened her eyes and smiled. "Tom?"

He flinched and opened his eyes. "Yes?"

"That should be enough for now. Use your canteen to wash off the dirt. Then let me know if there's anything else you need."

Tom almost blushed as he replied. "Yes, ma'am."

Trey snickered. "Woo-hoo! She has him hooked!"

Ben rolled his eyes at Trey. "Yeah, well what can you do?" He smiled.

Carl stepped up. "So, Annie, I suppose you found the door?"

"When the colors matched," she said, "when they were the same tint, I could suddenly see the door, like the entrance to a tunnel. In fact, it *was* a tunnel. I went in and figured that everyone else would follow me. After a few steps, I heard this terrible crashing noise, and when I looked, there you all were, beating on the wall."

"So why didn't you come back out and tell us?" Tom asked.

"I tried to, but with all of you still hitting the wall, I had to be careful. I could have had my head bashed in, so I had to time it between hits."

"Oh," Tom said slowly.

She smiled. "I understand."

"So you the door opened for you. How do the rest of us get in?" Carl asked.

"I don't know. Let me try an experiment," Annie said. "I'll see if I can open the door, but not go all the way through it." She put her hand on Tom's arm. "But if I do disappear, do me a favor, Tom: wait a little longer before coming to my rescue." She smiled.

Tom grinned. "No problem."

"All right, everyone," Ben said. "Step away from the mountain and turn your backs again. We're going to try it a different way."

Annie held the amulet in front of her and stepped towards the rock wall. "Wait…wait. Getting there. Closer. That's it." She paused. "The door is open, but I'm still here, right? Tom, turn slowly. Do you see the door?"

"Yup," Tom said. "I can see both you and the tunnel plain as day."

Annie smiled. "I thought that if I waited in the doorway, it would stay open, and it did."

Ben called to everyone. "Grab your stuff, and get moving. We're going through the mountain!"

Deezhlahmahs begged off. "Annie here help. I *Roadranusis* help."

"I understand, Deezhlahmahs," Ben said. "You have all those people to help out and can't be away from your patients for too long. When we get back, we'll let you know what we found."

"Good," Deezhlahmahs said, heading back to town, followed by her helpers.

Patrick was the first to go in. "Not bad. Tall enough so you don't need to duck but narrow."

Joe and Carl followed him. "Not too cold, but feels damp."

Fredekas pushed the three *nimre* through next, but when Trey, Bear, and Shess all tried to step through at the same time, someone up front yelled, "Hey! Who's blocking the doorway. It's getting dark in here."

Ben held up his hand. "Who has the lanterns?"

As the lanterns were brought out, Robb stepped up, lighter in hand. "Need a light?"

"Yeah, Robb. Thanks," Ben said. "Get 'em lit and pass 'em in."

Once all the lanterns were lit and shared, the group moved forward, single file, an occasional lantern lighting the way.

As Eric passed through the door, he muttered something about advanced technology using nothing but stone knives and bear claws. Everyone ignored him…as usual.

Tom was the last one through. "Thanks for holding the door open for all of us," he said to Annie.

"My pleasure." She smiled again at him.

"I'll have to return the favor sometime soon."

"I look forward to it, Tom," Annie said.

Trey faked a gag, and Ben laughed.

Annie stepped away from the doorway, and it darkened slightly in the tunnel, but the outside world was still faintly visible.

"Appears to be still open," Tom said.

Ben agreed. "That's good. We'll be able to find our way out without having the key, but not the other way around."

"Can we?" Tom asked. "We should test it."

"Yeah," Ben said. "But later when we aren't in such a hurry."

"But if it is a one-way door," Tom said. "We could have a problem. If someone accidently steps through, they'd get stuck on the other side."

"Stuck," Annie said, "unless someone opened the door for them."

Tom smiled. "I'd be glad to."

"Well, we can watch out for it…if we knew what to look for."

"Yeah. This *is* extraordinary," Tom said. "I can't wait to get back to tell those scientists what they missed. They won't believe any of it." He grinned at the door. "I wonder if the military would be interested in doors that are invisible one way but not the other."

Ben shrugged. "Could be. They're always on the lookout for weird stuff."

"Well, we've certainly come to the right place for weird. Keep that list close, Ben. I know they'll want a full report when we return."

Ben patted his shirt pocket. "It's right here." He checked the button on the flap. "Secured and waiting for their review."

Word came from the front of the line that the tunnel was sloping upwards, a slight slope at first, but it soon became steeper, becoming shallow stairs. Then stretches of level passages were interspersed with more flights of stairs. Every now and then, the slope increased more and the hand-carved steps were definitely steeper than Ben thought normal, but it didn't seem to bother the *nimre*, they stepped high in stride.

Suddenly Ben could hear yelling and shouting. "What's going on?" He frowned. "Who *is* in the lead anyway? I should have been up *there*, not back here!"

Tom up the passageway. "Too narrow for anyone to pass easily, but if folks squeeze to the side, we can see about getting up there."

Trey didn't wait—he yelled and pushed everyone to the side, Bear followed, yelling at the natives, and Ben followed as quickly as he could, easily making it through the gap left by those two, shouting back to Tom, "You stay back here, in case someone comes through the door!"

Tom shrugged and fell in behind Annie, but Ben could see that he probably would have preferred to walk *next* to her, probably even holding her hand, but the tunnel was too narrow. Ben fretted as he ran after Trey. *We don't need a distraction like that when his attention is needed elsewhere.*

Ben finally passed all the camp followers to find the scene of a battle. "What happened?"

Joe was squatting on the floor, wiping blood off his sword. "We had a delay."

"Oh? Care to expound on that?" Ben asked.

"Guards posted along the way, hidden in little cubby-holes in the walls."

Ben gawked at the three bodies sprawled across the tunnel floor. "So I see."

"Anyway, they were probably expecting more *nimre* because they didn't react at all until we had passed by. Then one of them jumped out right behind Carl and swiped at his back. Stupidly, the guard made his move right in front of me, so I easily skewered him from behind."

Ben blinked. "And the other two?"

"One from the right, one from the left. Both swung at me, but they didn't last long. I dropped both before anyone else was threatened." Joe stood up and slid his sword back into his scabbard. "That leaves the fourth one."

"And where is he?" Ben asked.

"He was in a cubby farther up. When the commotion started, he ran off to warn the others. Any chance of taking them by surprise is gone."

"You did your best, and it's regrettable, but as long as no one got hurt…"

Joe kicked one of the bodies. "As long as none of *us* got hurt."

"I stand corrected." He leaned to squint ahead, up the passageway. "Any clue how much farther this tunnel runs?"

Joe stepped into the alcove where the guard had been. "There's not much here—nothing but a chair and a lunch—an outpost. There must be something bigger, a guard station farther on."

Carl checked out the alcove on the other side. "Same thing here. They weren't at these stations long. We must be getting somewhere, though I could hear the other one running for quite a ways after Joe finished off these, so we're not there yet."

"Well, we haven't come across any branches or forks, so far, so the plan is to keep going 'til we get there," Ben said. "Where ever *there* is."

"Well, we won't get lost," Joe said. "Are we ready to move out?"

Ben checked with everyone. "All good here. Joe, will you head us out?"

"I'd be glad to," Joe said, then strode off, keeping his hand on the hilt of his sword.

"Move out, everyone, let's go." Ben leaned back against the wall and let the next group go past, then joined the procession.

A couple hundred meters on, Joe shouted back, "More cubbies, no guards."

Ben checked out where the guards had been waiting. In a slightly larger chamber off to the side, he saw indications that they had been there for quite a while: small padded stools, a rickety table with a card game in progress, and a half-eaten haunch of animal. They had been on guard duty, and Ben figured that they had been relieved every couple hours because he didn't see any sign of toiletries, nor any smell for that matter.

He yelled up to the front, "There might be more. Keep your eyes open." All he heard back was a grunt, but he knew that Joe would be careful.

The next time he heard something from Joe, a yell of triumph echoed back: "Light! We made it. We're out!"

Rounding one last curve, Ben sprinted up the last set of stairs into the open air. He burst out, blinking at the sudden brightness, then froze and whirled. "Be careful! We might get ambushed!"

"Fortunately not," Joe said. "No sign of those nimer guys here. They should have exploited our temporary blindness. Easy enough to sit outside the entrance and pick us off one at a time as we come out."

"Well, they aren't as smart as you are, Joe."

"Minor training is all they need. They're good at following orders. The problem is that the leadership here isn't all it should be. They assumed that no one would follow them back. Whoever is in charge didn't consider the possibility that anyone else would ever use the door. I'll bet those guards attacked late because they were asleep."

"Door!" Ben spun. "Can we see it on this end? Can we get back in?"

Fredekas had barely stepped out of the tunnel, so he spoke to the *nimre* for a moment, and relayed the answer, "No door, one tunnel."

"Oh, good. I forgot to check it as we came out." Ben examined the area before them. They were on a slight hill rising above a lightly wooded area. Past the trees a wide valley opened out, sunlight brightly lighting half, the other half shaded by tall snow-capped mountains. Lush short, yellow grass swayed as a cool breeze wafted small insects in circles. Scattered trees across the valley broke up the solid color. He blinked. "So, we're here, but where's here?"

The *nimre* spoke excitedly—Fredekas translated: "Home."

Ben surveyed the area. No *nimre*, no soldiers, no guards, but all his people were wandering in the trees right at the tunnel exit. Shess and most of the natives were grouped together, but some were mixed in with the scouts. "So, Fred, where do the *nimre* say that we should go now?"

"They say follow path home," Fredekas replied.

"You heard 'em, guys! Let's head out. Carl and Fred, you lead the group, even if all you're doing is following the *nimre*. Joe right behind them, but a bit slower this time. We don't want to get spread out again."

They followed a faint path that meandered through the patch of trees with no apparent destination. Hoping that the *nimre* knew where they were going, they followed through a most indirect route, but eventually, the trees opened out, revealing the entire valley.

In the middle of the valley, people, mostly women and children, were gathering edibles from the grasses in the open space. On the far side were tents and cook fires, with women and older children tending them. The handful of men they saw stood unmoving, alert, and wary.

"Congratulations, Ben. You've discovered yet another group of native folk here. The techies back home will have a field day studying them," Tom said.

The *nimre* escorts shouted, and the people in the nomadic village broke into action.

"Fred! Carl! Can you keep those guys quiet?" Joe yelled. "They might be calling out an attack on us!"

Fredekas and Carl tried to silence the prisoners, but the damage had already been done. Most of the women ran back to the tents and ducked inside. The men in the village charged towards the group, but they slowed down when they saw Joe and his group at the lead, with weapons drawn.

Ben noticed none of them had weapons, in fact they seemed to be a welcoming committee. The women who had gone into the tents were slowly coming back out in small groups.

"Hang on, Joe. They don't seem to be attacking," Ben shouted.

"Yeah, I noticed," Joe said, standing his ground. "What's going on?"

"I don't know," Ben said. "Hey, Fred, what are they saying?"

"They want go home. Those friends, family," Fredekas said.

"Hey, Shess. Do you see any problems with letting the prisoners go? If we need to, I'm certain we can retake them."

Shess spoke quickly to the natives near him. The townsfolk circled out to either side, weapons still at the ready. "Can go now. We ready."

"All right, Carl. You and Fred can release them. Let's see what they do."

Carl stepped aside, motioning the three *nimre* to go ahead.

They ran the short distance to the tents, greeted the women with hugs, and jabbered, then the men turned their backs on Ben and the group and headed back to the tents.

"Well, they aren't going to attack us," Joe said all but disappointedly.

"Yeah, and they aren't afraid that we'll attack them either," Ben said.

Carl frowned. "Fearless or foolish?"

"Could be a trick." Ben checked the sides of the valley for any movement.

Joe sheathed his sword. "I don't think so. They seem sincere enough."

"Keep up your guard, but put your weapons away," Ben said to the group. Shess echoed the command to the natives, and everyone complied, the natives sheathing any swords and knives, the scouts clicking their safeties on and slinging their rifles.

"Move out, slowly," Ben said.

As Ben neared the group of tents, he could see women running to greet the three *nimre* that had led them here. The rest of the women gathered the children, surrounding them to protect them. The three guides chatted with the others, obviously talking about Ben's group. One of the women stepped into a tent and came out carrying a long, dark cloak. She put it on the shoulders of one of the guides, then suddenly ran right up to Carl. Hesitating for only a moment, she pulled off her flower necklace and looped it over Carl's head, then hugged him tightly.

Carl stepped back in surprise and smiled. "Whoa, what's that all about?"

Fredekas frowned. "She not right speak. Her words strange. I think she say you bring home man, husband."

Within moments the other women came with more necklaces made of flowers or beads, each one picking someone from Ben's group to greet. They hugged back and forth, but then Ben had had enough. "Are we going to stand around hugging all day?" he shouted.

Shess translated his question to the group in general, and everyone replied by gathering near a central campfire. They made a big show of leaving a gap in the circle at one end.

Suddenly the flap of a large tent flew open and a dozen large men marched out solemnly…carrying the oldest guy Ben had ever seen on a chair high on their shoulders.

Ben leaned closer to Joe. "Impressive guys. Not on guard when we arrived."

"Maybe they only guard the chief." Joe watched as they made a parade of circling the fire three times before formally placing the chair on the upwind side of the fire. "Litter carriers?" He laughed.

The old man, the chief, spoke. One of the *nimre* guides stood to the side and translated the local speech to what Shess understood, while Patrick then translated that into English for the sake of the scouts.

"The guard in the tunnel told them we were on the way…and that we were bringing back three people from their tribe." Patrick glanced at their guides. "He thanks us for bringing them home and regrets the inadvertent loss of the guards we surprised in the tunnel, but understands how it could happen." He leaned in closer. "Now he's going into the history of his group. They've been isolated from the rest of the world for generations." He leaned back. "And they did it deliberately."

"That's what the Amish did," Joe interjected.

Patrick kept translating. "Having been so cut off from the rest of the world, they are happy to meet and share stories with us."

"That explains why they reacted the way they did." Ben said.

Patrick continued. "Their ancestors were opposed to the government because of all the wars and such. They wanted peace. They also did things differently from most others, because of religious issues, and so they were persecuted for it."

"Yup, sounds Amish to me," Tom agreed.

Patrick carried on, "Long ago, when they had had an extraordinarily charismatic leader, he decided to pull out of society in general. Taking advantage of a pagan holiday," Patrick leaned aside, "pagan from *their* point of view," he continued, "they all packed their things and walked out of the city in the middle of the celebration."

"Doesn't sound like the Amish, now," Eric said.

"Hey, let me keep up with what they're saying," Patrick frowned. They say that no one noticed for quite a while, and by then, they were well on their way to a new home. They lost some in the snow, but most managed to survive the trek over these peaks." Patrick indicated the formidable mountains surrounding them. "They had finally found a home where none would come to harm them."

Trey piped up. "Ah, not Amish, Mormons. Remember the Donner Party?"

Patrick shushed him. "They've been living here in this valley ever since, not building a permanent town, moving along as the food source is depleted."

Annie interrupted her private conversation with Tom. "Nope. Not Mormons either. They built huge cities. It's the *Jews* who are known to celebrate their impermanence as part of their religion."

Patrick ignored the speculative comments as he continued. "After they had been here for years, they noticed a lack of local meat. They'd over-hunted the valley, so they built those tunnels through the mountains and protected them with the invisible doors. Sometimes they'd send their men to hunt outside the valley, but lately, they haven't been coming back. They've been captured by the *nimre*, used as slaves."

The chief paused at the end of his story, giving Ben a chance to ask Shess, "How was it you happened to pick those guides, anyway?"

Shess said, "These three not fight. They do what told. Others bother them much, order them about."

"In other words, you picked them out because of their upbringing. They were the meek ones."

"Meek? Good word. Empty word. These people not *nimre*. They not violent, not animal. They good people. People without city. People of land. They *lahnpe*," Shess declared. "Like my people of town. You say townsfolk, we say *shmahseespe*."

"shmahseespe," Ben said. "That makes about as much sense as anything else."

"Of course it does," Patrick said. "Consider the roots of the word."

Ben stared at Patrick. "I'll leave the linguistics up to you."

The chief waited with apparent irritation until the interruption was done, then continued in a more deliberate tone.

Patrick continued to translate. "Anyway, word came back into the valley that the hunter groups weren't so much captured as they were bought out. The *nimre* groups bribed them with food and drink. They were influenced by an evil force and convinced to remain outside."

Ben whispered, "I'll bet Mr. Bentnose was involved in that!"

"Probably," Patrick said. "Regrettably, once they made that decision, they were considered outsiders, and the locals wouldn't let them return."

"I know! Shangri-La," Carl shouted.

Patrick frowned. "Quit trying to put these people into a category. Things are different in this world. We've already seen that. The people here are different, too. They have different backgrounds, different reasons for doing things. They aren't going to fit into your ideas from your world back home."

"Jeesh. Listen to him already," John said. "*Our* ideas from *our* world back home? It's *your* world, too!"

Patrick sat down. "I apologize, John, and to all of you as well. It's that since learning this language, things seem to make so much more sense. It's not how you *say* things that's different. It's how you *think*."

Carl stood up. "I know how you feel, Patrick. Even dressing this way makes me feel like I belong, as if they accept me for being *me*. I never had much of that back home." He smiled at Fredekas and patted him on the shoulder. "Thanks for helping me. *Gah-oo* for *selbah*." Carl grinned at Patrick. "See, I'm picking it up, too."

Ben addressed the scouts. "We're all under more stress than normal. This is not a typical campout, though it is more eye opening. We've all had experiences that we can learn from."

"Speaking of experiences," Joe said. "Remember when we were attacked that first day?"

All the scouts nodded.

"They had the map and the amulet from *here*," Joe said. "Were those guys I shot the *good* guys?"

"Can you ask them about that, Shess?" Patrick said.

Shess spoke to the chief, then faced the scouts. "Not *lahnpe. nimre* take things from *lahnpe*, kept *lahnpe* for slaves." Shess slowly raised an arm at the three guides they had used. "Those them."

"So the amulet belongs to them," Annie said, taking it off and offering it to the guides.

They shook their heads in unison, and one spoke.

"What did he say, Patrick?" Annie asked.

"He said for you to keep it. They've realized that you are a good person, that you aren't going to use it against them, and you might need it to find your way back here, so it's yours now." He spoke to the guides then said, "They also said that I can keep the scrolls, and they hope I can learn the second one, too. They said that later, if there's time, I can chat with one of their wise men to see if he can help me learn it." Patrick reddened. "They told the chief about me goofing off breaking rocks."

"Well, it's good to know we didn't hurt any *lahnpe* when we were attacked," Ben said. "It was just dumb, foolish *nimre* that attacked us."

"It's good to know?" Joe asked. "It would have been all my fault if I'd hurt any of the good guys."

"I don't think so," Ben said. "All you did was defend yourself from *their* attack, and you were hurt pretty bad in the process, too."

One of the guides spoke up, and Patrick translated, "He heard about the attack that first night. The *nimre* that survived came back to the main camp and told all about it." He listened more. "They had a lot to say about *you*, too." He motioned to Joe. "Anyway, the *nimre* attacked because they had been told to track us. One of the ones that ran away had a finder, not a door finder, but a power finder." Patrick paused. "I'm not exactly certain what that means, but that's what he said."

"A power finder?" Ben asked. "What power was it finding? We didn't have anything powerful, did we?"

Tom thought a moment. "I can't think of anything that they'd think was powerful. We certainly didn't have anything that *we'd* consider powerful. Not even the gunpowder, and none of the natives has ever commented on that on any previous trips."

The guide spoke up and talked with Patrick.

Patrick slowly stared at the scouts. "He says that they used their power finder to track something that Mr. Bentnose would want, and when they located it, they snagged it to bring to him."

"So? That affects us how? What did they find?" Ben asked.

"What they found was Melvin!"

"That's why they grabbed him and ran off," John said. "But why him? What was so special about him?"

Ben shrugged. "All we know is that they *did* target Melvin, but we still need to know where to go."

The guides chatted together quickly, then prostrated themselves before the chief. After a quick discussion, they stood up, accepting a small object from the chief. One of them formally handed the object to Ben, another amulet on a leather cord.

Patrick waited, then translated as they explained. "It's a power finder, another one. They say that if you use it, you'll be able to see where Melvin is, the same way the *nimre* were able to find him."

"I don't know how to use this," Ben complained.

Patrick leaned closer. "You could ask the chief how it works…but he's busy right now." He laughed at the almost somnambulant chief.

Ben agreed. "Maybe Annie can figure out how this one works, too."

"Maybe she can," Patrick said. "But later. Right now just accept it, accept any help we can find."

Ben faced the chief and made a big show of looping the cord over his head, tucking the amulet into his shirt, then patting it to show it was safely tucked away. He made a big, sweeping bow.

The chief stood up, raised his hands above his head, and shook his fists. All the *lahnpe*, the entire community, broke out into cheers. Shess and his people cheered back, followed by the scouts letting loose with a whoop and a holler. Ben smiled. *Wow, we managed to make a good impression, in spite of everything.*

Trying to quiet the crowd was futile, only making them yell all the more, so Ben waited for a moment or two, hoping it would die down. When he'd definitely had enough, he stepped closer to the chief to talk, and as the chief slowly sat, the crowd silenced, all except for Eric who had to be physically restrained by Annie.

Ben glanced at Patrick, then faced the chief and said, "We appreciate your benevolence in bestowing this precious gift to us. We will seek and endeavor to utilize it in the utmost proper manner in our search for our lost fellow, but we must now beg leave of you as we must go search for him."

A couple of the scouts snickered, and Patrick smirked as he translated, "*gah-oo.*"

Ben whispered, "That's it?"

As Shess relayed the message, Patrick leaned over to Ben. "You said 'thanks' right? Remember what I said about things being so much easier in this language?" He stuck his tongue out.

"Well, as long as the intent of the message gets through," Ben said.

"It will. As the mayor of his town, Shess knows how to make good with the verbosity all political leaders seem to like."

The chief and Shess spoke, then Shess spoke to Ben. "Chief returns thanks. Understand need find friend, but want you stay for meal."

The chief stood and spoke briefly, and all the *lahnpe* jumped to their feet and set up for lunch.

Ben stood in front of the scouts. "As you heard, we're going to stay for lunch, so try not to ruin the good impression we've made so far."

One of the *lahnpe* women stepped up to Ben, held his hand, and led him to sit on the ground right next to the chief's tall chair. Ben had to twist his head to see the chief, but the chief didn't seem to notice Ben's discomfort. Ben noticed that Shess was on the other side of the chief and the rest of their group had mixed in with the *lahnpe* men. Robb was at the campfire, getting it up into a roar.

No one complained about sitting on the ground, in fact they appeared to be quite comfortable sitting there. Ben watched as the younger women served the meal while the older women kept the children off to one side. "Typical hunter-gather society, with the men at the top of the food chain, the oldest and youngest at the bottom. Somewhat clan-like," Ben said to Tom who sat nearby.

Tom glanced at Ben. "Whatever you say," he said, then went back to talking to Annie.

Ben watched the scouts enjoying themselves, passing plates of food to each other, with the women replenishing the food when the plates were empty. On the other hand, one young woman had the singular job of bringing full plates to the chief, who would pick out a couple pieces, then wave for it to be offered to Ben and Shess.

Ben leaned towards Shess. "Such are the privileges of the ruler-class."

Shess merely grunted as he already had a mouthful, drips of juice running into his beard. Ben smiled and dug in. The first bite of a crunchy vegetable was tart, but the next bites were so sweet that Ben couldn't remember anything better. The next plates had small, thin strips of meat, like jerky, with a salty flavor. He noticed Patrick analyzing each item as it came by, and said, "Enjoy it now. Figure it out later."

"Yeah, I'll do that," Patrick said. "Love the taste, don't you?"

"Yeah," Ben said as he went back to eating, watching to see how the scouts were doing. All appeared fine as the meal progressed…until they were served the drink. A couple of large barrels were brought out, one being set at the head of the group, in front of the chief.

Women circled the fire, scooping from the barrels with half gourds and passing them to everyone in the circle…just like the cliché in the movies: sailors carousing and getting drunk with the natives. Ben knew how that always played out: the sailors would pass out and the natives would attack them in the middle of the night, no one surviving. Ben was glad that this was going to be a quick lunch before they headed out.

Along with the drink, the women served dessert. Ben bit into the pastry and found it filled with nut paste and honey. He was amazed at how flaky the crust was and wondered how they'd managed to bake it. He hadn't seen any kind of oven. Cooking at this level of excellence wasn't typical for a society like this. Then again, not a lot was typical here. These folk, these *lahnpe*, were advanced in some things yet were so backward in others. High-level technology to keep themselves safe from the outside world, yet they ate with their fingers.

Ben imagined that they probably had utensils, at a minimum spoons, when they had been part of the larger society, but probably because their food was now mostly small critters, there was no need, so they had reverted to using their fingers. Ben went back for more dessert, but passed on the proffered drink. He wanted to keep alert in case something happened. *It would be nice if more of the scouts did, too.*

After what felt to Ben like much too long of a "quick lunch," he stood up and mumbled thanks to the chief. He hoped that the chief understood him. Wanting to get a good start before they lost too much time, he gathered the scouts—half of them were missing. "Patrick, where is everyone?"

Patrick, still deep in conversation with the *lahnpe* women, shrugged. "I don't know. I wasn't paying attention. Did you know that they harvest their honey from domesticated bees? They have hives set up on carts and bring them along as they move. I've never heard of portable bee hives."

Ben frowned. "Portable bees? Who cares? We need to find the scouts and get moving if we're going to make it out of this valley before night."

Patrick blinked and shrugged. "Maybe they wandered off. Hang on, let me see if anyone knows." He spoke to the women around him, then explained to Ben, "They say that the ladies of this society wanted the scouts to feel appreciated after lunch, so they invited them out to the field, to lie in the sun, get a nap, or a massage, or something."

"Or something?" Ben started, then stared at Patrick closely. "Wait, have you picked up yet another language?"

"Yeah. Not too difficult. It's a morph of the standard, naturally simplified for their lifestyle. Minor vowel shifts and vocabulary changes. Less even than Chaucerian to Shakespearean English."

"Whatever. So where do I find all these napping scouts? I don't want to waste any more time here."

"I'll have one of these ladies escort you. She should be able to find most of them."

"Most is a start. Can you tear yourself away from your language lessons to help me?"

"We aren't having language lessons. I'm learning how they manage to cook such light crusts. Have you seen any evidence of fancy baking equipment?" Suddenly reacting to Ben's frown, Patrick stood up and apologized to the ladies. "Let's go get them."

"Patrick, you circle that way, and I'll go this way," Ben said. "We should meet on the other side of the field. Send everyone you find back to the campsite, and try to stay focused. I know you want to talk shop with these young ladies, but we need to get going."

"That's fine," Patrick replied. He quickly spoke to two of the ladies, then told Ben, "I've asked these two to go with you. If you have any troubles, you can send one back for help. Is Shess going to help search?"

"You see the chief snoozing?" Ben laughed. "Check out the feet sticking out from behind his chair. That's Shess, taking a nap right there. He didn't even get to his feet before passing out."

Patrick laughed. "Wow, that's what heavy carbs do for ya."

"Yeah, alcohol, too! Especially for lunch." Ben frowned. "Let's see if we can salvage this search operation. I'd hate to tell Melvin that we left him in the clutches of evil longer so we could nap a little longer."

"When you say it like that, it does sound pretty bad. See ya." Patrick headed off to search.

Ben circled the site with the two ladies in tow. After going past the halfway point, he hadn't found many scouts. The ones he had found were either napping or getting to know the *lahnpe* better. He sent all he found back to prep their gear for the trip out. Most of the natives, both *lahnpe* and *shmahseespe*, didn't think there was any need to be in such a hurry, and Ben noticed that the apathy in this valley was contagious. *This valley is going to suck all the life out of us, and we'll be stuck here forever.*

The last person Ben found before rendezvousing with Patrick was Eric. He was lying face down across a small hill, shirt off, with a young lady sitting astride his back, rubbing his shoulders. Stomping on the ground next to Eric's head, Ben shouted, "Yo! Eric! On your feet!"

Eric must have been asleep because he snorted and rolled as he tried to sit up, knocking the young lady to the ground.

Ben reached to help her up, but the two ladies who'd been following him pushed past him. They lifted the young lady to her feet carefully and hurriedly brushed off any grass, chittering the whole time. Ben shaded his eyes as he said, "Eric, put your shirt back on! The glare is too much."

Grabbing his shirt and stuffing his head into it, Eric said, "I don't spend much time in the sun, so I don't get a significant tan."

"Is that what you call it? Never mind, just get going." Ben watched the ladies fussing, noticing that they were spending entirely too much time for such a minor task. "Eric, who is this lady, anyway?"

Eric shrugged. "I don't know. She and I were the last ones left, and I helped her pick up stuff from the chief's chair, then she grabbed me and brought me out here. Do you know how nice and warm it is to spread out here in the sun?"

Ben frowned. "Warm is good, but we—"

The ladies screamed and jumped about.

Ben spun around and saw bugs crawling across the feet of all three women, and not little bugs but big, red ants, with gigantic pincers. The women ran back to the camp as Ben stared where they had been standing. "Eric, do you realize that you were on top of an ant hill? And not normal ants, check out their size."

Eric shied back. "I don't like ants. I'm allergic to them."

Ben checked Eric. "Well, I don't see any on you, but let's clear out before any do. Come on, follow me. We'll meet up with Patrick."

Moments later Patrick came into view, and Ben jogged to meet him. "Find any scouts?"

"Yeah, and I sent them all back. Joe was the last, and you know what he was doing? He had *two* women giving him a massage." Patrick shook his head. "I must say, he has a way with women *I* didn't know about, but he's up and dressed now." Patrick paused, then continued, "Shess' men were reluctant, but they're heading back to camp, too."

"Good. Let's head back and see how many we're still missing."

A brisk breeze kicked up as they arrived at the camp. Shivering slightly in the cool air, Ben counted the scouts, raising his hand. "Anyone not here, raise your hand, so we can come find you."

Eric raised his hand, but Annie poked him in the ribs as Tom stifled a laugh.

In the middle of the roll call, the chief's personal guards woke him. They gave him a short message, and he signaled for the three guides. He started to use them as translators, as he'd done before, but Patrick spoke up, addressing the chief directly. The chief was astonished but, after a quick discussion, accepted Patrick as translator. The chief managed to get to his feet and make an announcement, then dropped back into his chair.

Patrick faced the group. "Oh, boy, he did it this time," he said as he glared at Eric.

"Who did what?" Ben asked.

"That lady Eric was with, remember the one on the ant hill? She's the chief's daughter."

"What have you done this time?" Ben asked, staring at Eric. "Patrick, can you ask the chief exactly what the problem is? And how we fix it?"

Patrick explained slowly. "Well, the good news is that the ant bites aren't bad."

Ben groaned. "And?"

"And she's willing to let that go. Also, she doesn't have an issue with him not speaking her language. She's seen that I've picked it up, so she figures he can learn it eventually, too."

"What does that have to do with it?" Ben asked.

Patrick inhaled.

Ben stared. "There's more? They didn't have time to do much of anything else out there, did they?"

"That's precisely it, he didn't. The gist of it is that he was nice to her."

"That's the problem? He was nice?" Ben asked.

"Yeah, and she liked it. Being the chief's daughter, she's usually left out of things, snubbed by the other people, but Eric didn't know that she was somebody special, so he was nice to her. That's it…he was nice."

"That's good, right? Not a problem? Nothing we need to do."

"Not quite," Patrick continued. "She understands about his need to seek his friend, but she expects him to come back here after we've rescued Melvin…" he raised an eyebrow at Eric "…to marry her."

Eric gasped and would have fallen over, but Trey reached out to hold him up.

"Hang in there, buddy," Trey said, then smiled. "Hey, she's not bad looking at all, in fact, she's kinda pretty." He smacked Eric on the back. "You did quite well for yourself." He put his arm across Eric's shoulder as if to show support but mostly to keep Eric from sinking to the ground.

The chief's daughter had been lurking behind her father's chair as the conversation progressed but now stepped out and walked to Eric. She stood in front of him and smiled. As Eric stood there in abject horror, she reached up and gave him an unpretentious kiss on the cheek. Trey was still holding him up otherwise he'd've fainted dead away.

The focus of his concern then went to the chief and curtsied, holding out her hand. Her father stared at her for a moment, then slowly reached for a small dagger that hung across his chest. He leaned forward, pulled the cord loose, unlooped it off his shoulder, and handed it to her.

She then strode to Eric and curtsied again. When he didn't respond, Trey leaned on him slightly, making it look like he was bowing. Satisfied she stood up and looped the cord over his head and shoulder, bringing the dagger to rest diagonally in the middle of his chest.

Patrick bowed to Eric. "Hail, prince of the *lahnpe*, next to rule."

Trey had to pull Eric back upright but had a difficult time keeping hold of him because Trey was laughing so much. "Oh, boy! You've done it this time, Eric, ol' boy. Wait 'til you get home and tell your sister about this. She'll never believe it." Trey laughed again. "Heck, she'll probably kill you." He almost dropped Eric he was laughing so hard. "Don't lose that knife there. It's proof of your prince-hood!"

All the scouts cheered hesitantly until Ben encouraged them, "Keep it up, guys. Make it a good show. We have to survive this a little more, then we can leave."

Tom slapped Eric on the back. "Good show there. When we return, I want to keep in contact with you. You'll be our connection to these folks."

Everyone paraded by, giving the bridegroom their congratulations.

When Annie had her turn, she stepped in and hugged quickly, saying, "You don't know what you have here, lady…you *really* don't." She then frowned at Patrick. "If you even think about translating what I said, you'll regret it."

Patrick held up his hands. "I'm certain she knows your intent, whether she knows your words or not."

"That's quite enough," Annie said.

When everyone had had their chance to razz Eric, Ben stepped to the chief, pulling Patrick to his side. "Sir, with your permission, we would like to be leaving now. If you could have someone show us the way out of your wonderful valley, we'd gratefully get out of your hair."

Patrick chatted with the chief, then replied, "He says that it's too late." He paused. "What he really said is that the sun is too far across the sky."

Everyone could see that the sun was about to touch the top of the west mountains.

"I gather he won't let us leave now?" Ben asked.

"Nope," Patrick said. "He insists that we spend the night. It gets dark early in this deep valley, besides, he wants his new son-in-law-to-be to have a chance to spend the night with his daughter before he goes out to rescue Melvin." Patrick grinned at the group. "What? That's the way he said it."

"We're staying for the night." Ben said, trying to find a good place to set up camp. "Spread out by those trees to keep warm. Robb, can you can get us a good fire going?"

"I'll get right on it," Robb said.

Ben frowned. "There's a breeze picking up." He studied the mountains surrounding them. "I don't know why. With mountains like this, I would expect the valley to be calm, no wind at all."

Patrick shrugged. "The chief implied that it does this every evening."

"Well, make certain to pound in your stakes well. Whatever the reason for the wind, I don't want anyone getting blown away."

"The wind can get pretty tough," Patrick said. "So the chief offered the use of his tents for us. They've withstood the winds here before. Besides they have nice soft beds…warm beds, warmed up special-for-us beds, if you know what I mean." He elbowed Ben and winked.

"I may have had my overseas shots already," Joe said, "but I'm going to pass on catching anything this time around. No offense to you, Annie, but I don't see any medics with a silver bullet standing by."

"I understand, besides I don't think I'd want to treat such an 'injury.' You bring it on yourself, you cure it yourself," she replied.

Tom looked between the two of them, then said, "I'd hate to offend our hosts, but Joe's right. Besides, I'm saving myself for someone special." He pouted at Annie as she punched his arm.

Ben watched the scouts pause to consider Joe's idea, and most followed as he and Joe went to the trees, while the rest followed Shess and the natives to the tents. Ben hoped that this wouldn't end poorly—He hadn't seen any shrunken heads on display anywhere…yet.

As the scouts were bedding down, Ben overheard the conversation.

Patrick said, "Another night, another world. The people in this valley are so different from the others, it's like being in another world again."

John asked, "So, Patrick, did you see anything special about today, about Sunday?"

Patrick blinked. "Sunday? Oh, yeah. That was today. In all the excitement, I'd forgotten." He stopped to think. "I didn't see anything special going on, did you?"

"Nothing stood out to me," John said.

Patrick leaned back. "I'll admit that my speech about assuming things about these folks should apply to me as well. If they do have any significant holy days, they certainly won't match up with ours."

"Yeah, well, I wanted to prove a point, Mr. Pot."

Patrick blinked. "Yes, sir, Mr. Kettle. Message received."

A hush finally settled across the crew, and Ben was glad that his friends were able to work things out. This was certainly a new experience. Eric's uncle was right: an experience like they'd never had before. He looked forward to what the morning might bring, though he wasn't certain that they'd make it through the night.

The chief had told them that they didn't usually bother to post guards at night because there weren't any wild animals, none large enough that could do any damage. Besides, with the night so cold, everyone wanted to stay under cover. He insisted that no nocturnal animals lived in this valley either, but that didn't dissuade Ben from setting up watches, as they had done previously. They used Tom's trusty hourglass to set up shifts throughout the long night, manned by one of the scouts or a *shmahseespe*.

As much as the days had dragged on before, this night was even longer. They practically ran out of folks to tackle watch duty, but with so many shifts, everyone had time to sleep. By the time there was enough light to move out, they were well rested.

Hours after what should have been sunup, still no direct light reached the valley floor. Shess tried to rouse any sleepyheads that might be considering dozing more by sounding his horn. When he went closer to the campsite and sounded it again, a general stirring from the tents indicated life as both scouts and *shmahseespe* turned out and stumbled to the center of camp, joining Ben's group.

Eric was the last one out, and when he stepped out of the large tent in the middle, he had such a stupid grin on his face that Trey burst out in laughter. Slapping the nearest bystander on the back, Trey yelled, "His first time?" After shouting, Trey looked to see who he'd hit—Bear stood there, grinning—he understood completely what was going on and slapped Trey right back. They fell on each other and laughed together until Ben called for quiet.

Ben stepped up on a small stump and called to the group. "Do we want to wait for breakfast? Or do we want to hit the road now, stopping to eat after we've built up an appetite, when we're darned good and ready?"

"I've already had breakfast," Eric said, but that merely served to send Trey and Bear back into hysterical laughter.

The crowd murmured vaguely, but no one actively protested. Ben figured that the ones who weren't hung over were still so tired from sleeping that they didn't care. Ben asked one of the *lahnpe* to send for the chief, so they could say their good-byes and get a guide out of this lethargic valley. *Talk about a field of poppies, that's exactly what this is. I'm going to be more careful about relaxing too much. Keep active and keep alive, that's my new saying.*

Ben was told that the chief didn't usually rise this early, but at his request, the chief sent out the same three guides they'd had on the way in. Appreciating the help they now offered under no duress, the scouts followed their guides at an unhurried pace, going west: they were going to be heading out a different door than the one they had used to enter the valley. No need to backtrack, the chief had said.

They arrived at the foot of the mountains as the sun peeked over the eastern range, finally giving enough direct light to cast real shadows. Their *lahnpe* guides led them to the tunnel, then started to head back when Ben stopped them. "That's it? That's all the farther you're going to lead us?"

They all chattered, and Patrick translated, "They say that they've had enough of the outside world, and in spite of the fact that we were a nice change, they look forward to living out the rest of their lives in this little box." He paused. "I put in that last part. That's not what they said, but it's what they meant."

"I understand. If they want to live their whole lives in seclusion, who are we to say anything? It's their lives, but I'd prefer to be out there." Ben strode towards the tunnel entrance. "Out there being alive." He spoke to the guides. "I hope you have a wonderful life. If you ever want to join us out there, come on out and see what there is."

Patrick spoke to them for a moment, then they bowed curtly and wandered off, moving no faster heading home that they had leaving it this morning. Nothing in their world was rushed or hurried.

Ben shrugged and called for the group to move out. "Single file," he reminded them. "Robb, get those lanterns lit and spread out. I don't want anyone tripping. Joe, you have the lead and when you get to the other end, don't go out. If it's anything like the other door, we'll be able to see out, but no one will be able to see in, so we can check to see what's there without exposing ourselves. We know what to expect this time, so don't do anything rash."

They filed in but didn't come across anyone along the way. Any guard cubbies they found were unmanned and appeared dusty, unused for quite a while. The fact that this path wasn't as popular as the south tunnel gave Ben a feeling of dread. What would be outside this door?

Tromping along slowly, the line started and stopped fitfully. Ben was beginning to think the tunnel would never end when he realized that they had been stopped for entirely too long this time. "What's going on up there?" he yelled.

He heard his question echoing up the line as if it were a command in a submarine. A moment later, he heard an answer coming back: "Joe sees light." They had finally reached the end. He sent back the message, "Wait there. I'm coming up now." After each person had relayed the message, they stepped to one side, making room for Ben to squeeze by. As he passed Annie and Tom, he paused. "Come on, Annie. We'll need you and that finder in case we need to get back inside."

As they approached the end of the tunnel, he could see light, dim light, shining in up ahead. The doorway was as he'd expected. Light shining in as if through a screen door, filtered but anything right outside was visible.

"So, Joe, do you see anything out there?" he asked.

"Not much light yet," Joe said. "The sun hasn't risen far enough to get past these mountains, so there's no direct sunlight, but I can see bodies lying out there. Old bodies. Not much left but skin and bones."

Ben leaned forward to look. "You're right. Doesn't look like there's been much activity lately."

Tom stepped up, still holding Annie's hand, and squinted back and forth. "No movement. It could be safe. Should we go out?"

"We have to. Can't go back now," Ben said.

"I know that, but should we go out *now*? or wait until, I don't know, dark?"

Ben stared at Tom. *Getting soft, all because of Annie.* "Joe, hold your sword at the ready. Annie, grab that finder and follow me."

Annie pulled out the amulet, holding it tightly. "Ready."

"Joe, go out first, head left. I'll check right. Annie, you wait in the doorway until we give the go-ahead."

They both waited a moment, then stepped all three out together. Joe checked out a small outcropping to the left, and Ben investigated the area to the right. Trying to be quiet, they hesitantly stepped, cringing at the noise of gravel scraping underfoot. The scree here extended much farther, over a half click before any vegetation managed to get a foothold.

Seeing no issues, Ben inspected the mountain they had exited. He could see Annie, right in the doorway, half in, half out. As with the other door, this one sat at the base of a huge cliff. "Joe, anything?" he asked.

"Nothing," Joe said. "Seems safe. Tell them to come out."

"Before we do that," Ben said. "I want to see if we can find *this* door from the outside. We might need to head back this way, and I don't want to get locked out. Stay on top of things out here while I let them know." He walked back to the door and leaned in. "Everyone wait. We want to test this door first." He stepped back a ways. "Annie, come on out. Let's find out what you can see on this end."

Annie stepped towards Ben, and he watched the door suddenly vanish. It didn't so much disappear, as it just wasn't there, as if it had never been. "Wow. Better than a Copperfield trick," he said, doing an about face. "We're ready. See if the finder works."

Ben heard Annie shuffling on the rocks as she said, "I'm going to start farther away from where I know it is, to make certain." More shuffling. "I'm there, ready to test." She continued her monologue. "Get the light right. Good bright colors. Not the same as on the other door. There the colors were blues and greens, here they're more in the reds and oranges." Rocks shifting. "Getting the balance. It should be right here." Silence.

Ben spun to see a blank wall. No Annie. "Hello? Annie? Are you inside?"

Joe stepped back and stared at the rock wall. "Annie?"

Suddenly she stood in front of them, in the open doorway. "It worked?"

"Yeah," Joe said. "There was nothing but a wall, then a hole, with Annie standing there. And I can see Tom farther inside the tunnel."

"You can see me?" Tom asked. "Can you hear me?"

"Yes, to both," Joe said.

"Wait a minute," Ben said. "We never tested sound. Annie, go back inside, then try talking to us."

"I'll do that," she said, then was gone.

Ben and Joe leaned forward, straining to see if they could hear anything.

"HELLO!" Annie shouted.

Both Ben and Joe jumped back. Ben tripped on the rocks and landed on his butt.

Joe laughed at the blank wall. "Um, we aren't having any problem hearing you," he said as he gave Ben a hand up.

"Uh, yeah, really. Sound gets out fine," Ben muttered.

"And we can hear both of you, too." Tom's voice came out of the rocks in front of them.

Getting to his feet, Ben said, "Good that we kept quiet. Not needed in this case, but it's a good habit."

"Better safe than sorry," Joe said. "All done testing, Ben? Can we let them out now?"

"Oh, yeah. Annie, let 'em go!" Ben stepped away from the area in front of the doorway, guiding everyone to a level area free of any rocks…well away from the bodies. He put Carl and Fredekas in charge. "Keep them there. Let them get some fresh air and sunshine. It was kinda damp in that tunnel." He asked Robb, "Can you get a small fire going, to warm up everyone?"

"Easy peasy," Robb answered.

"Thanks." Ben paused. "Annie, I have another test for the door."

"What's that?" she asked.

"Well, we know that you have to be there with the amulet to open the door to go in, but can anyone come out? Even if they don't have the amulet?"

Still standing nearby, Joe blinked. "Hey, that could be useful. Let's test it. Annie, can you open the door for me?"

She faced the mountain, pulling out the amulet, pausing to say, "Not with everyone watching me, I can't."

"Oh, sorry," Ben said, spinning and waiting for Joe to do the same, then called out, "Testing the door! Everyone look at something else." He waited for Annie to find the door. Then when she announced it was open, he watched Joe step inside. "All's well, so far."

"Good for me," Joe said from inside the tunnel. "Go ahead and close the door, Annie, or let it close by itself, or whatever it is that you do."

Annie stepped away from the rock wall and the door vanished. "Can you see us, Joe?"

Momentary silence, then Joe said, "Well, as clearly as I can see you, obviously you can't see me. I've been jumping around like a maniac. As far as hearing you, that works just fine, as if you were standing right next to me. Ready for me to try coming out?"

Ben checked the area. "Yeah, we're ready. All you need to do is walk up to the door as if it were open."

"Here I come." Joe's voice emanated from the rock wall, then he was suddenly standing before them. "Oooh! That felt strange." He shuddered.

"What is it?" Annie asked, stepping towards Joe.

"A feeling, a peculiar one," he said. "Have you ever walked through a waterfall? Like that, but no water."

"Well, remember what it felt like. If you ever feel it again, you've passed through a door, a one-way door," Ben said.

"Could be useful information, but we're done experimenting. We need to get going," Annie said.

"Yeah," Joe said. "But let's examine those bodies first."

"Good suggestion," Ben said. "Annie, you're the medic, anyone else you think should help do the autopsy?"

"Any CSI guys in your group?" Tom almost laughed. "I wouldn't doubt it. You have all the other bases covered."

Ben paused for a moment. "Well, I don't know about before, but lately Carl has developed a good eye for things here."

Joe called to the group, "Send Carl."

Moments later both Carl and Fredekas showed up. "What's up?" Carl asked.

"We're getting ready to examine these bodies and figured you might have some input."

"Roll 'em and let's have a look," Carl said.

Ben watched as they inspected the remains. Like Joe had said earlier, not much to see, dry bones with loose skin draped on them.

"No colors in them at all, same as a rock wall to me," Annie said.

Carl studied the bones carefully. "Well, I don't see any evidence of movement. Nothing's touched these old bones for years."

"Well, are you guys going to *touch* them? Or just *look* at them?" Joe wanted to know.

Annie sat back. "Should we, Carl? Would it be right to disturb them?"

"If we want to know anything about them, we should," Carl said. He picked up a stick and poked at the ribs of the body in front of them.

Joe stepped up. "Here, let me help you," he said as he gave the hollow torso a swift kick.

Bones flew as Annie and Carl jumped back.

"You didn't need to do that, Joe." Annie frowned at him.

"Waste too much time and we'll never find Melvin. They're dead, long dead. No need to be gingerly."

"Knife," Fredekas said.

"Good catch, Fred. What else can you see?"

Fredekas picked up the hilt of a knife, more of a thin dagger, long enough to be a sword, though a short one. "No sheath." He used the blade to dig through the layers of bones, finally moving the pelvis to find the rotted remains of a sheath. "Here sheath, under body. Died with sword out."

"Ah, good detective work. Probably died in battle," Joe said. "Went down fighting. I like this guy, already. Check the other ones."

The other bodies yielded similar weapons, though one had a spear tip inside the rib cage.

"Easy enough to determine COD on that one," Carl said, eyeing Tom. "No need for a CSI here."

Joe stepped back and surveyed the scene. "There must have been a battle. No reason that I can see to be fighting right here. Nothing worth fighting about, no position, no battlements, no supply line." He put his hand on the rock wall. "Nothing but the door. They must have been defending it."

"What makes you think they were the defenders?" Annie asked.

"Note the position of the bodies," Joe said. "They fell with their backs to the mountain, to the door. The victors didn't retrieve the bodies, so they weren't part of them. The attackers must have come from the west. I don't see any reason to head north or south," he said as he sighted along the mountain ridge. "If these men were *lahnpe* defending their valley, it happened a long time ago, a *very* long time ago. They certainly don't have the backbone for anything like that anymore."

Annie looked from Joe to the invisible door. "I see what you mean, but can you imagine it?" She paused. "They were retreating into the safety of their valley, but were caught outside when the door was shut behind them."

"Yeah," Carl said. "They were stuck out here defending a rock wall that didn't need defending, not once the door was closed. They had nowhere to go. They must have been slaughtered."

Joe stood at attention and saluted the remains. "I would have been proud to serve with them. They kept to their post, defending their people right to the end, to the bitter end."

Annie stood up and assessed the battleground. "It's certainly too late for them, but if we plan on having any chance of helping Melvin, we need to get going, don't we?" She frowned at Ben. "The examination is done."

"Good point," Ben said. "But does anyone know which way?"

Joe spoke up. "Like I said, the attackers must have come from the west, so we should head in that direction, keeping the mountains to our backs."

"Generally, yes," Carl said. "But wouldn't now be a good time to use your new amulet, Ben?"

"Oh! I'd forgotten I even had it." Ben reached into his shirt and pulled out the power finder. "So how does it work? We neglected to get any kind of operating instructions before the *lahnpe* left us in the lurch."

"Patrick figured that if Annie could make the door finder work," Carl said, "then she would be able to use the power finder as well."

"That would be good," Ben said as he pulled off his amulet and studied it. Round and wooden like the other one, but this one had different carvings on the front. Instead of three circles in a triangle, this one had a series of concentric circles, fat ones near the center, getting skinnier closer to the outer edge.

Studying it over Ben's shoulder, Joe said, "A target?"

"We'll see," Ben said, offering the amulet to Annie.

"I'll give it a try. Let's hope that it works the same as the other one." She held the amulet close and stared at it. "Yes, colors, but not flickering like the door finder. This one is more stable, just in different patterns." She paused. "Everyone turn your backs to me, so I can see if that does anything different."

The group obediently turned their backs.

Ben asked, "So, anything different?"

"Doesn't appear to change," she said. "Apparently, you can go ahead and watch with this one. Carl, you could see something on the other finder. Do you see anything on this one?"

Carl leaned in closer. "Yeah, color swirls, like a rainbow on a puddle."

"That's formed by road oils floating on top of fresh rain," Eric said.

Ben spun. "Hello! I didn't see you coming. What's up?"

Eric shrugged. "What you were doing looked interesting."

"Well, thank you for the science lesson." Ben frowned. "Now get back with the others."

Eric mumbled about missing out on all the fun as he tromped back.

Ben watched him go. "Science stuff when we don't need it."

"Whatever the reason for the rainbows, that's what I saw, too," Annie said. "Well, Carl, now there's *two* of us who can use this amulet."

"Try tipping it. That worked on the other one," Carl suggested.

Annie tipped the amulet back and forth. "No real change, though the colors seem to slide like they're loose on top."

"Loose colors? Let me see it," Carl said as he leaned in closer.

Annie held the amulet out. "Oh! Now the colors are sliding all over."

"Turning it makes a difference?" Tom asked.

"Sort of. The colors move on the surface, but…let me try something." She rotated, stopping with her back to the group. "Now the colors are facing the other direction…from what they were before." She faced the group. "Now they're back."

"Tipping doesn't do anything, but twisting it does?" Carl said.

Annie twisted the amulet. "Yes, the colors are definitely sliding across the surface." She frowned. "Or the surface is sliding *under* the colors. They don't stay in the same place *on* the amulet—they stay in the same place *outside* the amulet."

Carl raised an eyebrow. "Ah, I have an idea. Let me try something."

Annie handed the amulet to Carl.

He held it flat on the palm of his hand, then rotated it, then rotated himself in place. "Yup. As I thought. It's a compass. The 'needle' always points the same way no matter how the case is oriented."

"Compasses don't work here," Tom said. "Something about magnetic fields. Ask Eugene if you want to know the techie stuff."

"This must be the local equivalent…with no magnetic field." Carl smiled.

"So it's a compass," Annie said. "But a compass to what? It certainly doesn't have a simple arrow showing north."

"According to the *lahnpe*, it's a compass to power," Ben said.

"So it's a compass…where does it point?" Joe asked.

"Is there a needle?" Tom said. "Annie, do you see any kind of needle, or pointer?"

Annie stared at the amulet in Carl's hand. "Nothing like a needle or a pointer exactly, but the colors do swirl in different spots on it."

"There are definite points where the colors group in tight circles," Carl said. "Those must be the points of interest, the centers of power." He frowned. "But there's not just one."

"I see a few of them," Annie said.

"A few targets?" Ben asked. "Are they near each other? Or are we going to be wandering all over kingdom come?"

Carl consulted the amulet. "Two are fairly close together…to the west."

"As I recommended," Joe reminded them.

Carl continued, "And one more or less south." He looked along the edge of the mountain range.

Tom looked off in the distance. "Towards *Roadranusis?*"

Carl compared the compass, the rising sun, and the mountain range. "Yeah, that'd be about right."

"What kind of power could be there?" Ben asked.

"Do you think it could be Deezh?" Annie asked. "With all the healing I've seen her do, she's a good candidate for being powerful, though I don't know what kind of power shows up on that thing."

"That makes sense," Carl said.

"Can we sit for this?" Annie asked. "My legs are getting tired."

Ben checked around for some place appropriate.

"As long as the compass isn't bothered by other people," Carl said, "We can go sit with the rest."

"You're right. Let's go," Ben said.

"Here, Annie, you can carry the power compass," Carl said, offering it to her.

"Thanks," Annie said as they followed Ben towards the main group.

"Not much to sit on," Tom commented.

"You get used to what you have available," Joe replied.

"I know that, Joe, but I was thinking of the lady."

Ben made a big point of peering all around. "What lady?" he asked.

Annie smacked him on the arm and pouted.

Tom shook his head at them. "You two."

They found roundish rocks to use as seats, and Tom suggested the best one for Annie.

She was making a big show of sitting on the rock when she gasped. "The compass! All the colors are pushed out to the edge."

Carl reached for the compass. "Show me."

Annie lifted it up to show him but paused. She slowly brought it back down, then raised it up again.

Carl leaned in close. "I see it, too. The colors shift as it moves. Closer to the ground, the colors move out. Higher up, they move in." His eyebrows shot up, as he said, "It not only shows the direction, but it also shows the *distance* to the target, *and* it's adjustable. It has zoom—the distance to the ground is somehow related to the distance to the target."

Tom raised an eyebrow. "Well, that certainly would be useful to know…once we figure out which target to chase."

Annie smiled. "Well, if it's based on what I learned from Deezh, then I may be able to help with that."

"Tell me what you think," Carl said.

"Do you see how the center of each circle, each target, ends in a different color?"

"Yes," Carl said. "Does that mean something to you?"

"It certainly does. Deezh showed me that colors are in a spectrum. The reddish-oranges are healing colors, and the blues and violets are disease colors. Do you see that one spot where Tom said *Roadranusis* was? It's a bright red, right? That's the same shade I saw on Deezh, I'll bet."

"And the others?" Carl asked.

"There's a dark purple one right next to a bright orange. See there?" She put her finger on the surface of the compass, Carl nodded, and she continued, "If they were using something like this to track Melvin, then I'd be willing to put money on it that those two are Mr. Bentnose and Melvin."

Ben shrugged as they marched west. "Joe was right about the direction, after all," he said.

Tom agreed. "But you can't always trust a gut feeling. Having a compass that shows us the way," he put his arm around Annie, "definitely makes it easier to convince me."

Ben checked the people behind. "They didn't seem to need much convincing."

"Not after *you* were involved. You have a natural gift for leadership. I can see why you were always the patrol leader when you guys were in scouts."

"They told you that?"

"Well, I've heard tell of your exploits," he tipped his head towards Annie, "from a fairly reliable source."

"Oh? I can only imagine." He glanced back at the group, keeping up a good pace. "Well, today is certainly better than yesterday."

"Yeah," Tom said. "Once we were stuck in that valley, I thought we'd never escape. Shangri-La? Ha!"

"Maybe the land of milk and honey…but nothing else," Ben said. "I feel sorry for the *lahnpe*. They're never going to get back what they had before." He hesitated. "From what I could tell, they had been fairly advanced at one time."

"Isolation will tend to do that to ya," Tom said.

They approached another ridge in the forest they were traversing, and Tom suggested they check the power compass. Annie stood on the crest of the hill, in as much of an open area as possible.

"We're still heading in generally the right direction." She paused. "Mostly west, but a bit south-ish."

"South-ish?" Tom asked. "Do you mean towards that tall tree?"

"The one all by itself at the top of the hill," Annie said.

"That's doable." He yelled to the group. "Ben, head 'em out. We'll get another reading when we get up there."

Annie kept an eye on the compass, guiding the group in the right direction…towards the two points ahead of them, the ones they assumed were Mr. Bentnose and Melvin. Every time she measured, she could see that the colored points shifted more and more across the compass face…the red one behind them getting farther away and the double one ahead of them getting closer, slowly but definitely closer: they were making progress. Based on the latest readings, she estimated that they were still a full day from their destination, assuming that Mr. Bentnose and Melvin didn't move.

The group kept up a good pace, except for stops to have a quick breakfast and an even quicker lunch, continuing until early afternoon. Cresting one more ridge, Tom dropped, froze, and motioned everyone to stop.

"What is it?" Ben asked.

"Smoke. I saw smoke in the next valley." Tom said.

Joe crawled up to the edge of the rise and smiled. "Well, you didn't think we were going to get away with walking right in to the enemy camp, did you? I'm certain Mr. Bentnose has advanced guards posted throughout the area." He smiled. "I know I would."

Tom frowned. "Why the smile, Joe?"

"Finally some action," he replied. "We're back into combat mode."

"As if we haven't had enough already? We barely survived that attack on the *nimre* campfire."

"That little skirmish? Ancient history. *Days* ago. I'm hoping for more, soon, real soon."

"Well, let's wait until we verify the need," Ben said. "Whoever it is might not be anything to stress about."

Joe sneered. "Yeah, right." He scooted away from the crest of the hill and leaned back. "We can wait for you to check it out. When you're done, let me know and the rest of us," he nodded at his group, "will go in there and clean up whatever is left. Then we can be on our way."

Tom blinked at Joe. "Thank you, Joe, but wait here. We'll let you know when to head in." He squinted into the trees at the bottom of the hill. "Ben, did anyone bring field glasses? Binoculars?" He shrugged. "Knowing you guys, a telescope?"

"I don't think so. Not that I noticed, but would a spotting scope work?" Ben suggested.

"Yeah, that'd be fine."

Ben trotted back to the waiting group and came back moments later. "John, the *only* real hunter here, or so he says, brought this." Ben offered Tom a small, squat telescope. "He says that he had to replace the original tripod with something more solid."

"Should do the trick," Tom said, putting the small scope on the top of the ridge and leaning in to squint through it.

Joe snorted loudly, a critical comment.

"What's wrong, Joe?" Ben asked.

"The scope is set up right on the edge of the ridge."

Tom leaned back. "So? I want a good chance of seeing them."

"Yeah? Well, this time you're hunting humans, not dumb animals. They'll have as good a chance of seeing you as you have of seeing them. You're silhouetted against the brightness of the open sky behind us."

"Good point, Joe," Tom said. "You have a better idea?"

"Yeah, want me to set it up for you?" Joe offered.

"Go ahead," Tom said and rolled away from the scope.

Joe pulled the scope back. "We should shift sideways to the base of those bushes first." He slowly crept back up to the edge, stopping three feet shy. "That may be the actual crest of the hill, but this is the Ranger Crest. We keep low to see but not be seen."

"That's an excellent idea," Tom said. "I didn't expect to have anyone on this trip with such good training, military training."

Joe planted the scope, then rolled to the side. "All yours, Tom."

Tom shifted then fiddled with the focus knob. "It's too sensitive, can't see where it's aimed."

Ben reached over and twisted another knob. "John says this one adjusts the zoom. It goes from 25 to 75x."

"Much better," Tom said. "Now I can see where I'm looking." He tweaked the knob and swiveled the scope back and forth across the sky. "That's a good little scope." Tom said, then locked in on the trail of smoke. Following the smoke into the trees, he zoomed in to get a better view, then frowned. "Too many trees. We need to get closer."

"Not necessarily closer, just better," Joe said as he scootched down the hill. "Let's shift along the ridge this way." He walked to the right. "We can circle to the side and get a different angle on the situation."

"Everyone, sit tight," Tom said. "Sit tight here but keep it quiet. We'll be back in a bit."

"Annie, you wait here, too." Ben frowned. "No arguing, and tell Robb no fires." He followed Tom and Joe along the ravine, staying low, keeping out of sight of anyone on the other side.

Joe kept going until they came to a slope in the ridge. "Here on the side of the hill. Check what you can see."

Tom placed the scope on the ground, swung it twice, and zoomed in. "Wow. I can see them."

"So what do we have?" Joe asked.

Keeping his eye on the targets, Tom listed what he saw. "Three of them. Not *nimre*, not like the ones we ran into earlier. These guys are bigger, but they don't look dangerous." He frowned. "Sitting around a fire like they're camping and are bored."

"I can guarantee you, they aren't on a camping trip," Joe said.

"I'd believe that," Ben said. "So what would you do, Joe?"

"What would *I* do?" Joe sat back. "My gut instinct would be to hit them fast and hit them hard." He paused. "You said there were three of them, Tom, but that's just what you *saw*. There are probably more hiding nearby." He sat up and indicated the area. "I'm amazed that this is the first time we've come across any of them."

"And?" Tom asked.

"And they are most likely lookouts for a larger group, which we'd like to avoid alerting until the last possible moment." He looked straight at Ben. "The best approach in this situation, if you're up to it, Ben, is for you and Patrick to approach them from there where everyone else is sitting, as if you wanted to talk, similar to your plan, *but* with Tom and me here, and maybe John with his scope, watching…down the barrel of a rifle.”

“I can go along with that,” Ben said. “I’ll go get John and send him here, then head out there.”

“With Patrick,” Joe added. “You’ll need him as a translator, in case there’s a language barrier, which I assume there will be. Send John and give him time to get settled before you head out.”

“Understood,” Ben said as he stood and walked back.

Finding John and Patrick was easy—telling them the plan wasn’t. John was all for it, but Patrick wanted to know why he had to be bait.

John went to join Joe and Tom, as Ben worked to convince Patrick that this was the right thing to do. “Like Joe said, it’s because you can speak the language. I don’t think they speak English, do you?”

“Probably not,” he said, “but why can’t Shess go with you?”

Ben saw the town leader standing in a group of *shmahseespe*, a full head taller than everyone else, leaning on his sword…a broadsword…a six-foot broadsword. Ben considered. “Well, if we want to keep a low profile, and not antagonize them, then we should head in with the least threatening look possible. That would be you and me.” He grinned at the two of them. “We’re certainly not threatening, are we?”

“I have to agree with you there,” Patrick said. “Well, if we’re going to risk our necks, let’s get on with it.”

“They’ll keep a watch from around that hill there.” Ben said. “If somehow something goes bad, we’ll drop to the ground and wait it out.”

“And here I signed up to be on the *other* end of a rifle.”

“I know, but it’s what we have to do to get Melvin back.”

“Oh, yeah. Melvin,” Patrick said. “This is all for him. Have you ever, just once, thought of leaving him behind and heading home, safe and sound?”

“Yeah,” Ben said. “I’ve had thoughts, but what would we tell his parents? What would we tell *our* parents?” Ben sighed. “Patrick, can you imagine sitting in church in the next pew over from his family?” He stared at Patrick. “You won’t be able to hide from them your whole life. If I do what I can, *then* if, for reasons beyond my control, I *can’t* get him back, I’ll know that I tried my best.”

Patrick agreed. “Do your best, then let the chips fall where they may.” He stood up. “John’s had plenty of time to get ready, so let’s get this thing done with.”

Ben followed Patrick up the ridge, down the other side, and through the trees. They approached the campfire slowly, not necessarily trying to be quiet, but when they were close enough to see it, no one was there. They paused for a moment when suddenly two guys stepped out from behind nearby trees. Like Tom had said, these weren’t any little, wimpy *nimre* guys…these guys were much bigger…and uglier.

Ben froze when the two uglies jumped out, one with a sword, the other with a long spear. They were yelling something—he thought it might be a warning but wasn't certain.

Patrick answered by bellowing right back at them.

They both stopped and stared at him.

Patrick barked out again. Ben didn't understand it, obviously but they did.

The one with a spear looked startled, leaning back and planting the base of his spear on the ground, though the one with a sword continued to keep it trained on them, as he stepped forward, the tip aimed right at Patrick.

Staring the ugly in the eye, Patrick stepped forward and shouted again, his hands gyrating.

Ben ducked, thinking Patrick was going to blast them, but he kept yelling. He stared at Patrick. *He has to have a pair to be facing these guys down like that.*

The one with a sword stopped, his blade mere feet from Patrick. He issued a command to the other one, and the spear-carrier stepped into the trees. Ben could hear him smashing though the woods for quite a ways. *So why didn't we hear them when they were coming this way?*

Moments later, after more crashing noise, two of them appeared. Another sword carrier followed spear-carrier, though he still had his sword in his scabbard. The new sword carrier, plainly the person in charge, spoke to the other swordsman, who complained about something, then lowered his sword, unwillingly.

Patrick straightened up and spoke directly to the leader as Ben stood there, watching. *Pretty handy that he speaks the lingo around here,* Ben thought. The leader was listening and nodding every now and then. Other than that, he had an occasional question, but Patrick answered easily, doing most of the talking.

Bored with what was going on, Ben let his attention wander, which was helpful, as he spotted movement in the distance, directly behind both Leader and Spearman. He smiled to himself. *Joe has circled behind and has them surrounded.* Trying not to attract attention to Joe, Ben kept a casual eye on him, watching him circle to the right. *Wait a minute,* Ben thought, *He should be coming* from *that direction, not heading towards it. He's going to get in John's line of sight.* Ben frowned. *Does he know what he's doing?*

Patrick was clearly trying to explain something, but Leader didn't look convinced. Ben continued to watch Joe moving through the underbrush making little noise. *Boy, he's good.* Ben suddenly had a better view as Joe moved quickly from one tree to another: dark brown leather. Ben paused—none of the scouts were wearing leather. Trying to look innocent, Ben watched the movement, and he saw a crossbow. That wasn't Joe—there were four of them!

Ben tried to get Patrick's attention, to warn him, but he was still deep in conversation with Leader, oblivious to Ben's subtle signals. Ben didn't want to tip their hand that they knew, not yet, so he quit trying to notify Patrick of the danger. Watching the progress of the crossbow, Ben had to turn a little bit as the crossbow circled directly behind them, trapping them. Ben must have moved too much, attracted too much attention, because the swordsman quickly stepped closer, his sword at the ready. Keeping his sword centered at Ben, he slid to the side, getting out of the line of flight of any quarrel that his friend might loose in their direction.

He knows! Ben thought. Checking the situation, he tried to find any exits. Spearman in front to the left, Leader dead center, Sword to their right, and Crossbow at their rear: they were surrounded.

Patrick's speech was petering out—he was running out of things to say, and Leader certainly didn't seem to be buying any of it. Shaking his head, Leader stepped to the left, letting Spearman complete the circle, his spear still targeting Patrick, and Sword continued to close in from the right.

Trapped between the crossbow and the sword, Ben didn't move, but Patrick had been so focused on the conversation that he had no idea about the crossbow right at his back, so when Spearman circled, Patrick backed up.

"Come on, Ben. This isn't going to work out. Let's go."

Whispering, Ben frantically said, "Why didn't we arrange a signal to let Joe and the others know that we were in trouble?"

Suddenly Crossbow stood up and stepped forward, not caring if he crackled branches this time. He wasn't trying to hide anymore. Patrick spun at the noise, saw the crossbow aimed at him, and threw his hands up into the air.

A single shot rang out, and Crossbow collapsed to the ground, the loosed quarrel going high into the branches overhead.

Ben glanced towards the hillside where Joe and the others were. They must have recognized the international signal for 'I'm giving up' and decided to take action, he thought.

The other three bad guys had jumped as the gunshot echoed through the small canyon. Leader drew his sword and moved cautiously to the left, glancing over his shoulder as he circled to trap Ben and Patrick between the two swords as Spearman continued to push forward.

A second shot, and Sword to Ben's right dropped. Leader screamed and charged as Ben dropped to the ground pulling Patrick with him. He stayed flat, his arm across Patrick's back. Two more shots, then a lot more noise as people ran back and forth through the vegetation.

After an extended silence, Ben heard, "You can get up now. It's all over." Joe stood above them, John was just feet away, and Tom was coming back through the woods.

Getting up cautiously, Ben offered a hand to Patrick. "Any injuries?"

Patrick patted himself down. "All good here, so what happened?"

Joe kicked one of the three bodies on the ground. "The boss guy and a couple others are down, but the guy with the spear was still up and running." He asked Tom, "Any luck tracking him down?"

"Too fast," Tom said, glaring. "He must know these woods. Besides, he had a head start."

"We may have lost the element of surprise with the one that escaped," Joe said. "But I hadn't anticipated the sound of the rifle, echoing all across this place." He waggled his head. "This world is naturally so quiet that I'd forgotten how loud a .30-'06 can be. We didn't even think to put in earplugs, but a couple shots won't hurt much…I hope."

John cupped his hand by his ear and said, "Huh?"

Joe started to repeat himself, then said, "Say again?"

John sniggered and asked, "What?"

They both laughed.

Ben cleared his throat. "Hello? We have dead bodies lying here."

Tom stepped up. "Yeah, and they're not *nimre*, certainly not like the ones we've run into before. These guys put up a good fight, and they're much better armed."

"Decent armor, too," Ben added. "None of the *nimre* had anything like that. Shess called them wild animal men, but these are real soldiers."

"Are they carrying anything we should salvage?" Patrick asked.

"Let's see," Joe said, as he rolled the swordsman. "Adequate sword here, if any of Shess' men want to upgrade."

"What's in his pouch? Any scrolls…or *just* money?" Patrick laughed.

John squatted to grab the pouch. "You don't want the money? Leave it for me."

"You can have it," Patrick said.

"Nope, no scrolls," John said. "No money either, just a patch of chain armor, too small to be useful." He frowned. "I don't know what it is."

"You mean a bunch of rings linked together in a chain?" Tom asked.

"Yeah, chains linked to chains," John said.

Tom laughed. "That's money, John. That's how it's done here."

John frowned. "Weird money, but as long as I can spend it, I'll keep it." He deposited the handful into his pocket.

Patrick walked to the body of the leader. "You can have it. I want to see what *he* has. I'm hoping the good stuff." He grabbed the pouch from the leader's belt and dumped it out. "Mostly more money." He tossed it over to John. "You can have that, too." Patrick smiled as he dug through the pile. "I'll take the rest: a map and a scroll…wait…scrolls. There's a couple of them." He smiled and held up his treasure.

Ben wandered to the last man. "Anyone want a crossbow?"

"Crossbow?" Joe asked. "Hmm, projectile, reloadable…and silent. Better than a rifle. Yeah, sounds good. How many quarrels?"

"Well there's one loaded, and…" Ben frowned. "Hey, wait, didn't he get a shot off when he was dropped?" Ben kicked at the crossbow then crouched beside it. "Interesting, it's a double shot. Oh, and, he has more quarrels in a pouch on his belt. Close to half a dozen."

"I'll take 'em all. Save ammo, *and* avoid announcing my attack. I like that," Joe said.

John stood up. "What do they have at their camp?" He headed towards the rising smoke.

"Don't run off," Tom warned. "Grab whatever you want, weapons, armor, helmets," he eyed John, "money, and let's get out of here. I don't want to be sitting at the bottom of this ravine if any other soldiers show up."

"I'll be quick," John said. "You guys head back. I'll join you when I'm done."

Tom raised his eyebrows. "I'm not leaving any of you out here alone. Ben, you and the others start back now." He stepped towards John. "*We* will check out their camp and be right there."

"See you." Ben grabbed the pouch of quarrels from the dead guy's belt and went up the hill followed by Patrick. Joe was close behind but stopped to grab the crossbow.

They walked along the back side of the ridge, and Joe asked, "So, Ben, how was it there in the middle of the action?"

"I may have to change my pants." Ben laughed. "Hey, Patrick, wait. What all did you say to them?"

Patrick raised an eyebrow. "Well, I basically told them the truth. That we were with a much larger group waiting behind the ridge, and we were searching for the bent-nosed guy." He stopped. "And you know what? They knew exactly who I was referring to."

"You told them all that? What if the spear guy warns them that we're coming?"

"I wasn't concerned with that right then," Patrick said.

"Bet on it, Ben," Joe said. "If he does his job right, and I assume he will, he'll report all of this to whoever sent them out here. And they'll set up more defenses, possibly even send out a small patrol to check us out, and it won't be the kind of patrol we had in scouts. They'll be heading right for us, but if we get enough of a start, we won't be anywhere near *here* when they arrive—we will be heading right for the main contingent."

Ben squinted into the sun, not quite on the horizon. His turn to be out in front, on point, leading the way, as Eric would say, so he was the first to crest this ridge and look into the valley beyond. He shaded his eyes, trying to see into the shadowy basin below. Suddenly movement caught his eye…large-scale movement. He froze and dove for cover, then spun, checking to see if anyone else was nearby. The main group was still quite a ways back.

He scootched to the bottom of the hill, pulled off his hat, and tried to get their attention. When someone finally noticed him, he waggled his hat, then slammed it to the ground. He could see everyone drop right on command, but instead of waiting until he could come back and explain, a small party broke off, disappearing into the trees to the side, then circling up to the hill. *Good ol' Joe. Always wanting to be right in the middle of things.*

The small group approached, circled to the side, and slowed as Joe moved closer to Ben then asked, "What is it?"

"I don't know. There's something in the next valley, something big."

Joe frowned. "An animal?"

"No, not *an* animal," Ben said. "More than one, and maybe more than animals. I couldn't tell. We're staring right into the sun from here."

Joe snapped a quick nod to Ben, then low-crawled up the rise. Ben followed, keeping as close to the ground as he could. As they crept to the top, Joe tipped his head towards the sun. "If we wait, the glare won't be in our eyes. See how the sun is touching the tops of those mountains. When it has moved completely behind, we should have a better view of what's there."

After waiting long enough, Ben asked, "Can you see anything now?"

Joe stretched his neck up and shaded his eyes with his hand. He stared into the valley beyond, then said, "Yup, you were right. Movement, like crawling ants." Then he quickly pulled back behind the brink.

"What?" Ben asked.

Joe frowned. "Could've sworn I saw light in there, a bunch of possibly campfires."

"Campfires? Then they aren't animals, are they?"

"Not unless animals on this planet use campfires…and we don't know that they don't," Joe said. "This may be the group we were expecting."

Tom crawled up behind them carrying the spotting scope. "Can you use this?"

Ben started to answer, but Joe interrupted, "No way." He glared at the sun. "This is a near-perfect example of the worst angle. The objective lens would reflect the sun right into the valley, revealing our location."

Tom paused. "Like they always show in the old cowboy movies?"

"Exactly, so we'll wait it out." Joe peered at the sun again. "Getting there, half-way now, so it won't be long."

"So, Ben, what did you see?" Tom asked, scooting up closer.

Ben replied, "Movement, a bunch of movement was all I saw, but Joe could see campfires."

"Probably close to a dozen," Joe said.

"Ah, so we run into them now. Annie's compass didn't show that we were that close yet."

"Well, whether this is the main group or not, we definitely have a skirmish ahead of us." Joe rolled onto his back and stared up at the sky. "May as well get comfortable for the next couple minutes, long enough for the sun to drop behind those mountains."

Ben and Tom followed his advice and relaxed. Ben closed his eyes and listened, focusing on what he could hear. Beyond the sounds of birds and critters in the bushes, Ben could swear that he could hear the goings on on the other side of the ridge: voices talking, metal clanking, animals pawing the ground…it sounded like horses. He suddenly realized that they hadn't seen any horses, nor had anyone talked about them. *I wonder what horses look like here, if they even have them.*

Moments later Ben noticed a dimming through his eyelids as a shadow passed across the group. Startled, he sat up and checked for movement. Nothing visible, but the sun had faded from sight. "Now?" he said to Joe.

Joe craned his neck, checking the sun. "Yup, now." He rolled back to face the valley and scooted up closer.

"So? What can you see?" Ben asked.

"Keep low, and you can see for yourself," Joe said.

Tom moved up on Joe's right as Ben came up on his left. Ben kept low as he crawled up to the edge of the ridge and peered into the valley beyond.

Scattered campfires were spread out surrounding a large tent that glowed from internal light in spite of the still dimming twilight. From the distance, Ben could make out knots of people sitting near each of the fires, though he could also see movement from fire to fire.

"Wow. I see hundreds of people," Tom said.

Ben rolled to his side. "Yeah, a bigger group than last time. Ideas?"

Tom shrugged. "Any chance of circling past them?"

Joe didn't respond as he pulled up the spotting scope and carefully investigated their options.

"Joe, can you see anything out there?"

Joe continued to stare through the scope as he listed off what they were facing. "A platoon of spearmen are drilling behind the main tent. A fairly large group of swordsmen are practicing on dummies set up to the south of the encampment. I don't see any archers, but there appear to be targets set up across the river." He adjusted the knobs on the scope. "The rest of the soldiers are resting near the fires, being fed dinner, no mess tent, instead women wandering through serving food. The cooks are working on the far side of the camp, on this side of the river."

"Tom suggested getting past them," Ben said. "Any chance of that? I mean, if we don't have to face them, why should we?"

"Any fight avoided is better than a fight won, right?" Tom said.

Joe frowned. "I suppose." He swung the scope, examining the northern path. "No chance of heading in that direction. The hills are too rocky. Even if we managed to get through, there's no cover. They'd be right on us." He aimed the scope to the south. "And the valley remains open and flat for quite a ways in that direction, so we won't be able to go that way without being seen."

"Oh, well. It was an idea," Ben said. "Any suggestions?"

Joe handed the spotting scope to Ben then trotted to his group, waiting at the base of the rise for Ben and Tom to join them.

Ben scrambled to his feet and followed Tom as they jogged up to the small group. "So what's the plan?"

"Hang on," Joe said. "We were discussing the situation."

Ben raised his eyebrows. "Can we include the rest of the group?"

"If you want to, but the more ideas, the longer it will take." Joe waited for a moment, then signaled a couple of his guys, directing them to the top of the ridge, one to the right, one to the far left. "They'll handle things back here and let us know if anything needs our attention." He headed back to the main group, the rest of his men right behind.

Tom put his hand on Ben's shoulder and stared at Joe's departing back. "Do we have a problem there?"

"I don't know. He's doing what he *thinks* is right. I'm just not convinced that he *is* right."

"Yeah," Tom said. "I know what you mean. Let's go hear his plan."

As they drew near the group, Annie jumped up and accosted Ben. "What's on the other side of that hill?"

"Hang on, Annie," Ben said. "Let's pull everyone in. We don't want to have to repeat it a bunch of times." He called Shess to join them.

Shess arrived with Bear and Shankaktos, followed by Doug and Trey.

As everyone gathered, Ben held up a hand, signaling Joe to wait. He walked to a couple of downed trees. "Let's sit." As soon as everyone was settled, he continued, "We have people in the next valley, a much larger group than what we've encountered before."

"Do we know who they are?" Annie asked.

"We assume they're baddies," Ben said. "What's the compass show?"

She pulled it out and studied it. "Not much different from before. Certainly nothing that close, if I'm reading it right."

"As I had hoped. These soldiers are plain old soldiers. Nothing special about them, no one powerful enough to show up on the compass. Annie, any idea how close the power points are?"

"We still don't know how to gauge distance, yet." She examined the compass, stretching her hand across the surface. "But our targets are less than half of the distance back to *Roadranusis*, in the other direction, so I'd say probably less than a day away."

"Good, so the *real* problems are far enough away to worry about later. Now we just have *this* one to deal with." Ben raised his eyebrows at Joe.

"Ready," Joe said.

"Now we're going to hear from Joe," Ben said. "He has an opinion he wants to share. Go ahead, Joe."

Joe caught everyone's eyes before he launched into his reasoning. "There are more of them than there are of us, many more. And although we'll be going up against a much larger group, we *may* have the element of surprise, as long as we beat that one guy that ran off." He paused. "I know we've been on the move all day, so we're not up to snuff, but if we attack now, we'll have the best chance of taking them out."

Annie blinked. "Hit them first, catch them off guard…" She paused. "Kill them in their sleep? Is that how the military taught you to fight?"

Joe jumped to his feet and ready to respond, but Ben interrupted. "Hold on there, Joe. She may have a view worth considering. What if we *do* win this battle, but then the boss, the king, the general or whoever is in charge of all those guys gets annoyed at us and sends in more troops, so many more that we can't handle them all?"

Joe backed off. "That's the difference between tactics and strategy. We learned tactics. They don't cover strategy until officer's school. In Ranger school, we learned to hit, and hit hard."

Tom spoke up. "But the objectives were assigned by the officers, right?"

Joe paused, then said, "Of course."

Tom looked directly into Joe's eyes. "Then all we have to do is figure out who the officers are, right?"

Joe intentionally looked past Ben. "Any volunteers to make command decisions?"

Before Ben could reply, Annie spoke up. "Shouldn't we check on the local attitude?" She paused. "Shess, what would you do in this situation?"

Shess stood up. "Would announce self. Ask for leader. Ask him move to side. If he not move, then we return to group and prepare attack."

"In other words, give up all chance at a surprise attack." Joe said.

"Is true," Shess said.

Joe pushed the point. "We didn't do that when we attacked the nimer campfire, the one where John was being held. No announcing ourselves *that* time. We just hit 'em fast. Why didn't we talk first then? Your way?"

Shess shrugged. "Not asked."

Joe glared at Annie. "But this time someone *did* ask, so *now* we're going to lose the surprise, by going with *their* way?"

Ben answered, "It may be the best thing if we want to get Melvin back. What if those guys out there don't mind us passing through? They might be from a different tribe or something. They might even be on our side, after the same bent-nosed guy."

"Not likely, but you do have a point. Why attack when you can talk your way through?" Joe sounded sarcastic, but then he continued. "In this case though, that might not be a bad thing, because the other force is so much bigger. We wouldn't have had an easy battle ahead of us."

"So we talk to them?" Ben asked.

"Politics may be a good alternative to combat," Joe said. "In this situation."

"When do we go talk, Shess?" Ben asked. "Now or in the morning?"

"Go now."

Ben stood up. "I'm ready. Who goes with us?"

Shess put a hand on Bear's shoulder. "And Trey-ss. They come, but stand behind, quiet."

"You heard him. Let's go." Ben headed up the hill.

"And the rest of us?" Joe asked.

"Yeah, do we just sit here?" Doug asked.

"Yes, I need the rest of you to wait," Ben said. "We don't know what will happen, so you need to be ready for whatever it is."

"We can do that," Doug said.

"I need and Shawn to keep everyone under control." Ben said. "Circle the group, including the camp followers, and keep everyone together, calm them all down." He asked, "You guys can handle it, right?"

Doug stood up. "Yes, we can." He grabbed Shankaktos, and they headed back to look after the sheep.

"Hey, Robb," Ben said. "As long as we aren't going to have surprise on our side, can you get a cook fire going?"

"How about if make a bunch of fires?" Robb asked. "That way they won't know how many of us there are."

"That works," Ben said. "Joe, have your guys watch from the ridge, making certain everyone stays on this side." He paused. "Unless, you see that we need help." He smiled.

Joe directed his troops to circle to the side, taking up positions all along the ridge.

Shess grabbed his staff and climbed the hill as Ben and Trey followed, Bear right behind them.

They crested the ridge and walked into the valley. Ben noticed the soldiers watch their approach, but no one stood up, no one came out to meet them. When they hit level ground at the bottom of the hill, sentries that they hadn't seen before popped up and challenged them.

White flag! We forgot to bring a white flag, Ben suddenly thought.

Shess bumped his staff on the ground twice, then flipped it upside-down and stuck the tip into the ground.

The local equivalent, Ben assumed. *Not very good scouts, are we? Hardly prepared at all.*

Shess replied to the sentries' challenge.

Ben leaned towards Trey. "Forgot about the language issue, too. Should have brought Patrick."

Trey shrugged. "Shess'll let us know what's going on."

"I certainly hope so," Ben said as the sentries surrounded them.

A scantily clad, skinny guy ran off, and everyone stood in silence as they waited for him to return. Moments later, he ran back and signaled for the group to enter the encampment. The sentries moved to push the group, but Shess headed out first, making the sentries try to keep up with his long strides, as they escorted the group into the middle of the camp.

As they passed each campfire, groups of soldiers stopped eating, rising to their feet to watch, lining up along the path, making Ben feel as if they were running a gauntlet. The corridor was so narrow that Ben and Shess had to go single file.

Trey and Bear weren't going to let the soldiers intimidate them, so they continued to walk side by side, pushing the soldiers back to let them through.

Ben felt uneasy. *What if the situation turns ugly? Joe's people are on the hill, but even if they had sniper scopes, it's getting too dark to do much good.*

They stopped in front of the big tent and waited. Ben knew that whoever was in charge intended that the wait put them at a disadvantage, and it worked. The leader of this group was certainly showing off who was in charge.

After making them wait a while, a boy stepped out and pulled the flap of the tent aside allowing two of the biggest soldiers Ben had ever seen step outside. He glanced back at Trey…and Bear…and smiled. *Woo!*

Once the guards had given the visitors a once over, one of them grunted at the other and received a nod. He stuck his head back into the tent and said something. The leader stepped out and approached Shess, seeming to examine him, then glanced quickly at Ben but, appropriately, ignored Trey and Bear completely.

Ben checked out the leader as well. He wasn't as big as Ben had expected, but the feeling of power that he exuded was enough to convince anyone that he was in charge.

He and Shess had a short conversation, sometimes gesturing at Ben, sometimes back at the hill where the rest waited. Finally the leader waved westward, the direction that the compass showed Mr. Bentnose and Melvin were. The discussion stopped with finality, and Shess gave up on the discussion and stepped back, not taking his eyes off the leader until he passed the guards, then just walking away.

Ben followed quickly, not wanting to wait to find out what had happened. "What did he say?"

Shess glanced at Ben as he continued walking, heading back through the gauntlet of soldiers. "They *betnahzbit* soldiers. He send them. They look for us. Now they found." Shess strode out of the encampment, with Ben and the rest trying to keep up. When they were out of earshot of the soldiers, Shess paused and said to Ben, "We battle in morning."

Ben plopped on a log by the campfire. "No hiding and having to eat a cold dinner."

Tom agreed. "As long as we *have* to go into battle, it's better on a full stomach."

"Unless you lose it all on the battlefield," Annie added.

Joe snickered. "And I can see them doing that."

Patrick wiped one last bite of bread across the bottom of his bowl. "I'd hate to lose *this*."

Annie stared at Patrick. "Are you eating already?"

"I'm getting a quick snack. It might be my last meal, right?"

"Don't talk like that. We're going to survive," Annie said.

"Well, now that we *are* going into battle," Ben said, "does anyone have any suggestions?" He waited for Joe to answer. "Any *tactical* suggestions?"

"Yes," Joe said. "We were surveying the encampment while you were there talking, and we've come up with a plan."

"We?" Ben asked.

"Yes, we," Joe said. "I've consulted with the *shmahseespe* on various aspects of the weapons and armor used here."

"Well, that would be helpful," Ben retorted.

Joe continued. "Most of the battles here are hand-to-hand. Hand to hand, mind you, but not necessarily one on one. They battle the same way we'd have a bar fight. If you best the guy you're facing, then you turn and hit the guy next to you. Hopefully that guy isn't one of your friends, but it's been known to happen."

The scouts snickered.

Joe frowned. "As I was saying, little use is made of long-distance weaponry, for example the bows used here are mostly for repelling foot soldiers on the charge, as are lances. No consideration of attacking the enemy overhead or of hitting their rear or flanks with high arching shots."

"Interesting," Ben said.

"You've no doubt noticed that there aren't any horses or anything similar. I've asked around." Joe paused. "Though Patrick has heard that such critters *do* exist...but only in legend, and *those* horses are much bigger, stronger, and breathe fire in the stories told to little kids. That aside, we won't be having any cavalry, nor on the other hand, will we need to defend against any."

Ben noticed the others nodding. "That's all interesting, but you're starting to sound like Eric." He stared at Joe. "Do you have a *plan* to take these guys on?"

"The first thing to consider would be how *they* plan to take *us* on. According to the locals, they would wait in the flat of the valley for us to come to them. From what I've found out, it's typical that the attacking force, that would be us, moves towards the defenders, that would be them. In other words, they would sit and rest, while we walk the distance." Joe scowled. "I don't think so. My idea is that we barely crest the rise, staying near the top of the hillside and then wait. They will get anxious and tired of waiting, so they'll come to us, probably in a rush, charging at full speed."

"And that's good?" Ben asked.

"As I have it planned, yes. We'll keep most of our archers hidden behind the hill until the last moment, then they'll step out and start pelting the rear of the enemy, making them charge even faster, wearing themselves out before they even get to us. Our troops can even retreat a little ways up the hill for an additional height advantage."

"What happens when the forces clash? How will the archers avoid hitting us?"

"Ah…" Joe paused and smiled. "The front troops will carry flags." He held up a hand. "Yes, I know we don't have any flags right now, but by morning, we'll have had plenty of time to fabricate makeshift ones from tree branches and spare cloth."

"And how will they fight if their hands are full?" Tom wanted to know.

"They won't be using their hands to carry the flags." Joe grinned. "We strap a tall branch to their backs, sticking above their heads. The flags will be high enough, so we can see them but not so high as to interfere with their movement. That way their hands will be free for fighting."

Tom leaned back. "Impressive."

"Go on," Ben said.

"So, the archers will continue shooting at anything beyond that line, and when our front line moves out of their range, the archers will pull back behind the ridge, circle to the north, and enter the valley on the enemy's flank, possibly even being able to circle to their rear."

"That's reasonable. You've conferred with the *shmahseespe* on this?"

"I have, and though they never would have considered this type of attack, they think it'll work."

"Good," Ben said. "But I have one question for you."

"Shoot," Joe said.

"Your plan will work fine for *shmahseespe* fighting other natives, and you'll probably tilt the balance of power…until someone analyses your tactics and ups the ante." Ben paused. "But aren't you forgetting something?"

Joe frowned. "I don't think so." He ticked off the points on his fingers. "I've taken into account the traditional native battle methods, considered all the possible attack and retreat routes including the surrounding terrain, and…" he acknowledged Annie, "…even consulted with Shess on what *he* would do." He sneered at Ben. "So, in your infinite wisdom, tell me what you *think* I've overlooked?"

"We have…" Ben paused and snickered. "…rifles."

Annie gasped.

Tom laughed. "Oops!"

Joe smacked himself on the forehead. "Wow. In all my discussions with the *shmahseespe*, I neglected to consider *our* distinct advantage."

"So, where in all this would the rifles be placed?" Ben asked.

"Hmm…for best tactical superiority, we shouldn't reveal that we even have such weapons until we have the enemy committed. If we let loose with a couple shots early, then they'll run and scatter. They won't make as good a target if they're spread out, so we'll want to try to keep them contained. Once loose they'd probably circle, regroup, and gang up on the shooters, I know I would. Not good, and if any of them make it back with word of our abilities, it would make it all the more difficult for the next battle, if there is one."

Annie spoke up. "Don't they already know? Remember those *nimre* that escaped when we rescued John, and then that one guy from this morning ran off, too."

"From what we've seen of this crew, the nimers are an entirely different group, so there's little chance of them sharing info, and as far as that spear guy goes, he might not have reported to *this* particular group. Even if he has, consider what he has: a single report, no corroboration, no witnesses, no evidence, and an entirely outlandish story." Joe laughed. "Heck, I wouldn't believe him.

"Yeah, me neither," Annie said.

Ben prodded, "So, the rifles? Where do we put them?"

Joe thought a moment. "Similar to the archers, we have them line the edge of the ridge but on the outer edges of the archers, so we can catch the enemy in as much of a cross fire as possible. Keep them low and at the top of the ridge." Joe thought a moment. "Yes, that should work fine."

"I like that plan," Ben said.

Joe continued. "The rifles will have the advantage of distance, so to avoid friendly fire, they should aim at the farthest back troops. If they get a bead on any leaders, get rid of them first and fast. Losing a leader will make for a good morale breaker. Sometimes that's all you have to do to win a battle. Like chess, take the king and the game's over."

"Yeah, but not until the pawns find out. With all the confusion I expect will be in this battle, the troops in the front probably won't have a clue about what's going on in the back, will they?" Ben asked.

"You're right," Joe said. "With the lack of technology, there probably isn't any effective battlefield communication. So unless we manage to make a big enough deal of taking out their leader, their captain, it won't make any difference to the soldiers on the front lines at all. Either way, the rifles should still check for any kind of command structure."

"Thank you, Joe. We'll do our best," Ben said. "Does anyone have any comments?" He waited.

After a moment, Annie raised her hand.

"Yes? What is it?" Ben asked.

She hesitated. "Do you want me out on the battlefield?"

Ben started to answer, but Joe replied quickly, "No, your talents are best used behind the lines. There is a small hillock to the south on our side of the valley. I was thinking you could set up a triage area there."

"Good. That's certainly a better use of my abilities, much better than trying to dodge through the action healing folks in the middle of a battle."

Ben stared at her. "It's interesting that you use the word 'healing' instead of 'treating.' Care to tell us about what you've learned?"

"Not much to tell. From what I've discovered, it's like Joe with that sword. Although he's had general combat training, he never had any explicit sword training, yet when he *doesn't* think, it comes naturally."

Joe blurted out, "Yeah, that's it. There's no thinking. It just…flows."

"I don't know about all that," Ben said, "but as long as you two know what you're doing…"

Annie glanced at Joe. "We do, Ben, but if we have any problems, we'll check with you first."

Joe stood up. "Well, if we're done here, I'm going to grab my guys and see about making flagpoles."

"Considering all the fires Robb has going," Ben said. "You might as well pick up more fuel while you're out there. We probably should keep those fires going all night."

"Easy enough," Joe said.

"I'll help with that, too," Tom said.

After supper, everyone hit the sack early. Lying in his sleeping bag, staring at the stars, Ben was glad that the weather was so temperate. They hadn't even bothered to set up tents this time, as they had on their first night here. Thinking back to that first night, he did the math: they had arrived on a Thursday, spent Friday in *Roadranusis*, Saturday they rescued John, if you could call it a rescue, Sunday they were in that *lahnpe* village. He thought, *What a colossal waste of time* that *was.*

That would make this Monday night. Assuming that they survive the battle in the morning, and find Melvin quickly, they would probably take all of Tuesday and part of Wednesday making their way back to Shess' village. That left two days to do any hunting—the main purpose of the trip. Then they would spend Saturday at the waypoint, and Sunday they'd get back home. Following the plan.

Wow, I felt ten days would be plenty long enough, he thought. But now we only have two days to do any hunting…the whole reason for the trip. That's cutting it close. Any longer to liberate Melvin, and we'll have to forgo the hunting completely.

Ben had to admit that they *had* seen and done things that they would never have had the chance to do back home, but was it worth it? With all the problems, assuming they made it out alive, did all the effort they'd put into it make the adventure worth all the hassle? Ben drifted off to sleep still considering the overall value of the trip.

The sun rose early, but thankfully, the honor of battle held through the night, as no interruptions had spoiled their sleep, other than the changing of the guard every couple of hours. A quick breakfast out of the way and Ben went to check on the activity in the valley. He stood on an outcropping of rock that had a view of the entire valley floor below. The sun was clearing the mountain peaks behind him, and the short grass, still wet with dew, was glistening as a breeze drifted across the open field.

Shess came up and stopped beside him. They watched the action below: soldiers crawling out of tents, stirring the coals of last night's fires, and generally wandering from tent to tent.

"Not organized much, are they?" Ben asked.

Shess grunted and gazed across the scene. "Not organized, yet many."

"I'm certain we can beat them. Between your swordsmen and my troops, we'll handle it."

Shaking his head slowly Shess said. "Many, many soldiers. You save guns. May need later. Use sword first…and arrows."

"Yes, save ammo," Ben said. "We can't get any more, but we can always recover arrows as we work our way through the mess." He paused. "I have an idea. Hey, Joe!"

Joe finished giving his group last-minute instructions then headed up the peak at a slight trot. "What's up, Ben?"

"Shess suggested that there are too many soldiers out there to waste bullets on," Ben said. "We should hold back until we *have* to use them"

"We could still use them as snipers…but only for *good* targets." Joe agreed. "Make every shot count."

"Yeah, that's it."

"I'll have the ground-pounders stay close, as close as possible," Joe said. "That'll give the archers more time to pick off the enemy.

Ben agreed. "We have to save the ammo."

"I'll spread the word to the others," Joe said. "Tell 'em to treat it like it's made out of gold." He laughed. "Where's Eric? I'll tell him that we've found the philosopher's stone here."

"While you're at it, can you let Annie know that if she has any of the camp followers not helping her that they can sweep through behind us, collecting arrows?"

"The archers may think they have plenty," Joe said. "But if some is good, more is better." He paused. "They can also haul our wounded back to Annie's hospital." He glanced at Ben. "Oh, and finish off any injured enemy soldiers."

Ben frowned at Joe's last suggestion, but he didn't see anything he could do.

"We have Annie's field hospital set up on the back side of that hill to the south," Joe said. "She'll be there along with anyone helping her."

Ben squinted. "I can't see anything from here. It's well hidden. Plenty of cover. The trees make it easy for her to see anyone approaching, yet they won't see her at all. We shouldn't have any problem keeping them protected."

Shess stepped to the side, staring at the north-west edge of the valley. "Cloud?"

Ben followed Shess' gaze, squinting across the expanse of the valley. "Where? I don't see anything."

Joe unslung his rifle, leaned on a nearby rock, and searched the mountains on the far side of the valley through the scope. "I see something, sorta like clouds, but not rain clouds. Too close to the ground, wrong color." He lowered his rifle. "Shess, you must have pretty good eyes to see anything that far away."

Shess grunted. "*aa-eh.*"

Ben shaded his eyes and looked where they were both staring. "I don't see anything." He lifted his rifle and sighted in on the far side of the valley. "Still nothing."

Joe passed his rifle to Ben. "Check the view here. I have a pretty good scope. I like to be able to hit a target before it's close enough to hit me."

Ben sighted through the scope but couldn't keep it from shaking. *Too much adrenaline this early in the morning,* he thought. He squatted, braced the rifle on a small rock, and swung it left and right, trying to see what they saw. Then he noticed a blur rising up near a low spot on the far ridge and locked in on it. "Ah, I see something now." He leaned back and trained the barrel of his rifle towards the disturbance. "Isn't that right where Annie said we should be heading?"

"I think you're right." Joe stepped forward. "Yeah, that's exactly where we're going to be heading when we finish off these guys, but it still shouldn't be too much of a problem."

Ben leaned in to sight through the scope. "You're right about the color, too. It doesn't look like rain. Those clouds are brown. What could cause clouds like that? Dirt? Dust?"

"But coming from where?" Joe asked. "The prevailing wind in this area is from the south." He considered the sky. "And it's cloudless in that direction, so we're going to have good weather for our battle."

"Then what's this cloud?" Ben asked.

"Can you see anything besides the clouds?" Joe asked.

Ben squinted through the scope. "Yeah, hang on, I see something now." He watched the clouds grow, resolving into shapes, though still blurry. The shapes became clearer, and what he saw made him catch his breath: The hillside was swarming with soldiers, lots of them. Hundreds–no, thousands—no, hundreds of thousands. A horde of ants coming into view, cresting the ridge, covering the hillside, billowing out into the valley. Reinforcements had arrived.

Ben stood up slowly, considered his pitiful army, and his head drooped. No matter how many swordsmen we have, no matter how many arrows we recover, no matter if we had an unlimited supply of ammo, there are too many of them, Ben thought. He now knew that they didn't have a chance. We aren't going to be victorious today—we're going to be overrun.

Ben sat despondent on the back of the ridge. After he explained what he'd seen, everyone else wanted to go see for themselves. Even after minutes, the flow hadn't stopped—the valley was slowly but steadily filling.

The scouts came up to sit next to Ben trying to console him.

John grabbed his spotting scope, checking the incoming horde. "It's not as bad as you think, Ben. All those guys showing up are plain ol' nimers. I don't see a weapon among them."

Patrick glanced around for Eric. "Talk about cannon fodder."

Joe agreed. "I wouldn't have expected nimers to join up with the soldiers, but if they are conscripted fighters, it would be to our advantage…if the actual soldiers are busy keeping the nimers in line, it means fewer trained and armed soldiers for us to tackle."

"Then again," John said, "maybe their tactic is to intimidate us with mere numbers."

"Well, it's working," Ben said.

"More isn't always better," Patrick said.

"Yeah," Joe said. "We have a better fighting force, a *much* better force, *and* we have rifles."

"Better force or not, rifles or not, their tactic is working. I'm ready to give up and run." Ben looked for support. "Tom?"

Tom leaned back. "Don't pull me into this. I don't mind helping you locate Melvin, but that's it."

"Yeah, do we just abandon Melvin?" Annie asked.

"Like she said, Melvin is still out there," added John.

"Let Melvin take care of himself," Ben said. "We tried, but they must want him pretty bad."

"Not as much as *we* do," Annie said forcefully.

"Do you see what's out there?" Ben asked. "You know we can't stand up to *that* many fighters. Besides, we're not just outnumbered—we're out classed. They know what they're doing, how to fight…we've just watched movies. Having rifles won't help that."

"Yes, we have rifles," Joe said. "But we also have Patrick. You saw what he did to that nimer campfire. Can you imagine what he could do to a platoon of soldiers?" He stepped to the top of the ridge.

Patrick stood up. "Yeah, I'm willing to give it a try."

John stood up beside him. "Me, too." He wrapped an arm across Patrick's shoulders and stood tall.

Patrick cringed, then smiled. "Yeah, we can face 'em down."

Annie added, "We're willing to try, and we have Joe to guide us."

"Yeah, and I'm not going to fail you guys now," Joe said.

"I appreciate what you're trying to do, Joe, and I know that you've had good training and all," Ben said, "but none of us have much experience, not only in battle but in life, too." He watched Shess forming up his men. "They *know* how to fight in this world, and they *have* fought, to protect their village."

"Remember what Zhahmonichas said?" Patrick asked. "Those guys may have old knowledge, but we have young power. He said that's why we're able to do the things we do."

"And what are we doing?" Ben sighed. "Just who do we think we are? A bunch of kids trying to act big. You know what's going to happen? We're going to get ourselves killed, *and* we're going to pull Shess' men down with us. We dragged them into this. They didn't *have* to help us find Melvin, and now we're putting their entire village at risk."

"I'll bet if you ask, Shess will say that he's helping us because he *wants* to," Annie said. She stepped towards Shess' group. "Shall I go get him?"

"No, no. I'm certain you're right," Ben said, standing up. "I know he feels that way, but I don't think enthusiasm, even as much as we have, will be enough to win the day. I wish that we had a secret weapon that we could use." He thought a moment. "John, you didn't happen to bring a bazooka, or a machine gun, did you? A hand grenade, perhaps?"

John blinked innocently. "Who, me? What makes you think that I would have brought something like that?" He blinked innocently. "Besides, if I had, I certainly wouldn't have waited *this* long to use it."

Patrick tried to stifle a laugh, but when he saw John's face, he couldn't help but let out a loud guffaw.

Tom rolled his eyes at the group. "There you guys go again."

Joe patted Ben on the shoulder. "Come on. We have work to do."

"You think we can handle what's out there?" Ben asked.

Joe gave the group a once over. "Oh, we can handle it, all right. I just hope it'll be enough."

Ben stepped to the top of the ridge and looked out across the valley. "So say we *do* try. Has the battle plan changed any?"

"Other than trying to conserve ammo, I don't think so, though we should probably limit it to two rifles, set up as snipers, one on each side of the ridge." Joe checked his crew. "Ben, would you say Carl should be one of the snipers…because he's still somewhat under the weather…and Eric, to keep him out of the way?"

"Yeah, that makes sense," Ben said.

"Everyone needs to get armed," Joe said. "We can borrow the archers' swords…they won't need them, not if things work out the way we hope."

Shess translated and the archers dropped their swords in a pile.

Doug patted the sword already hanging from his belt. "Shawn gave this to me a while ago. It'll do fine, thanks."

Robb took one last look across the campsite and dropped his lighter into his pocket. "Not much need for that in battle." He grabbed one of the swords offered by the archers and gave it a couple swings. "This'll have to do."

John dug through the pile to find a big one. "This is going to be fun!"

Ben blinked at John. "Try to keep it under control," he said, ducking as John swung the sword through the air.

Joe continued, "Don't use your firearms, unless it's necessary, but do keep them handy…loaded, ready, and holstered or slung on your back."

"Have shield, too," Shess said.

"Yeah. Shess is right," Joe said. "Everyone grab a shield." He eyed Trey, "Unless you need two hands to handle one of those big swords." He pumped his fist. "We're going to get down and dirty!"

"Well, if we're ready, there's no reason to put it off. Let's go," Ben said, heading across the ridge and towards the valley. The *shmahseespe* followed alongside. Joe and his group ran to the bottom of the slope, then spread out, hiding behind bushes. Although visible from the hillside, they were well hidden from the valley floor, hoping to catch soldiers off guard when they were closer.

Initially Mr. Bentnose's soldiers stood in neat lines across the valley floor, waiting, but Ben and the scouts had stopped on the side of the hill. Ben didn't know who it was, but someone yelled insults at the soldiers. Then all the other scouts joined in.

The soldiers didn't know what they were saying, but the tone of their voices was unmistakable. Then Shess pulled out his horn, and his folks raised a clamor that put the scouts to shame. It became a contest between *shmahseespe* and the scouts, each trying to out shout the other.

At first, the soldiers stood their ground as they stared at the noisy hillside, but then they joined in, yelling back. After yelling for a while, they tired of standing still, starting to creep forward, breaking their coordinated battle lines. Ben could see officer types trying to keep them in hand, but to no avail. At first one or two, but then just as Joe had predicted, more and more of them came towards the hill, running and drawing sporadic fire from the archers.

Joe yelled loud enough to pierce the commotion, "Hold your positions! They aren't close enough yet."

In spite of itching to join the battle, the scouts held back valiantly, forcing the soldiers to come to them. Holding them back until the last possible instant, Joe finally gave the command to attack, sprinting forward to lead the charge.

As the scouts and *shmahseespe* finally moved, the remaining soldiers still in formation broke into a run, right past all the officers—the groups finally meeting on the field of battle.

Ben stood on the ridge, watching the overall flow of the battle trying to figure out how to direct the effort. Patrick stood next to him and commenced intoning, building up power, concentrating on the middle of the surge. After being annoyed at how his blasts were turning out, he said, "This isn't working. I can't hit it if I can't see it, and they're too far away for me to focus on."

"Are you going to go in there?" Ben asked.

"Yeah," Patrick said. "I need to get closer, to *see* where I'm aiming."

"This shield might help." Ben handed Patrick a small wooden shield. "And this sword, too. You might need it."

"Thanks." Patrick grabbed the sword, hefting it. "I can still do my trick with full hands. Let's see how effective I can be." He trotted off into the fracas.

Ben was able to follow his progress by watching the clouds of dust that he kicked up with his explosions. He was putting a serious dent in the front line as the enemy soldiers realized what was happening and backed off, but then Ben heard another explosion, along with a bright flash of light, nowhere near Patrick.

He couldn't tell what had caused the flash, but he could see activity off to one side. Soldiers were backing up, opening a space that was quickly filled by his troops. Someone was poking a hole in their lines, the same as Patrick was doing. He checked Patrick and saw that he was still making progress, then the flash and explosion happened again.

He looked closer and could see someone swinging a sword, swinging it wildly. Ben continued to watch and noticed flashes of light. *Must be the sun reflecting off of his sword*, he thought, but the more he stared, the more he could tell that it was something else, not sunshine, not a reflection, no, it was something beyond that, a full circle of light…with the sword wielder in the middle. He stared as the flashing sword came to a stop and a couple of the scouts yelled back and forth. Suddenly the crowd opened up, and Ben could finally see that it was Robb with sword in hand.

* * *

Robb swung his sword again.

John downed his opponent, stepped towards Robb, and yelled through the crowd, "See? There it is again!"

Robb paused to stare at his sword. "There *what* was again?" he yelled to John, but John was in the middle of another fight and couldn't answer. Robb saw a wall of soldiers rushing him. He raised the sword above his head and grunted as he twisted, swinging at the soldiers. This time he definitely saw a flash of light. The end of the sword had lit up. He tried it again, but this time he put his full force into the swing and yelled at the same time.

The flash was bigger this time and not just light. He could see flame on the end of his sword. The soldiers he was facing backed off…the ones that could. The ones in front ran into each other, tripping as they retreated too quickly. Robb pressed his advantage, swinging hard and fast, spewing flame from the sword.

Unfortunately for Robb, they all didn't back off. One brave, or foolhardy, soldier charged and managed to get inside Robb's swing, close enough to block Robb's sword with a large shield. Although the sword stopped suddenly when it hit the shield, the flame on the tip broke loose and continued to fly into the crowd. The glob of fire hit the hapless group of soldiers targeted by Robb's sword, and they collapsed to the ground, screaming as they burned.

Robb and the brave soldier both froze as they stared in horror at the downed soldiers. Taking advantage of the momentary distraction, Robb reached over and grabbed the soldier's dagger, right out of his belt, and stabbed him in the leg, dropping him on the spot. Then he stepped forward and swung his sword again, hard, this time jerking the sword to a halt, actually aiming at a distant knot of soldiers. As he'd hoped, the flame broke loose again and pelted every one of them. After their screams faded out, there was a moment of silence, then the crowd opened up—even the scouts backed off, giving him plenty of elbowroom.

Finding himself in the middle of a breach of the enemy's line, he brandished his sword at them one more time, sticking out his tongue, yet they continued to back up even farther leaving him plenty of room, as he'd hoped. He yelled, "Hey, John, watch this!"

John blocked his current attacker and glanced at Robb, seeing him swing his sword like a golf club, barely scraping the ground. When it reached the top of the swing, Robb jerked the sword to a stop, gut-yelled, and sent a ball of flame launching high into the air, arching high to land farther back in the attacking horde. Distant screams filled the air as Robb shouted, "Mortar as well as flame-thrower!"

John yelled something in reply, but the comment was lost in the noise of combat.

* * *

Ben watched, amazed, as Robb continued to toss flame back and forth, breaking through the enemy lines, opening up a larger and larger breach. *I want to hear Tom's response when I tell him about* this *list item.* Watching Robb push his way through the crowd, Ben could see that he was advancing too far, too fast. Any moment now, he'd be in the middle of the enemy, and they'd envelop him, like a pincer movement in reverse. He glanced back at the archers hoping they knew to adjust their aim.

Ben tried to find a way to get a message to the folks in the valley. He needed a radio, a walkie-talkie, even good old scouting semaphore flags would be handy, but nothing was available.

To his right, a shot rang out, and Ben spun to see one of the snipers they'd kept behind celebrating: Eric. Ben had hoped that putting Eric on sniper would save ammo, because Eric would be too chicken to even fire a shot, but in spite of his fear of guns, there he was taking potshots at who knows what. Ben scooted in closer. "Save the ammo!"

Eric called back, "I hit the captain!"

"Are you certain?" Ben asked.

"Yup. I saw him drop. Good clean shot."

Ben raised his eyebrows. "Wow. If you're going to pick targets like that, then keep at it. See what else you can find."

"Gotcha covered!"

A moment later, another shot, again from Eric.

Ben spun. "Who'd you get this time?" he asked.

Eric muttered something.

"What?" Ben leaned in, so he wouldn't have to yell quite so much.

Eric said, "The captain…again."

"You missed the first time?"

Eric frowned. "No. I dropped him…I know I did, but then he popped back up, over a dozen meters away."

"Huh? Maybe it wasn't the captain the first time."

"Joe said to watch for shiny armor and fancy headgear. Both guys I shot were wearing a helmet with tall tassels, like a feather top. They were somebody important, so I dropped 'em."

"Well, they might have been somebody, but they weren't the captain. Watch for a kinda short guy with two hulking bodyguards."

"Do I go after the big guys or the little guy? Easy targets or more difficult?"

"If you can, get the little guy, if not, then go after either of the big guys. It might scare him into hiding, and if he's hiding, he can't direct the battle," Ben said.

"Can do," Eric said, going back to seeking targets on the battlefield.

Another shot, this time from the other sniper. Ben sat up, and Carl shouted, "Just took out the captain!"

Eric laughed. "Yeah, right, the one I was sighting in on."

"Hold your fire, Carl!" Ben yelled. "I'll be right there," then said to Eric, "Be right back."

"No rush. I'll be here."

Ben scrambled back to Carl, circling behind the archers.

Carl pumped his fist. "I hit him, did you hear?"

"Yeah. Check that same spot again. Tell me what you see."

"Same place? No one'll be there. They'll panic and run, seeing their captain taken out like that. They're not used to distance weapons."

"Check it anyway," Ben said.

Carl leaned back into his rifle, stared through the scope for a moment or two, then rolled to stare at Ben. "I don't believe it. I *know* I hit him."

"Yeah, well, so did Eric, twice!" Ben frowned. "Hold your fire. I'm going back to Eric. I'll let you know what we find."

Ben dashed back to Eric, as he was taking another shot. Ben hoped that he was hitting desired targets and not merely making a lot of noise. As he ran, he grabbed the spotting scope that they had left on the slope when they'd been planning the battle. He dropped in close to Eric and said, "Let me spot a couple of targets for you."

Eric pulled his eye from the riflescope. "Thanks." He frowned. "By the way, I shot him again, the captain, the same one Carl also got."

"I don't know what you're hitting," Ben said, "but there's only one captain." He looked down at Eric. "There can be only one, right?"

"Yeah, yeah, so I've heard," Eric said. "So look out there and let me know what *you* see."

Ben kneeled and set up John's spotting scope. Surveying the area near the big tent, he spotted movement. Zooming in, he saw the captain. It had to be him. He was sitting right outside the big tent, and two bodyguards were sitting with him. "Hey, Eric. I see a target for ya, near the big tent. Check out the guys sitting in front of it."

"Yeah, I can see 'em. Little guy sitting between two big guys, same hat, big red feathers. That him?"

"Same hat?" Ben asked.

"Yeah," Eric said. "The same hat, same big plume in it."

"That has to be him this time. Take the shot."

Eric paused. "What I don't understand is why he's sitting *there*. From that spot, he'd have the rising sun in his face. Easier for us to see him than for him to see us." Eric frowned. "How can he run a battle when he can't see what's happening?"

"Good question, but for later. Can you hit the guy in the middle?"

"Yeah, easy shot. Keep an eye on him."

Ben kept his eye on the group of three as Eric shot. The two big guys jumped up as the little guy in the middle blasted backwards, smacking the side of the tent. Ben laughed. "Yeah, you definitely hit him that time."

"Good! I was thinking my aim was off."

Ben zoomed in on the tent again to see what the bodyguards were doing. What he saw confused him: the captain was sitting between the two big guys again…or still? "Wait, Eric."

"What?" Eric sounded annoyed.

"He's back. The captain is back sitting between the guards again."

"Ha! I told you so. I knew I hit him before, twice. This makes three times *I* hit him, so he's been hit four times if you count Carl's, and five if you count the time I took him out by the water trough."

"By the water trough? Where's that?"

"Behind the main tent, to the left, not quite to the river. Where the cooks were doing dishes."

Ben moved the scope gingerly. "Hang on. I need to zoom out to refocus." Ben zoomed back far enough to see the whole encampment, then zoomed in where Eric had described. There he was again, the captain. No bodyguards this time, but it had to be him. Ben recognized the uniform from last night, and the tall red-feathered hat was so easy to spot. "I see him. Can you aim back there again?"

"Easy enough," Eric replied. A moment later, he said, "I'm there. Is that him leaning against a barrel?"

"Yeah, that's him. Go ahead. I'm keeping a watch on him this time."

A loud click told Ben that Eric had dropped the hammer on an empty chamber.

Eric cussed under his breath as he fumbled for an ammo pack. "Four round magazine?" He crammed in four more rounds, locked the bolt home, and sighted in. "Give me a moment. I need to settle in again." Getting his cheek lock the way he wanted, Eric said, "I'm there, and he hasn't moved at all. Still in the same place."

"Yeah, hasn't moved a muscle, right out there in the open, but I don't care what he's doing. I want to see what happens when you shoot."

"Ready?"

"Yeah."

Ben continued to watch as Eric shot again. This time he kept his eyes on the action and saw the captain get hit in the chest, a solid shot. Blood splattered across the water trough and the hat went flying. Ben waited, watching, then he saw the most amazing thing. A skinny, little *nimre* stumbled out from behind the barrel, as if someone had pushed him. He hesitantly picked up the red-feathered hat and put it on his head as a hand came out and pulled the downed body out of sight. He was back: The 'captain' was back, leaning on the barrel as if nothing had happened.

Ben sat back and tapped Eric on the shoulder. "You won't believe what happened."

Eric rolled up to look. "What, did I miss?"

"On the contrary, you had a clean shot. You dropped him, *but* then he was back up."

Eric blinked. "Zombies?"

Ben wasn't amused, but on consideration, Eric might have a point: In this world, there might *be* zombies. "No, not quite. *He* went down…and *stayed* down…but was replaced."

"Replaced?" Eric queried.

"Someone else put on the hat," Ben said slowly. "And the body was dragged away."

"Re-using the hat? Must be a different hat than the one by the tent. It's way across the encampment."

"I don't know." Ben frowned. "Two hats, but one captain?"

"Give me one more shot at him. He's such an easy target, out in the open, no activity nearby, bright red hat flopping in the sun." He rolled back to his belly and hugged the rifle into his shoulder.

"Let me get sighted on him." Ben said.

Both trained their respective scopes at the target. Ben grunted when he was ready. Eric returned a grunt.

Again, the shot was a good one, but this time a head shot. Red feathers flew in all directions, and Ben continued to watch carefully. Like before, someone popped out from behind the barrel, another little guy, but this time he couldn't find the hat. He stood there shrugging his shoulders, the feathers drifting in the breeze. He appeared to be talking to someone still hiding behind the barrel. A large soldier in full battle dress stood up and stared right at Ben, then scrutinized the area. He walked towards the remains of the hat and kicked it, then pushed the little guy to the side and strode behind the small tent next to them and out of sight.

Ben gasped and looked down at Eric. "Did you see that?" Ben asked.

"Most of it," Eric said. "I figured that if the hat was drawing our fire, then that's where I should aim, so I blew it into a hundred little pieces, to smithereens, shards, fragments."

"Yeah, well you certainly hit where you were aiming. I didn't know you were such a good shot."

"I didn't either." Eric shrugged. "I was never this good at scout camp. They would usually empty the two or three lanes next to mine." He smiled. "I do have quite a reputation."

Ben stifled a laugh. "Well, you're hitting where you're aiming now. *That* 'captain' is down for the count. What's your next target?"

"Did you notice how skinny he was?" Eric asked.

"Now that you mention it, yeah, he was kinda scrawny."

"Like those *nimre* types?" Eric prompted.

Ben stared at Eric. "You mean the ones that Joe said weren't allies with the soldiers?"

"Well," Eric said. "They might not be 'allies,' but they're certainly being used by the soldiers."

"Good point. Can you still see the one in front of the tent?"

"Yeah," Eric sighed. "Let's try him again. He's sitting between those other guys, so I don't know if I'll be able get a good head…er…hat shot."

"Aim at the hat if you want. I just want to see what happens there."

Ben adjusted his aim and focused in on the front of the tent again. When Eric shot, Ben saw the 'captain' fly back the same as before, but this time he saw another 'captain' get pushed out of the tent. One of the big guards grabbed the now deceased 'captain' by an ankle and pulled him to the tent door where someone else inside pulled him out of sight. The red feather hat popped back out the tent flap where the other bodyguard crammed it on the head of the new 'captain.' In moments, they were all sitting as if nothing happened.

"Sitting ducks. Easy targets that aren't worth wasting ammo on. None of those guys are the captain."

Eric stared at Ben. "Where'd they learn to do that? Certainly not something that anyone from *this* world should know about, not according to what Joe found out about their fighting methods."

"Yeah, that's certainly true. Why would they even *think* to do that?"

"It would make sense if they *knew* that we had long range weapons, and they *knew* that ammo was scarce, *then* they could intentionally draw our fire, making us waste ammo, using up a limited resource."

"Yeah, that *could* make sense but how would they know that we even *have* such weapons, *and* that ammo is a limited resource?" Ben looked out at the battlefield. "Do you think we have a spy in our midst, giving info to the enemy?"

Patrick stood in the middle of the battle, glanced into the melee, and saw a ball of flame land in an enemy mass. *Hey,* someone *has figured out a neat trick. I'll have to see who it is…when we're done here.* He fired off another blast, knocking the enemy back, and stepped into the opening, moving forward through the battle, leaving others to clean up the mess he left behind.

Another fireball landed, closer this time. *One problem with pushing through the enemy line so far, I have to keep an eye on my back as well.* He shouted into the air, "Hey! Watch where you're aiming!"

No one responded. The noise surrounding him was stifling, so he dealt with it by picturing himself in a bubble of silence, keeping up his concentration. It didn't seem that the racket of battle had affected his blasting…yet. He adjusted his aim in the direction of the fire.

More blasts, more steps closer. He watched another fireball launch, coming from right in the middle of the battle. *I wonder how they're launching that stuff. For that matter, how are they making those fireballs?* He shrugged and moved on, focusing his movement to intersect with the source of the fire. He was intrigued by it, and by getting closer to the origin, he was getting farther from the impact point. Whoever was firing off those fireballs was aiming into the crowd.

He turned his back on the main part of the battle and prepared to set off another blast. Unfortunately, as he was about to discover, turning your back on a fight is not good. He was half way through his vocalization when a random sword swing intersected with his forearm, cutting all the way to the bone. The pain was unbearable, Patrick dropped to the ground, his eyes closed tightly, and he screamed the last part of his chant.

Everything slowed as Patrick felt the pressure building, as if his whole body were in a vice, his gut felt slammed, his eardrums popped, and the force squeezed all the air out of his chest, stretching his shriek into a long, drawn out howl. An instant later, the pressure was gone, and the sudden release deafened him momentarily. He sat there trying to recover his breath. He opened his eyes to find no one nearby—at least no one on their feet. He pivoted, seeing nothing but bodies stretched out on all sides—even the grass, bushes, and a couple nearby trees had been flattened into a circle surrounding him, over ten meters across, all leaning away from him. Nothing was moving.

He stood up unsteadily, his hand gripped tightly on his arm to stop the bleeding. He staggered for a moment, then movement caught his eye, large movement. He saw a soldier, a huge soldier, the biggest soldier he'd ever seen, pushing his way through the crowd, yelling something, but Patrick, still deafened by the blast, couldn't hear a thing.

Patrick stared as the soldier charged, and in the slow motion that enveloped everything, he had plenty of time to notice that this soldier was big, *and* he was the ugliest person imaginable. Patrick checked him out, from top to bottom, from his immense, misshapen face, to his armor made of bones strung together as a shirt, to his madly pistoning legs.

Patrick calmly studied the scene. Small rocks bounced into the air as each deformed foot hit the ground. The grotesque chest expanded and contracted with every breath. Bulging biceps tensed and relaxed as the disfigured arms swung back and forth. Massive jowls vibrated on the monster's face in rhythm with the pounding feet. Sighting higher, Patrick finally saw the sword.

But not any sword, this one was longer than six feet and appeared so heavy that Patrick didn't think he could have ever been able to lift it, much less wave it high in the air like Ugly was doing. Patrick watched the wind up and knew that his head was the target. As he stared, he saw an arrow appear in Ugly's arm, then another. Two more materialized in his other arm, three landed in his chest, a couple in each leg. None of them did anything to slow him in the least. He kept coming, sword raised high. Unmoving, Patrick stared in morbid curiosity at the glint of the sun on the edge of the sword as it swayed in the air. With it coming straight at his head, he considered what it would feel like to have his head split in two.

With the sword in mid stroke, a rock, no, more of a boulder, flew in from behind. It hit Ugly's forearm, splintering through the armor, then through the arm itself, shattering the bone, sending the sword into a spin. With no force behind it, the sword spun through the air and the flat barely tapped Patrick on the side of the head, though enough to knock him to all fours as the sword landed in front of him.

Patrick sat back on his heels, still holding his injured arm, staring at the body twitching in front of him. Ugly's legs were still trying to run, in spite of the fact that he was lying there bleeding to death. The hatred in Ugly's eyes burned into Patrick's memory as the massive body quivered one last time, then went still. Patrick shivered himself as the eyes glazed over, and the monster finally stopped moving.

Taking a deep breath, Patrick saw Trey and Bear running up from one direction and Joe coming from the other. Trey dropped to his knee and put his hand on Patrick's shoulder. Patrick could see Trey saying something, but he still heard nothing. He drew in a breath and tried talking. "I can't hear you," he said, putting his hands over his ears. "Can't hear anything."

Trey grabbed Joe. They had a discussion—silent to him. Bear joined in, and in a moment, they grabbed Patrick and lifted him into the air, Trey on one side, Bear on the other. Joe led the way as they carried Patrick through the crowd, heading towards Annie's field hospital.

Patrick saw one more flash of light and finally saw Robb fling a ball of fire from his sword into the mass of enemies. *Ah, so that's who's doing it, but how is he doing it?* He didn't have time to find out as they rushed him out of the area.

* * *

Ben watched in horror as they rushed Patrick from the battlefield. He asked Eric. "Did you see that?"

Eric grunted. "Not soon enough. I would have taken some shots of my own at that big guy. I have news for ya, though, good news. I finally spotted the real captain."

"Are you certain?"

"The reason I didn't see all of what happened to Patrick is that when I saw that big guy heading through the crowd, I backtracked him and found where the real captain is hiding."

Ben grabbed the spotting scope. "Where? Guide me in."

"Left of the big tent, left farther than the cook area where we shot the first 'captain'…" Eric snorted in disgust. "…three times. Keep going until you see that small group of soldiers in the middle of a bunch of nimer guys, on that knoll. See 'em?"

Ben aimed the scope across the far side of the battlefield and zoomed in on the area. "I see them. Which one is he?" Ben zoomed in closer. "Wait. I see him now. Yeah, that must be him, the one in the middle. He's directing the other soldiers. Sending them as runners." Ben frowned. "*We* should have thought of that. We needed to arrange communication to co-ordinate things."

"Too late for this battle. Keep it in mind for the next one," Eric said.

"Next one? Not if I can help it, but thanks for the advice."

"So, do I dispose of him?"

"Yeah, and quick. Then take—"

Eric fired.

Ben checked the scope. All the soldiers had dropped to the ground. They looked through the crowd around them, then he saw a couple of them talking, facing right at them. "Do they know where the shot came from?"

"Someone must have informed them," Eric said. "As you thought: we have a spy."

Ben frowned. "I can't believe that any of Shess' guys would do that, and I *won't* believe that Melvin did it, either."

Without taking his eye from the scope, Eric fired twice more. "Ha! Took out a couple lieutenants right when they stood up. Can't get any more of 'em. All on the run now, scattered targets."

Ben watched the soldiers that had been with the captain run, and fast, spreading out, mixing in with the *nimre*. "Well, you took out the one that counts, finally. Let's see what they do with no leader." He continued to watch as the battle increased in fervor, then he frowned. "Those lieutenants are rousing the troops. It's getting worse."

Eric grunted. "Can't help that."

The noise on the field was getting louder when a horn sounded across the valley, a short tone, three toots, then a long blast—a signal for the soldiers, and they all knew what it meant. They turned tail and ran for the back lines, deserting the battle, abandoning the *nimre* to continue the fighting.

Ben jumped to his feet. "Hey, this might work. They're bugging out!"

The *nimre* saw the running soldiers and backed down. Most of them were confused at the departing soldiers, so Robb lobbed more fireballs, and then the *nimre* started running, too. The scouts and the *shmahseespe* caught wind of the change in tone of the battle and pressed on, turning the retreat into a full-fledged rout.

Shess, at the front of the battle, slowed the rush, holding his troops at the river's edge, though the *nimre* kept running. A cheer went up as the valley emptied out even faster than it had filled.

* * *

"Well, the battle went fairly well, mostly," Ben said to the assembled group who wanted to discuss the situation.

"What was the casualty count?" Joe asked.

Ben looked towards Annie's field hospital. "I don't have an exact count, but besides Patrick, there weren't many serious injuries. She's taking care of them now."

"That's good to hear." Joe said, pulling out a small notepad and pencil. "I have some questions." He ticked off his questions. "First, what did we *think* was going to happen?" He waited a moment. "Then what *did* happen. Also what went wrong? And finally, what went right?"

Ben frowned. "I'm not certain we can go into all that right now, Joe. Let's just clean up and care for the wounded."

"No After Action Report again?" Joe shrugged. "Maybe later." He put away his pad. "What do you have in mind?" he asked. "After seeing what happened *this* time, I'm open to any and *all* suggestions."

"Keeping an open mind?" Ben asked. "That's good,"

"As to the strategy," Joe continued, "Annie's idea was appropriate for this first battle, but after this, we may not have the opportunity for negotiations." He frowned. "Although there was one aspect of the battle that annoys me. Ben, do you think—"

Ben interrupted, hoping to contain the rumor of a spy situation, "Shess, what would you do now?"

Shess stood up. "Win battle, return home. No need go more."

"Yeah," Ben said. "Well that would work fine if we were defending a town. In this case, we have a different goal: We have to locate Melvin."

"True, but until Annie gets done treating…er healing the wounded and brings the compass, we can't do much but clean up and wait," Joe said.

Eric piped up. "And eat lunch."

"Yes, Eric, we can eat. We can't keep moving like this without food. Shess, could your people put a meal together? I want to talk to you and Tom…" Ben eyed the others meaningfully, "…in private."

"*aa-eh*, we talk," Shess said, giving the camp followers brief orders.

Ben continued, "Robb, do you think you can get a fire going…without incinerating the entire forest?"

Robb stood up. "Yeah, and if you don't mind, I'd like to try something new to start them."

"I figured that," Ben said. "I saw what you were doing out there. See about keeping it under control."

"I'll try." He pulled his sword as he headed off, twisting it in the air.

"Joe, can you see what's left out there?" Ben said.

"Clean up the carnage?" Joe asked.

"Mostly look for anything we could use," Ben said. "I didn't see the soldiers grab any of their equipment as they were running, so there might be something worth salvaging."

"Excellent." Joe saluted. "And if we come across any maps or papers, we'll pull them aside. We could use intelligence on these guys."

"That's your field of expertise, but if you find any scrolls or whatever, save them for Patrick."

"Speaking of which, any idea how he's doing?" Carl asked, then smiled. "Hey! I'm no longer the focus of attention here, being a wounded hero."

Ben shrugged. "Do you want to head there and check on him? Let the rest of us know."

"I'll report back as soon as Annie lets me," Carl said.

"Thanks, and when you get there, send Tom back. We need him here."

Carl trotted off towards the field hospital.

"Well, Shess. Everyone's been dealt with except the two of us."

"Hello?" Eric said. "I'm still here. What am I supposed to do?"

"As you suggested lunch, I figured you'd want to help ready it."

"In the kitchen, with the women?" Eric asked.

"Unless you have a better idea. You can supervise things there." Ben smiled at Eric. "I'll put you in charge of lunch."

Eric puffed his chest. "I can handle that. I'll make certain we all get properly fed," he said.

Ben smiled. *Sometimes you need to know which buttons to push.* "Good. Now then, Shess, let's head this way. Tom should be able to find us if we don't go too far." Ben strolled to the top of the ridge, to get a view of the entire battlefield. They surveyed the damage as they waited for Tom to show up.

"Good fight," Shess observed.

"You think so?"

"Not many hurt, none killed. Yes, good fight."

"None killed? Do you see that out there?" Ben asked.

"They killed, not us. They cause problem, not us. We talk first, ask. They not give." He tried to find the right words. "They make problem. We fix problem."

"Ah, we threw down the gauntlet and they picked it up, right?"

Shess frowned. "Not know 'gahnt-let.' Why throw?"

Ben tried to explain. "As you said, we asked, but they refused, so we did what we had to—demand satisfaction."

Shess was still confused at the reference, but Ben didn't get to explain as Tom walked up.

"So, what's up? Tom asked.

"Before we get into it, can you tell us how Annie's doing with the wounded?" Ben suggested.

"She says that most of the injuries are easy to handle, doing a quickie fix to stabilize them. She'd prefer to focus on the major injuries."

"Patrick among them?"

"No, Patrick was one of the relatively easy ones: bad cut, chipped bone, and a massive headache, but no concussion. Not what *I* would call easy, but that's what *she* said." Tom shrugged.

"If Patrick was an easy one, then what's she consider a difficult one?"

"The ones who were hit in the gut. She's concerned about infection."

"You know," Ben said. "The more we get into this, the more I'm glad we brought her along."

"Yeah, I'm glad, too." Tom smiled. "But you didn't want to talk about *that*, did you?"

"No, and what I have involves Shess, too." Ben stepped closer.

"You talk. I hear," Shess said.

Ben proceeded to tell them both about the *nimre* masquerading as a captain, that the bad guys knew about firearms and were trying to make them waste ammo, and his assumption that there must be a spy. "So, any idea who it might be?"

Shess didn't think any of his men could have done it. "They not leave camp, so how they tell?"

"True, besides, they wouldn't have any motive to throw the battle, would they?" Ben asked.

"We win, we go home. We lose, we become slaves." Shess frowned. "They want win."

"Exactly, unless they get a better offer, but most of them have families back in *Roadranusis*, right?"

"All have family."

"There you go. No reason for them to give up the info. Do you have any ideas, Tom?"

"I can't think of anything. On the previous trips, everyone was interested in hunting and getting back, no one wandered off. I haven't lost anyone…until Carl and his buddies disappeared."

"So, are you thinking that it might be Melvin that's telling them?"

"I wouldn't think so," Tom said, "but who else could it be?"

Ben sat on a nearby rock. "It doesn't make any sense. I can't see him telling anything…of his own free will. He may not be terribly happy with all of us right now, but he doesn't have any reason to stab us in the back like that."

Tom put his hand on Ben's shoulder. "Not unless, as you said, they gave him a better offer, but I can't see that happening. I certainly hope it's not him. There must be another answer."

A shout echoed across the battlefield as Joe and his crew came up the hillside.

Ben spoke to Tom and Shess. "Let's not say anything about this. Not until we know something more certain."

Tom agreed as Shess said, "No need say, yes."

Ben stood up and waited for Joe to get there. "What did you find?"

"You won't believe the sword we came across," Joe said. "The guy who had been carrying it was full of arrows, like a porcupine, lying there in the middle of an empty area."

"In the middle of a big circle? Everything flattened?" Ben asked.

"Yeah. What happened out there? Did someone set off a bomb?"

"Might have been where Patrick was almost taken out. I couldn't see what all was going on in there, but right about where he'd been there was this big blast, much bigger than anything else I'd seen him do." Ben glanced at Tom. "But it *must* have been him. Can anyone else do a blast?"

"Hey, I wouldn't put it past anyone here to pick up something like that, but, no, I haven't seen anyone else do those blasts like Patrick does."

Joe yelled back to the field, "Hey, you guys. Hurry up with that sword."

Ben leaned to look. "It takes two to carry it?"

"That's what I was saying. It's so big, I don't think anyone'll be able to use it," Joe said.

"Trey might be able to use it," Tom said. "He can carry a lot."

Shess spoke up. "Berahdahchurm can use, also."

"True," Ben said. "Someone fetch them and see if either of them wants it."

The guys carrying the sword dropped it at Ben's feet, jumping back as it clanged on the rocks, throwing up sparks.

"Hey, watch it," Ben said as he jumped back as well. "Leave it there. Head back out and see what else you guys can find." He poked at the sword with his toe and frowned. "But see if you can find something more useful," he called after them.

Joe tossed off another salute at Ben and jogged off with his men.

Tom kicked at the sword and watched Joe depart. "Yeah, it would be nice if they found something we could use."

"We need to get going," Ben said. "If we're going to have any chance of rescuing Melvin and getting back on time." He wondered, "Any clue how long Annie needs to get the wounded up and going?"

"Shouldn't be long," Tom said. "Not many and amazingly minor, too."

"Good." Ben smiled, then continued. "I'd like to get another reading on the compass, so we know where to head…unless you think following the crowd would work out." He considered the well-worn path exiting the valley.

"If we knew that they were heading the right direction, that would be good, but like you said, we don't have a lot of spare time to go chasing wild geese." Tom noticed Trey and Bear approaching. "They seem to be hitting it off quite nicely."

"The language barrier isn't preventing friendships," Ben said.

"They have so much in common, why not?" Tom watched them approach. "Although Trey is strong, you can *see* that Bear is strong."

"Trey is strong but not noticeably so. I wonder if that's related to the list," Ben said as the two arrived. "Who wants a sword?"

Bear patted the hilt of his sword. "Have. Not need more."

Trey bent to pick up the sword.

"Careful. It's kinda big," Ben said.

Trey grunted slightly as he hefted it. "Not bad." He twisted it once or twice and swung it back and forth. "Good balance." Trey glanced at Bear. "Now all I need is a proper scabbard, and I'll be ready."

Bear shaded his eyes as he scrutinized the valley floor. "Who had sword, had scabbard. We get?"

"Yes, we get," Trey said. "Hey, Ben, do you mind if we go hunting for gear?"

"Have at it, Trey. Tell the others, too," Ben said. "Joe and his guys are already salvaging what they can, so why not you?"

Trey whooped and yelled at the group still sitting by the campfire, "To the victor belong the spoils!" He ran off with his new sword. The others followed slower.

"Well, at this rate, we'll have the valley picked clean by time we eat."

"Speaking of picked clean, any plans for all the bodies?" Tom asked.

"Shess, what would you do?" Ben asked.

"As did before, take what we need, leave the bodies for the animals. They need eat, too."

"Less than what I'd've thought, but in the circle of life, it's either eat or be eaten," Ben said. "Even if we bury them, they'd still get eaten…by worms, but that way it would be out of sight."

"It's that harsh living again," Tom said. "You aren't going to get squeamish on us are you?"

"No. I can handle it." Ben looked across the valley, watching the scouts and friends picking through the detritus. He paused a moment, then said, "You know, there's one thing that's kinda bugging me."

"What's that?" Tom asked.

"That big guy that went after Patrick. Why would he run past easier targets or clear-cut threats, like where Trey and Bear were taking out dozens, and focus on that one target?"

Tom cocked his head and responded, "Good question. He even passed up Joe with his fancy martial arts sword stuff. Now *that* would have been a good target for them."

"So, what do they know about Patrick that we don't?" Ben wondered.

Ben's attention snapped to the battlefield when he heard yelling. "Seems they found someone alive, Tom." He ran to see what was going on, shouting back, "Come on!"

Tom and Shess scrambled after Ben, hurrying to see what was happening.

The three of them arrived to find Joe literally standing with one foot on a soldier.

"Do you need to do that?" Ben asked.

"Yes, I do," Joe said with a grin. "Barely hurt at all. Faking his injuries. Waiting for us to wander by, so he can attack from behind." He pushed a little harder with his foot. "I warned the others to watch out for anyone else playing the same game."

"Shess, can you question him? We'd like to know what we're up against here."

"Yes, find out," Shess said, then spoke at length to him as the others looked on.

Ben muttered, "Patrick is still recovering, or I'd have him out here getting his evaluation of these guys."

Shess finished and said, "His language not right, but can understand. He say they know you want back, so they block you."

"We want back?" Ben frowned.

"Friend, Melvin-ess," Shess said.

Ben frowned. "Yeah, we *do* want him back." Then Ben stared at the captive. "Does he know where Melvin is?"

"Melvin with *Betnahzbit*, in city," Shess said.

"That would explain why their two spots on the compass are so close together," Ben said.

Shess continued, "They know we here. They track us, same we track them."

"How did they track us?" Joe asked. "We didn't have any dots on the power compass, did we?"

Shess shrugged. "He say they track."

Ben interrupted Joe's next question. "We can check into that later. What I want to know is who told them about our rifles."

"Yeah," Joe said. "I was wondering that myself." He checked to see who was close by, then leaned in to Ben. "I didn't want to say anything earlier, but you know, the way they drew our fire like that, making us waste ammo, makes me think we have a double agent in our midst."

Tom rolled his eyes at Ben. "The cat's out of the bag now."

Joe stared. "So you guys came to the same conclusion?"

"Yeah, but keep it to yourself, will ya?" Ben asked.

"Will do," Joe said.

"So, Shess, does he have anything useful to say?" Ben asked, kicking at the prisoner.

"He say *Betnahzbit* tell them do that," Shess said. "Make *nimre* look captain. One captain, many *nimre*, not good for else, use to keep busy."

"We still don't know *how* they found out about our rifles, so that question will have to wait." Ben frowned. "Is there anything else anyone wants to know?"

"As talkative as he is," Tom said, "I'm not certain we trust him."

"True," Ben said. "And when he's done talking, then what? We can't treat him like the regular *nimre* we'd captured."

Joe spoke up. "Because there aren't many of them, assuming we find more, we can offer to let them swap sides. If they don't like that, or if *you* don't like it," he looked directly at Ben, "then we can strip them of any gear and turn them loose in their BVDs. I can't see them being much of a problem after that."

"That could work as long as we confiscate their shoes, too," Ben said.

"Their shoes…" Joe smiled. "Now you're thinking."

"Well, go ahead and search out any more. Keep them under control until Shess has a chance to question each one. We'll let him decide if they get the opportunity to swap sides."

"That'll work, right, Shess?" Joe asked.

"These good men," Shess said. "They need leader. You be leader."

"If that's what they want, we can give it to them, but let them know that we'll be monitoring them, too. One screw up and they're out. See if he's agreeable to that, Shess. Oh, and one more thing, who was their leader before?"

Shess spoke with the prisoner for a moment. "He agree." Then Shess abruptly started walking away.

"Wait, who was their leader?"

Shess said one word, "Roodahlf," then strode back towards the camp.

"What's with him? And what did he say?" Ben asked.

Tom shrugged and said, "Sounded to me like he said 'roodahlf' but what that means, I don't know."

Joe grabbed the prisoner, pulled him to his feet by the front of his shirt, and said, "What is this 'roodahlf'?"

The prisoner nodded fervently. Holding up a finger at the retreating Shess, he said, "Shessicheros," then he planted his finger on his chest and said, "Skarochub." Swinging his arm west, he said, "Roodahlf."

"Is it someone's name?" Ben asked. "Their leader. The name of their boss?"

"Their *boss* back home maybe, but not their *captain* here in battle," Joe said. "Not that far away. The captain is lying out here somewhere."

"Eric finished him off…finally," Ben said.

"Good," Joe said, trying to sight down the prisoner's arm. "So what's he showing us? Where all the soldiers ran?"

"Looks like it," Tom said. "So if that's where their big boss is, then what happened to Mr. Bentnose, that *Betnahzbit* guy?"

The prisoner almost bounced up and down as he directed their gaze to the west. He said, "*Betnahzbit*," paused and then said, "Roodahlf."

Joe's eyebrows shot up. "*Betnahzbit* and this Roodahlf are the same guy?" he asked. "Have him say it again, slower."

Ben patted himself on the chest and said, "Ben…ja…min." Then lifted his arm to the west with a questioning look.

The prisoner followed Ben's finger and said, "Roo…dahl…fff," emphasizing the last letter.

"I heard him say his boss' name is Rudolph. Is that what everyone else heard?" Joe asked.

Looking around, Ben saw agreement, so he said, "Well, now we know that Mr. Bentnose's first name is Rudolph."

"It isn't Adolph?" Joe asked with a grin. "So, we know his name, and that helps us how?"

"We can address him properly when we meet him?" Tom suggested.

"And that should be any minute now, right?" Joe asked.

"If we get moving quickly," Ben said.

Before starting lunch, they had found half a dozen men on the battlefield who weren't injured too badly, and Annie quickly fixed them up. Some of them opted to leave, but the rest joined the group, offering their knowledge. Not quite the level of intelligence Joe wanted, but "Something is better than nothing," he said.

Annie brought the wounded to the main camp for lunch. Not many needed help moving. "The rest are perfectly ambulatory," she said. "And using stretchers won't slow us much. Anyone who can't keep up can hold back with the camp followers and join us when they're up to it."

"That probably won't be an issue," Ben said. "When was the last compass reading?"

"Not recently enough," Annie said. She pulled out the compass and studied the surface. "Carl, what's your opinion?"

Carl leaned in to inspect the compass. "Well, we're still heading the right direction. We might not be able to tell distance, but I *can* say that we're definitely getting closer. In fact, we're so close to that pair of targets, Melvin might be right on the other side of those mountains."

"Based on how far the targets were when we first figured it out," Annie said. "And how much we've hiked, I'd say the same thing."

"That's certainly good news," Ben said. "Let's get packed up and on the road again."

Joe stood up. "If we push it a little, we should make it well into those mountains by this evening."

"That's a good goal," Tom said. "Now let's see if we can make it."

Carl led as the group traipsed across the valley. After crossing the small river running through the middle of the valley, the group found a clear path. It ran south into the distance, but to the north, it curved into the mountains. Following it to the north, the group was soon heading west, up into the hills, exactly the direction they had wanted to go.

As the path curved, Ben paused to look behind, to the south. "Wow, that's not a simple path. It's a real road heading straight through the entire valley, an actual *road*, a *paved* road."

Joe pulled up his rifle and used the scope to sight along the road. "This route has been used for quite a while." He stepped to the side and leaned on a large rock to steady his rifle. "And it's in use now, too."

"Oh? Do we need to do anything?" Ben asked.

"Doesn't look like it. I can see a small wagon, maybe a merchant wagon? Pulled by big critters. I can't make out what kind of critters, could be oxen or horses, or something, but whatever kind of wagon it is, it's heading in this direction."

"Should we send troops back to check it out?"

"I wouldn't. We need to keep going, and if the wagon is going as slow as I think, it won't catch up with us at all, but if it does get close enough to verify that it's a threat, *then* we can do something about it."

"Keep an eye on it and let us know," Ben said. "We'll keep moving."

They hadn't gone much farther when Joe stopped in the middle of the road, holding up his fist. Everyone froze and most jumped to the side, crouching behind whatever cover could be found.

Ben crept his way to Joe. "What's the problem?"

"High cliffs, narrow passage," Joe said. "Perfect for an ambush."

"What should we do?" Ben asked.

"Check it out before wandering into a situation we'd regret."

"How many should we send to check it out?" Ben asked.

"Only a couple. If they don't have any problems, they can circle back on the high ground. Once they pronounce it safe, we can all proceed."

"I assume that you'll want to be one of the ones going through, right?"

"Yeah," Joe said. "John's with me. He's a good shot and quick on the draw, maybe too quick, but that's better than being too slow."

Ben called for John to join them, then asked Joe, "Do you want to see what Shess has to say on this?"

"Yeah," Joe said, sighing. "We should check with him, too." He stood up and yelled, "Send Shess up, too!"

John crept along the edge of the road, skittering from bush to bush, but Shess walked in the middle, casually chatting with his men as he came. Tom followed, half dodging, half walking.

Joe explained what he wanted to do, but Shess merely shrugged.

"Not problem. Go visit city," was all he said.

Tom thought the plan was a good enough one. "Let's have a go at it."

But John had a question. "Why me? You guys don't trust me."

"Exactly. Your attitude is what we need right now," Joe said. "We may run into a problem, and you're good at getting out of sticky situations." He paused. "And that would be helpful, considering how many situations you keep getting *into*."

John stared at Joe and frowned.

Joe leaned back and said, "Never mind. I was kidding."

"Yeah, right." John paused. "But it's true. I do get myself in situations that I'd prefer to avoid…but I always get unstuck."

"Whatever works." Joe stood up, hefted his rifle, and said, "Ready? Let's go get 'em."

John followed, cocking his rifle loudly and flipping the safety.

As they disappeared out of sight, Shess kicked back and pulled a pouch of trail food out of his pack, some kind of dried meat. Ben thought, *What's with him lately? He's so quiet, so withdrawn. It's as if we aren't in the middle of a battle.* He frowned. *What's he know that he's not sharing?*

Tom waited patiently with Ben for a while, but then they noticed the others getting edgy.

"Keep it quiet, back there," Ben whispered loudly. "And keep your eyes open."

Finally, Ben noticed the two scouts strolling back along the road as if nothing unusual was going on. Ben thought, *They must have good news, with that attitude.*

"Well?" Ben asked.

Joe sat, laid his rifle across his lap, and began, "It wasn't what I expected, not at all. There was *no* ambush, and there isn't even a problem. Half way over the summit, right before the road starts back down the other side, there's a little guard shack, and guards."

John butted in, "Yeah. We walked right up to them, ready for anything."

"So, what did they do?" Ben asked.

"The strangest thing happened. They came out and greeted us. We don't have a clue what they were saying, but they were being extremely polite as they welcomed us."

Ben stared.

Joe continued, "To their city."

John added, "And it's a big city. You can see it from the guard shack."

"So they welcomed you to the city?" Ben asked.

"Yeah," Joe said. "Apparently, they were expecting us or expecting *somebody*. I don't think we look like any merchants that might come through here, but they didn't seem to have any problems with us walking right into the town, but we didn't. We came back here, and *that* confused them."

"So you think it's safe?" Ben asked.

"Completely. Either they don't know who we are, or they think their defense will protect them from whatever we have."

John added, "Neither of which is possible. If you think, they *have* to know who we are, and what kind of defense could they have? If they had anything like that, why wouldn't they have used it on us earlier?" John frowned. "They should be afraid of us, very afraid."

Ben noticed Shess was still subdued. "Well, we won't get far by just talking," he said. "We need to get going, time to dive into the hornet's nest."

"You've been hanging around with Eric too much," Joe said.

"Speaking of which, how's he doing?" Tom asked. "He brought you into this, after all, but he's not much of an outdoorsy kinda guy, is he?"

"Not much," Ben said. "But I've been keeping him busy. Mostly having him hang back with the camp followers. I figure he can't get into much trouble back there."

"Ah, keeping him back with the *rest* of the women," John said.

Ben ignored John, stood up, and called out. "Everyone, let's move out." He headed off, then yelled back, "Send Patrick up to the front." He paused. "Patrick *and* Shess. This time I want to be certain of what they're saying." Ben strode along the road, leading his flock into who-knows-what danger, no other way to avoid it.

The entire group inched along nervously. The scouts kept their eyes on the edge of the cliffs overhead, swinging their rifles around, wary for any unusual movement—none seen. Everything was quiet, unnervingly quiet.

Patrick caught up with Ben as they approached the guard shack.

Ben glanced at him. "So, Patrick, how're you feeling? You were given quite a bump back there."

"Yeah, well, I did it to myself mostly. I wasn't focused on any one target, so it just went off all round me." Patrick shrugged, then blushed. "I need to keep my eyes open when I blast."

"Is that what happened?" Ben asked.

"So I'm told."

"That big guy was pretty scary. When we saw him charging you, we were worried."

Patrick laughed. "*You* were worried? I was right in the middle of it."

Ben advanced on the guard shack, walking between Tom and Patrick, Joe right behind them, and as had been reported, the guards came out and spoke gently to them, giving a slight bow.

Ben tried to find Shess, but he was lollygagging behind with his men. "I don't know what's up with him lately, but it's all on you, Patrick. Do the introductions, will you?"

Patrick addressed the guards. After a momentary chat, he said, "Joe, you were right. They want us to come visit their city."

Ben blinked. "City?"

Patrick grabbed Ben and almost dragged him along the road. In the valley beyond, they could see a wide, straight road in the distance, running through extensive fields to a large city. "Behold Rudolph-seet, the City of Rudolph." He warned the group. "Remember, to these guys here, Mr. Bentnose is a good guy, so watch what you say."

The guards said something to Patrick, then walked out into the road to greet more visitors.

Ben watched the wagon they'd seen earlier pull up. "Ah, they caught up. We must have been waiting longer than I realized."

The group stepped to the side as the wagon approached. The team drawing the wagon were as big as horses, but they looked dog-like to Ben, huge dogs but skinny and without all the fur. A half-dozen of them were all harnessed like sled dogs, three across.

The guards stepped to the middle of the road and stood waiting, hands on the hilts of their sheathed swords, not threatening, but alert. The wagon master pulled the team to a stop, handed the reins to the woman on the wagon with him, climbed off, and waddled to the guards.

Ben leaned to Patrick. "Are you listening?"

Patrick stepped closer and eavesdropped. "They want to know what he's carrying…he says that he has a load of…I don't know…furs or skins…from animals. The guards are directing him to the right part of town…along the main road to the…sign of the…something…then to the left until he comes to…something else." Patrick sighed. "The vocabulary here is markedly different from Shess', though I can make out most of it."

"You're doing fine."

Patrick continued to translate the conversation. "The merchant is inviting the guards to come…celebrate later this evening…the drinks are on him, once he's been paid for the goods." Patrick frowned. "The one guard can't make it because his wife is…something, pregnant?" Patrick shrugged. "The other one says he'll be there, but he says he's paying for his own drinks. The merchant isn't happy with that for some reason."

The merchant's wife yelled out from the front seat of the wagon.

"She says she's not happy with a guard that can't be…bribed, or maybe rewarded…with a good…ale? woman? I don't know, something. Anyway, the guard is relenting, but he insists that he won't let the husband buy him a drink, though he will let the wife buy him one." Patrick leaned back. "They're all happy about that."

Ben looked closely at the woman in the wagon. She had to be close to sixty years old, the same as the man talking to the guards. *Must be a universal custom: bribing guards with wine and women. I wonder if they're going to sing to him, too.* He shrugged to himself as the old man trudged back to the wagon and clambered aboard. The guards stepped back towards Ben's group as the dogs headed out again. Ben watched as the old man had to stand on the brake as they rounded the first bend, heading out of sight. *Hmm…steep hill.*

Ben glanced at Patrick. "So we're done here? They don't want to quiz us about who we are, what we're carrying, check our luggage or anything?"

Patrick spoke to the guards again then said, "They don't need anything more from us, though it *does* appear that they were expecting us. They called us the 'ones to bring to the boss, Rudolph.' An escort will meet us once we get to the city proper, but until then, we're on our own."

Joe spoke up. "Ah, now it comes out. How much you want to bet that that 'escort' will be a bunch of big soldiers."

"I'm certain it will be, to keep us in control, *and* to protect us from the city folk. They may not appreciate us killing their kin back in that valley," Tom said.

"Good thought," Joe said. "Here, *we* could be considered the enemy."

Ben shielded his eyes from the late afternoon sun, considering what was at the end of the road. "Who has that spotting scope? I want to see where we're going."

A moment later John came to the front, digging out his scope. "Taking a look before we wander in?"

"Yeah, something like that." Ben stood on the edge of the road, braced himself on the rocks at the top of the cliff, and studied the road. The wagon ahead of them was barely making it through the switchbacks on the steep hill. He zoomed in, following the road to the city. Because of the great height, he could see right into the middle of everything. Definitely a large city, much larger than he would have expected, considering the level of technology here.

He continued to investigate as he muttered, "Interesting…it's laid out as a grid, with straight streets running north-south and east-west. Some intersections are larger than others, and others have a tower in the middle." He frowned. "They look like roundabouts, traffic circles. Why would they have traffic circles? Why would they even *need* them?" He frowned. "This city doesn't look like a typical medieval city, certainly not like the other places we've seen so far. Too much planning went into its construction."

Ben aimed the scope across the skyline and continued. "The buildings in the middle are taller than the rest…could be the government section, and there are residential areas on the outskirts." He frowned. "It's all laid out quite carefully. Nothing haphazardly added onto older, existing structures. It's as if the entire city was built all at one time, with a lot of advanced planning."

Ben handed the scope back to John, thinking, *So, who is this Rudolph guy, anyway?* Aloud, he said, "Well, we shouldn't keep our host waiting. Let's head out."

They gathered up and headed out. As they soon found, following the switchbacks was easier on foot than trying to drive a wagon through the tight corners. Ben stood to the side and watched the progress. He noticed that most of the *shmahseespe* waved to the guards as they passed by. The funny thing was that the guards waved back, as if their sole job was to sit there and watch parades march by in review. *Well, maybe it is.*

They traced the narrow road down the mountainside—straight sections not many hundreds of meters long, followed by hairpin turns, banked up on the outside to prevent run-away wagons from careening out of control. Tall trees from each lower level blocked the view to the west, so the fading sun made only occasional appearances through the tall trunks. A warm, moist breeze drifted through the trees putting a damper on everyone's mood. Conversation was low and muted as they continued trudging. Nearing the bottom, the road levelled out and finally changed from the monotonous back and forth pattern. One last turn and they stepped out into bright light. Open agricultural fields ran the distance to the city proper where tall gray walls stood.

Long shadows stretched across fields that encircled the city, fields that, like the city itself, appeared intentionally designed. Ben could see that little space was wasted between sections, and where the ground wasn't quite level, levees separated the terraced fields. Most of the levees had access roads across them, but others had mere footpaths. Peasants, hundreds of them, worked the fields on both sides of the road.

Ben was startled out of his reverie by a voice at his side.

"Keeping those big dog-like critters busy," Tom said.

Patrick spoke up. "Yeah. A lot of wagons going back and forth."

"Empty ones coming from the city, and full ones heading back in," Ben said.

"It's harvest season here," Eric said, squinting at the sun. "Already peaked at full zenith and is about to reach equinox."

Ben stared at Eric wondering what he was doing up here instead of being at the back of the movement. He tried to find Trey…to keep Eric out of the way.

In response to the sudden silence, Eric continued. "The seasons here don't match up with back home."

"Makes sense," Patrick said. "We've already noticed that the days don't feel like they're the same, so why should the rest of nature?"

"It's strange how things are so close, but not quite the same," Tom said.

"It establishes proof for the Parallel Evolution theory," Eric said, waiting for a response. "You know, that civilizations tend to end up the same no matter how differently they started."

Ben smiled at Eric, then spotted Trey in the back and called him to the front. When he was close enough, he leaned in and whispered, "Keep an eye on Eric will ya? I know you guys are tight, so see if you can keep him out of trouble."

Trey laughed. "I can't guarantee anything, but I'll do my best." He took up a position on one side of Eric as Bear took the other. They slowed to walk behind Ben and the others.

"Thanks." Ben squinted at a full wagon heading out of the field. "Is that guy an inspector there, checking the load?"

"I noticed, but he's not just checking how full it is. He's checking *what* is in there. They have quality inspectors," Tom said.

"See that one?" Patrick asked. "He's sending it back to the field. Must not be full enough."

"What's that guy doing?" Ben wondered. "Inspecting an empty cart coming *from* the city? For what?"

Tom frowned. "Good question."

"Those guys are definitely accountants," Patrick said. "And they're taking notes on what I'd swear is a clipboard, but they don't have those, do they?"

"I wouldn't think so. You're seeing what you expect." Ben's head swiveled as he examined the ditches on both sides of the road. "That look like irrigation to you?"

"It certainly has the appropriate configuration," Eric said. "Even has gates to allow the water to flow through smaller channels to the farther fields." He shaded his eyes as he checked out the distant fields.

Patrick looked up at the mountain, then stared at Ben. "Where's all the water coming from? Do you see any kind of river?"

"No, nothing like that," Ben said. "They must have a reservoir feeding the system. Does that mean they have pumps as well?"

"Well, you saw the small ones Shess had in his fields, but to run such a big operation as this, they'd need something on an entirely different scale," Tom said.

"Any idea what they're growing?" Ben asked Patrick.

Patrick shrugged and asked Eric.

Eric considered the different fields. "Way across there, up against the mountain, it could be corn or other stalk grain, and off that way, the fields are flooded, so a rice-like crop." He scrutinized the distant fields. "Up the road a ways, I can see smaller plants in fairly neat rows, so that would be vegetables, I'd assume." He looked through the other fields. "I don't see any fruit or nut trees, so they don't have all the possibilities covered." He shaded his eyes and looked towards the city walls. "But if you look closely, you can see there are vines growing up on latticework, so that'd be grapes or beans or something."

Trey leaned up from behind. "Could be hops, too." He smiled.

"I would have to concur. Definite possibility," Eric piped in.

Ben sidestepped one of the small towers along the road. "Notice how straight all the rows are and how square the fields are? They couldn't have plowed them by hand, could they?"

"I wouldn't think so," Tom said.

"I would tend to think not as well," Eric said. "And considering how many different kinds of plants there are, and how well they all seem to be growing, it's either a fluke that they chose to set up the fields here, or they've enhanced the soil with quite effective fertilizer."

Joe walked up to join the front group. "The agriculture here is curious, but did you notice the watchers?"

"The who?" Ben asked.

"I don't know what else to call them. Overseers? Supervisors?" He looked sharply at Ben. "Guards?"

Ben looked across the fields. "Ah, those guys. Yeah. I see them. There's a few of them out there."

Tom agreed. "Quite a few." He indicated a man with a wide-brim, straw hat. "There on the levee road, watching the ones working in the field, not doing much else."

"See that one yelling at the guy wiping his forehead?" Joe asked. "Getting slackers back to work." He laughed. "I'd recognize a drill sergeant anywhere."

"Do you think they're guards and not other helper guys?" Ben asked.

"Oh, unmistakably they're guards," Joe answered. "And those guys in the towers along the road? Those are guards guarding the guards." Joe stared at Ben. "If this isn't a slave culture, it's close enough."

"It might be," Patrick said. "I don't see much evidence of technology in use here, no real tools or anything, so they must have done it all by hand. The cheapest form of labor being slave labor."

"Slavery isn't a necessary step to civilization, but many cultures did use it as a side road to becoming a world power," Eric offered. "Especially after conquering a neighboring enemy. Seize their fields…and their labor as well."

"All I know," Ben said, "is that this place doesn't feel right, considering everything else we've encountered. Tom?"

"I've never seen anything like it either, and with the way Shess is keeping to himself back there, I'd bet he knows something but is keeping it to himself. I've never seen him so quiet on an outing. Patrick, if you could chat him up, I'd like to know what's going on."

"I'll try, but I haven't had a chance to speak with him much. He's staying focused on getting things done and has been acting cold lately. I can try one or two of the others, Beradatcurm or Shankaktos, or even Fredekas. They seem friendly enough."

"That'd be fine. I don't like walking into things blindfolded."

"I can't blame you for that. I don't think anyone does," Ben said. "Go ahead, Patrick. See what you can find out. Let us know if you come up with something interesting."

Patrick slowed then headed back. "See ya in a while!" he yelled as he joined the main group.

Ben continued, noticing that the wall encompassing the city was gray but didn't appear to be made of individual stones, rather a solid wall of concrete, but he knew that that had to be an illusion. The gate into the city stood wide open, and small, portable stalls lined both sides of the road leading in. The area between was filled with shoppers milling about, hardly any moving with purpose, most just casually wandering from booth to booth.

Besides the usual grocers, tinsmiths, and tanners, Ben could see textile vendors, shoemakers, and moneychangers, and somewhere up farther ahead, he could smell a blacksmith's forge belching out smoke. A couple of the booths were proffering other manufactured goods. One stall in particular caught his eye. "Tom, is that a crucifix being sold there?" He leaned closer to see.

Tom walked towards the stall where Ben was looking and stared at the wares. "It may look like it, but I can't imagine it *being* a Christian artifact. Must be something similar but different." He leaned closer. "Even though this booth is full of other religious-looking stuff."

"The Navaho culture used something that resembled a swastika in many of their art forms," Eric said, "but it had been in use well before the possibility of German influence."

"Yeah," Joe said. "Nothing else matches up, days, seasons, not even the development of technology, so why would there be any religious similarities?"

"You're right, but it caught by eye…" Ben's voice trailed off as all the other sights distracted him, gawking at everything like any tourist in a new country. "Hey, Tom, didn't those guards at the top of the hill say that we were supposed to be met by an escort?"

"Yeah, they did," Tom said. "I wonder where he is."

Ben shrugged. "If he's late, it not our fault. We'll keep going and see what's here." As went back to the shopping, he stared at the gate to the city itself. "Check out those gates."

Tall enough to close off the entire archway, the gate was a half meter thick. Iron bands extending from the hinges wrapped to the near edge then back to the other side. "Those doors are huge. I wonder how much force is needed to close them. I'll bet they stay open except in an emergency."

"Like an attack?" Joe suggested.

"Do you know why protective doors swing in instead of out," Eric butted in, "even though it would make more sense to have them close tighter the more an enemy pushed on them?"

No one responded, so Ben glared at them all, then said. "No, Eric. I don't know why. Do tell us."

Eric smiled. "It's because if they swung out, then the hinges would be on the outside and vulnerable to possible attack. The enemy could unhinge them and break right in."

"Oh," Ben said. "Thanks for the lesson in mechanics."

Eric started to answer, but a couple of kids rushed past, running into him, giving him a tumble.

The kids chased each other back and forth between the stalls earning the ire of many a shopkeeper, though entertaining the shoppers. Suddenly one of the merchants grabbed the first kid, and the second kid ran smack into the both of them, knocking them off their feet. Not letting go of his prisoner, the merchant tried to stand but ended up tripping over a pile of rugs. He let go as he hit the ground, flinging the kid into the massive, wooden door.

Ben winced as he expected major injuries, but the kid merely stood up and leaned on the door, giving it a gentle push, easily moving it out of his way. The second kid hurdled the merchant lying on the ground, caught up with his friend, and pushed the door back the other way blocking any attempt at catching them, and they both disappeared around a corner.

As the crowd tended to the merchant, Ben stared. "Did you see that? The hinges on those doors must be so well balanced that they can be moved with even the slightest pressure."

Joe glanced at Tom. "You thought one-way doors and that group in the mountains would interest your scientists? Well, here's another mystery for them: where'd this level of technology come from?"

"The scientists gave up much too easily." Tom laughed. "Once they determined that their fancy electronic tools wouldn't work and they couldn't type notes on their little computers, they basically quit trying. If they would fall back to paper and pencil, I'd bet they'd be overjoyed to come back and explore more."

Ben considered the different roads. "So, which way do we go now? Or do we wait here for our escort?"

Joe stopped and glanced around. "I don't see any escort." He surveyed the crowd. "No one stands out. Maybe we arrived early, moved quicker down the hill than they expected."

"So do we wander about, shopping?"

"No way, a waste of time," Joe said. "If they aren't ready for us, then we'll make use of the opportunity to explore on our own."

"What if we're late to the meeting with Rudolph?" Ben asked.

"Not our problem," Joe said. "We'll get there when we get there, but no rush. We'll see the sights," he added, "and reconnoiter the enemy."

"I tend to agree," Tom said. "The more we know about this guy, the better."

"Patrick, can you keep Annie and the others together?" Ben said. "We'll head out to see what we can find."

"No problem," Patrick said. "We'll explore here and meet up later."

"So which way do we go?" Ben asked.

"We're already on this side, so I say to the right." Joe picked a road at random. "That road."

Eric said, "Make it so," then followed the group.

Ben pushed his way through, but the mass of people was too tight. "I can't move," he yelled back to the others.

"What's with these guys? Can't they see we want by?" Joe asked.

Tom tried to push an old man out of the way, but the people were packed together so tightly that there was no place for him to go.

Joe dropped his shoulder to bulldoze his way but was blocked. "Ben, should I use my sword?"

"Do you think you could?" Tom yelled.

"No!" Ben shouted. "Don't even try it. It's way too crowded. You wouldn't be able control it."

Joe pushed harder on the masses, but nothing moved.

"Forget this," Ben said. "We'll try heading to the left. It's not as crowded."

Tom headed left but ran into Eric. "Head back the other way."

Eric stumbled and backed up. Tom followed with Ben and Joe right behind.

"Come on, Eric, go frontwards," Tom complained. He grabbed Eric's shoulders and faced him the right direction.

The crowd opened up, and although the foursome managed to step forward a bit, the overall flow acted to push them deeper into the city.

Tom put his hands on Eric's back and pushed. "More to the left."

Eric nearly fell into the crowd. "I'm trying, I'm trying." He searched for an opening. "Hey, there's room here," he said as he stepped into a gap to his right.

"Not that way, Eric. Head to that side road," Joe shouted.

Ben stopped in the middle of the roadway. "Where's Trey? He could open up the crowd."

Tom kept pushing Eric, steering him by twisting his shoulders. "I can't see any of the others," he yelled back at Ben.

Suddenly the crowd dispersed, the roadway emptied, the hawkers quieted, and the shoppers at the stalls went about their business. Everyone ignored the newcomers.

"Wow, this place is weird," Ben said shaking his shoulders.

"Yeah. I've never seen anything like it," Tom agreed. He suddenly realized that he still had his hands on Eric's shoulders. He let go quickly. "Didn't mean to push you around like that."

"You did what you had to." Eric dusted off his shirt and shrugged.

"Should we try that again?" Ben asked, noticing the road to the right looked open. "There's no one in the way now."

"We could, but let's try a different road this time," Joe said as he other roads. "Does that one to the left look good?"

"All's as good as any," Eric said. "Right?"

"Right," Ben said.

Joe grinned. "No, left."

Ben laughed. "Yeah, not right, left."

Tom stepped towards the side road.

"Come on, Eric. We won't push you around anymore," Joe said, then added, "much."

Ben joined Tom, and they strode ahead. As they neared the next intersection, the crowd parted, but only for a mere moment as a shepherd rounded the corner, driving a herd of small sheep-like critters, blocking the entire width of the narrow road.

"Not that way," Ben said. "Let's try the next one up farther."

Eric shied away from the small, furry animals. "Yeah, the next one can't be as crowded with these smelly beasts."

Ben hid his smile. "That's fine with me. The next one to the left it is." He headed up the road.

Joe whined, "Are we there yet?"

Ben looked over his shoulder at him. "If you make me stop this car…"

Joe laughed. "If we keep going, we can meet our escorts half way."

"That's the plan," Ben said, as he walked along in the middle of the road. After passing the open doorways of a handful of shops, they came to another small intersection. "Should we turn here?" he asked.

"Looks good to me," Tom said. "Then again, they all look good to me."

As they stepped towards the side street, a wagon piled with hay rounded the corner. They slowed to let it pass, but a fuss ensued as the driver had an altercation with a lady carrying a baby and leading a small child. The problem was where the wagon had stopped: blocking the path they had in mind.

Ben shrugged. "Let's skip that one. Let's try the one on the other side. Should we try going back to the right again?"

"I'm game," Tom said. "Like Joe suggested, let's see what we can see of this place before we're forced to meet up with the boss guy."

"Yeah, reconnoiter!" Joe said.

Ben headed to the right, but he noticed that the roadway was flooded. Three men were digging in the road, trying to guide burbling water into a drainage ditch. "I don't think we want to get stuck in that mess," Ben said holding his nose.

"Yuck," Joe said. "Go ahead and pick the next one up."

Tom went ahead and approached the next lane. Smaller than the others, but still wide enough to fit through with ease. "Come on this way. It isn't packed at all. Should be no issue getting through."

"Finally," Ben said. He reached for Eric. "Come on, follow Tom."

As Ben caught up, he saw Tom in the middle of a horde. "You said this road was open?"

"The road *was* open, but then it filled up," Tom bellowed. "I don't know where they all came from."

Ben checked the road ahead. "That next one's open. What do you see, Joe?"

"Not this one, the next one, no, wait, the one after that." Joe glared. "This side, that side. The more we try, the more we get pushed closer to the middle of town. We were trying to avoid that. Can't we pick a road and *go* there?"

"We were trying," Ben said. "Do you have a suggestion?"

"Yeah…make a run for it. It doesn't make any difference whether it's open or not. We'll just sprint through."

"Tom? Next one up on the right. Just run?"

"Yeah, but don't forget about Eric."

Ben spotted him standing in the middle of the road. "Hey, Eric! Don't just stand there." He urged him on. "This way! Run!"

Eric trotted, then picked up speed, running at full tilt, so Ben joined Tom and Joe. They all raced for the next opening and were part way through when they hit a wall of people, jammed so tightly together that no one could move. They stood there, locked in place.

Ben ran into Tom, and Joe was motionless with his back against the mass, pushing in vain.

Eric ran, slamming right into Ben's back, stepped back stunned, stiffened as he stared, then yelled, "Why this beast with the many heads? Wherefore the hoi polloi, the great unwashed, the vulgar herd? Whence this blunt monster with uncountable heads, the still-discordant wavering multitude? Get ye hence, thou uncontrolled, nay, uncontrollable slime of humanity! Move aside, all. Stand not on the order of your going, but go at once! Be gone, I say!"

The crowd silenced. No one moved, least of all the adventurers. After a momentary pause, the typical hubbub of the streets slowly filtered back, and movement began again.

Joe stared. "And here I thought *I* was getting frustrated."

"We've met our escort." He glared at the crowd. "The way is upward and onward."

Ben stood in the middle of the road. "We should wait here and give the others a chance to catch up."

"I like that idea," Tom said, stepping to the side and signaling Joe to follow. They huddled, talking quietly, repeatedly peering at Eric. Ben could see Joe shrugging in response to Tom's questioning.

Eric kept an eye on Tom and Joe as he approached Ben. "Was I out of hand back there?"

"Not at all, Eric. You were as annoyed as we were at the situation."

"I tolerated it as long as I could, but then the irritation at being stymied became too extreme…I sorta blew up." Eric stared at his shoes.

Ben put his hand on Eric's shoulder. "This has been frustrating for all of us."

Eric's head snapped up as he sniffed. "Do you smell fresh bread?"

Ben closed his eyes and inhaled. "Yeah, I do." He rotated, trying to catch the aroma, then stopped, facing one of the shops down from the intersection. "You mean like what they have there?"

Eric twisted his head around slowly. "Yeah, like that." He followed the scent to the shop, stared at the fresh, hot loaves on display, then said, "Are you hungry, Ben?"

"No. I've been snacking on fruit bars. Do you want one?"

"That's nice of you, Ben, but what I'd truly like is some of that bread in there," Eric said as he walked through the door of the shop.

Ben hurried to catch up. "Do you plan on ordering from a picture menu? You don't speak the language, do you?"

Eric smiled. "Ah, but I do, the universal language: barter."

"What are you going to use for that?" Ben asked.

"These," Eric said as he pulled a handful of linked rings from his pocket. "I won them in the craps game."

"Keep track of how many you spend," Ben said. "So we can pay them back when we leave."

"Fine," Eric said, sighing. He caught the attention of the shopkeeper and pointed to the bread on display.

The shopkeeper launched into a long speech, which neither of the scouts understood, so Eric pointed again and jingled the rings at the bread.

The shopkeeper stared at the rings, then at the bread and frowned, stepping away from the display case. Eric rattled the rings again and looked expectantly at the bread. The shopkeeper held up his hands for them to wait, then he wiped his hands on his apron and invited the two scouts to join him behind the counter. They followed him into the back room where workers were rolling carts of dough back and forth. He led them into what had to be his office where he opened a cupboard and pulled out a chisel and small hammer. Then he walked to the table at the side of the room, gestured with the chisel at the rings that Eric was still holding, and dropped the hammer on the top of the table. It rang out, metal on metal.

Eric smiled. He flopped the linked rings onto the table, and the shopkeeper spread them out, counting links. He put the chisel on one link, then struck with the hammer, cutting off a short chain about a centimeter long. Then he picked up the rest of the rings and bowed as he handed them back to Eric.

Eric pocketed the rings and said, "That's all he wants for a loaf of bread? The worth of these chains is exceeding my expectations—I'm richer than I thought."

"Remember, you still have to give all that back to Shess' people when we leave, and you'll have to replace the missing links."

The shopkeeper walked them back to the work floor where workers rolled carts of raw dough into large, walk-in ovens. He pulled aside one of the carts as it came out and tapped the still warm loaves, picking one out of the middle. He offered it to Eric and brought them to a nearby table where a small, wooden tub sat. Then he picked up a second loaf, broke off a piece, and swiped it across the tub, drenching it in soft butter. He bit into it and smiled, then waited for Eric to do the same.

Eric followed suit, rubbing a piece of bread through the butter, then he stood there and watched as it soaked into the still warm bread. He bit in and slurped, butter running down his chin. "Oh, wow!" His eyes widened in satisfaction. "This is good stuff. Here, have a taste." He poked the bit-off piece at Ben, but the shopkeeper stepped in between, handing Ben his own loaf.

Ben dipped the fresh, still warm bread into the tub and tasted it. "Hey, this *is* good, and that's not plain butter either. It has an interesting flavor to it. Wouldn't it be nice to import this stuff back home? We'd make a fortune selling it."

"Interesting idea," Eric said, then leaned in close to the shopkeeper and spoke excessively loudly, "Yes. Good. We like."

The shopkeeper appeared to understand Eric as he beamed, bouncing happily. He yelled at one of the workers who ran across the room then returned quickly with a big cloth bag, which he then filled with a dozen or more loaves from the cart and handed to Eric.

"This much? I wanted to buy *one* loaf."

The shopkeeper was shocked at the dismay in Eric's voice, so he smacked the worker, picked up the tub of butter, and handed it to Eric as well. The questioning look on his face a request for approval.

"Fine. Good," Eric said overly loudly. "Thank you," he shouted.

"Eric, talking louder won't help with the language issue."

"Oh, sorry," he said to Ben, then bellowed to the shopkeeper, "Sorry!"

The shopkeeper bowed deeper, heading back to the front of the shop.

Ben shook his head at Eric. "We'd better get back out to the street. Tom and Joe will be wondering where we are."

As they were leaving, Eric stopped to examine the plumbing running across the ceiling above the ovens. "Those pipes are rather solid for venting smoke outside, aren't they?"

Ben tipped his head to see what Eric was talking about. Overhead a series of pipes circled the room. He followed them to a large, round, machine on the other side.

The shopkeeper noticed and pulled them over, so he could show it off. He grabbed a deep wooden trowel and scooped up a bunch of grain from a basket on the floor, placed the grain into a hole in the side of the machine, then pulled a lever. A whistle tooted, startling the two as the machine moved, making a loud grinding noise. The shopkeeper reached into a bucket at the bottom and pulled out a handful of dark, brown flour. He picked up a pinch between his finger and thumb, rubbed it, and let it float back into his hand.

Ben stared. "Do you see what that is, Eric?"

"It's a flour mill, a *big* flour mill." He pinched a bit of powder from the shopkeeper's hand. "Grinds fairly fine flour, too."

"It's not an ordinary mill, Eric. It's a *steam-powered* mill. More technology that doesn't fit in with this world."

Eric bit into his loaf and shrugged. "Makes good bread is all I know."

Ben grabbed Eric's arm and led him out of the shop. "We need to get moving." Once on the street, he spotted both Tom and Joe standing in front of a shop serving fried meat on a stick. They were staring at the sizzling meat slowly rotating on a spit being turned by a small child.

Eric sauntered up. "You guys hungry?" he asked, holding his bag of bread. "I have butter, too."

"That would be wonderful, Eric," Tom said. "Thanks."

Joe grabbed a loaf and gnawed on it. "Hey, this stuff is tasty. Where'd you get it?"

Eric stuck out his elbow. "Over there."

"At a bakery using *steam power* to grind their flour," Ben said emphatically.

"Steam?" Tom asked. "Where'd they get that? It's well beyond anything we've seen so far."

"No clue," Ben said. "So, did anyone else show up while we were off shopping?" Ben asked.

"Nope. Nothing going on out here," Joe said around a bite of bread.

Ben checked the roads in all directions, trying to see over the crowd of natives shuttling back and forth. He was barely able to see the wall where the gateway was. "I know we split up to cover more ground, but I don't see the rest of our group. Do you?"

Eric searched the area. "Nothing seen." Then he hesitated, his gaze turning skywards. "It's getting kinda dark, too. Are we going to get anywhere before it gets to be too late?" He bit into another loaf of bread.

"Yes. We'll find an inn nearby in case we don't get all the way to the…the whatever." Ben noticed the look on Eric's face. "Hey, Eric, would you call it a castle?" Ben asked, trying to distract Eric from their dire situation.

Eric scrutinized the structure deep in the city, the location they were doomed to visit. "Less like a true European medieval castle than a mid-twentieth-century government stronghold, typical of Eastern Europe, possibly even of Russian design." He frowned. "The architecture is somewhat reminiscent of the communist regime of the mid to late twentieth century, wouldn't you say?"

"Yeah, it does." Ben said slowly. Well, I did manage to get his mind off of our present problems.

Eric glanced back in the opposite direction and pointed with a loaf of bread. "That gateway, on the other hand, certainly defies normal analysis. Having aspects of an entrance to both a castle, though lacking any visible portcullis or draw bridge, and a financial depository, with all that hardware securing it. That door is certainly designed to be impenetrable, as well it should be, but also not something to be expected here."

"Yeah," Ben agreed. "This town does seem like a tough nut to crack."

Eric reached out to pat him on the back. "Well phrased, Ben, well phrased!"

Ben wasn't certain what to say in response to a compliment like that, but he didn't have long to consider it because suddenly a small flash lit up the sky. He watched a small light slowly drift to the side as an upper breeze pushed it along. He asked Joe, "Hey, did any of you bring flares?"

Joe swallowed his bite of bread quickly and stared up. "Someone obviously did, but I didn't hear of it."

"Maybe it's Robb. You saw what he was doing in battle, didn't you?" Tom asked.

"Yeah," Ben said. "It could be him. Let's head that way…as long as the crowd lets us."

Tom stepped tentatively back along their path, then tried again, and a third time. "No problem so far."

Ben and Joe followed as Eric watched and waited.

"Come on, Eric. You can make it," Ben encouraged.

Eric followed quickly. "I wanted to make certain that we weren't going to end up in another mosh pit."

Another flare burst from farther ahead, lighting one of the intersections they had passed through earlier—no obelisk, merely a wider spot where crossroads met, the scene of yet another blocked passageway.

"Up there, where the burst sewer pipe was. That's where the flares are coming from," Ben yelled.

They entered the intersection from one side and saw Annie and Patrick leading the rest of the group in from the other side.

"Hey! Annie!" Ben shouted.

She yelled, "Find anything?"

"Not much," Ben said.

The groups met in the middle of a small plaza and a dozen conversations ensued as everyone caught up on what had been happening, and Eric shared his bread with everyone.

Annie frowned. "Have you had any troubles with the crowd?"

"You mean like not being able to go where we want?" Ben asked. "Being able to go where they let us and nowhere else?"

"Yeah. Exactly like that. What's going on?"

Tom joined them. "Remember what the guards said at the top of the hill?"

"That we were going to be met when we arrived," Annie said. "And be taken to the boss guy?"

"Patrick translated it as there would be an 'escort' to meet us. We didn't see anyone, but I think they found us." Ben frowned at the crowds.

Joe frowned. "Put a damper on our reconnoiter."

"We couldn't go where we wanted to," Tom said.

"We didn't get far either," Annie said. "That's when Trey noticed Eric wasn't with us. He thought he'd lost him in the crowd somewhere."

"We hadn't noticed," Ben said. "But he had followed us. It didn't bother me too much because I could keep an eye on him. Didn't think about you missing him."

"Anyway, we split up to find him," Annie said. "Trey and Bear went left with Patrick, Carl and Fred went back to the fields outside the city with the *shmahseespe* to search, and I convinced John to help me look up the road to the right."

"Where did Shess go?" Ben asked.

Patrick shrugged. "I think he went with Carl and Fred. I didn't see."

"So how successful was that searching?"

Annie glared at the crowd. "Not very. None of us got far."

"The crowd barged in?"

"Yeah," Annie said. "Blocked no matter which way we went."

"Same thing happened to us. The crowd *is* the 'escort' they sent to meet us." Ben frowned. "We even tried to push our way through at one point, but everyone closed up on us."

Tom glanced back at Eric. "Yeah, and you should have heard Eric. He cussed at the crowd. It sounded like cussing. I've never heard anything like it, not outside of a Shakespeare play."

Annie laughed. "Oh, yeah, that's Eric, quite erudite," she stood tall and waggled her head, "but a little out of touch with reality."

Ben raised an eyebrow. "Out of touch? Nice way to put it." He grinned. "We were afraid that he was going to wear his Trekkie uniform on the trip."

"Ah, that *does* explain some of the things I've noticed about him," Tom said thoughtfully. "I can see how he and Eugene would get along."

"His uncle? Yeah. They're two of a kind," Ben said.

"Did you know that Eugene was one of the founders of the company?" Tom asked. "He works directly with Frank on the Door. The two of them were working quite a while trying to figure out how to power up the whole system before they brought in more help."

"Wow," Ben said. "I knew Eric's uncle worked at that place, but I didn't know he was *that* well connected."

"Eric must consider you guys to be pretty good friends to bring you along," Tom said.

"Well, we did put up with him in scouts for years," Ben said. "We deserve something for that."

Annie smacked Ben. "You should be nicer than that. Eric might be strange, but he tries."

"Strange is a good word for it," Ben said. "So, Tom, how did you get involved in all this?"

"I'd been working on hunting trips, mostly big game in Africa, when Eugene and the rest started sending out exploratory trips, and they pulled me in. The first six months or so we just did the same as I had been doing before…just not Africa, but then they decided to expand their clientele."

"Expand their clientele? How's that?" Ben asked.

"I think it was mostly Eric's doing. I heard him trying to convince Eugene that the general public would be interested, that he should bring in outside folks to give it a try."

"What did Eugene have in mind instead?"

"Not so much Eugene as Frank. With his military background, he wanted something similar to NASA. Government control, with scientists doing Lewis and Clark type explorations. Nothing with the word 'fun' in it."

"We owe him…for thinking of us first," Ben said, "or even at all. I didn't know he could be so influential." He paused. "Maybe we should be nicer to him."

Annie poked Ben's arm. "*Maybe* we should be nicer to him? Of course we should be nice to him, but because it's nice to be nice, not because of who he knows."

Tom put his arm across Annie's shoulders. "Yeah, what she said."

"Fine," Ben said. "We should be nice to him, but where is he?"

"Right in the middle," Annie said. "There next to Robb."

"I see him. By the way, was that Robb that sent up a signal or did someone bring actual flares?"

"It was Robb," Annie answered. "When we realized that we weren't getting anywhere separately, I figured we should all get back together, so I asked him if he could send up a smaller version of the fireballs he'd been using in battle."

"Well, it worked fine," Tom said. "We're all here, but now, Ben, which way do we go?"

Ben thought a moment. "We could see where our 'escort' wants us to go. Any other ideas?"

"Well, you might want to hear what Patrick discovered before we get too far," Annie said.

"Oh, yeah. I asked him to find out why Shess had been hanging back so much, so what did he learn?"

"I could tell you," Annie said. "But that would be third hand, and I'd probably mess it up. Find him, and you can ask him yourself."

Tom stepped up into the back of a nearby wagon, earning a glare from the owner trying to sell his wares. He peered across the impromptu reunion. "There he is, on the other side of Eric, next to Trey." He shouted. "Patrick! Over here!" He stepped off the wagon, and the peasant frowned, pulling his load farther up the road. "He's on the way."

Patrick trotted up. "Hey, Ben. How's it going? Getting where you want to go?" He smirked.

"Not likely," Ben said. "You gonna tell us what you know?"

"Nah. Not enough time." He paused for effect. "But I *will* tell you what I learned from the *shmahseespe.*"

"I'll bite," Ben said. "What did you find out?"

"Mostly from Shankaktos, a talkative fellow, but it was confirmed by the others. Shess *did* know of this place but didn't bother to mention it because he never thought we'd end up here. In fact, he never thought *he'd* ever end up here." Patrick paused. "No one else expected to ever be here either, but they *have* all heard the stories. Not taught in school, but often talked about…by the older men in the village, including his grandfather."

"So all we have is rumors?" Ben asked. "And old rumors at that?"

"Sounds to me like old wives' tales," Tom said.

"Possibly so, but these rumors are well substantiated. This Rudolph guy came out of nowhere, popped up in the middle of *nimre* territory a couple generations ago. He set himself up as their leader, though he's not a *nimre* himself." Patrick walked to a bench and sat, stretching his legs out.

The others followed as Ben asked, "So, what did he do, as their leader?"

"He organized them, gave them stuff to do, and trained them, keeping them isolated up north for a while, but after a dozen or so years with him in charge, the *nimre* spread south into civilized space…nothing much, except minor attacks here and there."

"What did the people here do?" Annie asked.

"Well, they had been trying to keep the *nimre* under control, limited to the less desirable lands to the north, but with his lead, their interference with the civilized folks increased to an extreme level."

"Ah, and that's when the folks in charge became involved, right?"

"Exactly right," Patrick said. "The main government south of here sent up troops from the big cities to support the smaller cities closest to the unmarked *nimre* boundaries. At that time Shess' city was far from the border, but as the incursions continued, the border moved south, and now it's right on the edge."

"Sounds bad," Ben said.

"It's worse. When this Rudolph guy would approach a city to 'attack,' he had pretty unusual tactics. He would come into the city and talk with the local mayor types, offering to accept their surrender, but no one took him seriously."

"He's kinda gutsy," Tom said.

"That's not all. As he'd leave the meeting, he would say that he was going to curse the city, that he'd be back in a couple weeks to dump the dead and keep what he wanted. Then he'd basically leave them alone."

"That's it?"

"Well, except for some minor forays he'd send into the cities. The attackers used a catapult-like device, unknown here, and not doing any real damage, then they'd walk away, even leaving the catapult behind."

"Strange method for conquering a city. Curses don't work," Ben said.

"In most cases, yes, but this time they did work. Within days, people would start getting sick and dying. From what I heard, they went through some pretty awful times. Their hair would fall out, their teeth would fall out, and their bones would become brittle, breaking when they tried to walk. Eventually dark bruises would cover their bodies, then become open sores."

"Same as when the black plague hit Europe," Annie said.

"Yeah, like that. Then after two weeks, he would come back and do exactly what he'd said: clean out the dead and take what he wanted."

"Wow!" Ben said. "All that with curses?" He scratched his head. "Evidently they work here, but what kind of curse was it?"

"No one knows for certain, but after he conquered a half-dozen cities, when he'd walk up to the next one and announce himself, they'd run, leaving the entire city to him without a shot being fired. The local armies were helpless against him, and they pulled back, letting him have what he wanted."

"What stopped him? He could have conquered the entire planet." Ben said.

"If he had, I wouldn't have a job," Tom said.

Eric wandered up to Ben toting his bag of bread. "It's getting late. Where was that inn that you mentioned?"

Ben studied the small square. "The way the streets are lit up, I hadn't noticed it getting late. Those aren't electric lights, are they?"

"Most likely kerosene, couldn't possibly be gas, so someone must come through and fill them up every day as well as light them each night. Too much organization in this city he has here," Tom said.

"Yeah, and still too much advanced knowledge," Ben said. "Patrick, can you find us some place to stay for the night?"

"Should be easy." He chatted with the locals, coming back to report, "I've been told about a place a couple blocks ahead."

"Can we get there? Or are we going to be blocked?" Tom asked.

"We won't know until we try," Patrick said.

Ben faced the rest of the group. "It's too late to continue wandering the streets, so Patrick will guide us to an inn for the night."

"I will?" Patrick stared at Ben. "Oh, yeah, I will." He strode off through the crowd without any effort.

Tom followed. "No resistance so far. Keep going," he shouted to Patrick.

After two uneventful blocks, Patrick stopped before an open door, a sign above his head. "I can't read it, but the symbol is right." He paused, then said, "This must be the right place."

They all went in, with Patrick still leading the way. A quick conversation with the innkeeper and bowls were set up, followed by mugs. Serving wenches came by filling the bowls with slop and the mugs with a dark brew. Everyone found seats, though Shess and most of his people sequestered themselves into one corner of the room.

Ben pulled Patrick aside. "Hey, what's this going to cost us, and what kind of payment do they take? I don't want Shess and Tom to have to cover us all the time."

Patrick pulled Ben aside. "That's not an issue. When I asked about rooms, he said dinner was included, so I asked 'Included in what?' And he said that Rudolph was covering the tab."

"So we were expected here as well as at the top of the pass. This Rudolph guy is starting to get on my nerves." Ben shrugged. "Well, we can try to enjoy the meal," he said as he sat, watching Patrick find a spot across the room.

All was quiet as everyone ate, until Eric pulled out his bag of bread. This innkeeper didn't serve *that* kind of fancy bread here, only the normal stuff. Having *that* kind of bread meant that all the wenches in the room kept coming by to see that his mug was filled to the brim, much to his consternation. All the scouts laughed at his predicament, though silently jealous, wishing that they could garner that much attention.

Once everyone was satiated for the moment, conversations broke out again. Ben tracked down Patrick to get more details about Rudolph. Tom and Annie joined the conversation.

"So, other than saving Tom's job," Ben said, "Why did Rudolph stop his takeover of the planet?"

"No one knows. They say that once he picked through and kept what he wanted, he'd move on to the next city. After taking certain things from each city, he had it all shipped back here, as material to build this place."

"What kinds of things did he take?" Tom asked.

"Mostly tools and weapons, but he also dismantled the buildings, but again taking specific pieces and parts, leaving other buildings untouched."

"That's odd, but then again, most of what's happening here is odd," Tom said. "He wouldn't set himself up in the city itself?"

"After pillaging, he'd evacuate his men and leave the city empty."

"And the cities he left? What happened to them?" Ben asked.

"The ones that weren't cursed were reoccupied, but the ones he 'cursed' are *still* cursed. Whatever kind of curse he used, it stayed in effect. People moving back into those cities after decades still sicken and die within the same two weeks' span, so they've been marked as dead zones and are now generally avoided."

Tom blinked. "And somehow we've managed to miss running into any of those cities?"

"Well, most of them are farther west." Patrick put his hand on Tom's arm. "And your Door opens on the eastern edge of the civilized area, the north eastern edge."

"With the way they can't control the aim," Tom said. "They *could* have opened the Door right in the middle of a town." He gasped. "And in the middle of a cursed city would have been worse."

Patrick shuddered. "Yeah."

"Too bad they haven't figured out how to aim it yet," Ben said. "Then you could pick where to land."

Tom shrugged. "Maybe someday."

"So it was merely a fluke that you ended up out in the boonies," Annie said.

"A convenient fluke," Tom said. "On our first few trips, we could see that big desert…and the mountains on the far side, to the east."

"Those are the mountains you said glow at night?" Ben asked.

Tom smiled at Ben's interest. "Yes, those mountains, but don't even think of taking your troops there, Ben. We won't be visiting there soon, not until we get proper transportation to cross that desert."

Ben thought of the wagon Tom had been standing on. "You mean like a wagon or something?"

"Well, I was thinking of something closer to a deuce-and-a-half, but as we can't get anything like that to work here, we'd have to settle for wagons pulled by oxen."

"Oxen or those big dogs," Annie suggested.

Patrick piped up. "Oh, yeah, that's another thing that this Rudolph guy did. He domesticated wild animals, but *that* advance spread throughout the whole civilization."

"That was one thing Rudolph did good for this place," Annie said. "It's an ill wind that blows *no* good."

Ben though about Eric.

"Anyway," Tom continued, "East was out, so we headed west, found the river, then followed it downstream, figuring we'd find civilization, if there was any. Once we made contact with the natives, we didn't bother going north."

"So where'd all the people in this city come from?" Ben asked, seeing many different ethnicities. "They don't look like they *all* came from *nimre* stock."

"They didn't," Patrick said. "Although Rudolph did capture *some* folks from the cities he conquered, more folks saw his 'supernatural' powers and switched sides, swearing allegiance to him. They wanted to be on the winning side. That's how he built up this city so quickly. You can't do big projects like this exclusively with slaves, too much effort to keep them under control."

"And he's been sitting here ever since then? He's completely stopped his attacks?" Ben asked.

"That's what they said. For the last dozen years, he's been quiet, mostly keeping to himself. Though he has established unofficial trade routes, but everyone still wonders what he has in mind for the long haul. They still fear him and his unknown powers."

"So would I," Ben said. "We've seen his crowd control."

"Yeah, it is a neat trick, I must say. I wonder how he does it," Tom said.

"Well, we might be able to find out tomorrow, when we meet him," Patrick said.

"That said, we should encourage everyone to get to sleep," Ben said taking a quick glance for sleeping places. "Is there room for all of us?"

"The innkeeper has rooms upstairs for most of us," Patrick said. "And the rest can sack out by the fireplace right here."

"That should work." Ben said. "We can put the women closest to the toilets…I mean, closest to the door, so they can get outside in a hurry." He paused. "Unless there *are* toilets inside. Are there?" he asked with a grin.

"Yes, there are," Patrick said. "The sewer break out in the main road doesn't affect this establishment, not according to the innkeeper."

"Wait, you mean they *do* have indoor plumbing, *and* sewers?" Ben asked. "I was kidding." He hesitated. "At least I thought I was kidding. Well, Tom, there's yet another mystery to consider."

"With a city this size," Tom said, "I figured they'd have to have *some* kind of sewage system, but I assumed it would be chamber pots and gutters in the streets, not real indoor plumbing," He stared at Ben. "I'm getting to the point where nothing surprises me."

* * *

The smell of bacon drifting throughout the inn announced morning. Ben hoped that it was bacon that he smelled. Either way, one whiff of a hot breakfast and everyone was on the move. The lines at the toilets weren't as bad as Ben had imagined. Although the fixtures weren't porcelain, they were fully functional and even had a pull chain for flushing. Ben would have to talk to Tom about that later.

Breakfast was served, eaten, and left for the innkeeper to clean up, Ben shooed the scouts out into the street, and Shess, still saying little, followed with the rest. "So, do we trust the crowd to guide us, or is there another way to get through this city?" Ben asked Tom.

"Well, we were kind of assuming that we were heading to the city center, but now, I don't know if that's where they want us to go."

"Yeah, well it would be nice to have a real escort," Ben said, "so we don't have to wander through the city, bumping into invisible walls. It's like being a blind mouse in a maze." Wondering where Patrick was, he asked, "What would you say to getting directions? We can have Patrick check with the innkeeper or anyone else that might know."

"He could do that." Tom saw Patrick across the room. "There he is." He stood up. "Patrick! We have a job for you."

Patrick trotted across the room. "What's up?" he asked.

Tom waited for Ben. "Your idea."

Ben sat up. "Any possibility of *asking* where they want us to go?"

"You don't like being manhandled by the crowd?" Patrick chuckled. "Neither do I. Give me a moment, and I'll let you know what I find." Patrick scurried back into the inn.

As they were waiting, Joe strolled up. "I feel like I'm back home in the army, all hurry up and wait." He chortled.

"We're getting directions," Tom said. "So we don't keep butting up against the crowds again."

"Ah, I like that thought. Plan ahead." Joe said. "Nothing against you, Ben. There's no way you could have predicted where we are now." He smiled. "And, Tom, I certainly don't remember seeing anything in the flyer about getting kidnapped, fighting an entire army, engaging in political battles, and being hustled by mindless crowds, did you?"

"I'm in the middle of this right along with you guys," Tom replied.

Joe slapped Tom on the back. "And you're doing a fine job of keeping us alive. How much time did you spend in the military?" he asked.

"Standard six-year assignment, eleven-bravo, infantry, grunt. My dad was thirty-one-bravo." Tom grinned at Joe. "Though he still says ninety-five-bravo."

"An MP? That takes guts," Joe said appreciatively. "You've done well with your training." He tapped his own left shoulder and said, "There'd be a Ranger tab there if I were in uniform."

"Yes, I've seen what you've been doing with these guys, even keeping Shess' men in line."

"Rangers lead the way!" Joe shouted, then shrugged. "Shess has some good guys, and I have to work with what I have, right?" Joe asked.

"Right. OCS?"

"Maybe later. I want to get a good bunch of missions under my belt first."

"Well, let's see if we can count *this* one as a success, *then* you can go back tell some *real* war stories."

Joe checked out the roofline along the street, surveying the early morning crowd. "They wouldn't believe me." He laughed. "Hey, *I* wouldn't believe me."

"What did the flyer say about the trip? 'An experience like you've never had before.' Wasn't that it?" Ben asked.

"Well, they certainly lived up to *that* promise," Joe said. "Hey, here comes Patrick. What's the plan for today?"

"The innkeeper says that if we turn left at the next intersection and then head up three blocks, we won't be able to miss it."

"Easy enough," Joe said. "I'll head back with my platoon and keep your backside clean."

After Joe was out of earshot, Tom leaned to Ben. "I'm starting to like that guy."

"He's definitely handy to have available in the kinds of situations we seem to keep ending up in," Ben said.

"You know what, Ben? You have a good group overall: Trey for strength, Patrick with his languages, Joe has a military background…and the way he handles a sword…" Tom paused, then continued with his list. "Carl can track anything, and I still can't believe Robb with his fire thing."

Annie poked Tom in the ribs and cleared her throat.

"Oh, yeah, and Annie's useful, too!" Tom quickly added as he circled her waist with his arm.

Ben shook his head. "Yeah, well, we can't stand here in a mutual appreciation society. We need to get going if we're going to get there any time soon," Ben said, then yelled at the rest of the group. "Head out!" He stepped off in the direction Patrick had given them.

They went less than a hundred meters before they came to the first intersection, so Ben directed the group to the left, then followed, rounding the corner. This street looked similar to the others, though wider than the side street where the inn stood but narrower than the main road by the gate. A couple blocks later, they came to a larger crossroad with a massive obelisk rising up from the center of a circular pool. Everyone stopped to stare at the monument.

Ben searched for Patrick. "Hey, can you come read this for us?"

Patrick worked his way through the crowd and stood next to Ben. "Well, I can try, but the script is different from everything else I've seen here, quite different." He pulled out his notepad and flipped through the pages. He frowned and flipped more. "Not just different, totally different. Nothing matches." He frowned at the characters running the length of the obelisk. "I don't know what it says."

"Seems to me as if it's someone's name, a girl's name."

Everyone stared as Eric spoke up.

"You can read that?" Patrick asked.

"Well, not *read* it, but I recognize a Cyrillic font when I see one."

Patrick slapped himself on the forehead. "Ha! That's why it's not in my book. It's not from here. It's from Earth! It's Russian. And it *is* a girl's name. How did you know that, Eric?"

Eric leaned in closer to the letters. "See the ending? It's feminine, and I assumed a name would be the most likely thing etched into the obelisk—a shrine *in memoriam*."

Ben grabbed Tom's arm. "*That* could explain a lot. The Russians beat us here."

Tom jerked around. "The Russians have the tech to get here? I'll have to warn Eugene."

"Not necessarily Russian," Eric said. "But definitely Eastern European, though, with a touch of the British Empire. Notice the pool surrounding the monolith? See how the water comes right up to the edge *all* the way around. The edge is rounded like that, so you can't see it at all. It's called a reflecting pool. That's more of a western European characteristic." Eric continued talking as he circled the pool. "Excellent job of levelling it, too. Not one edge is even a tiny bit higher than the others." He reached out and slapped the surface of the water splashing water over the edge. "Observe how any excess water is directed by the curved edge into a drain circling the entire pool." He leaned over the edge, studying the middle. "And notice how evenly the transverse wave spreads. Every crest and trough equal across the whole thing. The base of the pool must be exceptionally smooth and even."

Annie snickered and poked Tom. "And we have Eric in case we need an encyclopedia."

"Well, *someone* was here before you, Tom," Ben said. "That must be who Rudolph is." He stared at the buildings around them. "But when did he have the time to build all this?"

Tom shrugged. "From rumors I've heard in the lab, although they had developed the *concept* of the Door years ago, it needed a lot of power to open big enough for anyone to get through. That was barely over a year ago." He slowly perused the buildings surrounding them. "Nowhere near enough time for any of this to be done."

"Now I'm intrigued to meet this Mr. Rudolph Bentnose," Ben said. "I think we're done sightseeing. Where do we go from here?" he asked.

Eric rotated and stretched out an arm. "I'd dare say that *that* would be our destination."

Everyone froze and stared at the imposing building before them. Dark walls, practically black, filled their view. As tall as it was wide, the edifice was an immense cube sitting on a pedestal of hundreds of steps, all leading up to nowhere but solid, blank walls.

"The innkeeper said that we couldn't miss it, and he was right," Ben said, breaking the silence. "So what now? Is there a door up there?"

"We did come up on it from the side because of our detour to the inn," Tom said. "If we had continued up the main street, we would be coming up on it from what would be the front."

"So we circle the building?" Ben asked.

Tom glanced back. "Where's Joe, and his guys? I'd like to have them close at hand."

"That would be them, heading down that alley," Ben said. "Already starting a skirting maneuver."

"Why are they doing that? Are they expecting an attack from a building?" Tom noticed the empty area in front of the building. "Not even any guards standing duty."

"Good question, but Joe thinks there's *something* he needs to do."

"Do we follow them?"

"No. That would draw undue attention to their movements. If anyone *is* watching, we want to draw their attention to *us*. That'll give Joe and his guys more freedom to do what they need to." Ben walked to the open space in front of the building. As he walked by the corner of the stairs, he looked closer. "The stairs are shiny black, but not shiny from being used. They're polished all the way across each step."

"Possibly polished," Eric said as he bent to rub the surface, frowning. "Interesting. They appear to be made of obsidian, volcanic glass, resulting from intense heat on certain rock types." He ran his hand along the steps. "The edges of each step can be extremely sharp, so be careful." He jerked his hand back and checked his finger for blood. "Ancient cavemen used obsidian for spear tips due to the cutting edges they could easily make."

"Steps of obsidian? That must have taken some advanced expertise," Ben said. "Do you think anything like that could be built back home?"

"Highly unlikely," Eric said. "It would be immensely difficult, and there'd be no reason for it. Obsidian, being a glass, would be subject to weathering and cracking. Besides, sharp edges on stairs would be counter-productive. Can you imagine if it rained, and you slipped on the slick surface? Hitting those edges would slice you to ribbons," he explained. "If they didn't want you to leave, they could flood those stairs…no one would try to escape that way." Then he paused, realizing the potential. "Ingenious."

Tom followed but shied away from the stairs, putting himself between them and Annie. "Then why have stairs made of obsidian? To show off?"

"Why else would anyone build such a place as this?" Eric said. "To sway your visitors. You have to convince them to kowtow before your greatness." He half bowed. "It's done all the time by the big-wigs in politics."

"Ah, yes, but it's still all a façade," Ben added, smiling at Eric. "A case of pay no attention to the man behind the curtain."

Eric agreed emphatically. "Yes, the reality of many is belied by their appearance."

"Huh?" Tom said looking around. "What curtain?"

"Never mind," Patrick said. "It's scout code for keep your eyes open. Don't get distracted by the humbug."

"If you say so," Tom said slowly.

Ben stopped in the middle of the square in front and squinted. "It's bright up there. From the side it was dark, but from out here in front, it glows as if it were on fire. I can barely see if there's a door in that wall, and it's a huge wall. What would you say, a half-dozen meters tall?"

"Close to a dozen," Tom said.

"Not at all," Eric said. "With the slope of the stairs, the shine of the building, and the fact that you are already viewing *up* to the *bottom* of the wall, the angle makes it look as if it were that tall. It is *also* an illusion. Probably only a couple meters tall, standard height." He squinted. "Though the glow emanating from that wall is interesting." Eric glanced back at the still rising sun. "The height of the adjacent mountain makes the first direct light hit the wall at such a high angle that it is probable you could see a second shadow…behind you."

Annie looked. "You're right. I can see one, but no one else but you would know to look for it, Eric."

"Physics bears out the truth," he said. "Remember physics is phun."

Ben groaned. "You've been using that pun ever since you read it on that pocket slide rule in Jr. High."

Eric smiled. "Haven't needed it yet on this trip. I should have brought it anyway…just in case."

Tom shrugged.

"Do we head up now?" Annie asked.

Ben checked the square. "Joe is in place and ready." He noticed the *shmahseespe* were cowering at the edges. "It would be nice if Shess and his men could join us, but they seem afraid of this place." He shrugged. "We're it."

"Who first?" Tom asked.

"You and Annie with me in the front, Eric, you and Patrick follow, but keep your distance in case something happens."

"Let's go," Annie said, taking Ben's arm in her left and Tom's in her right.

The three of them marched to the stairs and up to the door.

In lockstep, the three climbed the shiny, black stairs. They were part way up when Ben slipped. "Wow. The rubber soles on my boots are *designed* to grip, so can you imagine trying to climb these steps in a leather soled shoe? It's good that Shess stayed behind."

Farther up the flight of steps, Annie called for a rest. "I've done stairs at the gym, but nothing like this. With the sun shining on my back *and* reflecting from that door right into my eyes, it's hotter than I expected, and the steps are taller than I'm used to," she said.

Tom put his hands on his knees and stretched. "We'll make it."

She breathed deeply. "Anyone think about counting the steps?"

Ben checked on Eric and Patrick. They were close behind, still following, slowly but steadily. "Oh, I'm certain *someone* will give us a proper count, as soon as we get to the top."

Tom shaded his eyes, trying to see the building. "I still can't see much detail. The glow in the middle must be the door, but it's reflecting so much light that nothing about the building itself is visible. It fades away, a big, black hole in the sky."

"Should have brought sunglasses," Ben said as he looked across the city. "Impressive view from here."

Tom agreed. "And it'll be even better from the top."

"Well, we aren't there yet, so let's keep going," Ben said.

Annie put her canteen away. "Ready."

They trudged up more steps, getting closer. Finally, they reached the top, stumbling onto the platform in front of the door itself.

"I lost track of the steps along the way and thought there was one more," Annie said. "I could even see it."

"Yeah, you get into a monotonous pattern and want to keep going even if it ends," Ben said. "The illusion of more fooled me, too. Must be because of the reflection." He waited for the two followers. "I'm certain we'll get an explanation when *they* get here."

Annie smiled. "Eric *is* helpful, isn't he?"

Ben moaned as he bent over, rubbing his thighs. "What a workout. I'll bet Rudolph has an elevator somewhere."

"I wouldn't doubt it," Tom said. "He has so many other things here."

"Either that or he never goes out," Annie said.

Ben dragged himself closer to the building as they waited for the last two to arrive at the top. He slid his hand across the wall. "Interesting brickwork. I've never seen such dark bricks, and the mortar is dark, too, a shade of brown. It blends in at a short distance, making it look like a solid wall." He hobbled to the wide, double door to examine it. "It's shiny, metallic. It didn't look like that from down there in the square."

Annie limped up to run her hand across the door. "So smooth and polished, as if it were gold plated."

Ben tapped on it, not expecting anyone to answer, and it rang like a bell. He stared. "It can't be pure gold, can it?"

"I wouldn't put it past Rudolph to have a solid gold door," Tom said.

Annie spoke up. "Solid gold? That would be something!"

"Unlikely," Eric said as he arrived at the top of the stairs. He stopped to catch his breath, then rubbed his legs and continued. "Not a good material to work with, too soft…and heavy, and it certainly wouldn't ring like that—an alloy, I'd assume."

"Besides, where would he get that much?" Annie asked.

"Gold may be uncommon on our world, but that doesn't mean it's the same here," Eric said. "Likely, the composition of minerals is entirely dissimilar. In fact, Tom, the lack of an iron core and its accompanying electromagnetic field might explain why electricity doesn't work here."

"I'll mention that to Eugene and see what he says," Tom said. "Ben, you said something about importing bread when we get home. I have a different idea." He put his hand on the door. "We could do gold instead."

Ben stared at Tom. "Oh!"

"Get me a wagon to carry *one* of these doors." Tom grinned. "And I'll get you enough bread to keep you happy for the rest of your life."

Eric stepped closer and ran his hand along the edge of the door. "No hinges, too. That means it swings *in* to open, as expected."

"So why couldn't we see it shining?" Ben asked. "From down there, it looked as dark as the building itself."

"See how the door itself is recessed back from this large area, this patio?" Eric asked as he stepped to the top of the stairs behind them and looked down. "It's the angle again." He smiled. "Rudolph must like trigonometry. I'll have to ask him."

"Save your questions until *after* we get Melvin," Ben said.

Patrick examined the relief on the left door. "Intriguing design." He put his hand on the door. "Eric, check this out."

Eric ran his fingers across the carvings. "Hieroglyphs? Egyptian?"

"I don't think so," Patrick said. "The pictographs aren't familiar, but the links between them are what caught my eye." He started at the top of the door, barely a meter above his head.

Eric followed his gaze. "Yes, they form a pattern."

"Exactly," Patrick said. "One dot, two dots, three, then four, making a triangle of ten. I'm certain that that's a Pythagorean symbol."

"Yes," Eric agreed. "It's called a tetractys. One of the secret symbols the Pythagorean society used. I'm impressed, Patrick."

"Hey, I'm no dummy."

"That's apparent, considering your command of the local language." Eric swept his hat off his head. "I bow to your superior knowledge."

Tom frowned. "Can we get back to the door, you guys?"

Eric recovered and stepped back to study the other door. "Fascinating way to count here. The dots progress from one to three, then there's a bar. The enumeration then continues with a bar representing four. Mayan?"

"Three dots followed by a bar." Patrick studied the next symbols on the door. "And three bars with three dots are then followed by a box. Yes, it does look Mayan, but in groups of four instead of five. Strange counting method," Patrick said. "And somewhat primitive."

"Speaking of counting, did anyone count the steps?" Annie asked.

Eric tore his gaze from the door. "I had estimated there to be greater than a hundred steps, possibly upwards of two hundred, but from the angle, I wasn't able to more accurately calculate the total."

"So how many steps *are* there?"

"I counted exactly two-hundred-fifty-six steps. Why they used that particular number, I can't say. It certainly doesn't match up with any form of architecture I've studied before. Not a multiple of ten, nor even five as a subset of ten, not prime, not magic, not triangular, though it is a square. The square of sixteen."

"I've heard of primes, but what's magic about numbers?" Tom asked.

Annie shushed Tom. "Never mind him, Eric. You can give the lecture on magic numbers later, after this is all done."

Tom amiably kept his mouth shut, though he did pull Annie aside for a quick whisper. He then spoke to the whole group, "Analyzing the door and everything is good, but I have a question that's bugging me."

Eric raised an eyebrow, appearing noticeably Vulcan. "Oh? And what might that be?"

Tom shrugged. "Has anyone found the doorbell?"

Ben's loud laugh was quickly joined by Patrick's, but then they all froze as another, deeper laugh echoed from nowhere. Everyone spun to find the source of the menacing outburst, but they were alone.

Suddenly, silently, the doors swung inward, opening to a dark passage, the floor illuminated by the long rays of the early sun.

"Enter, please," a disembodied voice commanded.

Eric shook as he obediently stepped towards the gaping hole. Annie reached out to stop him, but he was out of reach. She glanced back at Tom who signaled that they should follow, so she stepped through, following the beam of light, the others right behind.

Their eyes hadn't had a chance to adjust to the dim light when the door shut behind them with a soft whir. In the darkness, they saw rainbows illuminating each of them.

Light from high above made brightly colored patterns. The walls near the ceiling were filled with beautiful abstract stained glass windows that had prisms scattered throughout.

Annie whispered to Tom, "I didn't see any windows on the outside. Did you?"

"I didn't notice any," Tom said.

Ben said, "One-way doors in the tunnels, and now one-way windows, visible from the inside but not the outside? It makes sense, right?"

Eric paused in the middle of a red-blue streak. "I can't see that the windows would necessarily be visible from the outside if done properly. The light is all being directed inside, none reflected back out."

"Thank you, Eric," Annie said.

Tom checked out the room. "In spite of all the gloom and doom, it *is* kinda pretty, isn't it?" he said.

"Not as dark as I'd expected," Annie said.

"And it doesn't echo either," Ben added. "From the way the steps were built, I figured it would all be dark and shiny, nothing to soften any sound, but it's not like that at all."

As their eyes adjusted to the light, they could see gentle movement in the large room, people coming and going, courtly conversations going on.

Sitting at a small table to one side sat an older gentleman with a large book open. He crooked his finger at them, waiting for them to approach. Holding a quill poised above the book, he spoke hesitantly, "Wha…What name?"

Ben stared. "English?"

Eric squinted at the man. "Interesting."

The man frowned as he repeated, "What name?"

Ben stepped in and replied, "You could use my name: Ben."

The man frowned as he started to write.

Patrick stepped up. "May I?"

"Please. Have at it," Ben said.

Patrick stooped to speak to the greeter, who was relieved that he didn't have to use such a difficult foreign tongue. After a moment or two, Patrick said, "He says Rudolph is kinda busy today. Affairs of the land keep him busy." Patrick shrugged. "He says that running a kingdom is difficult work."

"He said that?" Annie asked.

"He did," Patrick said. "Though, he said he might be able to squeeze us in next. After all, they *have* been told that we would be arriving any time soon."

The man spoke again, indicating a small man sitting at the head of a large T-shaped table, surrounded by paperwork. A line of men had formed along the long side of the table, waiting their turn.

Patrick stared. "That's Rudolph?"

The man nodded briskly and spoke more.

Patrick translated, "Those other men are from nearby cities. They're here to establish trade routes with Rudolph. I'm told he has a monopoly on all the food." He spoke to the greeter again. "Wait, his monopoly isn't on *all* the food, just on the good stuff, the healthful stuff. Basic foodstuffs are available to all the towns, and most grow their own, but the *good* stuff, the stuff with flavor and essential vitamins and minerals are grown exclusively here." He frowned. "The thing is only the elite have access to it. The peasants still get slop."

"If he has so much, why not share with everyone?" Annie asked.

Patrick shrugged. "Same as back home, I'd assume: those that have want to keep."

"So why can't the other towns grow their *own* good food?" Tom asked.

"Let me ask," Patrick said. After another short conversation with the greeter Patrick explained, "Rudolph doesn't share the *seeds*. The food he trades to other towns is de-seeded, already partially processed. That's the reason for all the guards we saw in the fields. They aren't guarding the slaves so much as they're guarding the plants themselves."

"So they aren't slaves?"

"Oh, no, they're still slaves, but the people aren't worth as much as the plants. Easier to replace peasants than to lose a seed monopoly."

"What little regard for human life." Annie frowned. "His focus is to be the boss of everyone."

"He can be the boss of whatever he wants, as long as he lets Melvin go," Ben said. "Is it our turn yet?"

Patrick asked the greeter and received an answer. "He says that we can go stand on the other side of the table. We'll get called up right away."

Ben stormed to the line, and the rest had to hurry to keep up, Eric trailing the group.

Rudolph barely acknowledged them, continuing to talk to the man fawning in front of him.

Ben whispered, "I don't see what's so scary about him now that we're standing so close, but I can see why they called him Bentnose. Take a gander at that schnoz." Ben stifled a snicker. "A little bit more and he could touch his ear with that nose of his."

"That's not polite," Annie said. "Though it is an ugly nose. I wonder if he's considered surgery."

Eric spoke up, "Yeah, he's not scary. Simply an old guy."

"I wouldn't say *old*, Eric. He's probably not over forty," Patrick said.

"He might be forty," Tom said. "But he's been able to accomplish quite a bit in the last few years."

Annie put her hand on Tom's arm. "The last few years? Patrick, when did you say that Rudolph arrived here? A couple generations ago? He doesn't look old enough to be *that* Rudolph. Maybe his name is a title like king that's passed on from generation to generation."

Ben and Patrick both said, "Dread Pirate Roberts!"

"Yeah, that could be it," Patrick said.

"As long as he doesn't say, 'I'll most likely kill you in the morning' I'm fine with it," Ben said. "And I don't care if he's the original or a descendant—we're getting Melvin back and getting out of here."

The man in front of Rudolph stopped talking, bowed, and backed away from the table.

"That would be our cue. Let's go," Ben said, stepping forward.

Rudolph pushed aside the papers in front of him and weighed up the group. "I didn't think you'd ever get here."

"Why not?" Ben asked.

"I expected you to bolt at the first sign of difficulty," he leaned back, "but here you are." He ignored them as he pulled a random document from a pile and glanced at it. He spoke to himself, "Such a ragtag bunch of misfits. It's amazing that they even manage to find the privy in the morning." He squinted at them. "Then again, maybe they didn't. Any close bush would do as well."

Ben frowned. "Hey, we're right here. Don't talk like we can't hear what you're saying."

"Good point, young man. No one around here understands me when I speak English, and I've become so used to it. They think I'm casting a spell, so it keeps them on the defensive." He mumbled as he went back to his papers. "Casting a spell, ha! Such things don't exist."

"We've heard about the spells you cast on those cities, those curses you used," Annie said. "You or your *grandfather*."

Rudolph blinked in surprise. "My grandfather? He's never been here, and those weren't curses…they were a matter of physics and medicine." He shook his head. "Even after I explained it to them," he wafted a hand at the crowd of men waiting their turn, "they still refused to understand."

Annie waggled a finger at Rudolph as she said, "You couldn't possibly have done all this, as old as you are."

He sat up and leaned forward. "How old do you think I am?" he asked.

Annie shrugged. "Certainly not in your forties yet. Probably mid-thirties."

Rudolph leaned back and smiled. "Thirties? You think I'm in my thirties? What a nice thing to say." He sneered. "I was in my late 50s when I was trapped here, in the mid-80s, 1986, April, as I recall." He frowned. "I don't know how long I've been here. Time is different in this world."

Ben frowned. "1986?"

Eric did the math. "Thirty-five years ago?"

Rudolph stood up. "In that case, I should be well into my 90s, yet what do you see?" He flexed his arms.

"How is that possible?" Tom asked.

"I could tell you, or I could show you, but that's not why you're here, is it?" he prodded.

"No, it isn't," Ben said stepping forward. "We're here to get Melvin."

"Ah, that's the boy's name? I never did find out. It's so much easier when there's no resistance. I usually keep them sedated except for feeding time. That way I can get what I need, when I need it."

"So where is he?" Annie asked.

"Let me show you the way," Rudolph said, heading out of the hall. The men waiting in line stared, disappointed that their opportunity to beg was leaving.

Ben and Annie followed Rudolph through the room to a door and along a hallway off the side of the main hall.

Patrick caught up with Ben and said, "I don't have to translate for you this time, but did you notice an accent?"

"He speaks English quite well, but plainly it's not his native tongue."

Eric joined in. "As I had noted earlier about the architecture, it has a heavy eastern European influence."

"Yeah, that's what I thought, too." Patrick patted Eric on the shoulder. "Good to have you with us."

Eric smiled. "Nice to be of help."

Tom leaned to Ben. "Did you notice that he didn't bring any guards?"

Ben stared back. "Come to think of it, I didn't see any guards back in the big room either."

"Does he have everyone here so enchanted that he doesn't need any protection?" Patrick asked.

Ben shrugged. "Well, that won't work with us. We can see through his masquerade."

They followed Rudolph through a hallway lined with identical doors on each side that continued for a long ways.

He suddenly stopped in front one of the doors. "I can't remember which one it is. I usually have them brought to me." He released the latch and swung the door open, leaning in to look.

Ben looked past Rudolph and saw a small square room. A short stool sat next to a table in the corner, and a bed was along the back wall. No other furniture. On the bed, a small boy was sleeping.

"No, not this one," Rudolph said. He closed the door, replaced the latch, and moved farther along the hall.

Rudolph picked a door on the other side of the hall this time, opening to reveal an identical room, but this time the occupant of the bed was an old lady. The door banged as he shut it. "Need to replace that one soon," he muttered.

As they approached the third door, Ben noticed how long the hallway was. *How many prisoners does he have?* he thought.

The next door opened was the one they wanted. Melvin was on the bed, deep asleep.

Annie rushed past Rudolph to check on him.

Rudolph strolled into the room. "Care to see how it works?"

Ben leaned through the doorway and watched as Rudolph put his hand on Melvin's forehead and closed his eyes. Melvin writhed on the bed, moaning in pain, though still asleep. Rudolph leaned his head back and whispered in relief. "Ah, yes. That feels so good. He still has plenty of power to give."

Annie slapped Rudolph's hand away.

Rudolph leered at her, then laughed and faced Ben.

Ben stared as the one or two wrinkles on Rudolph's face twisted, snaking back and forth, finally smoothing out, giving him a younger, more energetic, look.

"So, how old do I look now?" Rudolph said, showing off his face.

Eric leaned in from the hallway. "Certainly not older than 30, I'd say."

Ben frowned. "Don't play his game, Eric."

Rudolph flexed his legs, stretched his arms out, and smiled. "See? This one has a lot of natural energy." He put his hand on Melvin's shoulder. "Much too much to keep it all to himself."

Annie glanced at Ben, still out in the hall. "I could see it draining from Melvin." She frowned at Rudolph. "He was sucking the life-force right out of him." She put her hand on Rudolph's chest and pushed him out of the room. "We aren't going to have any more of *that* going on."

Rudolph stumbled back out of the room, into the hallway where Ben was waiting.

Ben stared at Rudolph, then stepped back, resting his hand on his pistol. "So, he goes with us, right?"

Rudolph stumbled back against the wall halfway to the next door. "You mean to take him by force?" he whimpered.

"If that's what's necessary," Ben said.

Tom pushed Eric towards the door to Melvin's room then circled to the other side of the hallway, watching to see what Rudolph was going to do. Patrick stood next to Ben, blocking any exit back towards the big room.

Rudolph cowered against the wall, holding his hands in front of himself. "You aren't going to hurt me, are you?" he pleaded.

Ben relaxed. "No, that's not our intent."

From inside the room, Annie stepped to the doorway. "Melvin's fine, but he's unconscious." She glared at Rudolph. "As if he's been drugged."

Rudolph raised his shoulders. "I have to keep them under control somehow," he squeaked.

"Can you guys get in here and help me lift him?" Annie asked.

Eric was closest, but as he stepped into the small room, Rudolph stood straight and moved to the middle of the hallway. He raised his arm, curling his fingers into a fist, and the door to the room slammed shut, then he twisted his wrist and the latch locked into place. "I don't think so," he said, his voice hard. "I don't know what I'm going to do with the new boy," he sneered, "but I have plans for that little girl."

Ben jumped back as Annie and Eric pounded on the door. He could hear them yelling.

"Don't know what to do?" Rudolph taunted. "Do your best. Let's see what you have."

Tom already had his pistol out and levelled at Rudolph, and Ben could see the hammer cocked back. *Good planning, Tom. Joe would be proud of you,* Ben thought.

Ben reached to unsnap the strap on his holster, flipped it out of the way, slipped his fingers around the butt, and slowly drew out his pistol. He reached across and deliberately pulled the slide back, letting it fly home with a solid ka-chunk. "That's my sister you have in there," he said through gritted teeth.

"Ooh! So you aren't her boyfriend?" Rudolph asked.

"No," Tom growled. "That'd be me." He glared at Rudolph. "And I'm not happy about what you've done to her."

"Not happy? What ever shall we do about that?" Rudolph said mocking them.

Patrick stepped between Ben and Tom, starting to wave his hands in circles. "Save the ammo," he mumbled back at them.

"Ah, so *you're* the one who has the power. I wondered why they'd brought you along." Rudolph looked Patrick up and down, then sneered. "Not good for much else, are you?"

"Hang on, guys," Patrick said as he stepped forward. He lifted his hands, inhaled purposefully, and stared straight into Rudolph's eyes, then slammed his hands down, screaming out the phrase he'd been studying.

Silence filled the hallway. No one moved. Patrick held his hands up to his neck, coughing as Rudolph smiled. "Can't speak, little one?" Rudolph strode towards Patrick, his fingers held up as if he were strangling him in spite of being across the hallway. "No sound, no control, is there?" He tipped his head. "You've been able to learn so much in such a short time. It would have been fascinating to see what you could have accomplished…if you had had more time." He snorted. "Like say…as much time as *I've* had?"

Ben finally broke out of his trance and pulled the trigger. The blast echoed back and forth along the hallway, snapping Tom into action as well. A second shot echoed out. At that range, neither shot could have missed, yet Rudolph didn't even blink as both rounds hit him and tumbled to the ground, landing with a soft thud, softer even than the noise the brass made clinking to the floor.

Rudolph sneered at Ben. "Wasting ammo, are we now?" He waggled his fingers and Patrick stretched up onto tiptoes, gagging and choking, trying to breathe.

Ben fired again, a double-tap. Both rounds hit Rudolph in the middle of his chest— neither did any damage.

Tom leaped at Rudolph, swinging his pistol, but Rudolph merely stepped to the side, drawing his head back an insignificant distance, and the butt of Tom's pistol glanced off Rudolph's forehead, leaving no mark. Tom fell to the floor. Rudolph leered, still keeping his invisible grip on Patrick.

Ben adjusted his aim, focusing on the back of Rudolph's head. He let loose a volley, emptying his clip. Each shot hit, barely managing to shove Rudolph's head down a little each time.

Rudolph twisted to stare at Ben. "I *was* planning on letting you go, after I disposed of this…this difficulty here." He shook Patrick like a puppet on strings, except he had no strings. "But you're starting to annoy me, and now you're out of ammo. Planning to survive out there without ammo? You're certainly not smart enough on your own."

Before Ben could reply, Tom fired from the ground aiming up right into Rudolph's face. The first shot hit him in the chin, knocking his head back. The second one missed completely, ricocheting off the ceiling and hitting the latch on the door. As Rudolph shifted to tackle Tom, the door burst open, slamming into the wall, and Eric fell into the middle of the action. Annie managed to keep her balance and ducked back into the room, but Eric had to struggle to gain his footing, stumbling across the hall.

Rudolph watched Eric's painfully ludicrous efforts, laughing at the idiocy. He jerked Patrick's head one last time from across the room, then tossed him aside where he landed with a thud, unmoving. He shifted his aim, reaching for Eric.

Ben saw Rudolph target Eric and charged him, hitting his outstretched arm. It felt as if he'd hit a stone statue. The force of the impact knocked the air out of Ben's lungs, but he hung onto Rudolph's arm, trying to upset his targeting, but that wasn't necessary as every time Rudolph reached for Eric with his invisible grasp, Eric would slip and fall, and Rudolph would miss.

The frustration on Rudolph's face grew as his inability to capture such a simple mark agitated him, and he continued snatching at the air, as if he were trying to catch a gnat buzzing his face.

As everyone else was watching Eric's antics, Tom scrambled to his feet and snuck up on Rudolph from behind.

Eric, still attempting to stand up, managed to trip over Patrick, kicking him in the ribs, acting like a precordial thump, bringing him back to consciousness. Patrick rolled to his knees, coughing.

Still concentrating on grabbing Eric, Rudolph wasn't paying attention to anyone else, so Tom jumped up and snaked his arm around Rudolph's head, covering his eyes. With Rudolph suddenly blinded by Tom, his arm went limp, and Ben grabbed it, keeping it from moving.

Realizing that Rudolph's transparent shield was gone, Ben pounded his fist into Rudolph's ribs. At the same time, Patrick managed to get to his feet and charge, his shoulder slamming Rudolph in the gut.

Rudolph collapsed to the ground with a thud, pulling Tom to the floor with him, and his arms flailed about as he yelled incoherently.

"Keep his eyes covered!" Ben told Tom. "He can't do anything if he can't see."

"Trying," Tom replied. "Get his legs under control. He's a slimy little punk."

"I have one arm," Ben yelled. "Patrick, can you get his legs?"

Patrick dove onto Rudolph's ankles and scooped them up in a bear hug.

"We have him, Annie," Ben said. "Do you want to question him?"

Annie looked out of the room and rushed up. "Deezh warned me, but I have to try." She put her hand on Rudolph's leg and closed her eyes. A loud crack, and Rudolph screamed. She gasped and leaned back on her heels. *So much easier to break his leg than to heal it.* She reached for the other one, but Rudolph suddenly relaxed and all movement ceased.

Patrick sat up, still holding Rudolph's legs, Ben shifted his grip on the arm he had, and Tom loosened his grip on Rudolph's head. Suddenly Tom yelped and pulled his arm back. "He bit me!" Tom was reaching back to slug him again when Rudolph opened his eyes, glared at everyone, narrowed his eyes at the ceiling, and vanished.

"Where'd he go?" Tom asked, his arms suddenly empty.

"I don't know, and I don't care," Ben said. "Let's grab Melvin and get out of this place."

"I'm all for that," Patrick said hoarsely, rubbing his throat. "But I'd like to know how he did that remote choke thing."

Eric was still sitting in the middle of the floor and shrugged. "What? My feet kept slipping."

"Never mind, Eric," Annie said. "You distracted him long enough for us to get the upper hand."

Ben stood up. "How's your throat, Patrick? Good enough for a two-man carry?"

"For Melvin?" Patrick choked out. "Yeah, let's get him."

They went into the small room where Melvin still slept, and Annie shifted Melvin leaning him back into the seat that Ben and Patrick had made with their arms. They stood up, Annie wrapped Melvin's arms across their shoulders, and they all headed for the main hall with Tom leading the way. Eric and Annie brought up the rear, easily keeping up with the group.

"Remember the way back?" Annie shouted as they ran.

Tom yelled back, "Yeah, I paid attention…in case we needed to hurry."

"Good," Ben said huffing and puffing with the extra load he shared.

They burst out into the main hall, startling all the petitioners still waiting their turn. As they ran across the room, the hubbub increased, and the braver souls attempted to get in their way.

Tom figured that as a common enemy makes friends, a common friend made enemies, so he didn't hesitate to shoot at anyone in their way. As soon as the first ones went down, the resistance quickly subsided, everyone else panicking and running for cover.

As they approached the outer door, Annie yelled, "It's closed. How do we open it? It opened by itself before."

Ben gasped for breath. "Patrick, are you up to opening a door for us?"

"I could try, but let's drop Melvin somewhere. I could *try* with my arms full, but for such a big task, it would be easier if they were empty."

"Go ahead and drop him on the floor right by the door," Tom said.

"Not that close," Patrick warned. "If I make the blast big enough to open the door, it'll have a back blast big enough to hurt anyone close."

"Especially as you're pushing against the hinges," Eric stated.

Tom grabbed Melvin and dragged him back. "Eric and I can carry him for a while, as long as none of these idiots gets in our way."

"You scared most of them off with the first couple shots," Eric said. "They don't know about firearms. Not unless Rudolph told them."

"Eric, that's it!" Ben shouted. "*That's* why the soldiers were using the *nimre* as fake captains. The idea came from Rudolph. We *don't* have a spy. It was Rudolph who wanted us to waste our ammo. *He* knows about firearms."

"Makes sense," Patrick said. "Stay back there. Any closer and I won't be able to use a big enough blast."

They stopped and set Melvin on the floor. Annie sat by his side, checking his colors. "He's fine…for now."

"Plug your ears," Patrick warned as he faced the door and built up a charge. Swinging his arms overhead, he yelled, and the blast rattled the glass above, cracking the windows, but the door didn't budge. "Let me try again." He stepped closer and planted his feet, staring right at the door. "Ready?" His hands circled, his arms snaked, and his body swayed.

Ben could feel the power building, like static electricity, making the hairs on his arms stand up.

When Patrick released the blast this time, the windows overhead shattered, glass flying in all directions, raining beautifully colored daggers.

"Duck!" Tom yelled, then crawled away from the door. Ben grabbed Melvin's arm and dragged him as Eric and Annie used Melvin's coat to cover him, helping to move him away from the wreckage.

"Oops!" Patrick said, sucking in air. "Give me one more shot at it." As Patrick was catching his breath, another blast hit the door, but from the other side. "Hey! What was that?"

"Someone else trying to break the door?" Ben said. "From the outside?"

"Well, it would be preferable to have it burst *out* than in. More room out there, *and* we're not in the way," Patrick said.

"Then have at it, but you might want to hit low," Eric shouted. "I'll bet whoever's out there is aiming high. Remember the angle of the steps."

"Ah, yes." Patrick wound up, ready to blast again, this time concentrating on the bottom edge of the door. Trying to time it right, he waited, then let loose. The timing was perfect. His blast hit the bottom at the same time the outer blast hit the top. The doors unhinged, letting in tongues of flame. Flying through the air, the doors twisted about, surrounded by fire. The massive blocks sparkled in a golden blaze, dropping to the ground in a decisive crash.

Ben could feel the heat from outside as well as the shock wave from the inside, but once the flames and smoke dissipated, he could see rays of light shining through the dust—it was open. "Let's go!" He lifted Melvin onto his shoulders and ran for the door. He could feel other hands supporting Melvin, helping him. They found that it still wasn't going to be easy. Although the doors were no longer there, debris was scattered across the entryway making it difficult to wend their way through.

Ben noticed Patrick doubled up, hands on knees. "Are you hurt?"

"No," Patrick said. "Just feels like I ran a full marathon," he panted.

"Don't overdo it," Ben said.

Tom grabbed Melvin. "Ben, can you get Annie and Eric through?"

"Yeah, we can make it."

Patrick stood up and tripped over the clutter. "Hang back. I'm going to open a path for us." He climbed onto one of the larger fragments and yelled down the stairs to the people in the square, hoping they could hear him, "Back off! Incoming!"

Ben passed Melvin to Tom. "We'd better get under cover, too," he said, pulling Eric back into the building far enough to duck behind a large chunk of ruined door.

Tom managed to half carry, half drag Melvin to another safe spot.

Annie dove behind Tom and stayed low.

Patrick started a series of small blasts, aiming first at the pieces tottering at the top edge of the stairs, sending them tumbling across the obsidian steps, then moving on to the larger pieces. Shards of black glass split off the steps, joining the remains of one of the doors in a deadly avalanche.

Ben hoped that everyone in the square was aware of the wreckage they were sending their direction. He realized that Eric was mumbling to himself and when he checked on him, saw a crowd approaching from inside. "Patrick! Can you send a blast this way?"

From his vantage point, Patrick aimed at the ceiling, blasting it, dropping chunks of rock onto anyone inside, and blocking the doorway in the process. "That should do it," he yelled, taking a deep breath and continuing to blast at the rubble.

"Thanks," Ben shouted, then noticed Eric crawling in circles on the floor picking up specks of dirt and cramming them into his pockets. "*What* are you doing, Eric?"

Eric stared at Ben. "Do you realize that we're crawling in gold dust? There are nuggets lying all over the place."

Ben stared in bewilderment. "If you're going to steal, do it right," he said, grabbing a hunk of solid gold the size of a goose egg and tossing it. "Grab the ones that'll impress everyone when you get back, and watch out for flying fragments."

"Wow! Thanks, Ben," Eric said as he caught the huge nugget.

The next couple of blasts were closer, and Ben poked his head up to watch Patrick control each blast, budging the debris enough to open a path.

"Can you make it through now?" Patrick yelled back.

"We'll try," Ben shouted. He stepped towards Eric. "Come on now. You have plenty enough gold."

Tom stood up and hefted Melvin into a fireman's carry, then managed to get a hold of Annie's hand, helping her to her feet. They wound their way through the loose chunks and met up with Patrick barely in front of Ben and Eric.

"Good job, Patrick," Ben said. "We have a clear path."

"You're getting so good with that," Annie said. "I'm going to ask you to sweep the walk when we get home."

Patrick stepped off the piece he was standing on. "I may do that."

They approached the edge of the stairs and looked into the square. Broken door pieces spread across the extent of the open area, people were frantically running, and screams filled the air.

"Oops. Maybe we should have warned them," Ben said.

"They should have had enough notice when we blasted the door," Patrick said.

A ball of fire burst on the other side of the mess, sending up a greasy cloud of black smoke. A pattering of gunfire followed.

"Save the ammo," Ben muttered under his breath.

Another fireball exploded in the middle of the crowd below.

"Well, we know where Robb is," Annie said.

"Yeah. Easy to spot," Ben said. "Patrick, you definitely have a rivalry for new tricks now."

"Robb and I should combine efforts more often," Patrick said, grinning at what was left of the door.

"That could be interesting," Ben said raising his eyebrows.

Tom cleared his throat. "Can we get a move on? Melvin here isn't getting any lighter."

Annie stared at the black staircase. "There are huge pieces all across, but the worst part is that the steps themselves have been shattered. There's no place to walk. Any plans for getting out of here?"

"Oh, great," Tom said as he sat on a small, flat piece and slid Melvin off his back. "Let me know when you get something figured out."

Eric kicked at a large, flat piece of the door. "What if we sit on that and slide down?"

"What's that, Eric?" Ben asked. "We do what?"

"Use that section of the door as a toboggan. It's big enough for all of us to fit on. We could skim right across the sharp edges."

Ben frowned. "Is that even possible, Tom? Can we do that?"

Tom shifted Melvin to see what they meant. "Hmm…Well, it *could* be done, if it were closer to the edge, but then we'd need to ride it all the way *down* the stairs."

"Patrick, do you think you could ease it closer to the edge, using your blasts?"

Patrick walked to the flat piece, then circled it. "Maybe. Let me try."

"Everyone get back," Ben said. "Who knows what kind of shrapnel he'll send flying."

"I'm going to open out an area in front of it first," Patrick said as he walked to the stair side. He swept his arms back and forth as he blasted the area, knocking the larger pieces aside. "Annie, interesting comment you had earlier: sweeping the sidewalk. It works!"

Annie peeked out from her hiding place. "You're welcome."

"Now to move the slab itself," he said. He stood a couple meters behind the hunk of door and used a pushing motion with his hands, sending out little blasts as he walked. "It's working!"

Annie stuck her head back up. "Good. Let us know when you're ready for us to get on."

Tom reached up and grabbed Annie by the shoulder. "Hey! Sit tight. He's doing fine on his own."

Patrick continued urging the soon-to-be sled until the front end extended a ways out, above the steps. "That's as close as I want to get until we're on board. Everyone climb on," he said, pausing to breathe.

Ben and Tom manhandled the still unconscious Melvin into a spot in the middle, then sat on either side, supporting him between them. Eric and Annie sat in front of them, and Patrick climbed up right behind.

"A warning," Patrick said. "When I was moving this block, pieces were chipping off where I was blasting. I didn't see any big cracks though, so it *might* hold together until we get to the bottom.

Ben twisted to stare at Patrick. "How will you slow us when we get there? Any brakes on this thing?" He raised an eyebrow.

"I figure that if I blast away at the front, it might work. Hopefully, there will be enough left to sit on by the time we get to the bottom that we aren't sent flying."

Annie glanced at the front of the sled. "Oh, so *now* you tell us."

Patrick kneeled behind Melvin, then stretched out to Tom and Ben. "If you guys hang on to me, I'll be able to keep both hands free to do this. Ready to start now?"

Ben reached back with one hand, holding Patrick's waist and reached forward with the other to encircle Eric. Tom did the same, linking hands with Ben behind Patrick's back, holding on to Annie in front.

"I wish we had rope to tie us all together," Ben said.

"We'll make it," Tom said as he pulled Annie closer.

Ben held tight, then checked out the conflict still going on in the square. "Well, we're as ready as we'll be. Do you think they'll move?" He tipped his head downhill.

Patrick shrugged. "We'll see." He looked behind and aimed at the back of the slab.

Sharp jerks shook the passengers as the door scooted forward—finally hitting the tipping point, and Annie let out a screech. The ride down the stairs was anything but smooth, and the vibrations threatened to dump the entire load. As they slid faster and faster, the remaining pieces of the wrecked door still on the stairs slowed them at first, but soon joined them in a landslide heading right for the middle of the square.

Patrick swiveled to the front, blasting the rocks ahead, opening the path before them, but it sped their descent, so he shifted to the sides, pushing away any loose rocks that were tumbling in their direction.

"Slow!" Ben shouted. "Can you slow us?"

"I'm trying," Patrick said, taking a breath. He aimed and blasted away at the front of their rocky sled, slowing it somewhat, but they continued to pick up speed, rapidly approaching the bottom. He paused for a moment to catch his breath, then continued.

With every blast, the slab slowed slightly, but every blast jerked their sled, making the five of them slide forward. It wouldn't be much of a problem, but the blasting was also wearing away at the front, so the closer they slid to the front, the closer the front crumbled to them.

They finally hit the bottom and careened onto the level part of the square. The journey suddenly became more stable, but they were still moving so fast that they continued to slide across the square, heading straight for the buildings on the other side.

Patrick tried slowing them, but there wasn't enough of the slab left—Eric's feet were already dangling. If he blasted away any more, they'd *all* fall off the front.

Ben could see the predicament, too, so he shouted, "Ground too smooth! Break up the cobbles."

Patrick shifted his aim, trying to shatter the pavement into dips and bumps. It was working, but he was running out of breath, and their speed barely decreased, still moving too fast as they continued to slide all the way across the square.

The huge slab finally came to a stop, mere centimeters from hitting the wall, and Ben started breathing again as the rest tumbled off the remains. Tom held on to Annie as Eric jumped off, tripping and all but landing on his face. Patrick dropped to sit, focusing on his breathing.

"None too quiet getting out of there, are you?" Joe shouted to Ben through a shattered window of the building they just about plowed into.

"We didn't have many options," Ben said. "Anyone available to help carry Melvin?"

"You found him? Good!" Joe shouted into the dark room behind him. A couple *shmahseespe* scrambled out of a nearby doorway to lift Melvin off what remained of the slab.

"We knew when you were coming, what with all that noise, so we ducked behind something solid," Joe said as he came out of the building where they'd been hiding. "Some of the locals didn't." He indicated the bodies scattered to the side. "And you made so much noise trying to open that door, that Robb had to join in. Blasting that door helped him figure out a way to make fireballs that explode."

"Yeah, we figured it must have been him," Ben said. "So what've you been up to?"

"Well, until you came sliding in, we were having a small fire fight. We held to the edges, waiting for you, then moments before you started blasting the door, they attacked us with no warning. Most of our targets were peasants who suddenly turned vicious. Like that crowd-control thing but worse. Ever shoot unarmed civilians? There's not much worse than that." Joe frowned. "The problem was that every time we dropped one, another one stepped up to fill his place. They could have been zombies for all I know."

"Eric mentioned zombies earlier," Ben said, "and I laughed, but he might be right."

Tom rushed up. "Can't hang around here. Have your reunion later."

"If those peasants start moving again," Joe said. We'll have to waste more ammo on them."

"That would be a problem," Tom said, his head snapping up. "And more are arriving…from both sides of Rudolph's place." He gasped. "We're going to be surrounded."

"And they aren't peasants," Joe said, grabbing his gear. "Those guys are soldiers. And they're armed!"

"In that case, Tom's right, but we don't need to get out of just this square, we need to get out of this town…completely," Ben said.

"We *could* stay and fight," Joe suggested. "Good cover," he indicated the building, "and we have rifles. We could do quite a number on them." He looked across the square, then paused. "But considering how many I see coming, you could be right. It might be a better idea to bug out." He shouted orders then ran down the street.

Joe's troops, both the *shmahseespe* and the scouts, popped out of holes all along the side of the square and trotted up. They grabbed Melvin and loaded him onto their shoulders, jogging through any remaining crowd, either firing pistols or using their rifles one handed, a noisy affair.

"And we don't need to search our way out," Annie said. "The main road out of town is right there."

"Then let's get on it," Ben said as he urged her ahead. "Patrick, can you get them off our tail?"

"No problem," Patrick said as he blasted the ground, throwing loose shrapnel into the air at the soldiers. Some of the soldiers were hiding behind convenient barricades and launching arrows, so he adjusted his aim.

From across the square a fireball bloomed above the soldiers coming from the other side.

"Good job, Robb. Keep at it," Patrick said, watching his compatriot do some damage. Patrick blasted more holes in the ground sending rocks and dirt flying across the open space, then hightailed it after Ben, running backwards. He glanced up to see Robb come running across the square, heading his way. When Patrick saw that they were both well out of the square, he blasted the nearby buildings, filling the road with rubble.

Robb shouted, "Thanks!" then spun to face the pile of destroyed buildings.

Patrick stared as Robb twirled his empty hands in the air, and a small ball of flame suddenly appeared. The ball expanded as he kneaded it, swelling to the size of a basketball, then Robb compressed it to the size of a baseball, and pitching it into the middle of the road. It hit the pile of rubble and exploded, creating a conflagration that covered the entire width of the road.

"That should keep them busy," Robb shouted. "Let's go!"

"Neat trick, Robb. You'll need to show me how you do that," Patrick shouted as they ran.

"Sure. Next time we're kicking back with nothing to do—" He spun and hurled another fireball down a side street to engulf the soldiers who were scurrying to cut them off. "A little busy right now."

The two ran to catch up with the others, following the sound of gunfire. Based on the body count, Tom and Ben weren't putting up with any crowd blockades this time, no conserving ammo in this situation.

They slowed as they approached the rest of the crew, all hunched behind the remains of the abandoned sales stands that had filled the gateway the day before.

They ducked behind an overturned table between Ben and Annie. Patrick lifted his head to look. "There's the wall," he shouted.

"And there's the gate," Robb shouted back.

"But it's closed now, so what do we do?"

"Right now, we keep our heads down," Ben yelled. "There are archers on the wall above the gate."

"And we have company coming from behind," Patrick said. "We slowed them as much as we could, but they'll be here any moment."

"Can you keep our backside covered, Tom?" Ben shouted.

Tom spoke up from behind a cart lying on its side. "We've got it!"

"Patrick, Robb, now that you guys are here," Ben said, "can you do something with that gate?"

Patrick grabbed Robb's arm. "Let's get closer and see what we can do."

They crawled through the wreckage, getting as close to the gate as possible, then kept under cover as they started their respective tasks. Blasting and firebombing the center of the gate, they went through their routines again and again, getting nowhere but tired.

"That thing is too solid," Patrick finally said, out of breath. "It's not going to break."

"Yeah," Robb said, also breathing heavily.

"You guys need to rest, both of you," Ben said. "We'll have to figure something else out."

Robb frowned. "The way that gate is built, it's closed up against solid rock walls. The more we push it, the tighter it gets."

Ben ducked again. "Yeah, I remember Eric saying that when we first walked into the city. Can you hit the hinges? The weak spot?"

"If I soften them, Patrick, could you blast them?" Robb suggested.

"Might work. Can you keep a flame going long enough…at that distance?" Patrick asked, trying to catch his breath.

"Haven't tried, but even if it works, the gate is still up against the frame. We'd have to pull to open it." Robb sat down. "We opened that last door by hitting it on both sides at the same time. Can you blast the other side of the gate?"

Patrick shook his head. "Can't blast if I can't see it," he said. "The last time I blasted without focusing, the whole area was laid flat."

Ben remembered the flat circle in the big battle. "Well, that's out."

"Robb, keep the archers at bay," Patrick said. "I have a second scroll and two more from those guys by the campfire. Maybe I can figure something out."

"Not a problem," Robb said. "I'll fling fire at them every time they pop their heads up." He faced the gate.

"Hey, Joe," Ben called. "Help Tom watch for anyone behind. Patrick's gonna try something."

Joe and his group joined Tom, hiding behind piles of rubble, keeping watch back towards the city center.

Ben and Patrick ducked beneath broken tables as Patrick removed his backpack, dug through it, and pulled out the scroll.

"What's it going to do?" Ben asked.

Patrick shrugged. "No idea."

"Do we have time to experiment?"

"We need to *make* time." Patrick sent a blast at the archers still firing at them. "I don't see anything else that needs our attention."

"I have the archers covered." Robb stood up and juggled a couple small balls of fire back and forth, then pitched them right below the archers. As the flames licked up the wall, he said, "That should keep them busy for a while."

"Don't forget the road, too," Ben said. "Those soldiers might be coming through any time now."

Robb checked the road behind them and sent fireballs that direction as a precaution. He laughed. "Go ahead and play with your scrolls."

Patrick pulled out his pad, checked his notes, then shrugged. "Without Zhahmonichas, I'm going at this blind."

"Do you know what you're doing?" Ben asked.

Patrick shrugged. "I have no idea about the two new scrolls, but based on what Zhahmonichas showed me and what I learned from the first one, I think I've figured out the active part of the second one. The problem is that I haven't tried it out."

"No time like the present," Ben said.

"Ready or not, here goes," Patrick said.

"What's your target?" Ben asked.

"How about that wagon wheel?" Patrick asked, suggesting the remains of a crashed cart.

"Good enough, no one near it. Go ahead."

Patrick practiced the new phrase a couple times, then spoke aloud. The wagon wheel burst into flame.

Startled, Ben yelled, "Hey, Robb, was that you?"

"Was what me?" Robb asked.

"That fire on Patrick's target," Ben said.

Robb stared. "That no fire." He walked to the wheel and held his hand in the flames. "There's no heat."

Ben and Patrick joined him and examined the wagon wheel.

"But it *appears* to be fire," Patrick said.

"Appearances can be deceiving," Robb said. "It may put out light, but it's not normal. Doesn't even *look* like fire to me."

Ben put his hand right through the flame and grabbed a spoke of the wheel. "Robb is right. It's not hot, not burning at all. It's imitation fire."

Patrick frowned. "Light, but no heat? What good is that?"

"Beats me," Robb said. "Unless you were in a dark place where fire would be too dangerous to use."

"Like in a powder keg in a cartoon?" Ben asked. "Not going to happen here."

"Either way, it won't help," Patrick said as he let the small light fade and die out.

Ben looked back into the city. The streets were quiet, too quiet. The silence broken by occasional gunfire as Joe and his crew kept the soldiers at bay.

Suddenly Robb shouted, "Duck!" as he threw a fireball over Patrick's head. "The soldiers are sneaking up, circling us." Robb tossed more into both side streets. "That should keep them back for now."

"Thanks!" Joe said, spreading out his crew to cover the far side of the open area.

"This far, then we get stuck," Ben said. "We have to keep going. Can't give up now." He plopped on the ground, and the others came to sit with him.

As they were pondering the fate of their doomed mission, Annie came up. "I don't know what you guys are doing, but you should know that Melvin is awake now. He's not up to running a marathon, but he's eating like there's no tomorrow."

Ben wondered at Annie's turn of phrase. *There might not be a tomorrow for any of us,* he thought.

"Well, we can go see how the target of our rescue is doing," Patrick said, standing up. "After all, we're all here because of him."

"Now don't you go and make him feel bad, Patrick," Annie said as she followed him. "He's been through enough as it is."

"Yeah, I know. I'll be nice."

Ben and Robb joined them as they wandered to Melvin. They found him eating earnestly but in otherwise good health.

"Getting enough to eat?" Ben asked.

"Yeah, thanks," Melvin said. "I haven't eaten a good meal for weeks!"

"It hasn't been that long, as today is Wednesday," Eric said. "It's been barely five days you've been missing."

"Well, it feels like a month," Melvin said around a mouthful of food.

Robb reached to pat Melvin on the shoulder. "Go ahead and eat…it could be your last meal."

Ben frowned. "You don't need to put it like that."

"Incoming!" someone shouted. "The archers are at it again."

Robb tossed a couple of small balls of fire at the archers, but instead a deluge of fire erupted from his hand, drenching the parapet where the archers were. Short screams erupted as bodies flew from the top of the wall, landing below. "Wow! Didn't expect that," Robb said to everyone.

"Watch it," Annie shouted. "We don't want to injure any of *our* folks."

Ben had tumbled to the ground. "I don't think I have any eyebrows left!"

"I didn't mean to," Robb complained. "It just happened."

"It *didn't just* happen." Annie frowned. "Look what you've done to Melvin."

Melvin, with a half bite of food still in his hand, was lying on the ground, unconscious.

"What *I* did? I didn't do anything."

"Yes, you did. When you sent that last blast of fire, you had your hand on his shoulder, and I could see energy flowing from him."

Robb aimed at what remained of the archers' location, but this time only sputters of flame danced across his fingers, then he frowned and tried again. This time a larger ball flew across the battlefield. "It's usually easy to control the size of the flame."

"The energy flow must have boosted it," Annie said.

"Energy flow?" Ben asked. "Like what Rudolph was doing?"

"Yes, *like* but not quite as strong," Annie said.

Ben looked slowly from Melvin to Robb. "And it made Robb's fire bigger?"

"It certainly felt like it did." Robb shrugged. "I'll have to be more careful."

Annie tended to Melvin, helping him sit up.

Ben asked, "So, did he faint or what?"

"It could have been something like that," Annie said, then frowned at Robb. "But we won't be trying anything like that again."

"Not even for an experiment?" Patrick blinked. "We still need to get that gate opened up."

Annie frowned. "No experiments, not if it causes him to pass out."

"What if we control the energy flow?"

"And how're you going to do that?" Annie frowned. "You don't even know how it works, much less how to control it."

Patrick shrugged. "I was hoping you'd have a suggestion."

"My suggestion is that we leave it alone," she frowned, "until we can discuss it properly."

"Not now," Robb started then tossed a couple fireballs at soldiers sneaking up. "We *don't* have time now. We have to vacate this city."

Patrick grabbed Robb's shoulder. "Remember that gold door?"

"*Was* it made of gold?" Robb asked.

"Never mind that now," Patrick continued, "If you hit high and I hit low, do you think we can open that gate?"

"One moment." Eric stood and held up a hand. "With the apparent offensive abilities we have, there might be a better way to tackle it."

"What's that?" Ben asked.

"I overheard Robb saying something about softening the hinges. If he could do that, then Patrick could blast the bottom center of the gate. The angular force, translated through the fulcrum of the rock wall that's supporting the gate, might be enough unhinge it."

Robb stepped closer and stared at the gate. "I'm willing to give it a try, but someone will have to watch our backside. I don't know how long it'll take to warm up those hinges."

"Ben, you and the others spot for me," Patrick said. "I'll blast anyone coming close until the hinges are soft enough. Then when we're ready, I'll blast the gate like Eric said."

"Good," Ben said.

Robb dropped to a knee behind the remains of a small wall. "Good thing we don't need to watch out for the archers anymore. That accidental fire bomb did a real number on them." He focused on the gate, directing a stream of fire across the open space, hitting one hinge, then switching to the other, back and forth.

"Focus on the top hinges," Eric said. "That's where the angular force will be the greatest."

Robb nodded slowly. "Whatever you say," he said as Patrick watched for anything that moved up the street.

A couple minutes later Robb wilted. "It's tough keeping this up. My arms are getting tired."

Patrick glanced back. "Should I try it now?"

Robb shrugged. "Now or never. Hit it!"

Patrick spun, stepped forward, and launched into his chant.

Ben watched. "Keep the flame going, if you can, Robb. Don't let the hinges cool off."

"Easy for you to say," Robb complained but went back to being a human blowtorch.

Patrick paused, waiting for everyone to get down, and they all ducked behind something substantial as he let loose. The blast echoed and a cloud of dust billowed up.

No one could see anything, then as the dust drifted away, they all saw light shining through where the gate had once stood. The bottom hinges had held, though twisted and misshapen, but the top ones were torn to shreds, making a gap at the bottom easily large enough to get through.

Breaking the silence that followed, everyone cheered, though most could hardly hear it, their ears still ringing from the backlash of the concussion. Before Ben could hear again, he directed everyone to proceed through the breach, and proceed they did, at a full run.

Patrick and Robb waited for Annie to escort the now awake Melvin on ahead as the two of them held back to ensure their escape. Tom and Joe brought up the rear, though with a detonation like that to announce their capabilities, there wasn't any resistance from the soldiers behind them.

With the still-recovering Melvin finally on his feet, stumbling but mobile, no one had to carry him, so the group ran at full tilt through the fields. What little resistance they encountered, they dealt with harshly. Still at close to a full run, they traversed the switchbacks, arriving at the top quickly, but completely out of breath.

They quickly passed the abandoned guard shack, and they could tell why: the front gates to the city below were easy to see, still enveloped in flame, and the guards wanted nothing to do with anyone who could do that.

Ben stopped at the top of the climb, watching the now-burning city, and checked off each group as they entered the mountain pass. When Shess showed up, he called to him, "Hey, can you make certain all of your folks have made it out?"

"*aa-eh*. Shankaktos helping," Shess said, walking to Ben and speaking softly. "When heard name Rudolph, I knew where headed. I expect none return. Without power of big city to help, all be slaves or killed."

"Now that I've seen what that Rudolph guy does, I understand why you were reluctant to go along with us. Yet you did. For that I thank you," Ben said bowing to Shess. "You would have been entirely within your rights to give up on us and head back to the safety of your town, but you didn't. You stuck with us. Thanks."

"You friends have power," Shess said. "More than we knew. They help us return."

Ben ticked the scouts off his mental list as they jogged past. "They have more power than *we* knew. It's surprised *all* of us."

"How we get away from Rudolph's soldiers?" Shess asked as he bent over the rocks at the edge to see the city below.

Ben joined Shess and watched hundreds of people milling about, getting organized, forming up into groups, and heading along the road from the city. He yelled at the slowly moving group, "We have incoming!"

Ben tried to get the scouts moving, but the more he yelled at them, the more it encouraged them to yell at the soldiers in the flaming valley. A group of *shmahseespe* joined them, and they all shouted at the soldiers, egged on by John.

"With all those soldiers heading our way," Tom said. "This isn't like that last battle we were in. We aren't prepared for this at all."

"We injured, need heal," Shess said. "Escape good."

Eric stepped up. "A case of run away to fight again another day."

Tom agreed. "Yeah, it may not be what we want, but it's what we have to do."

Ben yelled at the group by the edge. "You plan on loafing here until they arrive?" He frowned. "Yeah, escape or run away, whatever. If we move fast enough, we can get some serious distance on them, but do you think we should delay the soldiers on our way out?"

"Delay?" Shess asked.

"Yeah," Eric said. "We could block their movement."

"Something like that," Ben said. "And those guys standing around yelling aren't helping much, though I can't blame them. After our escape from the city, they think they're hot stuff, but we need to move." Ben leaned over the edge. "Way too many solders for us to handle down there."

Joe stepped up. "How many soldiers there are isn't the real problem. Considering the terrain—we're in a world of hurt here." He pointed to the road ahead of them. "If they caught us in this canyon, we'd be cramped. Tight quarters. No room to maneuver."

"Yeah, do you think that we should try to delay the soldiers?"

"That would be nice if we had the time, but I think we should get moving first…and fast," Joe said.

"What about them?" Ben asked, frowning at a cluster yelling at the soldiers below.

"Gotcha covered," Joe said. He grabbed a couple of his followers, then stomped towards the crowd to get them moving.

John and the others were reluctant to leave, forcing Joe to bodily push them away from the edge, finally getting most of them to follow the group, though some still tried to hang back.

"Good, they're on the way." Ben watched the group head through the canyon. "Hey, Shess, I have an idea."

"Idea good. What is?" Shess asked.

"When we're through the pass," Ben said, "do you think we should have Patrick bring down the rock walls on both sides, with Robb's help, of course?"

"This way to Rudolph city," Shess said. "One way. He not come out, others not go in. Could work."

"A landslide? Hmm…" Eric considered the walls of the canyon.

"Let me go find them and explain what I have in mind," Ben said as he headed back.

"I tell others move more," Shess said.

"Good." Ben found Patrick in the middle of a congratulatory circle, Carl at the forefront, happy to give up his 'hero' title and the attention that went with it, though some thought that blasting a gate from a distance, even with the help of Robb, was nothing compared to actual hand-to-hand combat. Ben managed to drag Patrick away from the crowd, explaining his plan as they searched for Robb.

"There he is, in that group," Patrick said, "with Annie and Tom. He's helping them with Melvin."

They went to explain the plan, and Eric continued following Ben.

Robb wasn't thrilled with the idea. "I'm still tired after that last attempt, and then to have run up that hill. That didn't help any."

Eric butted in. "I'm not certain it would work even if Robb *could* pull it off."

Robb glared at Eric. "Are *you* willing to give it a try?"

Eric blinked and stared. "I certainly don't have your ability, Robb, but let me get this straight. Ben, you plan to have Robb weaken the rock walls with heat, then Patrick will drop them, creating a wall to block the oncoming soldiers, right?"

"That was the plan," Ben said. "I've seen them work together, so I figured it would work."

Eric continued. "Last time they were working on a door with hinges, metallic hinges, steel hinges, man-made hinges. This is different. Heating up the rock won't be quite as easy to do. It's not the same as heating metal. Attempting to soften the rock would be like trying to build a mini volcano. The problem isn't so much one of temperature. After all, iron melts at 1500 degrees, and rock can get soft enough to flow at a mere 1200, but metal is a good conductor of heat—it transfers it so much better. Rock tends to isolate the heat, and if you consider the thermal mass…" Eric paused. "Even more difficult to heat the rock."

"We don't have time for long drawn out science lessons," Ben said, "but if you have a quick idea, we'd love to hear it."

"I'll get right to it," Eric said. "Considering the height of the canyon and the width of the road, I don't think you'd be able to move enough material to block it entirely, and without complete blockage, the effort will be futile."

"Don't you mean, 'Resistance is futile'?" John muttered as he walked past.

"So what's your idea, Eric?" Ben asked.

Eric stepped towards the top of the switchbacks. "If we could block the trail, at the narrowest point, there would be fewer options for the soldiers. Hit the path at the most restricted spot, not up here in the much wider canyon."

"Yeah, that could work," Ben said. "Can you do that, Patrick?"

Patrick glanced at the road. "Yeah, I see trees and rocks that I could knock loose. I'm certain I could get an avalanche going. Probably faster than building a volcano." He looked intently at Ben. "Though not as much fun."

"If that's all you want, I could catch some trees on fire along there, too," Robb said. "That wouldn't be too difficult, right, Eric?"

"The combustion point of wood is certainly well below that of liquid iron, even fresh wood. Besides the underbrush would make good kindling," Eric said. "Excellent idea, Robb."

Melvin finally pulled back from Annie's ministrations. "Anyone care to let me in on what you guys are suggesting?"

"Do we have time for a quick demo?" Patrick asked. "Seeing is believing, right?"

Ben checked the progress of the soldiers below. "Yes, yes," he said. "But make it quick. We don't have all day."

"Yeah, quick *and* little," Annie said. "Remember, he hasn't been with us this last week. He hasn't seen any of what's been going on."

Tom shook his head. "Here we go again."

"Melvin, since you've been out of the picture, we've discovered a few things," Patrick started. "Some of us have developed…shall we say abilities? Things that until now, I would have believed impossible."

"Yeah? So Eric was right about this place?" Melvin asked.

They all nodded in unison as Patrick continued. "See that rock?" he said, picking out one at random.

"Yeah," Melvin said.

"Keep an eye on it," Patrick said as he raised a hand.

The rock shattered, spraying fragments, leaving nothing but a dust cloud.

A couple scouts farther ahead jumped and laughed as Melvin dropped his jaw and stared.

"And Robb has a different talent. Watch him," Patrick said.

Robb leaned down to Melvin and opened his hand, offering a ball of flame.

"Yow!" Melvin screeched.

"That's enough," Ben yelled. "Let's get moving,"

Most of the group headed out, but Patrick and Robb stayed behind. Their plan was to do as much damage as they could do quickly, then run to catch up with everyone else.

Eric waited, wandered up to watch.

Robb frowned. "You ought to be up with Ben and the others."

Eric ignored him and said, "After seeing what Robb did with Melvin's help, though unintentional, can you imagine what Patrick could do?" His eyes lost focus as he thought about it. "The explosion could be as much as an atomic bomb going off."

Patrick laughed. "Yeah, that would be neat. Can you see turning that whole city into one big crater?"

"Yeah," Robb said. "But if we try something like that, we'd need to make certain Annie is out of the way first, for a short while. She won't let us do any experiments if she thinks it'll hurt Melvin."

"She may have a point there, but it would still be neat to try," Patrick said.

Eric continued, "As opposed to an atomic bomb, a blast like that wouldn't have any fallout, but with enough energy released it could have a similar effect. Similar conventional explosions have happened in the past, the far past, when meteors impacted the Earth leaving huge craters, though most have long since been grown over."

Patrick stood there, considering the possibilities, then slowly said, "Yeah, but if I ever try *that*, I have *got* to maintain control. No misfires."

"That goes twice for me," Robb agreed.

"Well, let's get on with blocking the road," Patrick said.

Eric was helpful in identifying good targets as the two of them alternately blasted and flamed anything in sight. Once they were satisfied with the mayhem they'd created, they caught up with the group, looking one last time at the flames flickering behind them, then made their way through the group to find Ben at the front.

"Hey, Ben. We've done what we can back there. Anything else for us to do?" Patrick asked.

"Keep going?" Ben glanced back at the glow shining through the canyon. "Not much smoke, is there?"

Eric piped up, "With the breeze trending from the east, and the cold mountain air flowing down the slope, the smoke will be pushed into the far valley. We won't see much of it from this side of the mountain, but it should be definitely visible for anyone in the town, and with the rocky canyon pass, there isn't any possibility of the fire spreading in our direction."

"Good," Ben said. "And it'll certainly discourage any followers."

The road exited the mountains and headed south, opening out onto the battlefield that they'd recently left behind. The group slowed and bunched up, all staring across the small valley.

"What's the hold up?" Ben asked. He stared as everyone spread out, sitting somewhat casually in shady spots along the path. "Once the danger is out of sight, everything is back to normal?"

Shess stood next to Ben. "Not see, not worry."

"Yeah, we have that saying, too," Ben said. "But I do have a real question: which way do we go?"

Eric blinked. "We head home, right?"

"That's all you're interested in? Going home?" John teased.

"Yes, Eric, we head home." Ben pulled Eric by the shoulders away from John. "We plan to head home right now. What I meant was which path to use."

"Why not back the way we came?" Patrick asked. "Back across the valley where we fought."

"That's a good start, but we don't have the time to retrace our exact path," Ben said. "Think about going through the *lahnpe* valley again. That would be out of our way and take more time than we have."

"True, but not going that way would mean going cross country," Patrick said, "crossing fresh territory."

Tom gazed to the south. "On the other hand, following the road would be faster, and we'd be in known areas, known to *this* civilization that is."

"Yeah," Ben said. "That might be better than possibly running into wildlife, either animal or human."

"Road south goes far. Cross river far, go back north to *Roadranusis*," Shess said.

"Thanks, Shess," Patrick said. "So following the road would definitely be longer, distance-wise, and although it might be faster to travel on, it will probably end up being longer, time-wise."

"Yeah, and timing is important. We don't want to miss our date with the Door, so we might not have enough time to go the long way," Ben said.

"How much time *do* we have?" Eric asked.

"Well you said that today is Wednesday, right?" Ben asked.

"Exactly," Eric said.

"Four days to get here, Saturday to Wednesday." Ben counted. "So another four days to get back, and we won't get there until early Sunday."

"If we leave quickly and push it, we can make it back by Saturday evening," Tom said. "Doesn't leave us much time for hunting if we're going to be at the pick-up spot by Sunday noon."

"Cutting it kinda close, aren't we?" Patrick asked.

"Well, if we subtract the Sunday we spent with the *lahnpe*, then we have an extra day in case we run into something," Ben said. "We could make it back by Friday."

"Cut out Sunday? Right, and what a way to spend a Sunday," Tom said. "I'm willing to avoid that again."

John reached over and patted the dagger strapped across Eric's chest. "From what I remember, *somebody* wouldn't want to miss out on *that* part of the return trip," John said. "He still has to pick up his bride, right, Eric?"

Eric jumped back and managed to squeak out, "I'm willing to avoid that valley again, especially if it means getting home on time."

"That's good," Ben said, "as I'm not even certain we'd be able to find the way back in. Did anyone look behind us as we left that area?"

"Not that I heard," Patrick said. "And I don't think that the finder would help us get there. We'd have to get close to the mountain, the *right* mountain, before it could show us an invisible door."

"For that matter," Tom butted in, "can any of us backtrack our path at all?"

"Head east until we hit the river," Ben said, "then turn south until we get to the village, right?"

"Which river? Do you know how many rivers and streams we crossed on the way here?" Tom asked.

"In that case, we follow the road," Ben said. "To guarantee that we'll be able to find the right place, but it'll be a longer trip."

Tom looked across at the small groups sitting in the shade. "Can we do that?"

"I don't see that we have any other choice. Anyone else have any ideas?" Ben waited hopefully.

No one spoke up.

"Shess, any suggestions?"

"I not hurry. You need hurry. We break group. Fast you go, slow rest go."

"That could work. Thanks, Shess," Ben said. "John, can you round up the troops and get them ready to head out?"

"No problem," John said, starting to round up the troops.

"Good," Ben said, glancing back at the canyon road. "Less talking, more doing." He followed Tom towards Annie to give her the news. *We've been pushing things as it is, but now we need to seriously hurry, and she's still focused on Melvin.*

Annie was standing by Melvin as they approached, but she stood in front of Melvin, blocking Ben. Glancing at Melvin, she said, "He isn't doing as well as I'd hoped. That last run up the mountain was tough on him. If we could get to a place where he can rest, I'd greatly appreciate it."

Tom hugged Annie and shook his head. "Stop to rest? Not likely to happen for a while. No place near here, and we need to get moving to make it back on time."

"Ben, can *you* do something?"

"According to our calculations," Ben said, "we're already going to be hard pressed to get back in time."

"Oh." Annie thought about Melvin. "Does that mean if we slow down for his sake, we'll *all* miss the exit?"

Tom gave her a squeeze. "Not a problem. We don't mention it, but Eugene came up with a contingency plan. If we aren't at the drop-off point when they first open the Door, they'll close it quickly to save power, then re-open it every 24 hours until they make contact." He smiled.

"So we won't have to wait long if we're a little late?" Annie asked.

"Any late is too late, but it'll only be one extra day," Tom said.

"That'll have to work," she said.

"Well, we've never had to rely on that plan yet, but that would be the best scenario. The thing is that with all those rapid openings and closings, they can't fully recharge the system, so each opening would be shorter and shorter. If we aren't there on time, they might not be able to hold it open long enough for *all* of us to get through in one pass."

Annie stared. "Some of us will get left behind?"

"Not intentionally," Tom said. "The sick and injured go through first, and you, of course. The rest of us would have to wait for the next chance. With a crew this big, it might be more than a couple days to get all of us through, but we'll make it."

Ben frowned. "Has this emergency plan ever had to be used before?"

"Well, no," Tom said. "But they *did* consider what might happen when they first sent someone through the Door. 'Expect the best, but design for the worst,' as the engineers say."

Annie glanced at Melvin again. "Any possibility of getting a carrier? Did Joe bring one of those army stretchers?"

"Nothing like that, but we could build a temporary one, like we learned in scouts, then when we arrive in the towns to the south, we could see about getting a cart to carry him," Ben said.

Annie's head snapped to stare at Ben. "Town to the south? Why would we go that direction?"

"It would be easier travelling if we kept to the roads, besides there's a good chance the cross country route would be even longer." Ben glanced back towards the canyon. "And we don't have any time to waste if we want to avoid another battle."

"Do you think the people in those cities would be happy," Annie said, "if you came running through their town being chased by that hoard?"

"Probably not," Tom said. "But, now that you mention it, going through the cities might slow down the soldiers."

Annie frowned. "We were being nice to the natives…the ones that were being nice to us."

Tom shrugged.

"Too bad Shess doesn't have a map of this area. I'd be more willing to risk the more direct path," Ben said.

Annie stared back and forth at the two of them. "What's wrong with going back the same way we came?" Before either could answer, she pulled out the power compass. "Using *this* to go directly to Deezh…and *Roadranusis*."

"Traveling light helps," Ben said as they were rushing across the valley floor, bringing up the rear.

Tom ran alongside. "Smart sister you have there, Ben."

Ben shrugged. "I have nothing to do with that. She's smart on her own."

"Well, I'm sure glad you brought her." Tom squinted back along their path. "Nothing from the canyon yet."

Ben slowed and jogged backwards as he searched the distance. "Sun setting. Too much glare."

"Dark soon," Tom said. "Stop for the night?"

"And let those soldiers catch up?"

"Think they made it past the fire?"

"Could be. Can't tell."

"Can't keep this pace long," Tom panted.

"Keep going as long as we can." Ben climbed the hill they had descended yesterday morning as they attacked Rudolph's army and stopped to catch his breath. Squinting at the mountains across the valley, he said, "Happy to have *that* place behind us."

"Good riddance," Tom said. "Let's keep going."

He and Ben strode past the small incline, the view of the valley falling behind the crest. Ben suddenly stopped. "I have an idea. Get Joe back here."

Tom shouted up the column, the word travelled quickly, and Joe arrived right as they were passing through their last campsite before the battle.

"Now *this* is what I call a quick march," Joe said, barely out of breath at all.

"What can you and your guys do to hinder any pursuit?" Ben asked.

"I've been thinking about that," Joe said. "If we set up snipers along the ridge on this side of the valley, we'll be able to make them think seriously before they cross."

"Do you have enough men for that?"

"Won't need many," Joe said. Two in addition to me should be enough. I'll take center, John the north side, and Tom the south side."

Tom slowed. "You want me on your fire team again?"

"Yeah. You did such a fine job last time." Joe smiled. "I certainly could use your help again."

"But I didn't do anything last time," Tom protested. "In fact, I froze."

Joe looked Tom up and down. "Yeah, I know."

Ben interrupted, "If Joe thinks you're needed, then why not?"

Tom shrugged. "Look after your sister, will ya, Ben?"

"Well, duh." Ben laughed. "You two get going. I'll send John back to join you." He jogged through the group, found John, and told him about the plan.

"I like the way Joe thinks. I'd love to get those guys in my sights." John ran back to set up his position.

Ben ran up to the front, past Annie and the main group. When he found Trey and Bear, they were wielding swords as if they were machetes, cutting back the brush and making a path for everyone else to follow. "Good work, you two. How's it going?"

Trey slowed slightly as he answered. "Doing fine. The vegetation's not too thick here. Still kinda green, so it's easy to remove."

"So I see. The problem is that you are making an obvious path."

"Easier for the folks to follow." Trey said. "It's getting dark and not everyone has a lantern."

"True," Ben said. "But remember those guys following us? They'll be able to see where to go, too."

Trey stopped swinging his sword and put a hand on Bear's shoulder. "Change of plans. We need to make an obvious path *and* a separate path that we are going to follow. That'll get them off our tails for a while. It might even force them to split up their group. Half an angry horde is better than a whole angry horde, right?"

"I'll have Carl lead the main part of the group off to the side," Ben said. "You two keep hacking away on a false trail."

"Gotcha covered," Trey said, going back to slashing the underbrush. "Veer left, Bear. We have another path to make."

Bear understood, so Ben let them continue, checking on everyone as he patrolled back through the group. When he found Carl and Fredekas regaling the others with stories of bravado, he stopped them. "I need the two of you to lead the march. We need to get through this forest quickly, quietly, and without leaving a trace. Trey and Bear are cutting a fake path to detour our pursuers, but I need you guys to keep the group going."

"Easy enough," Carl said. "Fred and I will head straight out a ways, and find an easy path for the group to follow, then circle back and cover up any evidence that any one has ever been here."

Fredekas smiled. "Good do. We go."

"I trust you to do an amazing job," Ben said, "based on what I've seen you do before."

"Come on, Fred. We have real work to do," Carl said, heading towards the front.

Ben continued his journey making certain that everyone was keeping up. Passing the middle, he came across Annie and Patrick still helping Melvin along. "Is he any better?"

"He's not doing too bad," she said. "Though at this pace, none of us will last much longer."

"I know, I know. We're going to stop as soon as we can, but not yet."

"Melvin isn't alone in slowing us," Patrick said. "You should see how far back Eric and the camp followers are."

"Hey, I'm not that slow...am I?" Melvin said.

"No, you're doing fine, but we're all tuckered out and need a rest."

"Yeah," Annie said. "And we'll need to bed down soon. Can we find a clearing or something?"

"I'll have Carl and Fred work on that. They're up front trying to locate an easy path." Ben glanced farther back into the deepening night. "Have any of you heard any shots? Joe was hanging back with John to slow those soldiers from the city." Ben intentionally didn't mention Tom to avoid worrying Annie.

Both Annie and Patrick shook their heads.

"Oh, well. With Joe back there, I'm certain they'll catch up soon enough." He shrugged and checked the rear one last time. "The rest will have to keep up. Let me go tell Carl to find us a stopping place."

"Thanks," Annie said. "Soon, too. It's not just *getting* dark."

Ben jogged back up the line again. *I'm certainly getting my exercise today.* He encouraged everyone as he passed by, finally catching up to Trey and Bear at the front. He asked, "Where's Carl?"

"They're up there a ways," Trey said.

"They far," Bear said.

"We had been right behind them," Trey said. "But then they went on ahead to find a good place for us to cut to the side."

"Thanks," Ben said and hurried off into the darkness of the woods. Not too much farther on, he managed to find the trailblazers and asked Carl about stopping.

Carl grinned at Fredekas. "We were just talking about that, Ben." Carl gazed into the darkness behind them. "We were noticing that those folks were having a tough time keeping up."

Ben squinted back in the same direction. "You can see them back there?"

"Yeah," Carl said absentmindedly. "We had planned to cross that stream in a couple hundred meters, but we can travel along it to hide our path instead, *then* we can stop for the night."

"There's a stream?" Ben asked. "You've been there and back? How far out have you scouted?"

"We haven't been farther than here." Carl stared at Ben. "You can't smell the water? You don't hear it?"

"Never mind, Carl. Just get us to a stopping place," Ben said. *More evidence for the list.* He headed back. "I'll let the others know. They've been waiting long enough for it."

Carl continued tracking as Ben headed back to the sagging crew.

When Ben caught up to Trey and Bear, he told them about the plan to hide their tracks in a stream.

"I like that idea," Trey said. "In fact, Bear and I will make *another* phony path, straight across the stream. Everyone else can head crosswise through the water. That'll make it even tougher for them to track us."

"Go far enough that they won't notice the side path," Ben said. "*Then* circle back and join us."

Trey grinned at Bear. "Yeah. That'll be fun."

Ben smiled. *Someone's enjoying this trip.* He went back to the main group and explained the plan, then headed towards the stream to help direct the traffic. As he neared the stream, he found Fredekas and Bear keeping out of the way, as Carl and Trey continued a heated discussion.

"Downstream."

"Upstream."

"Downstream is easier."

"That's why we should avoid it."

"You like climbing climb wet rocks?"

"Better than slipping on them."

"They're already tired."

"I'll bet the soldiers are, too."

"So we need to move faster, right?"

"Yes, faster, but safer at the same time."

"You want them stumbling in the dark?"

"You want them blinded by the moonlight?"

"Moonlight isn't a problem, not with all those clouds."

"Then it'll be even darker."

"So we should go on the easy route, downstream."

As Ben walked up to the two of them, they both said in unison, "Ben, will you tell him—?"

Ben shushed them. "Let's hope that there aren't any soldiers within a click or two. They'd hear all the noise and know right where to go."

Sheepishly, both waited for Ben to continue.

Ben paused, letting them think, then asked, "So, what's the problem?"

They both spoke at the same time, and Ben tried to make sense of their argument. He finally figured out what each wanted: Trey felt the group should go downstream, the easier path and Carl thought it would be better to head upstream, to further delay their followers. Both had good points. Ben would have preferred to make the decision with Joe's military expertise, but he had to do this one on his own.

He asked the two of them, "No one wants to split the group? Some head upstream, some down?" He stared. "And maybe have some continue straight across?"

Both Carl and Trey stared at Ben, then at each other.

"No way," Carl said. "Splitting up the group would invite more trouble."

"Yeah. That would be dumb," Trey said.

Ben smiled as the two finally agreed on something.

"So then, we have a head start," Ben said. "And we haven't heard any shots, so they haven't run into Joe yet." He paused. "We do need to hit the sack soon, and it would be easier to hear anyone following us tripping *up* through the stream than if they *snuck* downstream, right?" He waited.

They both nodded, Carl a little more enthusiastically than Trey.

"Then we'll head upstream?" Ben raised his eyebrows.

"Yeah, that makes sense," Trey said reluctantly.

"Ha!" Carl said, not quite sticking out his tongue.

Trey shrugged for a moment, then slapped Carl on the shoulder, just about knocking him to the ground. "Oops!" He reached down and helped him back to his feet.

"You two are still friends?" Ben asked.

They grinned at each other, and Carl said, "Why wouldn't we be?"

"Yeah," Trey said. "We've been through worse and survived."

Ben smiled. *I don't know what I'd do with these guys if they were ever serious.*

Trey grabbed Bear and said, "As much as I'd like to wait and watch those two scramble across the rocks upstream, we have chopping to do." They headed across the stream and started slashing through the trees.

"With all that chopping, the soldiers won't even notice our side trip. They'll follow the path Trey and Bear are making."

"That should give us extra time," Carl said. "But you realize that no matter which way we go, we'll have to walk through the middle of the stream. We can't leave any tracks on the sides."

"That means we'll *all* have wet feet before we stop," Ben said. "And we won't be able to build a fire to dry out our socks. That would be a searchlight to direct *anyone* in the forest to find us." He shrugged. "We'll have to make do in the dark."

"Joe won't be happy, and Annie certainly won't want to treat a bunch of foot rot," Carl yelled back as he and Fredekas picked their way through the rocks at the edge of the stream.

With Trey and Bear beating the false path straight ahead, Ben stood on the far side of the stream, directing everyone upstream. He felt like a traffic cop, controlling the traffic through an intersection. He watched as folks stumbled and tripped through the water. The upstream path was more difficult than Carl had assumed. *Maybe Trey was right. Maybe I'm sending everyone to their doom, or not.* He didn't know.

Every now and then, another cloud passed across the moon, making it even more difficult to traverse the rocky bottom of the stream. Folks were slipping and getting wet, and not just their feet. *Foot rot may be the least of our worries,* Ben thought. *What if we all catch the chills?* He expected that Carl was right about Annie and the foot rot, but if Annie herself came down with something, then what would they do? He'd have to keep her safe, safer than he'd expected. She was valuable cargo.

When Ben saw Robb coming through, he stopped him. "I know we can't get a big fire going, but do you think you can make something small but warm enough to dry us out?"

Robb paused for a moment, then said, "Yeah. I may be able to help. I don't know if you've noticed, but when I use a fireball to light a regular fire, then there's smoke…from the wood burning, but if I use *just* a fireball, there's no wood, so no smoke. If I keep it in my hands, then it should be more difficult to detect at a distance."

"Good," Ben said. "That's what we'll need. Thanks."

"I'll get one going as soon as we settle for the night," Robb said as he splashed off.

That's taken care of, Ben thought.

Annie's group coming through the opening interrupted Ben's reveries. They stopped at the edge of the stream, and she looked across at Ben on the other side and raised her eyebrows. "No bridge? We have to get our feet wet?" She started hopping across on rocks, trying to stay dry.

"No bridge," Ben said. "We turn here, head upstream."

Annie stopped mid-stream and looked past Ben. "Then why do I see a path right there behind you?"

"That's where Trey and Bear went."

"And we aren't following them?" she asked. "That's why they were cutting the path, right? For us to follow?"

"That was the original plan," Ben said, "but now *that* path is to lead the soldiers astray. We're heading *this* way, upstream."

"I don't see any path." Annie squinted. "*Where* are we going?"

"That's the idea. The soldiers won't see any path either. They'll keep going forward as we cut to the side."

Annie frowned as she examined the sides of the stream. "You expect us to walk through the middle of this? We'll all get wet."

"Try to not get *all* wet, maybe keep it to your feet," Ben said.

Annie stared at him. "And then you'll be letting Robb build a big bonfire, so we can all dry out?"

"We can't risk a bonfire," Ben said, "but he has something in mind that might work."

"As long as you don't expect us to sleep with wet feet. I don't like the sound of that."

"I don't either, but there's no other way. We have to get these guys off our tail."

"Are they even following us? Has anyone even seen them yet?"

"Not yet," Ben said, "but we're assuming that they must be back there. Rudolph certainly wasn't happy when we escaped with Melvin, so I'd be surprised if he doesn't try to snatch him back."

Annie spoke to Melvin, sitting next to Patrick "I know you're tired, but now we have to *swim* upstream." She glared at Ben. "If he gets sicker…" She let her threat go unstated as she stepped back to seize Melvin's arm. "Patrick?"

Patrick grabbed Melvin's other arm as they waded into the middle of the stream. They splashed upstream for a ways, then continued into the darkness until they disappeared as another cloud passed by.

Suddenly Ben heard a big splash followed by a short shriek. He rushed up to see what had happened.

"Just a minor slip," Patrick said.

Annie frowned. "He slipped on a rock and fell in. Now he's wet up to his knees, *and* up to his elbows."

"Hey, I didn't fall in completely." Patrick tried to smile as his teeth chattered. "Wow, that water is cold."

"It might be easier if we could see where we're going," Annie complained.

"I don't know if the lanterns would help much," Ben said. "They aren't bright to start with, certainly not enough for this, and we didn't bring enough. No one thought we'd be wandering through the woods in the middle of the night."

"Well, I would think that you'd've planned for that. Not awfully prepared, are you?"

Melvin slowly stood up taller. "Annie, I don't think you should hold it against Ben. This certainly isn't a typical campout. I don't remember any other campouts where we were being chased by a troop of soldiers, another Scout troop maybe, but that only happened once." He grinned. "At the Scout-o-rama, remember?"

Patrick snorted. "You must be feeling worse than I thought, Melvin. You're starting to sound like Eric."

Melvin actually laughed. "Eric? As I recall, that whole ruckus started up because of something he said to that other troop."

"Never mind that now," Annie said. "We *have* to get out of this water and to dry land…in the dark." She glared at Ben.

"What do you expect me to do? It's night time," Ben said wide eyed.

"And the clouds passing by make it even darker," she said.

"Ben may not be able to solve the problem with the darkness," Melvin said, "but there's something *you* could try, Patrick."

Patrick blinked. "Me? What do you expect me to do about the dark?"

"When you were trying open the city gate, didn't we see you make heatless light?"

"Yeah," Annie said. "You were playing with one of your scrolls. We were watching you do that as Melvin was eating."

"Hang on," Patrick said. "I'll see."

"We've been heading upstream for a while now," Ben said. "Most likely far enough away from the path that it won't make much difference if we leave a trail leading out of the water now."

The four of them climbed up the bank and plopped on dry ground. Patrick pulled off his backpack and searched through the pockets. As he continued digging, Eric came splashing up with the camp followers.

"Hold up over there," Ben said. "Sit for a bit while we work on this."

"Thanks, Ben," Eric said. "We'll do that."

Patrick finally pulled out a scroll and held it up, the paper shaking in his still shivering hands. "Here it is."

"Well, what's it say?" Annie asked.

Patrick held it in the fading moonlight and compared with the notes written in his pad. He mumbled a couple times, spoke aloud twice, then said, "Ready or not, here I come." He held out an empty hand, curled his fingers shut, and stared into it, then whispered. A soft glow came from inside his cupped hand. He slowly opened it all the way and the glow grew to light all the faces staring at it.

Eric stepped up to see it better.

"If I didn't know better, I'd call it a fairy light," Annie said. "It's so soft and fuzzy, grayish but not quite white, yet no heat?"

"That's why we didn't consider it useful before," Patrick said. "We were trying to bust open the gate."

"It might not be good as a weapon," Ben said, "but as a flashlight it works brilliantly!" He laughed at his own joke.

"Can you make it bigger?" Annie asked. "It won't do us much good sitting there in your hand."

Patrick stood to make more room, but as he did so, he tipped his hand and the light fell out, drifting to the ground where it bounced slightly and moved in the gentle breeze.

"Hey, now that could be useful," Melvin said. "What else does it do?" He bent to pick it up, and held it out in his hand. "Doesn't weigh much." He blew on it, and it floated up out of his hand, carried on the breeze, and settled on Eric's head.

Eric jumped up and danced as if he'd walked through a spider web. "Get that thing off of me," he shouted.

"Sit down, Eric. As soon as you stood up, it fell off," Ben said. "If fell is the right word. It floated away like a dandelion seed being blown by the wind." He reached out and snagged the light as it drifted past. "Can you make another one, Patrick?"

"I can try." Patrick cupped his hands together and blew into them, quoting the scroll as he did. A brighter glow sprang out between his fingers, lighting up the whole area. "Here, Annie," he said as he handed it to her. "Keep a grip on it, so it won't get loose."

She held it in her hand and twisted it. "That works well. I can aim it like a flashlight."

Eric stood back and watched. "It isn't burning?"

"No. That's the neat part. It sorta tickles, but that's it. Ben was right when he compared it to a dandelion. Soft, fluffy, no weight, but it lights up."

Eric stepped forward slowly. "May I see?"

"Certainly. Hold out your hand." She gently released the ball of light into Eric's outstretched hand. "See? Pure light. Nothing else."

Eric stared at his glowing hand. "Interesting. Similar to *ignis fatuus*," he dragged his eyes away from the light. "That's Latin for foolish fire, what you might call a will-o'-the-wisp or St. Elmo's fire." He stepped forward hesitantly. "Annie, you called it a fairy light?"

"Well, yeah, that's what I *called* it, but there's no such thing as fairies," Annie stated firmly.

"Yeah, right, Annie," Ben said. "And Robb can't throw flame from a sword, and Patrick can't blast rocks by talking to them, and," he looked her in the eye, "you can't heal by touch."

Annie abruptly dropped to the ground. "When you put it that way, I'd have to admit that there *could* be fairies."

"Patrick, if you could be so kind as to make more of those, we can be on our way," Ben said. "Be careful not to make them too bright. We want to be able to see the ground, but not light up the forest, giving the soldiers a target."

"That's do able," Patrick said.

"I want to get everyone to get enough sleep tonight," Ben said as he looked at Annie, "and dried out."

"Thank you," Annie said as Patrick worked to make enough fairy lights for everyone. Then taking their newly-created flashlights, they all continued up the stream.

Joe crawled to the edge of the ridge, and squinted into the darkness. He looked towards Tom. "See anything?" he whispered loudly.

Tom glanced across the valley, staring at the mountains they'd barely left and replied quietly, "Nothing visible from over here. Can John see anything?"

Joe called out to his other side, "John? Anything?"

John shook his head in the dark, then whispered, "No movement."

"Do you still have that spotting scope?" Joe asked.

"Yeah, I have it." John hefted his rifle off his field-expedient bipod: his backpack, and opened it up. He snuck across the slope to Joe.

"Thanks. Keep an eye out while I have a look. I don't want to get caught by surprise."

"None of us want to," John said, creeping back to his position.

Joe focused the scope at the peak of the mountains across the valley. *I can see where to aim because stars silhouette the peak. Makes it easy to spot.* He then panned the scope across to the low spot near the canyon. Slowly moving the scope, he zoomed in on where the canyon opened out. Although the moon kept going behind the clouds, he had enough light to see if there was any movement across the valley.

"See anything?" John asked.

"Nothing. Even if they were wearing dark clothing, I would see *something*. Even a shadow of a movement would be enough."

"Or is that the movement of a shadow?" John teased.

Joe sat back and spoke aloud. "Do you think we've waited long enough?"

Tom sat up. "It's been a couple hours already, hasn't it?"

"Could be. Can't tell. Need a watch," Joe said. "When all you're doing is sitting on a post, waiting and watching, time does funny things. Five minutes can seem like an hour, an hour can seem like all night, and all night feels like a week." He scoped out the sky. "I don't know…maybe we *have* been sitting here a whole week already."

"I don't think it's been a week," John said. "I would have noticed my stomach growling."

"Yeah, that's a good clue," Joe said. "So should we head up?"

"Well, we haven't seen anyone coming, so maybe that fire, death, and destruction that Robb and Patrick pulled off worked. It might be safe to join up with the rest now," John said.

"Yeah, and the sooner we get going, the easier it will be to find the rest of them," Tom said.

"With as many of them as there are, and with the training, or lack thereof," Joe paused, "it should be easy to spot the trail." He picked up the scope and folded the legs.

"Hey, John. Be careful with this thing. It's come in handy, but I don't think we're done with it."

John walked up. "Well, it's good for hunting…hunting animals, I mean. I like to set up a blind and sit tight, waiting for the prey to come to me."

Tom raised his eyebrows. "Like what we're doing now?"

"Yeah, but like I said, hunting animals was my goal, not survival of the fittest. Hey, where's Darwin now?" John laughed as he slung his rifle on his shoulder. "Let's get going."

The group headed out, Joe in the lead, at a slow jog. Once they were on their way, it became easy to follow the rest of the scouts.

"I can't believe the damage they've done to the trees here," Joe said.

"I didn't know you were a tree hugger," John joked.

"Not a tree hugger, but if we're followed, no one would have to look twice to find us."

"A little more discreet, you're saying?" Tom asked.

"Yeah. Wasn't that the point? Avoid being followed." Joe frowned. "Someone up there missed the memo."

Tom shrugged. "Can't do much now, but now we won't get lost."

They went silent as they continued their jog through the forest. An hour or so later, after winding through the trees and crossing a dozen streams, the path suddenly came to an abrupt end.

Tom plowed into Joe who had unexpectedly stopped. "What's wrong?" he asked.

"The path stops here," Joe said.

"Stops? It can't," John stated. "Where'd they go?"

Joe stepped back. "The trees and bushes have been hacked all the way to here. Now they aren't touched."

John circled the area, studying the undergrowth. "You're right. Nothing is smashed past this point. Certainly not like we've seen before."

Tom examined the ground. "Not much in the way of footprints, so where did they go?"

Joe shrugged, then checked the canopy overhead. "No room for a Huey, so I don't think they were airlifted out."

Tom stared at Joe. "Huey? Airlifted?"

"Not an actual Huey, but there's no room to land *anything*, whatever they might have around here." Joe shrugged. "Just trying to consider all the possibilities, eliminating the ones I can. So, what's left?"

"They turned off to the side somewhere back there," John suggested, "and we didn't notice."

"And they kept cutting a path in this direction?" Joe asked.

"They might have done it to throw off any pursuers," Tom said.

"Yeah, but there's two problems with that thinking," Joe said.

"Oh? What problems are those?" John asked.

"One, no one in that group is smart enough to think of it." Joe headed out, backtracking their path.

"That's harsh." Tom followed slowly. "And the second?"

Joe stopped suddenly and spun. "The second problem is that they forgot to tell us."

* * *

Ben suddenly sat up in his sleeping bag. He stared up at the still dark sky, then noticed it starting to lighten to the east. *What time is it?* he wondered. He searched for anyone about and noticed a soft glow bouncing around the circle of tents. He waited until the sentry came around to his side of the camp, then called out quietly, "Hello?"

The light stopped its patrol, moved towards him, and slowly revealed Patrick. "Ben? What's up? You ought to be sleeping. Get all the rest you can."

"I asked to be woken when Joe and his snipers caught up, and it's already starting to get light. How long have they been here?"

"They aren't here, yet," Patrick said. "No one's seen them."

Ben rolled out of his bag and pulled his shoes on. "We manage to get Melvin, and now we've lost Joe?"

"And John, not to mention Tom." Patrick shrugged. "But I'm certain *he'll* survive. He has all the proper connections with the natives."

"Doesn't do *us* any good." Ben stood up and gave his sleeping bag a kick. "Is there way to let them know where we are?"

"Let me send up a fairy light," Patrick said. "A big one." He paused. "Wait. Wouldn't that notify the bad guys as well?"

"Probably," Ben said. "But at this point, I don't think it matters much. We need to get them back before they get left too far behind." He glanced up at the remaining stars. "And you'd better hurry. If it gets too light, they won't be able to see such a soft light."

"We could always get Robb to send up a smoke signal. One of his fireballs can be seen for quite a ways."

"True, but I'd like to avoid catching the whole forest on fire to rescue our lost souls," Ben said. "Go ahead and try your method."

Patrick stepped away, checked for obstacles, then cupped his hands together and formed a small ball of light. He kept talking to it as it grew to the size of a basketball, then a beach ball, then a huge ball two meters across. He hefted it, giving it a gentle toss into the air, then as it drifted, he sent it higher and higher with little pop noises. As it floated above the treetops, he glanced at Ben. "Here goes."

Ben watched as Patrick stared right at it and slapped his hands together, making the ball squish, then suddenly burst out bright white, illuminating everything in stark shadows. It didn't make much noise, but the light was certainly brighter than he had expected. Blinking, he tried to get his vision back, but before he could see, he could hear that many in the camp had been awakened by the sudden light and were wondering what was happening.

"Well, that should work…as long as they see it," Ben said. "Thanks."

"Welcome," Patrick replied. "I'll get everyone else back to sleep. We still have an hour or so before it'll be light enough to get moving."

"They need all the rest they can get. If Carl happens to be up, send him this way. I'm going to backtrack, see if we can lead the guys home."

"Well, don't you get lost either."

Ben guffawed. "Wouldn't that be a hoot? What did I say last night about sending out search parties to search for the searchers?" He paused and frowned. "That *was* last night, wasn't it?"

Patrick shrugged as he went back to walk his beat, circling the campsite.

Ben quickly rolled his sleeping bag, strapped it to his backpack, slipped it on, and headed out. As he left the campsite, he came upon Patrick, still making his rounds.

"Carl moved quickly," Patrick said. "He and Fred are already out there somewhere."

"Good. I'll keep my eye out for them."

"You should leave your pack here," Patrick suggested. "You could cover more ground if you aren't carrying all your stuff."

"Yeah, but what if I need something?" Ben said. "And what if I don't get back until after you have to leave? I don't want to make someone else carry my stuff."

Patrick shrugged. "Good point. See ya!" He continued his patrol.

Ben continued back towards the stream, stopping every now and then to look towards the campsite, hoping to hear that Carl had returned. When he arrived at the stream, he turned west, heading downstream, listening carefully, but still hearing nothing. Suddenly he heard a crunch to his right, across the creek. *Footsteps?* He froze and scrutinized the shadows in that direction.

A soft voice spoke by his left shoulder, startling him, and he jumped.

Carl spoke again, whispering, "See anything over there?"

"I didn't even see *you*." Ben stared. "How long have you been here?"

"We just barely arrived."

"We?" Ben looked past Carl, seeing nothing.

"Yeah, we." Carl said as Fredekas faded into view.

Ben blinked. "Hello, Fred. I didn't see you there."

Fredekas gestured silently.

Carl examined the trees. "So, what's out there?" He tipped his head to Ben's right.

Ben shrugged. "I don't know, but I heard a noise. Can't see much in this light, but I figured it might be you."

"Sounding like an elephant tromping around? Not likely."

"I didn't hear a thing," Ben said. "You blend in nicely."

"Learning from an expert." Carl signaled Fredekas.

"So how'd you find me out here?"

"Easy enough to track you. Not quite an elephant, but noisy enough."

"It *shairvoo*," Fredekas said. "Good eat. Catch not easy, fast run."

"A deer?" Ben asked. "Tell Patrick when we get back."

"If we get any hunting time in," Carl said. "He can cook us a feast."

"Hunting?" Ben winced. "Wasn't that the whole point of this trip?"

"It was," Carl said. "But if we ever get home, I'll bet Tom'll let us come back on another trip…either that or he'll have to refund us our money." He laughed. "On the next trip though, Ben, let's focus on hunting, no fooling with native politics."

"We didn't exactly volunteer to get involved this time," Ben said.

"True, but now that we know what's going on here, we'll be better prepared next time."

"If there is a next time." Ben frowned. "And we still don't know where Joe is."

Fredekas twisted sharply and silently. Carl grabbed Ben's shoulder, motioning him to stay put and keep quiet.

Ben froze, then mouthed, "What?"

Carl gazed into the distance and held up two fingers, hesitated, then raised three fingers.

Ben concentrated in that direction, but he couldn't hear anything. He cupped his hands behind his ears and listened back and forth, then shrugged again.

Carl shook his head at Ben's hands around his ears, putting his finger on the tip of his nose.

Ben stared. *He can* smell *them coming?* He continued to peer into the darkness, still nothing visible, and he couldn't hear anything either. Then suddenly, he saw a shaft of moonlight blink out and back, followed by another one nearby. Something was definitely there, but whatever it was, it moved like a shadow, *in* the shadows, silent yet quick, not staying in one place long enough to pin down.

Fredekas headed out with Carl close on his tail. Ben took one step, and though he didn't hear anything, both of them spun and stared. Ben stopped awkwardly and sat back on his heels, waiting for either one of them to give him permission to move.

With Carl and Fredekas fading quickly into the distance, and the unknown heading straight for him, Ben had to be satisfied to sit tight and wait. He leaned back and closed his eyes, concentrating on sound alone, listening for any sign of movement. This early in the morning, Ben would have expected more activity. *Unless disturbed by a bunch of trespassers,* he thought, but the usually active nocturnal wildlife was keeping still.

A slight vibration caught his attention a couple of times but nothing strong enough to identify, but then a new sound caught his attention. At first minor, it slowly grew to fill the forest. It sounded as if a breeze were coming and going, a whoosh, a pause, then another whoosh, rhythmically. Ben counted between whooshes and could predict the next one.

Then silence. Whatever had been making the whooshing had moved on.

Everything blinked dark. Startled, Ben opened his eyes and stared up. Nothing. Although the sky was still generally gray, the lighter sky to the east let him know that morning was arriving. Seconds later, Ben heard the normal forest noises pick up. He frowned and looked out through the trees. *I wonder why everything went quiet. That was bizarre,* he thought.

He slowly stood, feeling his knees creak. He'd been sitting still too long. Stretching his legs, he noticed movement off in the direction Carl had gone. Watching closely, Carl and Fredekas slowly came into view…followed by Joe, John, and Tom. They were found!

As they approached, Ben could hear Joe explaining how they saw the signal that Patrick had sent up. "Not exactly a standard flare that burns a while as it drifts. That one popped like a flash bulb and lit everything up."

"You should have seen it from camp," Ben said. "It woke up most of the guys."

John moaned. "Woke them up? What would I give to get some sleep right now."

"Not in the cards," Joe said. "Not everyone gets the luxury of sleep."

"As long as they're awake," Tom said, "we can get going right away."

"So, what happened back there, Tom?" Ben asked, hurrying through the forest.

"Nothing." Joe scowled. "Absolutely nothing. We waited for hours but no one ever showed up."

"Yeah," John said. "A total waste of time."

"So, do you think they're after us?" Carl asked.

"We couldn't tell," Joe said. "But if they are, they're way back there."

"Either way," Tom said, "it's high time that we get a move on."

"Can't agree more," Ben said.

Joe looked ahead. "I remember drill sergeants rousing us in Basic Training, and I've been wanting to do the same to someone else for quite a while."

They arrived at the camp site in time to see Trey and Patrick rounding up the troops. Bear and Shess were doing the same for the *shmahseespe*.

"Ah, shucks," Joe said. "Maybe next time." He glanced at Ben.

Ben yelled, "Where's Annie? We need to get a reading."

Annie stuck her head out of a small tent that hadn't been dropped yet. "I'm checking up on Melvin. He's not quite ready to head out."

"But he's feeling better?" Ben asked.

"The sleep did him good," Annie said. "And he says he's ready for normal duty, whatever that would entail." She smiled as she saw Tom standing next to Ben. She crawled out of the tent and said, "I wondered if you were going to make it back."

Tom walked up and let his arms enfold her as he smiled. "There's not much that can keep me away from you."

She gave him a gentle hug. "Glad that you feel that way."

He glanced around at the camp. "Are we ready to go?"

She stepped back and said, "More tents to drop and pack up."

Ben grabbed a tent stake and pulled. "Let me help you with that."

She frowned. "Let's get Melvin out of the tent first."

Joe jumped up and grabbed another stake. "Or not." He slapped the side of the tent. "Hey, Melvin! Up and at 'em. We have places to go."

Ben laughed as he pulled the tent cord.

Melvin crawled out of the tent as it collapsed, dragging his backpack. "No need to make a total mess of things." He frowned at Joe. "Give me a moment to get my shoes on, and I'll be glad to help out."

Annie stepped up. "Not unless you're feeling up to it, Melvin."

Melvin shrugged Annie's hand off his shoulder. "I'm not a cripple, but that rest helped. Whatever sleep I had in that city wasn't right."

"Probably the drugs," Annie said. "Either that or the power sucking thing that Rudolph did to you."

"Whatever it was, I feel fine now." Melvin stood up, tossed his backpack aside, and rolled up the tent. "The pack they gave me is pretty much empty," he glanced towards Ben, "trying to be easy on me. I'll get this tent."

"If you feel you can handle it, go ahead," Ben said. He left Melvin to finish packing up the tent and found Patrick hurrying the others along. "I assume everyone else is already prepped. Anyone think about breakfast?"

"A couple guys were asking, but I told them that if they still had any snack bars left, now would be the time to dig into them. I don't think anyone has any trail mix left, and I'm afraid that the locals are on their own."

"I'll check with Shess." Ben wove through folks still packing and came to a group of *shmahseespe* in the middle of a heated discussion. "Shess, what's up? What's the problem?"

Shess silenced his group, then told Ben, "They worry not get home. Want go back, follow road, go towns, not lost in forest."

"I understand. If we had the time, I'd head that route, too." Ben suddenly frowned. "Hey. I forgot to have Annie to check the compass."

"Compass good. Not lost," Shess said. He spoke quickly to his group, and they all relaxed, ready to move out.

"Thanks, Shess. I'll let you know when we're ready to go." He went back across the camp to find Tom and Annie studying the power compass. "So? Which direction do we head?"

Tom shrugged. "I still can't see anything on that compass."

"The bright red spot is mostly east," Annie said. "In the direction of the rising sun." She squinted. "I'll be able to get a better reading once the sun has risen far enough so that I'm not staring right into it, but, that's the direction we go."

"Does it show anything about Mr. Bentnose?"

Annie studied the compass again. "Well, we know that the orange spot in the middle is Melvin because he's with us, and the dark purple one to the west is Mr. Bentnose."

"So he's still in his city?" Tom asked.

"That's what it shows," Annie confirmed.

"That'd better be right," Ben said, shaking his head. "Let's get going!"

Using the same method as on their trip out, they kept an eye on the compass, stopping briefly and only when necessary. They ate breakfast, as well as lunch, on the fly, continuing as quickly as they could. They filled canteens at every creek and stream they encountered, because the next one might be too far away.

Twice they ran smack into rivers too large to ford comfortably. Although they had headed upstream in the dark last night to trick the soldiers, now that they knew which way to go, they headed downstream, in the general direction of *Roadranusis*, to find a place to safely cross.

Where they couldn't find a natural bridge, usually a fallen tree, they created a temporary bridge by chopping down a nearby tree, letting it drop across the river. The third time they hit a big river, they headed south, as they had before, but this time, they hiked quite a ways and still couldn't find a good spot to cross. This river was much wider and swifter than the others had been, and the bluffs on this side were tall and steep.

Ben, Shess, and Tom, again leading the group, called a halt to discuss the problem, letting everyone rest for a moment. They stood on a small outcropping of rock hanging over the rapidly flowing water.

"According to the last reading, the town is still south of here, so even if we stay on this side of the river, we aren't likely to overshoot," Ben said.

"Yeah, whatever," Tom said distractedly, staring across the river.

"We soon arrive?" Shess asked.

"That's what Annie thinks," Ben said. "As long as she's right that the spot she's been tracking on the compass is Deezh." He crossed his fingers. "It better be, or we're lost." Ben asked Tom, "Should we call her up here to check the compass?"

Tom continued to focus across the river.

Ben poked him. "Tom?"

Tom jumped as he pulled his eyes away from whatever had kept his interest. "What?"

"Do you think we should have Annie take another reading?"

"Yeah, yeah. We should do that." Tom went back to staring across the river again.

Ben followed Tom's gaze but didn't see anything that stood out. "Do you see something over there, Tom?"

Frowning, Tom said, "I don't know. There's something about that section of shore…"

Ben stared at the expanse of white sand across the river. "I don't see anything special. Though it would be easier to get to the water from that side. The cliffs here drop straight to the river."

Tom shrugged. "Maybe that's it. Maybe I want to be able to walk to the water's edge." He stepped close to the edge of the bluff and looked. "Quite a ways to fall."

Ben studied the drop. "And not much to grab a hold of either. You'd have a tough time getting back up."

Tom glanced back at the resting group. "Do we need to keep an eye on Eric?"

"You're getting to know us better than I thought, aren't you?" Ben said. "He *would* be the first to go over, and not voluntarily either."

"So I've heard. If half of what Annie tells me is true, it's amazing that he's still alive."

"We've wondered about that, too." Ben walked towards a downed tree and patted it. "You guys have a seat. I'm going to find Annie."

"Let *me* go find her and *you* sit here." Tom chuckled.

"Yeah, somehow that makes more sense," Ben said as he sat and pulled out his canteen.

Shess sat on a log across from him and smiled. "Rest good."

Ben leaned back on a warm rock, enjoying the momentary stillness. The soft sound of the water rushing past below drowned out any distant conversation, and now that they were sitting, the scouts had stopped singing, had stopped teaching the *shmahseespe* any more hiking songs, had finally started to relax.

Moments later, Ben snapped awake as Tom and Annie stepped up.

"Enjoying your nap?" Annie teased.

"Yeah, as a matter of fact, I was." Ben stood. "So, does the compass show anything useful?"

Annie pulled the string hanging on her neck, lifting a small cloth sack and drawing out the compass. She balanced it on her open palm. "Mr. Bentnose hasn't moved. He's still off to the west."

"That's good news." Ben looked west. "But I wonder why he's not coming after us."

"Why would he be after us *himself*?" Tom asked. "He'd be smart and just send his armies."

"He might have done that," Ben said. "But if he had, we wouldn't be able to track them on the compass."

"That would put us at a disadvantage," Tom said.

"And he may still be healing from our last encounter." A faint grin traced across her face.

"That could be our only saving grace," Ben said.

Tom leaned against Annie's shoulder and squinted. "So does it show which way we need to go?"

Annie glanced at the compass. "It shows that Deezh is right down that way, directly downstream from here."

"Due south?" Tom asked. "Following the river? That's where we need to go?"

"That's what the compass shows," she said.

Tom slapped himself on the forehead. "*That's* why it's familiar! *This* is the river that runs past *Roadranusis*." He grabbed Ben's shoulder and shook it. "That beach is our waypoint, where we camped the first night!"

Ben stared. "If you say so. We didn't have much time to see it in the light. When we made it there, it was all but dark, and we headed out early the next morning. No time for sightseeing."

"Well, I've seen it many times, both in the dark and in the middle of the day, but never from this side."

Annie squealed, "We're home!"

Tom put his hands on her shoulders. "Not quite. A dozen clicks to the waterfall, then more to town." He paused. "*And* a river to cross. *Then* we're home."

Ben shook his head. "Then *Shess* is home. *We* still have to get back to the Door…on time."

Annie whooped. "Close enough, and it's still Thursday. We made it back a whole day earlier than expected."

"Well, that's certainly good," Tom said. "Gives us plenty of time to make the connection."

Annie pulled at the string around her neck, getting out the bag to put the compass away. Suddenly she cried out, "Tom! Look!" She pushed the compass at him.

He stared at the disk but saw nothing. "What is it?"

Ben crowded up to see as well, and Shess stood, noticeably concerned.

Annie held the compass on her hand excitedly. "The spot, the purple one, it's moving. I can *see* it moving."

Tom put his arm across her shoulders. "Which way, Annie? Which way do you see it going?"

"Right at us, and fast. It's covering the entire distance from his city to here in a matter of seconds."

"How is that possible?" Ben asked. "Does he have a car or something?"

"Even a car couldn't make it cross country like that. There'd have to be a road, and I haven't seen any roads that could handle *that* kind of traffic." Tom stood there staring off into the distance. "I've never seen anything that moves *that* fast anywhere here." He paused. "Shess, do you know of anything that can cover two days travel in mere seconds?"

"Not fast," Shess said. "Walk, or use animal who walk. That fast."

"How about something that flies?" Ben asked.

"Not even close." Tom stared at the sky. "Where is it now, Annie?"

"Getting close. Coming in from a little north of west." Annie paused. "Wait, not quite. Still getting closer, but now it's going to miss us, pass by us to the north."

Ben and Tom instinctively adjusted their gaze as Annie continued.

"Directly upstream of us now." Annie glanced at the compass and gasped. "Now it's heading straight down the river."

Ben squinted as Tom tried to see it.

"Do you see anything?" Tom asked.

Annie held her breath.

"I see a dark spot on the surface of the river," Ben said. "What is it?"

Tom shrugged. "Can't tell. Too far away."

The dark shape hugged the surface of the river, drifting closer, then it closed to within a couple hundred meters and swooped up to veer over the bluffs where they stood. A shadow engulfed the group as something big momentarily eclipsed the sun.

Most of the people who had been resting farther back came up, clamoring and trying to see what was going on. Ben and Shess tried to keep them from getting too close to the edge of the bluff.

Tom yelled, "What did you see, Ben?"

"A bird? A big one?" Ben yelled back.

"Could have been," Tom said. "But it looked more reptilian to me."

"Reptilian?" Ben asked.

Tom shrugged. "Something about the way the wings were formed. Where is your walking encyclopedia when you need him?" Tom asked.

Ben looked though the crowd but didn't see Eric. "Out of harm's way, I hope!" He paused, then stared at Tom. Are you telling me that we have fairy lights *and* dragons?"

"I'm not saying dragons, but it looked more like a lizard than a bird."

"Yeah, it might have looked that way. We'll see what Eric says when he inspects it." Ben squinted downstream. "Annie! Where is it now?"

Annie snapped her eyes back to the compass. "Mr. Bentnose's purple point is heading downstream, towards *Roadranusis*," she said.

"*Where* is it going?" Ben asked again, glancing at Shess.

"I see it circling the Deezh dot. Once, twice…now it stopped, right next to her." Annie dragged her eyes from the compass. "That means…if Deezh is at home, then Rudolph could be right in the middle of the town, in the middle of *Roadranusis*."

Tom yelled to Shess, "Where's the closest place to cross this river?"

Shess looked downstream, then said, "We not cross river. Animal land, same above waterfall."

"So, there's no way to get across?" Tom asked.

"Next town south. They cross, have bridge," Shess replied.

"That's too far to go. We have to find another way." Ben peered across the river. "Shess, is there a narrow spot anywhere near here? Maybe we can drop a tree across like we did at the other rivers."

"Not know. Not look," Shess said.

"Well, we're going to look now," Ben said. "Tom, let's get this group on the road. We can't waste any time. *Roadranusis* is under attack!" He pushed folks to move, then left the job up to Tom and went to find Carl.

"What *was* that that went by?" Carl asked.

Ben shrugged. "Don't know, and right now, don't care. All we know is that we need to get across the river, quickly. Can you and Fred, and anyone else you need, scout on ahead? Find a narrow spot where we can build a crossing."

Carl slung his pack on his shoulder, grabbed Fredekas, and started off. "We'll let you know what we find."

"Put a rush on it, will ya? Annie says that Mr. Bentnose just landed a dragon in the middle of *Roadranusis*."

Carl blinked and stared. "Oh, is that all? Just a dragon? Nothing more?" He shrugged. "In that case we'd better get moving." A couple others sitting under the trees jumped up to join him as he called out, "Hey, Patrick. You available? We might need you up here." He jogged south.

Patrick grabbed his backpack and hurried to catch up with Carl, heading downstream at a run. As soon as they were out of sight, Joe came out of the trees. "We've been keeping tabs on our back trail. No sign of followers yet," he reported.

"That's good, but you may have missed something," Ben said.

Joe frowned. "What've we missed?"

"Air power."

"Where?" Joe asked as he examined the skies.

"Downstream now. Possibly in the village," Ben said. "Are you ready for real work?"

"Waiting for orders," Joe said as he jumped to attention. He signaled to his group, his platoon as he called them, and waited to see what Ben needed.

Ben explained that they needed a way to cross the river, then stepped back as Joe and his guys ran off. Carl and Patrick had a head start, but Joe would catch up quickly. Ben chuckled. *The way they're moving, you wouldn't know that they've been up all night. When do they rest?* He approached the remaining stragglers. "Can't stay here. We don't yet know where we're going to cross, but wherever it is, it'll be downstream, so let's get moving. We have a dragon to catch."

Everyone stared when what Ben said was passed down the line, but no one hesitated, and they moved out quickly. Hurrying along, they continued as the high bluffs soon gave way to gentle hills, leaving the river a gentle slope away.

Suddenly the group stopped. They had come to the long line of cliffs that split the region in two: South was where Shess and his people lived, North, where they were now, was *nimre* land, but they were still on the wrong side of the river.

Ben walked to the water's edge and stared across the river at the path that they'd used to navigate the cliffs earlier, then stared down the cliffs in front of him—no way were they going to make it here, no trail on this side of the river.

Suddenly he heard shouts and the crash of a tree falling, so he ran to check out the noise. He found Carl and Joe hacking on the trunks of trees, felling them, then stripping off any larger branches.

"What's up?" Ben asked.

Joe pushed a tree into the river. "Patrick hopes to get enough trees stuck on the rocks at the top of the falls, that we can just walk across."

Ben strolled along a slight hill to the edge of the water. The *shmahseespe* were busy rolling the cut trees into the water. Patrick was standing on a large rock at the edge of the falls, directing the trees out into the middle of the river. Blasts under the ends of the trunks threw up sprays of water as the trees drifted to the rocks. The force of the flowing water already held a handful against the rocks.

"Good so far, Patrick. It might work," Ben yelled up to him.

"Not enough yet," Patrick said. "Need more."

"Keep steering those, and I'll get more heading your way." He patted the blade hanging from his belt. "They do come in handy, don't they?"

"Yeah, can't fell too many trees with a pocket knife," Patrick yelled, then returned to directing trees.

Ben trotted up the hill and went back to the majority of the group, still waiting at the top of the cliffs. He sent them to help with the trees. "Stay next to the river and drop as many large trees as you can." He directed the rest of the group, "Trim the branches and roll the trees into the river." He thought about Eric. "And stay away from the edge."

On his way to see how the cutting was going, he came across scouts standing near the river, watching the trees settle into place.

John laughed. "He's building a dam, not a bridge, so does that make it a dam bridge?"

Laughing along with him, Ben said, "Yeah, it does, but let's focus on getting the trees cut."

John hoisted his sword above his head, a sword much bigger than needed. "Back at it!"

Ben climbed up onto the rock next to Patrick and watched him maneuver more trees into the bridge. He already had a decent pile of lumber stacked up against the rocks, but as Ben watched, they shifted, then barreled into the water, disappearing into the mist. Moments later, Ben watched splintered segments drift out of the pond at the bottom of the falls.

"How's it going, Patrick?" Ben asked.

"Could be better. The trees aren't stable. Once I get some set, with the top ones out of the water, the pressure builds up, and they all topple into the water."

"Yeah," Ben said. "There's a limit to how high you can stack them. What if you stop a little below that limit?"

"Tried that, too. They stay put fairly well, but the top ones have a *lot* of water rushing across them. I don't think anyone would be able to keep their footing in that current."

"Hmm…you know, John had a comment that might shed light on this. He called your bridge a dam bridge."

"Leave it up to John to start cussing." Patrick faked a smile at Ben. "Any *useful* comments from him?"

"Maybe that *was* a useful comment," Ben said. "He didn't mean 'damn' with an 'n'. He meant 'dam' as in stopping the water, so it *is* a dam, blocking the flow." He considered the width of the river. "Can't dam the up the entire thing. The water has to have *some* place to flow."

Patrick paused and considered the area. "Too much rock at the edge of the cliff to build a spillway."

Yeah," Ben agreed. "But if you pile up the trees on the edges, keeping the middle open, you can let the water continue to flow, underneath the logs."

Patrick leaned back and studied the bridge, the dam bridge. "Yeah, makes sense. To make it work, I'll need to build up the sides, then remove the middle, at the bottom of the middle. That should let the water through and relieve the pressure." He leaned back and considered the layout. "Tell John that I apologize for thinking poorly of him."

"You can tell him yourself, once we get to the other side," Ben said.

Patrick stacked the tree trunks according to his new plan. First on the edges, then the middle, then cross-stacked from edge to middle to form an arch of sorts. It was tough to do it right, but when pressure increased too much, he'd knock the bottom logs out of the way, letting the water flow under, making a funnel, with all the water directed through the gap. "Yes! That works." He added more logs to the sides, then stepped back to check it out. "Anyone ready to cross?"

"Is it stable?" Ben asked

Patrick jumped onto the first log, bouncing. "Solid enough for me."

"Well, I trust you," Ben said. "Let's get everyone rounded up."

He and Patrick ran back along the shore, calling all the small groups to stop chopping and start heading to the bridge. "Grab everything and head to the bridge." He called out as they ran off, "But wait on the shore until we get there."

Last out was Joe and his troops. Ben ran up to the group still chopping trees and yelled, "Enough! You can stop now." He was impressed with the assembly line they had going, one group felling trees, another group trimming branches, and the last group rolling the stripped trees into the water. Ben hoped that the extra trees wouldn't get stuck under the bridge, creating the same dam problem.

Joe called out orders, and the rest formed up quickly, ready to head out. "Let's go."

Ben followed at a quick trot but found it difficult to keep up with Joe's group, in spite of the fact that they had been working so hard.

Arriving at the bridge, Ben walked up to Tom.

Tom smiled. "I'm amazed at the engineering. Built to hold together long enough for all of us to get across."

"So who do we send across first?" Annie asked.

"We could start with the weak and wounded," Tom smiled at Annie, "and end with the big guys."

"That would work if we thought that it might collapse under the extra weight. We'd get the majority across first," Ben said.

"Thanks for the suggestion, Tom," Annie said. "But if it's going to fall apart at all, don't we want to send the big guys across first? They can stress test it, and Patrick can reinforce the weak spots for the rest of us."

"That could work," Ben said, "but I think there's a better idea."

"So what's your idea, Ben?" Tom asked.

"Let's send *some* of the 'big guys,' as you call them, across first, then everyone else, followed by the *rest* of the big guys. That way we can keep fighting power on both sides of the river until we're all across."

"Much better idea," Tom said. "Get 'em lined up."

Ben arranged the group with Trey and Bear first, followed by Shess and many of the *shmahseespe*, then the rest of the scouts, except for Joe and his crew. They wanted to hang behind, acting as the rear guard, while Patrick stayed on the rock overlooking the bridge, to make adjustments as necessary.

"Ready to cross?" Ben shouted.

Trey and Bear shouted back. "Ready!"

"Now, Patrick?" Ben asked.

Patrick checked it one last time, then yelled, "Go for it!"

Trey and Bear gingerly stepped up onto the first log and started across. Picking their way gingerly, they slowly negotiated the narrow bridge. Stopping in the middle, Trey started yelling.

Ben couldn't make out what he was saying, but he was leaning out over the waterfall. He frowned and shouted to them, "Don't stop to chat. Get going!"

"I don't think they can hear you," Tom said. "The waterfall would be too noisy right there."

"Well, they need to get going," Ben said. "Wish we had a bullhorn."

"No electronics, remember?" Tom said.

"I remember, but I don't have to like it." Ben yelled up to those at the front of the line, "Could anyone make out what they were saying?"

Annie answered from the water's edge. "He said something about not stopping, not looking down."

"Oh, great," Ben said. "Like we need that kind of advice."

Trey and Bear finished crossing and stepped off the logs on the other side, then stood there and yelled. No one could hear any of what they said this time, but they looked fine, so Ben sent on the next group. "Not too many at a time. Spread out, keep moving." He continued to cheer on everyone as they headed across.

"Getting to be our turn," Tom said as he checked to see who was left. "We can go right after Annie gets Melvin across."

"Then let's get there." Ben checked the tree line and saw Joe directing his group. They were walking backwards to the river's edge, keeping their eyes open for anyone approaching. "Joe's group will cross last."

Stepping up onto the first log, Ben followed Tom and sidestepped across. The tops of the upper logs were wet, but the bark made it rough enough to keep a good grip. As they neared the end of one log, getting ready to step to the next, Ben glanced to his right. The sight was startling, and he swayed for a moment. *Wow. Trey was right. Don't look down.*

Stepping from one log to the next was intimidating, but they managed it. They were passing the half-way point, when Ben saw movement out of the corner of his eye—logs drifting right at them. *The last of the trees that Joe's crew dropped must have slipped into the river!* He spun to wave at Joe, wobbling. Tom reached back, grabbed his arm, and stabilized him. "Thanks," Ben said. "Did you see—?"

"I see them," Tom said. "So move faster." He rushed across the rest of the bridge.

Ben ran across the last part of the bridge, pumping his fist for Joe to get moving. When he jumped off the last log, he stood in the shallow water at the edge and watched Joe's group cross. The loose logs floating on the river were approaching the base of the bridge, but half of Joe's group still had to get across.

The water was rising, splashing higher and higher, inundating the top logs, pouring over them, washing across the boots of the last ones trying to cross. Ben stared as the men froze, mid-bridge, flailing their arms to keep their balance. Suddenly one, two, then three slipped, disappearing into the mist. Ben fell to his knees. Those were his friends. They might even be natives, but no matter, it was his fault—no one else could be blamed that they had perished.

Joe hit land and yelled back, "Hurry! When those logs hit the bridge, it'll break! You have to make it across!" He knew they would rush, but would they be fast enough? He had to hope that the short time he had would be sufficient time for all the training he'd attempted. He'd drilled them in combat skills, in survival skills, in following orders, now he had to trust that they would follow through as he'd instructed.

Grabbing the rope around his waist with his gloved hands, he waded back into the water, backing upstream from the bridge. All he could think of was the water pulling him towards the channel, towards a cold, wet death, but he held his own. Planting his feet on the sides of the rocks, he tightened the rope and leaned back. The next man in line took up the slack and pulled along with him. Joe planted one foot on the rocky bottom and lurched towards shore, but the slimy moss growing on the rocks made it slipperier than he'd expected.

He lost his footing twice, but managed to regain it quickly. He slowly backed his way towards shore, pulling the next man along. When Joe saw two, no, three men lose their balance and disappear into the mist, he braced himself for the shock. The rope pulled tight as each man fell, pulling him back towards the deeper water each time, but he held, the rope held, and he pulled back. He was in hip deep water when he felt arms grab him, pulling him back. He kept his grip on the rope and pulled as hard as he could. Other hands reached past him and helped pull on the rope, taking the pressure off his hands.

He hit solid ground and collapsed, letting someone else pull his troops from the water. "Did they make it?" he asked.

Annie rushed up and kneeled next to him. "Yes. They all made it." She didn't mention the two still in the water, not yet pulled all the way to shore—they weren't going to come out unscathed.

She stepped away from him and ran to the limp bodies as Shess pulled them onto dry land. "Someone start CPR," she yelled as she glanced at the first one: Doug. She assessed his injuries: minor lacerations where the rope had scraped his skin, minor internal injuries where it dug in, bumps and bruises probably from bouncing on the rocks, and lack of breathing due to drowning. She was satisfied that CPR would fix the major issues. She could get to the rest later.

The other person was in worse shape, so she concentrated her efforts there. She sat by his side and evaluated him: major lacerations to the abdomen and back, crush injury to a leg resulting in a broken bone, a concussion and possible fracture of the skull, but the worst appeared to be a broken back. He had been caught in the rushing current…upside down, the rope tied to his waist serving to bend him in half—backwards. *If he had been facing the other direction, like Doug was, the injuries would be much easier to deal with.*

Checking to see that someone was performing CPR on Doug, she focused on his spinal cord. *If I can prevent paralysis, I'll be one step ahead.* She sat back on her heels. "Can anyone tell me his name?"

Shess spoke. "Name Shankaktos."

Ben squatted next to Annie. "We call him Shawn. He's the one that had a .50 caliber bullet as a protection amulet. Doesn't look like it protected him this time."

Joe stepped up. "Yeah, he and Doug were tight, always watching out for each other."

Ignoring the fact that he was unconscious, Annie spoke to him, "Shawn," she glanced at Shess, "Shankaktos, I know you're in pain right now, but give me a moment, and I'll fix that right up."

Ben scooted up, lining up his hands on Shawn's chest, ready to start CPR.

Annie grabbed his arm. "Wait. Don't do that."

"But he's not breathing."

"That may be true, but if you start pumping on his chest, you'll sever his spinal cord—he'll never walk again."

Ben pulled back quickly, giving Annie plenty of room. "Let me know when I can start."

She directed her gaze to the patient, trying to decide what she could do. *If I roll him over to examine his back, I'll do just as much damage as Ben doing CPR on him.* She put her hands on his stomach and slid them down his sides, into the soft, wet sand where he lay. "Because he's still half in the water, I can get to his injuries without making them worse," she said, worming her fingers through the moist sand until they barely touched behind him.

Joe leaned and put his hand on Ben's shoulder. "Any way I can help?"

"I don't think so," Ben said. "It's all on Annie now." He paused. "Unless you know of an ambulance service, with a dozen EMTs, connected to a big hospital."

Joe paused, then stood up. "No, no ambulance, but maybe something close. Wait here."

Ben stared at Joe as he jogged off, then started to talk to Annie, but she was concentrating on her patient, so he held his question. *I wonder what Joe has in mind.*

Ben reached out and held Shawn's hand.

To his surprise, Joe ran up dragging Melvin. "If we ever needed a power boost, this is it."

"Melvin? Power boost? Do you think it'll work?" Ben asked.

"What'll work?" Melvin was confused.

"Remember that trick Robb showed you? The fire in his hand?" Joe asked.

Melvin nodded vacantly.

"Eric told me that he showed you," Joe said. "At the top of the climb out of the city."

"Yeah," Melvin said. "I remember. So what?"

"Well, Annie has a power, too. The power to heal, and right now, she could use a boost."

"And? What am I supposed to do?"

Ben smiled. "*You* can boost. When Robb tried a standard fireball against the archers, he accidentally incinerated them, *only* because he was touching you at the time."

"You think *I* had something to do with that?"

"Definitely," Ben said. "Annie could even see the power flowing from you."

"So if I want to help…how…what do I do?" Melvin asked.

Ben shrugged. "Just touch her," he said pulling Melvin's arm towards Annie.

Melvin let his arm reach out, then dropped his hand on her shoulder. As soon as he made contact, Annie inhaled sharply, flipped her head back, and grimaced.

She groaned momentarily, then shouted, "Yes!" Her eyes flew wide open, and she pulled her hands out from under Shawn. "That did it!"

Melvin stumbled back managing to squeak out, "It worked?" as his knees buckled, and he dropped to the ground.

Joe caught Melvin in mid fall and lowered him to a sitting position, then laid him back. "Wow. Did you see that? When he boosted Annie, he drained his own battery."

"Well, we can't do that again," Ben said. "CPR now, Annie?"

"Yes, start now," Annie said vigorously. "His back is healed!"

Ben jumped to it and began pumping on Shawn's chest. "Joe. On. Five," he said in rhythm with the compressions.

Joe stepped away from Melvin and dropped to do rescue breaths, as Annie sat back on her heels.

"Wow. Invigorating boost," she said as she shook her shoulders. "Thank you, Joe, for thinking of it."

Joe made a circle with his fingers as a makeshift mouth guard on Shawn's lips and gave two puffs, then sat up. "You needed help." He checked with Ben to get the count and continued breathing for Shawn.

Annie tipped her head at Melvin. "Regrettably, we now have another patient."

Melvin rolled and tried to sit up. "Woo, I don't know what that was, but…" He dropped back to the sand. "If you don't mind, I think I'll sit here for a bit."

Annie probed Melvin. "Nothing terribly amiss, though he does look under the weather. Let him rest, and I'll check up on him in a bit."

"So what did I do?" Melvin asked.

"You. Gave. A. Boost," Ben managed between compressions.

"I couldn't have done it without you," Annie said.

Melvin stared at her. "I don't mind helping, even though I have no idea what happened."

"What happened here was that you saved Shawn's life." Annie slowly stood up. "And one of these days, you'll understand what you did." She held Melvin's hand and squeezed it. "Thank you again."

He hesitated, uncertain how to react, then returned the squeeze. "You're welcome." He shrugged.

Tom stepped up and congratulated Melvin. "Rescuing you was helpful. You're a valuable part of Ben's troop. I can see why he'd want to make certain you came along." He paused. "And I can see why Mr. Bentnose wanted you, too."

Melvin blinked in surprise. "Uh, yeah."

Annie stood up. "How're the others?" she asked as she stepped past Tom, approaching all the activity on the beach.

"Most are being cared for. We didn't get far trying to do CPR on Doug. As we were starting, he pushed us away."

"Oh? I could have sworn that he wasn't breathing." Annie frowned. "With as much time as he was under water, both dangling in the falls and while being dragged to shore by Joe, I can't see how he'd be breathing at all."

Tom shrugged. "Anyway, he's conscious and breathing on his own, so you go ahead and focus on Shawn. He's the one that needs help now."

"He's not the only one who needs help," Annie insisted.

"The rest of the injuries are minor," Tom said. "A couple of hands with rope burns and bumps and bruises. We can handle it. You need to rest, Annie."

"No time to rest. Shawn's back is good, but he still has a broken leg, and I need to see to Doug's other injuries."

"What injuries?" Tom asked. "I don't see anything wrong with him. He may not be *fine*, but he's not bad."

"That's the problem—you can't see internal injuries." She stepped up to Doug, kneeled, and inspected him, starting with his lungs. *Nothing unusual, no residual water, no pulmonary edema, no evidence of injury.* "Hmmm…You have excellent lungs there, Doug."

"How's it going, Annie?" Doug squeaked out, then coughed.

"Don't try to talk, Doug. In spite of your lungs doing better than expected, you may have other issues that need to be cleaned up before I let you get up and run off." She pressed her fingers into his abdomen, probing for any damage. Doug grunted. She paused. "Sorry. I'll be more careful."

"That's fine, but you hit something in there," Doug said.

Annie probed again, watching Doug's eyes for any sign of pain as well as watching for any color change that would indicate where she would need to focus more. "It's not as bad as I thought. You'll survive. Don't try anything strenuous for a while. And do me a favor, don't start smoking. I'd hate to see those lungs damaged."

"Yes, Doctor Annie." Doug flopped his hand to his forehead in a mock salute. "I won't do anything more strenuous than trying to save a civilization, get back to the Door on time, oh, and get some hunting done in my spare time."

"Good," she said as she smiled and headed back to Shawn.

Shess was standing by Shawn, watching Ben and Joe doing CPR.

"How's it going, Ben?" Annie asked.

Ben replied between compressions, "Still. Going. No. Response."

"I don't know if we're doing any good," Joe said.

Annie put her hand on his shoulder. "You are. Keep that oxygenated blood circulating. I'll see about doing the rest."

Joe leaned in for another couple of breaths.

Annie crouched next to Shawn's leg and fixed her attention on the broken bone. She pulled his ankle, straightening his leg, realigning the bones, keeping an eye on his colors. Once the bones were straight, she let the muscles pull the broken ends back together. *The pain of setting a bone must be terrible. If he weren't unconscious...* She sat back, shaking her head. *Fixing his leg with his heart stopped isn't doing much good.* "Tom, I don't suppose you brought along an AED, did you?"

Tom shook his head. "Nothing like that."

"Besides…" Ben said as he continued to pump Shawn's chest, "It. Takes. Electricity. None here."

"Ben, you have that list, anyone on it who can restart a heart?"

"No," Ben said as he kept pumping. "What. Can. *You.* Do?"

"I don't know," Tom said. "But unless we can get his heart going again, it's all for nothing."

Doug stepped up. "His heart stopped?" He frowned.

Annie looked into Doug's face. "I know he's your friend, Doug, but I'm afraid that I can't do much for him. I've never restarted a heart."

"You've never needed to before," Doug said, squatting next to Annie. "But I have faith in you. All you have to do is direct your energy where it's needed." He put his hand on her shoulder.

Annie tried to smile. "I appreciate your faith, but I have no idea what to do."

"Yes, you do," Doug said as he leaned in closer. "You've seen those scenes on TV: paramedics on the side of the road, paddles in hand, charging to 300, then yelling, 'Clear!' and zapping the guy. You know. Do that." He dropped to the ground across from Ben and reached out, taking Shawn's hand.

"I wonder if you're right, Doug." Annie blinked at him. "Everything else I've done was by instinct. I didn't think. It just happened."

"Do your best," Doug said.

She closed her eyes, raised her hands in front of her, and tried to picture the proper rhythm of a heart, tried to visualize the correct QRS wave, then keeping her eyes closed, she slowly spoke, "Everyone, stand back. I'm charging to 300."

Ben and Joe jumped, grabbing Doug as they stumbled back. Ben yelled, "Clear!"

Annie slapped her hands on Shawn's chest and let loose with a guttural noise.

Shawn's body arched up and dropped to the ground.

Annie gave one shriek and collapsed.

Ben dove forward, to listen to Shawn's chest. "Nothing…wait…Yes!" He leaned back. "And he's breathing, too!" Ben smiled at Annie. "You did it!"

Annie didn't respond.

Tom spun. "Annie!" He reached to pick her up. "Annie." He held her in his arms.

Ben grabbed her wrist. "Pulse and still breathing. Did she faint?"

"I don't know," Tom said. "But she's finished helping everyone else."

"Let her rest. She's the patient, now." He glanced at Shawn. "But she did manage to bring him back before she passed out."

Shess dropped to a knee, putting a hand on Shawn's chest. "He alive, breathing." He looked with awe at Annie lying in Tom's arms. "How she do?"

Tom shrugged. "I don't know. We'll have to wait for her to explain…if she wants to."

Ben added, "If she even can."

Joe stood up. "We've tended to the wounded, so now don't you think we should get going? We still have a problem in *Roadranusis*, and we're going to run out of daylight unless we hurry."

"Yeah, the dragon," Ben said. "Can you gather everyone together? I have something to say."

Joe whistled at his group. He gave quick instructions, then reached to put a hand on Shawn's shoulder. "Still working on building a stretcher for you," he glanced at Tom, "but I'll have a second one built right away for Annie." He asked Ben, "Can Doug walk?"

"Possibly, but not by himself. We'll have to get someone to help him."

"It won't be Annie," Tom said.

"So we'll be heading into town blind," Joe said. "She won't be able to guide us with the compass."

"That shouldn't be too much of a problem," Tom said. "After all, I've been on this route more times than I want to count. We know where we're going."

"But do we know *who* we're facing? That's where the compass could come into play," Joe replied.

"Yeah. That could be useful, but it isn't going to happen," Tom said, holding Annie tenderly.

Ben stared at his sister, resting in Tom's arms. "We've been too dependent on her, expecting her to fix everything, patch us up after combat, tend to all the problems we get ourselves into." He frowned. "We need to be more aware of what we've been putting her through."

"I didn't think we'd have so much of a need for a medic," Tom said. "Or I would have brought one along."

"Would your medic be able to do what Annie has done?" Ben asked.

Tom thought for a moment. "No. Certainly not. Not even close."

"Didn't think so," Ben said. "We certainly aren't working out much as a *hunting* party, are we?"

"Like I said before, this trip isn't like any of the others. You guys are way out in front of anything I've ever seen."

310

"But you *are* enjoying the trip this time, aren't you?" Ben asked.

Tom smiled at Annie. "Yeah, I'd have to agree with you there."

Joe interrupted. "They're ready for you, Ben. All gathered on the beach and facing that hill, so you can have yourself a podium."

"Thanks." Ben circled the crowd, climbed the small mound, and faced the late afternoon sun, motioning the throng to quiet down.

Thinking back over the recent days, he wondered, What have I got them into? Should I lead them into battle yet again? Or would it be better to head straight to the Door and wait it out? He shook himself back to reality. Shirk responsibility? No. We can't abandon Shess and his people now. We've dragged them into this mess, so we need to see them through to the end. He cleared his throat and waited a moment.

"I know that we've been through a lot." He glanced at the stretchers, one with Annie, one with Shankaktos. "Some of us more than others."

The crowd followed his gaze, murmuring assent.

"We've managed to survive, though not unscathed." He led their gaze to the many bandaged limbs. "Yet, in spite of all these difficulties, we've managed to make friends." He directed their attention to Shess encircled by his men. "In fact, those self-same predicaments have merely served to solidify those friendships." Now he focused them towards Trey and Bear standing shoulder to shoulder, Carl and Fredekas ready to lead the group, and Doug kneeling next to Shankaktos lying on a stretcher. They all blushed at the attention.

"When this is all done and finished, when we have to leave, I know that there will be some of you who will be saddened by our departure." He paused, letting them think. "On the other hand, most will be glad to be back home." He saw Eric trying to hide behind Trey.

"Then there are others who've formed…shall I say relationships…that I expect will endure beyond this trip." He grinned at Tom kneeling beside the stretcher holding Annie.

Everyone smiled, and Ben heard a couple cheers of encouragement from the scouts.

"We must hope that the possibility exists of our quick return, of our *safe* return." He saw Tom's head snap in his direction. "But would that require us to head straight to the Door…now?" He indicated the path that lead into the trees behind him. "If we did, we'd have to sit and wait for a while as we aren't expected for a couple days yet." He slowly stared at the crowd. "More importantly, it would *also* mean walking out on our newly found friends and allies."

The mood of the crowd was getting dark, and Ben thought, *Good. Now let's turn it around.*

"Do we want that?" he yelled over the murmuring. "No! And so we *won't* have it. Running to *safety* is not what we do. No, we run to *trouble*. We welcome it, we embrace it, we feel right at home in the middle of it." Ben felt the passion of the crowd building, so he kept up the pace. "We wouldn't be happy, we *couldn't* be happy, unless we were in the middle of conflict." He stirred up the gathering. "And so to seek that action, we will head south, back to Shess' town, back into *Roadranusis*, to face whatever fate awaits us there."

The noise from the crowd drowned out Ben's next statements, but they all knew what he was saying.

He swung his arm wide, encompassing everyone. "So, everyone, let's move out!" He picked up his backpack and swung it on his shoulder and trotted off his makeshift stage, heading for the cliff at the top of the falls.

Everyone followed noisily.

Ben watched the mob surge forward to the path ahead. It's been such a short time since we first climbed down that cliff on our way to Shess' town. Feels as if it's been two or three weeks if not that many months.

John ran to catch up with Ben. "I've caught rumors about what we have waiting for us up there. Mind clarifying?"

"Did you see that big shadow that hit us before we crossed the river?"

"I saw something, but I didn't look up fast enough to see what it was."

"Well, I thought it was a bird, but Tom saw a lizard, a flying lizard, and it was carrying Rudolph right to the middle of town."

John gawked. "Flying lizards *and* Rudolph? Any plans for that?"

As they were about to exit the forest to the north of *Roadranusis*, Ben called a halt. Keeping everyone else back, he summoned Joe up to the front. "Before we step into the fields outside the town," he glanced at the tree branches overhead, "and out from under this cover, I wanted to get your opinion on what we might be heading into."

"Good thinking." Joe sent for the spotting scope and crawled to the base of a tree at the edge of the open fields. He examined the seemingly empty fields, checking closely for anyone that might be hiding in the tall growth. "I don't see anything, but that doesn't mean much. Not if they're good. Besides, this angle is too low, too flat out there." He considered the trees over their heads. "Not much chance of climbing up to get a better view, is there?"

Ben shrugged. "Did anyone bring a portable ladder?"

Joe laughed. "Check Trey's pack. He has everything else in there."

"Maybe we need to get Carl up here," Ben suggested.

"Yeah, with his enhanced ability to spot things at a distance, he might see something that we can't."

They sent word back for Carl, and while they waited, Ben and Joe traded the spotting scope back and forth, hoping to see something, but nothing moved. Moments later, Carl showed up with Fredekas, and Ben apprised them of the situation.

"We haven't seen anyone," Ben said. "But we wanted to get another opinion."

"Better safe than sorry," Carl agreed. He headed left as Fredekas went right. They wriggled out into the field, and Ben watched as a head would pop up, twist quickly, and disappear back into the tall grass. After they both worked their way back to Ben and Joe, Carl said, "Your instincts are working overtime, Ben. There's a dozen guys out there waiting for us."

"What?" Joe sat up. "A dozen? Where?" He grabbed the scope. "Show me one."

Ben waited with Fredekas as the other two crawled off to the side of the road, circling through the bushes to higher ground, getting a better angle to see the fields.

They waited in silence, then Ben tried to start up a conversation. "So, Fred, how's your day been?"

"Day not good. Walk much, swim some, walk more. Feet wet still, cold."

"Yeah, I know what you mean. Well, as soon as we get this Rudolph guy out of the way, we'll put our feet up and have a nice, warm meal, on me."

Fredekas frowned. "Warm meal good. On you, not."

Ben laughed. "Fred, you're a hoot."

Frowning more, Fredekas said, "Hoot not sound good."

"Oh, it's good, Fred. You ask Carl when they get back."

"I do," Fredekas said, then went silent.

Ben received the message loud and clear and also waited quietly.

After a long wait, Carl and Joe came slinking back.

"He's right," Joe said. "I couldn't believe it, but we spotted a bunch of guys out there."

"And there's probably more that we didn't see," Carl said.

"See who?" Fredekas asked.

"We couldn't see faces or anything, but slight movements in the grass weren't natural."

"Not natural? How's that?" Ben asked.

"Not going with the wind. Plants move in patterns when the wind blows, but the movement we saw wasn't normal," Carl explained.

"I know," Fredekas said.

Carl glanced at Fredekas. "Yeah, you're good at spotting that stuff, too."

"I know," Fredekas repeated.

"You know?" Ben said to Fredekas.

"*aa-eh*," Fredekas said.

"Wait," Ben said. "You *know* who's out there?"

"*aa-eh*," Fredekas said more fervently. "Friend."

"You better make certain of that before you step out into the open," Joe said.

"I certain. Make certain more," Fredekas said. He stood up, walked next to the tree they'd been hiding behind, cupped his hands around his mouth, and made a soft noise.

Ben thought it sounded like an owl purring, if owls could purr.

A brief wait and an echoing noise came floating by. Fredekas stepped away from the tree and called out again with that same strange noise, warbling up and down.

Carl stood up and followed Fredekas as Ben peered past one side of the tree and Joe the other. They both saw movement as a couple people popped up, smiling at Fredekas and Carl.

Fredekas smiled back, walking to meet them with Carl right behind.

Ben waited with Joe until Fredekas and Carl returned. "So? Who are they? What's going on?"

"They wait for more," Fredekas started. "Afraid more come. *betnahzbit* wait for you. Not fight."

"*Betnahzbit* is waiting for us? Here in town?" Ben asked. "And he's not fighting?"

"That so," Fredekas said.

"How many are with him?" Joe asked.

"Only." Fredekas smiled raising his hands.

"Only *Betnahzbit*? No one else?"

Fredekas checked with the people now standing up in the fields. "They say."

"Good that he can't get an entire army on that dragon of his," Ben said. "But what's he doing there? What's he want?"

"We won't find that out until we ask him, so let's get going," Joe said.

Ben held up his hand. "Wait, not all of us."

Joe paused. "Oh? Why not?"

"Well, with Annie and a couple others out of the picture, I figured that while *we* head to Rudolph, *they* should head directly to the medic's hut, along with the other slightly less wounded. We have to get them taken care of."

"I'll send a couple of my guys along, to keep an eye on things," Joe said. "You get going, and we'll join you as soon as we can."

"Thanks." Ben said. "Everyone else, grab your stuff. We're heading into town," he said as he stepped out into the late afternoon sun.

As they paraded through the fields, more *shmahseespe* joined the group, all chatting quietly, trekking into the town square where they came to a sudden halt.

Something was different, something was wrong. Blocking the door to the meeting hall was an enormous chair—a throne on a pedestal—flanked by a half-dozen guards in bright armor, and sitting atop the chair was Rudolph himself.

Ben froze. He stared. Then he stood taller and slowly moved closer.

Rudolph leaned forward, elbow on knee, and looked down on them as Ben approached, trailed by Shess and Tom. He smiled slowly, then spoke. "So, my little gnats, what have you been up to?"

"Your leg's better," Ben retorted as he stared. Where'd all the guards come from? he thought. Fred had said that Rudolph was alone.

Rudolph reached to rub his leg. "Yes, I'm impressed with your friend's abilities." He skimmed the group. "Where *is* your little healer, anyway? I'd like to have a word with her."

"You're not dealing with her…nor anyone else." Ben glanced at Shess then at Tom. "Tell us what you want or buzz off."

Rudolph flicked a finger at the guards to his right, then left. "And my friends here? No concern? No worry about them?"

Ben kept his eyes locked on Rudolph. "They are of no matter to us. We've defeated your soldiers before, twice as a matter of fact. And many more than this. Why should this handful concern us?"

Rudolph leaned back and laughed gently. "Ah, getting cocky, are we? A bit too cocky, I'd say. What would you do if I called them into service?" He raised his hand, then slowly lifted his little finger, and the guards on each side raised their swords to the ready.

Ben stepped back, reaching out to grab Shess' arm. Suddenly there was the solid click of a rifle cocking…a dozen rifles. *Ah, Joe. Good timing!*

Rudolph paused to study the crowd, locking in on the muzzles aimed at him. "Yes! Gunpowder. That would have been a useful tool to 'invent' here. Having not anticipated the need, I didn't manage to get the resources to make a proper barrel. I'll keep it in mind, though." He slowly lowered his finger, and the guards relaxed but kept their swords in hand—the rifles never wavered. "An impasse," he said as he leaned back into his chair.

"You may think that…if you wish, but with one trigger pull, you'd be gone, and then what?" Ben stepped forward and stared at Rudolph.

"Go ahead," Rudolph said. "I'd like to see you try. I *am* curious to see if it will stop a bullet."

Ben frowned. "If what will stop a bullet?"

Rudolph leaned back and sneered. "My shield. Do you think I'd be sitting out here in the elements without protection?"

Ben leaned to peer around the throne. "I don't see any shield."

"Of course you don't. I don't want you to, besides I want to be able to *see* you," Rudolph said. "Go ahead, give it a test."

Ben leaned back to Tom and whispered, "Should we?"

Tom shrugged and whispered back, "At this point, it's your game."

"Would you try it?" Ben asked. "I mean, if his shield doesn't work, we've eliminated the problem."

"Yeah, but if it does…" Tom tipped his head at the guards. "…then we're in a world of trouble."

Rudolph leaned back and thrummed his fingers on the arm of the throne. "I'm waiting…"

Ben glanced back at him, then said, "Joe, give it a shot."

Joe stood up and shouldered his crossbow. "Save the ammo," he shouted as he loosed a quarrel.

There was a sharp ping as the quarrel stopped dead in the air a couple meters from Rudolph. It hung there for a moment, then slowly drifted to the ground.

Rudolph stood up and yelled, "I *know* it will stop an arrow! I want to see if it will stop a bullet."

"I don't care what *you* want," Ben said. "We aren't going to be part of your little experiment."

Rudolph slowly sat back. "Ah, yes, the brave, little souls refusing to do what they're told. You may end up regretting that."

Ben shrugged. "So you have a shield." Ben frowned at the huge throne. "But how did you get this eyesore here?"

"We flew in. Didn't you see me as I cut right above your little party? On the side of the river."

"We saw something," Ben said.

"But did you *see* what I was flying?" Rudolph asked slowly.

Ben shrugged. "Not well enough."

"Look over there." Rudolph sneered. "On that hillside."

Ben looked towards the hill where Shess' house sat above the town.

"You can see it easily from here," Rudolph said. "My transportation."

Ben looked in that direction and froze as the afternoon sun lit up the biggest creature he'd ever seen, a cross between an eagle and a 747. The thing was huge. Ben stared. "What *is* that thing?"

A small voice piped up behind him. "Could be a roc."

Ben spun to see Eric studying the creature. "Eric, get back!"

Eric stopped and gawked at Ben. "What's wrong?"

"Let the little man speak," Rudolph said. "What were you saying?"

Eric faced Rudolph, then stiffened. "I…uh…"

Rudolph laughed. "Can't speak in my presence? I sometimes have that effect on folks." Then he leaned in closer. "Wait, aren't you the little mug that caused me such trouble in my castle?" He raised his hand and clenched his fist at Eric. "Too bad this shield works both ways or I'd teach you a lesson or two."

Eric stared at Rudolph and mumbled, "Two-way shield?" Then he shrugged off his hesitation, straightened up, and faced the giant bird again. "As I was saying, before I was so rudely interrupted, it has the appearance of a roc." He explained, "That's R O C, not R O C K. A creature from Arabian mythology." He paused. "Well maybe not so mythical now, reputed to carry off elephants to feed its young."

Ben stared at him. Wow, Eric's getting mouthy. And he has a spine. I'm going to have to keep an eye on him in case he gets out of control.

Eric continued, "More related to a gryphon than an eagle, though undeniably from the same family." He glanced at Tom as he explained. "The wings of an eagle are differentiated from those of a gryphon by the alula." He ignored Rudolph and continued addressing the group. "That's the equivalent of the bird's thumb. It acts similar to flaps on an airplane, allowing a higher than normal angle of attack without running the risk of stalling out." Suddenly he stopped talking and stepped past Ben, trying to hide from the spotlight.

Rudolph leaned back in his seat. "Remarkable. He definitely has a tad of useful knowledge…and some not so useful, as well. I may need to take the little piss-ant with me."

Eric paused a moment to answer Rudolph, "*Formica pratensis starkei*, common meadow ant, now extinct in the UK," then he disappeared into the crowd.

Ben confronted Rudolph. "I don't know why you think you're going to take anyone. You are going back to your city. Stay there and you'll be safe. Come out again, and we'll be here to tackle you."

"Wait, Ben," Tom said quietly. "Don't make threats you can't carry through. You know we're not going to be here for much longer. We're going back in a couple days."

Ben shushed Tom and whispered, "He doesn't know that—"

Rudolph's voice boomed. "You're going *back*?" He sat on the edge of his throne, leaning forward, just about falling out of the seat. "You have a way to get *back*? Back to the *real* world?" He shook his fist in the air. "I *will* have that knowledge…but not from behind this shield." He frantically signaled the guards. They stared at him for a moment wondering if the command had in fact been given, then they all raised their swords and charged the crowd.

Gunfire rang out and everyone hit the ground, some pulled by others, some tripping as they tried to run. Sparks flew as bullets ricocheted off armor. The guards spun and jerked as they, too, went down—not to get up again. A huge gust of wind blew across the open area, blinding those who were still trying to get a shot off.

Joe yelled something about where to aim, but the wind ate anything he tried to say.

The sky darkened as the roc swooped in, landing on top of some folks. It leaned forward and hissed at the crowd, a roaring hiss. Everyone still on their feet backed away, running for cover, and shots rang out, but the giant bird didn't seem to mind. It reached out, grabbed the throne in its huge talons, and, giving one last downward beat with his wings, lifted off, with the throne, Rudolph, and all, into the sky.

Coughing and gagging from the swirling dust, Ben scrambled to his feet. He shielded his eyes from the sun and tried to see where the giant bird had gone, but it had already flown out of sight. He started to help Shess and Tom, but they were already helping others get back to their feet. As Ben wandered through the group, he found that there weren't any injuries worse than dirt in the eyes or mouth, both of which he fixed with a splash of water from his canteen.

When he came across Joe, he said, "Good shooting. I don't think any of our folks got more than dust in the eyes."

"Easier than the last couple battles. This was basically sniping. Those idiots stood their ground." Joe kicked at one of the bodies. "And it's easier to hit stationary targets."

"Speaking of targets, did anyone get a shot at Rudolph and his shield?" Ben asked.

"I know I shot his way a couple good times, but with all the wind, I don't know if any hit. If they did, then that shield of his works the way he expected."

"It's unbelievable how much dust that bird kicked up."

"Worse than a helicopter, even a chinook." Joe glanced at Ben. "That's a big, two-bladed transport helicopter for you non-military types."

"I didn't think you meant one of those little ones from the news stations."

Joe laughed. "Not quite." He glanced at the sky. "We need to hurry and get this mess cleaned up before it gets too dark. As soon as we get done with them," he kicked one of the bodies, "we can go check on how the sick, lame, and lazy are doing."

"I'd like to see if Annie is doing any better, too."

"You and Tom both." Joe said, watching Tom tending to folks.

Ben hefted his canteen. "Still plenty left. I'll go help him out, then we can head up there together."

"I'll get Trey and Bear to help us with the bodies," Joe said. "I figure they can handle it."

"Good idea," Ben said as he trotted over to help. "Need to wash out any eyes or mouths?" he asked as he sloshed the water in his canteen.

"Yeah, both," Tom said. "I was surprised with the way you handled yourself with Rudolph. You were fairly convincing. If I didn't know we were leaving, I'd be scared, too."

"Well, I might have gone overboard on that." Ben shook his head. "He overheard us say that we're heading back, and now he wants *that*, too."

"Well, he's not coming back on my watch," Tom said firmly.

"So, what's he going to do after we've gone?" Ben asked. "Will he ever leave Shess alone? Will there even be a village here when you return with your next expedition?"

Tom sighed. "I shouldn't have gotten you guys involved at all. If we'd kept out of the local politics, we could have had time to do some hunting, Shess would be fighting off the *nimre*, and Rudolph wouldn't have any interest in what's going on here."

Ben grabbed Tom's shoulder. "And Melvin would still be missing."

"Considering that," Tom said slowly, "I have to admit Rudolph did bring it on himself. He started it, and all we did was react."

"Exactly. So it's not so much that we were dragged *into* it. We need to figure out how to get *out* of it." Ben shook his canteen. "I'm empty. Head to the river or up to the medic's hut?"

Tom hefted his canteen. "I'm empty, too, so let's do both. Besides, you don't want to be caught with an empty canteen, do you? Aren't you always supposed to be ready for anything?"

"The phrase is 'Be Prepared,'" Ben said. "And, yes, a full canteen sounds better than an empty one."

They circled the lodge and strolled to the edge of the river, finding a stream of water running from a trough, a half pipe, draining into a small well, built directly in the water.

Ben stood on the small platform surrounding the well and reached into the falling water. "Ooh! That's cold stuff."

Tom stretched up to look along the length of the pipe. "It's being fed from a small half-dam upstream farther." He looked into the well. "And the river flows right through below. Well, here's Annie's running water. No knobs to turn it on or off, but it should do to keep her toothbrush happy."

"Didn't she ask for hot and cold?" Ben asked.

Tom laughed. "She'll have to find a coffee pot for that."

Ben uncapped his canteen and held it in the flowing water, filling it quickly. He recapped it and stepped back, so Tom could do the same. Once they had filled both canteens, they trotted through the town to the medic's hut.

They hesitated at the bottom of the steps.

"Do we knock?" Ben asked.

Tom shrugged. "We could try."

Ben climbed the short stairs to the door and reached up to knock when the door swung open.

Deezhlahmahs stared at them. "Come," she said pulling the door open.

Ben stepped into the cool darkness.

Annie was sitting on the edge of the table where Carl had been treated. "Hey, Ben," she said, then jumped off the table and ran past him. "Tom!" They hugged a moment, then she said, "Ben, how's the rest of the group?"

"That's what we came here to ask."

Annie stepped towards a door at the back of the room. "We'll go check on the malingerers in a moment. I want to know what happened."

Tom hugged her. "You want to know what happened? What happened is that you revived Shawn. We don't know how you did it, but I saw it with my own eyes."

"I remember working on him, then trying that AED thing, but the next thing I know, I was waking up here." She asked Deezhlahmahs, "Can you tell them what you told me?"

"Annie-ss put her heart into Shawn's," Deezhlahmahs said. "Then brought back."

Ben frowned. "I don't understand."

"Neither do I," Annie said. "But that's the way she describes it." She shrugged. "Whatever I did, it worked."

Tom squeezed his arm on Annie's waist. "As long as you survived it. We didn't know what to do."

Annie smiled at Tom. "Shall we check on the others now?"

Deezhlahmahs led the way into the infirmary. There were a dozen beds along each side of the main aisle, but Ben was relieved to see that less than half of them had anyone in them. He followed Annie as she strolled up one side and back down the other, reading off the injuries. Mostly cuts and scrapes—she called them lacerations—abrasions, and a handful of blisters. Most of these guys were ready to head back out, but at the far end of the room, next to what could be a nurse's station, were the ones that were worse off.

When they made it to Doug's bed, he was sitting up sipping soup.

"How're you feeling, Doug?" Tom asked.

"I feel fine, but they wanted me to stay here. Besides," he waggled his spoon at Shawn in the next bed, "I'm waiting for him to heal up."

"You should be resting," Annie said. "Sit there and finish your soup."

"Annie, shouldn't *you* be resting, too? After that CPR thing, you probably need a break, too."

"That's the same thing Deezh said," Annie said. "Those assistants of hers can rotate duties, giving each one a chance to rest."

Ben asked Deezhlahmahs, "Can you spare an assistant or two to help Annie out in the field?"

Yes, I able do," Deezhlahmahs said. "Tomorrow. Need all today."

"I can see that. Thank you," Ben said.

Annie elbowed Ben and whispered, "*mi garshoo gu.*"

"What?"

"Say it. Say, '*mi garshoo gu*'," Annie insisted.

Ben tried it. "*mi garshoo gu.*" He bowed to Deezhlahmahs.

She smiled at him and replied, "*mi towk-shoo gu*, you welcome."

"Now then, Doug," Annie said, "you finish your soup, then lie back and rest."

"Yes, ma'am," Doug said.

They stepped to the last bed, where Shankaktos lay. An assistant stood by, monitoring his status. Annie checked, then reported, "He's doing much better than expected. Although his injuries weren't as extensive as Carl's, they did need careful attention," she said. "We should be glad that he didn't have any encounters with poisoned blades, nor did we have to knock him out to clean any deep wounds, either. All in all, he's coming along quite well." She glanced at Deezhlahmahs, then continued. "Other than his leg, we could expect him to be up and about by tomorrow morning."

Doug leaned out of his bed. "How long for his leg to heal?"

"Well, now that's a problem," Annie said. "Deezh says that in my rush for an emergency fix, I may have set his leg a little crookedly." She blushed. "She says that we have two options here: re-break it and set it properly, but that'll put him out of action for days, or let it finish healing as it is, and he'll have a limp for the rest of his life, and possibly pain, too."

"Out of action for days?" Doug asked. "We'll be gone by then."

"Well, we certainly can't leave him an invalid for the rest of his life," Ben said. "So we'll have to slog along without him."

Doug swung his legs out of bed and stood up. "If he's going to be incapacitated for that long, I don't need to waste time here." He walked to the bed. "So I'll wait until he's out of surgery," he hesitated, "or whatever you do to him. Then I'll go deal with that Rudolph guy and be right back to help him recover." He slapped Shankaktos on the shoulder. "How's that for ya?"

Shankaktos winced then tried to smile up at Doug. "That good. Bring trophy."

"You betcha. I'll bring you a scalp or something."

"You will not!" Annie said. "That's gross."

Doug laughed. "Then I'll get him something else for all the troubles he's gone through for us."

"Something better than a .50 cal round?" Ben asked.

"Yeah, I'll find a bigger bullet for him," Doug declared. "Or a grenade if I have to."

"A grenade?" Tom asked. "And you're going to let him hang it on a string around his neck?"

Ben laughed. "That might not work."

Doug shrugged. "Maybe not a grenade, but *something* special."

"Doug, if you're feeling so much better," Annie said, "then you can head out now. Deezh and I have work to do." She shooed Doug and Ben out, then gave Tom a quick hug. "You'd better go, too."

Ben glanced back as they crossed the infirmary porch, and he thought he saw Tom lean down to Annie, right as the door closed. A moment later, the door swung open, and Tom strode past the two of them as if nothing was amiss. Ben and Doug followed Tom, heading to the lodge for the night.

All the able-bodied were in the lodge, already eating dinner. Before the three of them sat, Ben stepped to the front. "As soon as I'm done eating, I'm heading to bed. It's early, but I've had too many long days and late nights." He stared down the group. "I need to be well rested to be ready for whatever Rudolph has in store for us."

The group agreed, but Ben heard minor grumblings.

Tom joined in, "Yeah, as long as I have the chance, I'm going to enjoy a decent, hot meal, sitting at a real table. I don't remember the last time I had a chance to *sit* for a meal…and I don't mean on a rock." He looked across the room. "I can't tell you what to do, but you have a real table here, so take advantage of it and dig in. Have dessert, too, if you want."

The grumbling increased, and it sounded like most were unhappy with the suggestions. "What dessert?" a voice yelled out.

"I'll check back in the kitchen," he said. "We might be able to find something, but even if we don't, I want to be ready for whatever happens in the morning."

"We don't know what Rudolph is planning," Tom said. "So it would be safer to be ready for anything. Remember, there's power in numbers."

The crowd agreed and relaxed.

Ben and Tom went to join Doug who had already started eating. "I wanted to set a good example for the other guys," he said.

"Yeah, right," Ben said. "You're just hungry for *real* food. I've heard from Carl about that soup they serve up at the infirmary."

"That's terrible stuff. I wouldn't eat it except they force you to, and Annie's the worst."

"She's doing what she can," Ben said.

"And doing quite a good job from what I've seen," Tom said.

"Yeah, Tom, like you don't have any prejudices in that direction, do you?"

Tom shrugged. "What can I say?"

Ben crammed a large bite into his mouth and mumbled around it, "Nothing."

Tom followed suit, and soon they were all enjoying the meal.

As they were finishing up and still anticipating the hoped-for dessert, Ben leaned to Tom. "First thing in the morning, I'm heading up to check on Shawn, uh, Shankaktos. Do you want to join me?"

"As soon as the sun's up."

Ben tried to find someone in charge. "Can we leave a wakeup call?"

"Leave a message with whoever is on watch. They'll pass it on."

"I'll do that."

"If that doesn't work, I'll come by and pound on your door," Tom said. "How's that for a wakeup call?"

"That'll have to do," Ben said as he stood. "See you then." He checked out who was left. "Not many still here…and I never did see that dessert show up." He frowned then shrugged. "Oh, well."

"Yeah, most have hit the sack already," Tom said.

"There's still some left." Ben checked the room. "Patrick, trading recipes with the cook, and Doug, sitting there fretting about Shawn."

"And there's Eric, too, over by the fireplace," Tom said. "What's he got? A book or something?"

"Yeah, he tends to do that. Always has a book with him and sneaks off in the middle of anything, even a campout, to read. It tends to keep him out of trouble…as opposed to some of the other scouts," Ben hesitated. "It keeps him out of trouble *most* of the time."

"*Most* of the time? How would he manage to get in trouble by reading a book?" Tom asked.

"Let me tell you. We were on a campout one time where he wandered off, book in hand, and found himself a nice rock in the sun to sit and read. What he'd forgotten to do was tell anyone where he was going or even that he'd gone."

"That doesn't sound too bad."

"Not by itself, but when it came time for a group activity, the scout master couldn't find him, so we wasted half a day searching for him. We still couldn't find him, so the scout leaders contacted the forest rangers, and *they* called out the helicopters."

"Oh, now *that* could be a problem." Tom laughed.

"They found him a couple miles from camp sitting on the top of a rocky peak, still reading," Ben said. "When the helicopters buzzed close enough, he shooed them off, because 'they were interrupting' his reading."

"I would have loved to read the report the rangers turned in on that rescue: Victim claims he's busy, 'Leave me alone. I'm reading.' So reading *can* get him into trouble." Tom laughed again.

"Once he gets into a book," Ben said. "It takes an act of God to bring him back out. I'll see if I can get him to bed now." Ben walked across the room. "See you in the morning."

* * *

Morning came, and Ben was sitting on the side of his bed when Tom came by. "Internal alarm clock still works as expected," Ben said.

"That's the best way. Come on, let's get going."

They made their way quietly towards the front, intent on letting everyone else keep sleeping, but a couple doors popped open as they went towards the front room. Most went back to bed, but some needed to visit the privy first. And then there was Doug. He was wide awake, dressed, and sitting in the main room, ready to go, insisting on going along to see how Shawn was doing.

"Well, you do have a vested interest in his recovery, after all the stuff the two of you've been through," Ben said. "Let's go."

The rising sun had yet to peek above the hills behind the medic's hut, but the sky was light enough to find their way up the small hill. As they approached the stairs, they could see someone sitting on the top step.

"Halloo!" Ben said as they came through the gate into the herb garden.

The figure flinched and stood up. "Hello, Ben," Annie said. "Why are you up so early?"

"Checking up on Shawn's status."

"Good news. The operation, if you could call it that, went well. Deezh let me keep him sedated last night as she broke and reset the leg, and as of this morning, the leg is doing quite well."

"Does that mean he's ready to help us with Rudolph?" Doug asked hopefully.

Annie raised her eyebrows. "No, nothing that soon. We don't want him putting any stress on that leg until it has healed up more. Remember, it's already been broken twice, once intentionally."

"Ben, if you guys don't need me, I'll hang out here," Doug said. "I could do fetch-and-carry chores, Annie. If you want."

Ben glanced at Tom and shrugged. "Does that work for you, Annie?"

"I'm certain we can find something to keep him busy," Annie said. "Tom, have you had breakfast yet?"

Ben answered, "No *we* haven't. Anything up here other than that tasteless medicine you call soup?"

"It's not tasteless, besides it's good for you. It has all kinds of herbals that help injuries heal faster."

"I'm not injured, so, if you don't mind, I'll head back to the lodge for a *real* breakfast."

"You go right ahead and do that, Ben." Annie paused. "My question wasn't directed at you anyway. I was asking Tom if *he* wanted to take breakfast with me," she said glaring at Ben.

Tom stepped back holding his hands up. "If you two are quite done, may I speak?"

"Yes, Tom, go ahead," Ben said.

"Yes, Annie," Tom said. "I'd be glad to take breakfast with you." He pointedly paused. "Ben, we'll head to the lodge after breakfast."

"And we'll bring any of the guys that are ready to go," Annie said.

Ben started to go but hesitated. "Annie, when you come, don't forget that compass. We need to monitor Rudolph's location."

"Oh! Speaking of Rudolph, what ever happened to that dragon in town?" she asked.

"Something for your breakfast conversation," Ben said as he walked away, sauntering into town.

Arriving at the lodge, Ben found breakfast well underway, so he quickly grabbed a plate, filled it with food, and sat between Shess and Bear. Trey was right across the table, so once Ben had quelled his gurgling stomach, he asked how things were going.

Trey shrugged and mumbled through a mouthful, "Fine, now that I have breakfast well in hand."

"Um…Shess, are the *shmahseespe* satisfied with how we're handling this problem with Rudolph?"

"Ones not go with, stay here in town, want you leave, all you. Ones who go who with, who fight with you, want go get him, remove him, so no more problem."

Bear pounded his fist on the table. "We take out, right, Trey-ss?"

"Close enough," Trey said. "Hey, Ben, have you noticed the reception here?"

"What's that?" Ben asked.

"Well, although Bear and the others are all for getting rid of Rudolph, we're getting the cold shoulder from the innkeeper here. No real problem with his serving, but he's just not being very polite." He shrugged. "I'd say that because he's not making any profit with us here, he'd prefer that we leave and take our problems with us."

"I had that feeling," Ben said. "Hate to consider it, but it *is* our fault. We brought this problem to these people." Ben sighed. "Shess, do *you* have anything to say?"

"I say Rudolph want you, not me, not us. When you leave, he have no need be here, he go his city, and we go ours. We done."

"We hope so, and if we leave the compass behind, Fred can use it to keep an eye on Rudolph. Then you'd have advance warning if he moves."

"Fredekas or Zhahmonichas," Shess said. "Could read compass."

"Zhahmonichas? That's the guy that taught Patrick the language?"

"He teach children in town all they need," Shess said.

"That would be a good place to start," Ben said as he scraped up the last of his food. Right as he emptied his plate, the innkeeper came by and snatched it away, saying nothing. Ben stared at him as he stormed away. "Wow, I see what you mean about the service here."

"You should see it at the other tables." Trey said. "We get better service at this table because Shess and Bear are here. From what I've seen, the innkeeper is intimidated by them."

Ben regarded the two natives. "I can see why."

"Oh, it's not for the reason you think," Trey said. "Townsfolk don't usually eat here in this tavern, not unless there's an out-of-towner visiting, and with this town being on the frontier, that doesn't happen often."

Ben thought for a moment. "Unless they come from *way* out of town, or even off-world, like we did." He paused. "Before Tom and everyone showed up, the commerce they had here was limited to the grain that they exported to the towns south of here, right? But now that Tom's company has made a connection, well, that changes things, doesn't it?"

"Yeah, and now that Rudolph knows there's a way back," Tom said slowly, "I don't imagine that he will give up once we leave, either."

"True. Whether we're here or not, Rudolph will still be a problem to this whole area until he gets what he wants."

"And what's that?" Trey asked.

"Well, the last thing he said before flying off on that portable throne of his was that he wanted to get back, back home, back to the normal world. He's been trapped here for decades and isn't happy."

Tom inhaled. "So, Ben, if we let him come back with us, do you think he'd be satisfied and leave everyone else alone?"

"That's a nice idea, but from what I've seen, not with his attitude." Ben shook his head. "And I don't think being nice to him would change a thing, as much as we'd like it to."

Ben was about to continue when Annie and Tom burst in. They paused in the doorway, then came straight to the table, Annie holding the compass in front of her.

"What's up?" Ben asked.

"Rudolph is on the move again, but this time he's heading cross country and moving slower."

Trey sat up. "Slower? You mean not flying?"

"Much slower. As if he's walking," Annie said bouncing the compass.

Shess stepped closer. "Rudolph not alone. He lead army."

Ben stood up. "Well, we have advance warning. We may not know *what* he's planning, but we can keep track of his whereabouts."

Joe walked up with his troops. "Did I hear someone say we have incoming?"

"The compass shows movement," Tom said. "And they're heading this direction, so yes, you could say we have incoming."

"Not much rest before the next encounter." Joe studied the group. "Any clue how much time we have, Annie?"

"I still don't have the scale figured out on this thing," she held the compass up, "but *we* spent a couple days to make the journey."

"A couple days because we didn't know where we were going," Joe said, then added, "And I'll bet he has his army marching double time. It won't be long before they arrive. We'd best get things prepped." He called to his men. "Ready for action?"

They all shouted their willingness to head into battle again. Ben even noticed a couple of the natives shouting, "Oo-rah." He smiled. *Joe is going to make one heck of a good soldier…if we ever get him back to reality.*

Trey raised his hand. "I have a question, Ben."

"What is it?" Ben asked.

"It'll be a couple days before they get here, so won't we be well and gone by then?"

Ben scratched the stubble on his chin. "Hmm, could be. Tom, how much time do we have left?"

Tom pulled a small notebook out of his pocket. "I was keeping track of it. Never had to do that before. Usually we stick close to the drop-off point, but this time we've been wandering all across the countryside."

Trey and the others counted the days. "Here we go again."

Annie smiled at Trey. "So, Tom, what's your list show?"

Tom unfolded a wrinkled piece of paper. "Arrived Thursday and hiked to the beach, spent the night there. That's normal for most trips." He went down the list. "In town Friday. Saturday we blew the heck out of the *nimre* and found John. Sunday was the hidden valley with the *lahnpe* folks." He nodded to Ben. "Remind me to tell the techies about them."

"Sounds to me like you need a journal to keep track of all the stuff going on," Ben said.

"I'll put that on the list, too," Tom said. "Continuing, after we got out of that valley on Monday, we hiked a bunch. Tuesday morning we were in battle, and arrived at Rudolph's city that evening." He glanced at Ben. "More to tell the techies." He resumed his list. "Wednesday we met Rudolph and managed to break out of his city." He raised his eyebrows. "Thursday we hiked the whole day, crossed the river, and chased Rudolph out of town, so that makes today Friday." He stretched his arms, holding his list high. "Sound right to everyone?"

Everyone agreed.

"Good, then that means we have two days left to get to the Door, and the plan was to spend one night along the way, at the same beach, so…except for the hunting…we're right on schedule."

John's eyebrows shot up. "…except for hunting." He grinned at Tom. "Oh, shucks." He snapped his fingers. "We'll have to come back for that."

Eric wandered up. "What's going on?"

Annie gripped the compass. "Rudolph is heading this way."

"So why is everyone so excited? Isn't that even more bad news?" Eric sat and propped his chin in hands, elbows on the edge of the table.

"It's probably bad news that he's coming our way," Ben said, "but it's good news that we can *see* him coming."

"It is?" Eric dropped into a chair. "All that means is that we'll *see* our eventual destruction coming right at us. We'll *know* when we are about to buy the farm, kick the bucket, go we know not where."

"Oh, it can't be that bad, Eric." Ben put his hand on Eric's shoulder. "We've been through pretty tough situations, but we're doing fine, in fact we're all the better for it."

"Yeah, yeah, I know. 'That which does not kill you makes you stronger.' But what everyone forgets is the rest of that quote: 'It hurts like heck until it's done.' I'm all for growth and change, but I'd like to avoid the painful part, if you don't mind."

"Don't we all?" Tom said. "But life is what it is, so sometimes, we have to fight to survive."

"My point exactly," Joe said. "And this time we have to fight, so let's take the fight to Rudolph instead of letting him bring it to us."

"You may have something there, Joe," Ben said. "Tom, if we don't do anything, where do you expect this battle is going to happen?"

Joe jumped in, looking over Tom's shoulder at the list. "Depending on timing, it could be right at the drop-off point…unless Rudolph is faster than we think, then he'll be bringing the conflict to us, here in town."

"That sounds about right," Tom said, then noticed Shess and Bear, both sitting quietly watching the group decide their fate. "What did you have in mind, Joe?"

"Well, if we stay here, Rudolph will bring all his troops right down Shess' throat and probably wipe this village off the map, but if you think about what Rudolph *really* wants, it isn't even here." Joe paused. "We have no way to send him home from *here in town*."

"I see where you're going with that," Ben said. "If we head to the pickup point *right now*, we might be able to encourage Rudolph to follow us *away* from town."

"That would definitely bring the confrontation to the drop-off point," Joe said.

"*We* would control the location," Ben said, "give Rudolph the chance to get what he wants, *and* keep Shess and his folks out of harm's way."

Tom leaned back. "I like that idea, Ben. It certainly addresses all the problems, right, Shess?"

"No battle here," Shess said. "Take *betnahzbit* and leave."

Ben leaned to Joe and whispered, "Wow! We have *definitely* worn out our welcome here. Our focus should be to get the heck out of Dodge, and soon." He sat up and addressed the group. "So what that means is that we need to head out quickly tomorrow morning if we want to have any time to get things ready for Rudolph's arrival."

"Thank you," Annie said. "I'd prefer an extra day to let the guys heal up. We'd be pushing it to leave sooner," she said.

"And that's also assuming he won't be here until then," Joe said. "As Annie said, we still don't know the scale of things on the compass."

Eric piped up, "Would it help to triangulate his exact location if you had another point on your compass?"

Everyone stared at Eric, and Ben spoke up. "Another point? How would that work?"

Eric leaned back. "If we know where Rudolph is, and we know where *we* are, then a third point, of known distance, would set the scale of everything, right?"

"Are you taking us back to trigonometry?" Tom asked.

"Not trig with sines and cosines, but if you mean similar triangles, then yes, but that's all elementary stuff, right?" Eric smiled his little I-know-something-you-don't smile.

Joe stood to shush any response. "Yes, Eric. That *would* help." He reminded everyone, "Remember, we covered that stuff when we were learning mapping. We need to identify the scale of the map."

Eric continued, "Well, as I see it, we already have three points. Four if we count the holder of the compass, Annie's location."

Annie frowned. "Don't tease us, Eric. Tell us what you have in mind."

Eric leaned back. "Well, you know where Rudolph is, where Deezh is, and where Melvin is."

Annie looked across the room. "That doesn't do us much good because both Deezh and Melvin are right here in town with us. I can't see them as separate points unless I zoom in so much that I can't see Rudolph."

"Yes, at the present time all three points coincide," Eric said, tallying on his fingers, "Deezh, Melvin, and the compass, but they don't have to. What if a small contingent rushed Melvin to the drop-off point? We could then get a point on the map, on the compass, of where we're heading."

"Yeah, I can see that helping," Annie said slowly.

"Distance *and* direction," Eric added. "Moreover, if we leave Deezh here in the village, we could use that point to verify Rudolph's direction. Will he be heading here, to the village, or will he be heading to the Door...and home?"

The whole group broke out into heated discussion as Eric started carving a diagram on the tabletop, but the innkeeper quickly discouraged that. Eventually, Ben caught the room's attention.

"So, we've decided that we like Eric's idea of sending Melvin on ahead, with Joe and his troops as escorts, to the drop-off point, but to ensure that *they* don't get lost we need to send Tom along with them." He raised a hand to shush Annie before she could complain. "And although that would make it difficult for the rest of us to find the way home, all we have to do is let Annie monitor the compass allowing us to move from Deezh to Melvin, trying to stay ahead of Rudolph."

Everyone spoke at once.

Joe's voice carried above the crowd. "I like the idea of going on ahead, and I don't mind leading the operation, but I have one request: Let *me* pick the ones that will come with us."

The hubbub grew as complaints were bantered back and forth.

"It's not that I have anything against any of you." Joe continued. "But we'll need to go as fast as possible, so no one to slow us down." He paused. "Also we'll be wanting to lighten our load, if we can, so, Ben, if we could offload some of our gear…?"

"I'm certain we'll be able to pick up the extra." Ben said. "Trey, what say you?"

"We'll handle it," Trey said.

Annie frowned. "That's all well and good, but taking on the extra load means we're going to be even slower than before, and we might have a problem getting to the Door on time."

Tom spoke up. "If carrying Joe's droppings makes us slower, we'll just catch the Door the next time it opens. They typically open it at noon, local time, but if we miss it, we'll wait for the next opening…if we have to. Might be just an extra day or so." He glanced at Annie and smiled. "We'll wait for you before stepping through…Ben."

"I'd prefer to avoid that, if we can," Ben said. "I don't feel like sitting on my duff expecting to be rescued when the Door opens, with Rudolph and his followers still out loose."

"In that case, push it," Joe said. "And if you get tuckered out, remember: Once you're through the Door, you're home safe."

"Ha!" Tom said. "We'll slam the Door right in Rudolph's face, then stop to breathe once we're all on the other side."

Ben frowned. "Leaving Rudolph over here to wreak havoc?"

"Not much we can do about that," Tom said. "But I'll let Eugene know. He might have an idea or two."

"I have one more request," Joe said. "Shess, if you don't mind, I'd like to pick up extra gear that we hadn't brought, don't usually need on a camping trip."

Shess frowned. "What need?"

"Not much. Maybe some digging equipment, shovels, pickaxes, and things like that." Joe thought for a moment. "Oh, and something that can be used to fell a tree…it would be handier than using our swords."

Ben stared at Joe. "What's all that stuff for?"

"I have ideas on things to get ready for Rudolph," Joe said. "Stuff we learned when we covered booby traps in training."

"Booby traps? Hmm… That could be good," Ben said. "Shess, can you do that?"

Shess stood up and spoke to Fredekas and the townsfolk. After a quick exchange, he said, "All you need, they get. They go with, bring back later."

Ben smiled. "Thanks, Shess."

Shess sat, mumbling.

Ben glanced at Patrick who shrugged then leaned in. "He said something about doing anything necessary to get us out of town."

"Can't hold it against him," Ben said. "Ever since we've been here, he's had bigger issues than ever before. The sooner we leave this place the way we found it, the better."

Joe stood up and headed for the door. "I'm going to grab my guys and head out. Carl will be joining us as a guide, along with Fred, if that's all right with you, Shess."

"*aa-eh*," Shess said. "Is good Fredekas help."

"Getting such a late start," Joe continued. "We'll need to push it to make the beach before it gets too dark. We'll set up a quickie camp there, then head out early in the morning." He paused. "That should give you a wide enough spread to see Eric's triangle, right, Annie?"

"Oh, yes, that would be fine," she said.

"Good," Joe said. "Everyone else get a good night's rest and head out first thing in the morning. Maintain a good pace, spend Saturday night at the beach, and you'll easily arrive at the drop-off point by Sunday morning. Remember, noon is it." He glanced at Annie and Tom. "If you have anything to say, Tom, you'd better say it quickly. See you outside in a bit." He pulled his group off to the side, giving instructions on what to carry and what to leave behind.

Tom guided Annie by the elbow, leading her to a somewhat quiet corner, where they had a private conversation, well out of earshot of the others, so no one heard what was said. When they were done, she was openly upset but reluctantly accepted the plan.

Ben stepped to the other side of the lodge and yelled, "Yo! Melvin. You're at the top of the list again."

"I am? For what."

Ben hesitated. "Well, you could say we need you as a target. We have to give Rudolph someplace to go, and he's bent on getting home."

"So what does that have to do with me being a target?"

"We're assuming that he has a compass similar to the one Annie has. She's been tracking him on it, and we think that he'll be tracking you."

"There you go again, assuming. Why would he track *me*?" Melvin paused. "No, wait, *how* would he track me?"

Ben shrugged. "Rules are different here. Remember helping Annie?"

"Yeah," Melvin said. "That was weird."

"Well, that ability shows up on her compass thingy. She can see you on it."

"She can see me? Like on television?"

"No, not your picture," Ben said. "More like radar, just a blip showing your location."

"Why does it do that?" Melvin asked.

"There's something special about you," Ben shrugged. "And we know that Rudolph wants to get home, so we're thinking that he'll try following *you*. That way he has a good chance of getting what he wants. That's how his troops zeroed in on you before."

"And you want me to stand out there like a sitting duck waiting for him to come find me?"

"Well, not exactly, but close enough. The problem is that we don't want him coming here, to this town, so we're going to send you back to the drop-off point. We're hoping that will draw him off in that direction, and we can keep him out of Shess' town."

"So this is all for the natives?" Melvin said.

"Well, you *do* want to get home, don't you?"

"Of course!" Melvin frowned.

"Well, all we want is to send you back to the drop-off point *early*. We want you there *tomorrow* morning, instead of waiting until Sunday. You'll have an entire day to wait for the rest of us to catch up."

"I hear a 'but' coming on," Melvin said slowly.

"You're not as dumb as you look." Ben smiled. "The 'but' is we want you to leave tonight, *now* as a matter of fact, and if I know Joe, you may end up running most of the way. It shouldn't be too difficult because we're going to lighten your load. We'll haul any equipment that you leave behind when we follow you in the morning."

"That's good, but when you say right now, you mean it? As in *now* now?"

"If you need any help lightening your load," Ben said, "let Trey know. He'll most likely be carrying anything left behind."

"You said Joe, right? The two of us?"

"Joe will be bringing his troops," Ben said, "and Tom will be going, too, to lead the way, so there'll be a small group with you."

"As long as it's not John trying to push me up a hill in the dark, I'm certain I can handle it."

"We weren't planning on sending John in that group."

"Well, I'd best get going then," Melvin said. "See you in a couple days…if I survive."

Ben patted Melvin on the back. "You'll do fine." Going outside to check on Joe's group, Ben noticed most of the scouts and townsfolk were already in the town square to see the advance group off.

Joe stood at the front of the group, glancing up at the sun as it approached the horizon. "If we hurry, we might make it, as long as no one slows us." He glared at Melvin as he came out of the lodge.

"Don't push him too hard, Joe," Ben said. "He's been out of it for most of the trip. You guys have had time to figure things out, to accept what's going on with Patrick, Robb, Trey," he hesitated, "and all the rest."

"Don't forget Carl, too." Joe laughed at his crew. "I don't know if I'll ever get used to him dressed like that."

"Oh, well. We do what we can." Ben shrugged. "Be careful on your trip. Leave messages along the way, if you need to."

"If we have time." Joe said. "Move out…Melvin, you too! Let's hit the road."

They started off at a slow trot to give Tom a chance to catch up. He was slow in coming out of the lodge with Annie in arm. Ben could see that before they were out of sight, Joe was already starting to push them a little faster. *I hope Melvin survives Joe's boot camp.*

Everyone stood there a while, waiting for the group to pass through the fields and disappear into the woods. As soon as they were out of sight, the crowd dissipated, some folks wandering back into the lodge, some heading home. Ben stood in the doorway, keeping an eye on everyone. The last to come in was Annie who had stood there the longest watching Tom depart. Ben could see that in spite of the short time, some pretty significant feelings had developed between those two. *I'm going to have to keep tabs on them.*

Ben came back inside and sat near Annie. "All good?" he asked.

She shrugged. "Fine, I suppose."

Ben raised an eyebrow at her. "Getting serious?"

"Not intentionally, but it feels nice to pass the time with him, to talk to him, to be with him."

"Sounds to me like a valid definition of 'serious.' Cool it, though, will ya?" Ben asked. "Let's wait until we get back before you commit to anything major. I can't fault you for what's going on *here*. It's like Vegas: What happens in…uh…wherever we are, stays here, but when we get back to the real world, things might change."

"Yeah, I know. I'll be careful."

"Thanks. So…other than that, how're things? Can you see the Melvin spot moving away from here?"

"Oh! I hadn't thought to check." She fumbled to get the compass out. "I should be keeping track of their progress." She held the compass in the flat of her hand and stared at it.

Ben leaned in. "I still can't see anything on it."

Annie studied the compass. "It's difficult to tell. The points are close together."

"Why don't you try the zoom thing? Put it closer to the floor."

Annie crouched and slowly lowered the compass. "Yes, that works. If I zoom in close enough for the Rudolph dot to be right on the edge, I can see a difference between Melvin and Deezh. That means Joe's group is on their way."

"That's good," Ben said.

Annie stood up. "I wonder what I'll get if I hold it higher. I should be able to zoom the picture out farther, right?"

"If you say so," Ben said.

Annie stood up and held the compass as high as she could, continuing to watch the top surface. "Yes, that pulls everything in closer. Now I can't see *any* difference between Melvin and Deezh. The colors seem to blend, and Rudolph is close to them. Let me try even higher." She climbed up onto the bench, standing next to Ben, and studied the compass. "Now all three are almost merged, and," she squinted, "and I can see something on the *extreme* edge."

"There are more spots, more people out there?" Ben asked.

"Yes, people, but not ordinary people, ones that have enough power to show up."

"Tom should hear about that. He'll want to investigate."

"Let me try more," Annie said as she climbed on the table, stretching as high as possible, suddenly gasping. "I can see *beyond* where Rudolph's city must be, way beyond. There are other spots out there, lots of them. Mostly downstream, but I see a couple that way, too." She swung her arm to point east, then slowly move north. "Way far away."

Ben followed her arm off into the distance. "Towards the drop-off point? Tom could be running into an ambush!"

Annie took one last look then stepped off the table. "No, Ben. Those spots are way far away, twice as far from us as Rudolph is. Over a week's travel to traipse that far."

"That far away…but in the direction of the drop-off point? Wait until Tom hears about *that*," Ben said . "They never explored in *that* direction."

"And you remember why, don't you?"

"The desert…blocking the path to those glowing mountains," Ben said slowly, then grinned. "Now we have an excuse to cross the desert and explore those mountains."

"And when do you think you'll have time to do all that?" she asked.

Ben blinked at her in surprise. "The next time we're here."

Joe glanced back as they crested the first rise. The village was out of sight by now. "Come on, guys. Pick up the pace." He kept an eye on Melvin to make certain he wasn't going to drop behind. *Good troops. We'll make the beach on time.*

They passed quickly through the fields and entered the woods. As bright as the sun had been before, in here the air glowed with an anxious green, but Joe was pleased that a cool breeze kept the joggers from overheating. Sooner than they expected, they arrived at the base of the cliff next to the waterfall.

Everyone sat on the rocks by the pool. Carl squinted at the path up the cliff. "With the sun up, we can actually see where we're going this time."

Melvin, out of breath, pulled out his canteen. "Yeah."

"If we were going to stay here longer," Joe said, using his canteen to point. "I'd have to put in some stairs. That or an elevator."

"Handholds would be good enough for me," said Carl.

"While you're at it, why not add a gondola?" Tom suggested. "We'd welcome not having to clamber up and down this cliff all the time."

Joe laughed. "Yeah, I'll put it on my to-do list, right after Annie's hot and cold running water."

"So you heard about that, too?" Tom asked.

"Yeah. All the scouts have been laughing at it. We've had to put up with cold water on *all* our campouts, and all the *running* water we had was in the river or stream we camped next to."

"Well, I wouldn't expect that she'd live up to all the scouting ideals, though it would be nice to have her along on a regular campout," Tom said.

Joe choked on the mouthful of water he was sipping, all but spraying it on Tom. "Yeah, you *would* think that."

Carl stepped out of the shadows of the trees and tipped his head back to stare at the top of the cliff. "May as well get going." He grinned at Fred. "Don't want to make Sergeant Joe unhappy." He started climbing, followed by the rest of the advance group.

Following the trail was easy, and when it was too dark, Joe called for a quick break to light the lanterns. "No need to go running off into the dark, is there, Carl? Melvin?"

"Not if we have a choice, but John kept pushing us," Melvin said.

"So you didn't want to go along with him?" Joe asked.

Melvin hesitated. "No. I mean, yes…I mean. I don't know." He shrugged.

Carl stood up. "We wanted to go hunting, not sit on our butts and talk."

Joe stared at the two of them. "So have you had enough hunting? Or didn't that quite work out as expected?"

"Yeah, we sorta messed up," Melvin admitted.

"I don't think *any* of our plans have worked out as we expected," Carl said. "And where are we now?"

Tom stepped up. "Speaking of where we *are*, where *should* we be?"

Joe agreed. "Let's get moving. No time to waste talking." He looked intentionally at Carl.

They grabbed their backpacks, and passing out a lantern to every other person, they were soon on their way again. Frequently swapping out point, they pushed on, making good time, but no singing on this trek. They kept quiet in case there were any *nimre* out there. The path was easy to follow, stay near the river but not too close to the edge.

The moon was high in the heavens when they finally arrived at the beach. They set up the single six-man tent that they had brought and rotated the watch, though they didn't anticipate any action. Morning came quietly, a quick breakfast, pack up all the gear, then back on the road again. This time Joe let Tom run lead.

"It's not that I wouldn't be able to find my way," Joe said. "But you've made the trip enough times to recognize landmarks."

"I'll let you in on a secret, Joe," Tom said in a stage whisper. "From here it's pretty much a straight shot. See that mountain there? The one with the tall, skinny peak? Just a bit north of due east. I head generally in that direction, until we hit a creek that comes up on the south, pushing us more north. From there it's a quick jaunt up the creek until you see the big field where we landed. It's a pretty wide open place. It has a bunch of trees on the far side, so it isn't difficult to find."

"Up the creek? Do we have a paddle?" Joe teased.

"Why would you need a paddle, with no canoe?" Tom shot back.

Joe laughed. "Well, it's good to know which direction we're going. Give me a moment, and I'll notify Ben."

"Notify Ben? How? He's still back in *Roadranusis*," Tom said.

"Watch. I'll show you how scouts communicate." Joe called to Carl and Melvin. "You guys, set up some ducks."

"On it, Joe," Carl said, dragging Fredekas along.

"Follow me, Tom." They went to one of the trees on the north side of the campsite, and Joe pulled out his knife. "We leave messages like this." He hacked at the trunk, making a series of tall rectangular marks, two above and below, and one to the side. "This is a blaze that says the trail continues but turns." He faced east. "That way."

Carl came up with a handful of rocks, followed by Fredekas and Melvin with more. "Where do you want them set up?"

"Start right in the middle of camp," Joe said. "So they won't miss them. Point them towards that triangular peak." He checked with Tom.

"Generally eastward," Tom said.

"I'll get the near ones, Carl," Melvin said. "You guys keep the line going."

Tom watched Carl set up piles of rocks at the edge of camp, leading in a line, bearing due east. *Interesting technique these scouts have. Compass or not, Ben will know the right heading.*

Joe and Carl finished marking the trail and headed to the rest.

"Ready? Then let's move out," Tom shouted.

They headed off, Joe and Carl keeping abreast of Tom on the wide trail, Fredekas right behind.

Carl squinted into the rising sun. "As long as we have the sun to lock in on, it shouldn't be a problem keeping on the right course. It's a pain not having a real compass. I wouldn't want anyone to get lost out here."

"Not a problem. I've been back and forth enough times to get you home safely," Tom said.

Joe glanced back. "Considering who, or what, we may have on our tail, getting home *safely* is no longer a consideration. Get us home in as few pieces as possible, and I'll be satisfied."

"Yeah, this trip has been a doozy. I'm wondering if all the politics will make the bosses want to pack it in. This might be the last trip out here."

Carl gasped. "No! I plan to return as many times as I can." He reached out and slapped Fredekas on the back.

Joe smiled. "I'm certain we can convince them, politics or no. This has been an eye-opening trip, and I wouldn't mind coming back for another. Of course, it would have to wait until I can save up enough leave. A short trip would be nice, but a long one would be even nicer."

The group hiked at a quick pace during the cool morning hours, making good time, pausing as Tom verified landmarks. "Getting close," he finally announced.

Joe noted the sun's position. "If Ben got everyone up and out of the lodge quickly this morning, they should be well past the waterfall by now, and we're practically there, right on time, except one day early."

"It's not far from here, so even if they're slow, they'll have plenty of time," Tom said.

"Yeah, I remember this creek." Carl picked up a small, flat stone and sent it bouncing across the water. "Not a problem, Joe. Easy squeezy."

"Out here all the creeks look the same." Joe frowned. "Are you certain *this* is the right one?" He asked Tom, "Is this the right one?"

Before Tom could answer, Carl explained. "Well, besides seeing where they had been skipping rocks." He wandered up a bit of a slope. "And seeing where Trey smashed through the bushes as he clomped around, leaving distinct foot prints, boot prints to be exact, in the mud." He stopped to face them. "The biggest clue that this is the right creek is…" He slowly raised an arm targeting the nearby field. "…the bright orange flag right there."

Joe saw the small stick with a surveyor's flag gently fluttering in the breeze and said, "Duh!" He laughed and ran ahead to a small rise, then stopped at the top, looked back at everyone, and solemnly intoned, "This is the place."

The other scouts chuckled, pulled off their packs, and headed for the shade under the trees by the creek.

"Hey, wait! We're not finished yet," Joe yelled. "In fact, we're just starting. Stash your gear under those trees, then follow me. We have work to do!"

Melvin dropped his pack in the middle of the road. "We just got here. Isn't it time for a break?" He stared. "What do you want now?"

Joe walked to the group. "We know Ben will be here in the morning." He smiled. "We *hope* he makes it by then. We also know that Rudolph is heading our direction, but because we don't have Annie, we have no idea where he is or when he'll arrive, so we need to be ready for anything." He grabbed Melvin's pack and headed towards the trees near the creek as he continued talking. "What we need to do is set up an ambush."

He slid off his pack and dropped it and Melvin's. "When the soldiers pass that last clump of trees, they'll be in the open, right where we want them." He stepped down the slope heading to the creek and said, "We'll set up some *trou de loup* here."

"True de who?" Carl asked.

"Wolf holes. They're called punji sticks in Viet Nam," Joe explained. "Been used in combat since the Romans."

Carl stared at Joe. "Are you channeling Eric?"

"Yeah, must be," Joe said, laughing. "Anyway, we learned about traps in military history class, and with the lack of technology here, I figure they'd be perfect."

"You going to show us how to build a Roman troodle-de-do?"

"Basically dig a pit and put sharpened sticks at the bottom. When the soldiers get here, we attack from one side, and the soldiers dive for cover to the other side, to be impaled by the sticks."

"Sounds pretty nasty," Tom said.

"Well, if we weren't fighting for our lives, I wouldn't suggest it."

"Good point," Tom said.

Joe split up the group, directing both scouts and *shmahseespe* in various tasks. One crew was set up cutting and sharpening sticks while another dug the pits. When they were ready, he showed them how to use a rock to pound a skinny stick into each pit first, then pull it out and put a sharpened stick into the pre-made hole.

After the traps were set, Joe concealed them with long twigs, then smaller sticks and pebbles to make them virtually invisible.

Even Carl agreed that they blended in quite well. "Good job, Joe. The covering seems fairly natural…to an untrained eye, that is."

"Thanks…I think." Joe addressed the crew. "Now that we're done with the field-expedient traps, we need to dig foxholes. We'll start here on the side." He led the group to two small bushes near the path across from the creek. "Dig 'em shallow but long.

You'll be prone, so give yourselves enough room to be comfortable. We'll have two, one on this side, and one closer to the creek."

"So, who gets the sniper jobs?" Carl asked.

"Based on experience," Joe said. "It would have to be Tom and me. The rest of you guys set up behind us in the trees by the creek. You'll be farther away, but you'll have a wider view and can keep watch on the goings on to see where you're needed."

"Do you mind if I set up a couple deer blinds in those trees along the path?" Carl asked.

Joe gazed in that direction. "That might be a work. You'd have a better vantage point to see when they approach. But," Joe stared at Carl, "you *have* to do one thing for me…"

"What?" Carl asked.

"Hold your fire until we start shooting from back here. If they are alerted too early, we won't have a chance to target any of them."

"So, wait until they're in the kill zone," Carl said. "Then open fire on their flanks?"

Joe blinked. "You *have* been listening, haven't you? Yes, that would be fine. Tom and I are going to head out to dig more *trou de loups*."

"Melvin, feel like sitting in a tree?" Carl asked.

"Me?" Melvin asked.

"Yeah, you. Tom and Joe are pulling sniper duty, so you could help out in the deer blinds." Carl walked down the path. "I hesitate giving a rifle to an inexperienced native." He patted Fredekas on the shoulder. "Nothing against you, Fred, but I can't see you hitting the side of a barn. You're better at close combat." He shrugged. "So, Melvin, that leaves you and me."

"Well we wanted to get some hunting done, but I didn't think it would be *people* we'd be hunting."

"That wasn't part of the plan," Tom said. "But that's where we are now."

"As far as close combat," Joe said, "once we're out of ammo," he pulled out a magazine and held it high, "we'll *all* be in close combat, on the ground, shoulder to shoulder. When that happens, I'm following Fred and his buddies as the experts."

"So am I, but until that happens, we need to make the most of what we have," Carl said.

"When you need help, look to the experts," Joe said.

"You were pretty much an expert with that thing back at the lodge," Carl said, patting Joe's sword.

"Yeah, I have to admit that it felt good swinging it in practice," Joe said. "But combat is different."

Fredekas spoke up. "You good in fight. We see you." The other natives gathered around, agreeing.

"Well, thanks, guys. My preference is still to keep out of sight and shoot, but when it comes right down to it, I'll be out there in front along with the rest of you guys."

The natives stepped up and patted Joe on the back. Fredekas said, "We with you."

Joe shrugged off the backslapping. "Enough of the mutual admiration society," he said. "We have to finish up these defensive positions."

"True," Tom said. "So, you guys go build deer blinds, Joe and I are going to dig more holes, and we'll meet back here for lunch."

"Come on, Melvin," Carl said. "I'm going to show you how to build an invisible hidey hole." He grabbed Melvin's arm, and they walked off.

"This is working out better than I expected, Joe," Tom said. "You guys seem to have everything under control. You and me sniping from up here. Melvin and Carl in the deer blinds. Everyone else waiting across the field. They won't know where we are until we hit them."

Joe stepped away, then froze and pivoted. "They won't know where we are…"

"Yeah, that's what I said."

Joe gawked at Melvin walking away. "Wait! Come back here."

"What's wrong?" Carl asked.

"The problem is that they *do* know where we are," Joe said. "They know *exactly* where Melvin is, that is, Rudolph knows."

Tom frowned. "So?"

"So if Rudolph is tracking Melvin and can't see him when he comes tooling in on that dragon of his, then he'll know that Melvin is hiding, and why else hide unless we're planning an ambush? He'll warn his troops, telling them exactly where we are, or at least where he sees Melvin is."

Melvin stopped and stared. "So what am I supposed to do?"

"The best plan would be to put you out in the open. He'll see you where his compass shows you. All he would know is what he already knows. Keep the fog of war intact, and we won't lose the element of surprise."

"Out in the open? Sitting there?" Melvin blinked. "*Literally* a sitting duck. Won't he be suspicious if I'm sitting out there all alone?"

"Yeah, he might." Joe frowned. "Tell you what, keep the campfire going big, and have lots of green branches, so you can make a lot of smoke when you see him. You'll have your rifle, so take pot shots at him. That should keep him busy enough that he won't realize you're alone."

"I can handle that." Melvin shrugged. "I'll be able to see when they get here, or hear them with all the noise I expect you guys to make."

"Trying to avoid the fighting?" Joe asked.

"Never," Melvin said. "But I don't mind *not* being in the middle of combat."

"True, you won't be in the middle of *combat…*" Joe said. "But you *will* be in the middle of my *kill zone*, so be ready to vacate when the soldiers get here!"

Melvin stepped back. "Let me know when, and I'll be gone in a jiff."

"Good. That's under control," Tom said.

Melvin started to walk away but then stopped. "Hey, wait. If Rudolph can see me on his compass, won't he also see Ben's group and know that we've split up?"

"From what I've gathered," Joe said. "The compass we have shows where power is, and we assume Rudolph has the same kind. Melvin shows up, but no one else…other than the healer back in town."

"So, we have a Plan B: *one* deer blind…" Tom snickered. "…and a sitting duck. Let's get to it."

After a couple hours of setting up digging holes and setting up a deer blind, Joe pulled everyone back to the middle. "Before we stop for lunch, I want all of you to follow the creek downstream, back where we expect the attack to be coming from. Just a quick check, about a click or two, then circle back this way, look for any evidence that we've been here. I want everything cleaned up. Don't leave a clue."

"Don't forget that Ben is going to be leading his group right up this path," Tom said. "Won't he fall into the traps when he gets here?"

"Hey, Carl, have you marked the path? All your ducks in a row?"

"And the traps are flagged with a triple duck," Carl said.

"Good enough for you, Tom?"

"I can see that you guys have done this before," Tom said slowly.

"Not combat," Joe quickly clarified. "But the ducks are a good way to mark hiking paths. You saw us set some up back at the beach. Anyone who's been on a campout with us knows what to watch for."

"And the traps? Did you learn that stuff in scouts, too?" Tom asked.

Joe shook his head. "The traps are more my specialty. Stuff we learned in Ranger training. Never had much of a use for it outside of training, though, but they should work as planned."

"Carl says he marked the traps with a triple duck, right?" Tom asked.

"Yeah. What of it?" Joe asked.

"Well," Tom paused, "What *is* a triple duck? For that matter, what's a single duck?"

Joe stepped closer to a small pile of three rocks stacked in a triangle. "See that?"

"A pile of rocks," Tom said. "Doesn't mean a thing."

"Rocks don't usually pile themselves up like that. Ben will notice it, and he knows that it means 'avoid', so he's unlikely to stumble into any of the traps."

"Assuming he's in the lead," Tom said.

"Any of the scouts should recognize it, but Ben will probably be leading the group, next to Annie. He's careful that way."

"Also assuming he's not pressed for time," Tom added.

"A lot of assumptions, but that's all we have to go on," Joe said.

"We'll see when he gets here," Tom said.

"He's bright enough to keep an eye out," Carl said.

"If they didn't get a good start out of town this morn," Joe said, "or if they get delayed leaving the beach tomorrow, we should set up some advance markers to make certain. We'll cover that as we circle back doing the clean-up. Now let's head out. I want this place policed. No sign that anything's amiss."

They all spread out, heading generally to the west, in the direction of the beach, sometimes shouting back and forth to keep in contact. As Carl had the skill to spot minor details, they let him make the last pass, slowly walking along the ridge paralleling the creek.

"It's all good for me," Carl said. "Though that deer blind up in the tree stands out like a sore thumb."

"It does?" Tom said. "I couldn't see it even when you stuck your arm out."

"Well," Carl started, "to someone who can't see a turned leaf…" He laughed. "It's fine."

Joe glanced at his wrist. "You know, it would be nice to have a watch. I'd like to know what time it is."

Fredekas checked the sun. "Not high, not set. You say 'afternoon.' We say *foahmeezhdeh*, past middle day." He shrugged. "You hungry? Time eat. You thirsty? Time drink. Now tired, so is time rest."

"Yeah, let's sit in the shade for our lunch." Tom walked to where all the extra gear was piled.

They all sat to enjoy a restful meal, and the chit-chat continued.

"There's still the matter of timing," Joe said. "If we have to depend on Ben arriving before the Door opens, it would be helpful if we had a clock." He raised an eyebrow at Tom. "Well?"

"Hey, I have that hour glass, but it shows *passing* time, not what time it is now."

"So you're saying if I want a clock, I'll have to put it on my list, right after Annie's hot and cold running water?"

Tom started to laugh. "Back to that, are we?"

"Between that and Eric's non-interference policy, I don't know which is worse."

"Worse? Or more hilarious?" Tom stifled another laugh. "Both are pretty foolish."

"Yeah, but in a situation like this," Carl said, "It doesn't hurt to have a bit of levity."

The group had a good laugh, releasing the stress and tension that had beleaguered them of late, but instead of resolving the issues at hand, the laughter merely masked them. Shortly, as the laughter faded away, the conversation resumed, discussing the problems facing them.

"We still won't have any idea of where Rudolph is until Annie gets here," Carl said. "And if Rudolph gets here before Ben does, we'll be in the middle of a battle when they arrive."

"That could be a problem," Tom said.

"It could be, but doesn't have to be," Joe said. "If Ben *does* get here after Rudolph, he'll be at their back while we'll have their front occupied. He'll be our reinforcements. A pincer movement. That would be to our advantage."

"So does Ben know to do that?"

Joe stared at Tom. "Ah, communications, or in this case, lack of. That *is* an important aspect to keep in mind in warfare." He shook his head. "Well, it's not going to happen *this* time. Too bad we didn't think of it before, so we could've made arrangements before splitting up."

"We'll have to come up with something for future trips," Tom said.

"Tell you what, Tom," Joe said. "Before you get us watches, even before running water, I'd like to have radios."

Fredekas spoke up. "Far talk?"

"Yeah, Fred," Joe said. "Far talk. That's what we need. In spite of all the bleeps and bloops and silly noises that cell phones make, it would be helpful to know where Ben is right now."

"And Rudolph," Tom said.

Carl spoke up. "Annie will know where both of them are."

"Well, we can *hope* that Annie knows," Joe said.

Annie sat on the bench with the compass still in hand. "Now the zoom is back to normal, so I can see Rudolph to the west, and there is a definite space between Melvin and Deezh now. Melvin is making good time."

"As long as they don't push him too hard," Ben said. "I don't know if he's had a chance to recover from Rudolph's treatment."

"I checked on him, between other patients, and he's fine enough. About as well as any of the rest of the injured." Annie looked up the hill towards the infirmary. "Deezh thinks she can handle all the rest of the injuries, though this is the most she's had to care for all at once."

"Oh? From the size of that infirmary, I would have thought she often treated a lot of people."

"The way she explained it to me was that this town used to be on the front lines of a major war…a long time ago, so back then they *did* need that many beds, but they haven't needed them for generations. This part of the building has been closed up, unused, until we showed up, most of it sat here gathering dust."

"Until we showed up?" Ben asked. "I keep hearing that. Despite Eric's non-interference directive, we are still managing to interfere with the civilization here."

At the mention of Eric, Annie noticed him sitting at the next table, staring right at her.

"Did I hear my name mentioned?" Eric asked.

"Yeah, Eric," Ben said. "We didn't stick with your plans of not interfering, and now we've done some real damage here."

"I know," Eric said. "As much as our intent was to avoid hindering normal progression of the peoples here, change may be unavoidable. The mere fact that we've encountered someone different from ourselves will tend to alter their situation, much as it alters ours." His shoulders slumped. "The most effective way to circumvent modification is to eschew contact entirely."

"That wouldn't be much fun, would it?" Ben asked.

"True. We would have had to stay in the forest, never even meeting any natives."

"Wait a minute. Remember being attacked that first night?" Annie asked. "We didn't do anything to deserve that, did we?"

Eric thought a moment. "This world affected us before we had a chance to affect it, but we still could have forestalled any additional contact. That would have helped to prevent any unintentional modification of their life styles."

"That could have worked," Annie said.

Eric paused. "Though…I hate to bring it up, but remember what happened when the Europeans arrived in the Americas? I wonder if we are going to have a long-term influence on history here." He leaned back and thought. "Consider the possibilities. Future history books may present us as that weird group that changed everything, merely by arriving."

Annie gasped. "That would be bad."

"As bad as that might be," Eric said, "I'm certain our influence won't be as bad as smallpox or anything similar."

Annie stared at Eric. "Smallpox? Have we done that here?"

"No evidence of it…yet," Eric said. "And we *are* making a conscious effort to *not* change things here."

"That may be the limit of our ability to avoid messing things up," Ben said.

Patrick strolled up. "Hey, Ben, do you mind if I head back to the school? There's some things I'd like to discuss with Zhahmonichas."

"More talk with the school teacher?" Ben asked.

"Yeah. We figured out enough of that second scroll to make it work, but now I have those new ones," Patrick patted his pack, "the ones from the advanced guard, the guys sitting by the campfire."

"I remember them," Ben said. "That should be fine." He hesitated. "You aren't planning on going anywhere else, are you?"

"If I do, I'll stop by here and let you know. That good with you?"

"Yeah. Is someone going with you? You know, to stay in pairs, the buddy system," Ben said.

"I didn't ask, but I assumed no one else wants to spend time in school on this trip."

"Good point," Ben said. "But the more we know about what's going on, the better, just try to be back before dark. I don't want you wandering around getting yourself lost."

Patrick blew into his cupped hand. Light flared up, glowing through his fingers. "Gotcha covered, Ben. Flashlight's right here."

"Oh, quit showing off." Ben laughed. "See you later!"

Patrick double-timed it to the door and was gone.

"Remember that list I was making?" Ben asked.

"Yeah. Tom mentioned it," Annie said.

"Too much work, so I've given up on it. Too much to write. Too many weird things going on here."

"I'm not certain weird is the right word, more like unexpected."

"More like impossible," Ben countered. "How can you explain any of this?"

Annie shrugged. "I can't, so I don't." She stood up. "I should head back to the infirmary. We left Doug up there helping Deezh, and I want to check on the patients."

"Send word if you need anything," Ben said. "I'm going to go see how the guys are handling the spare time with no Doug and no dice."

Annie stepped out of the lodge, and Ben joined the group sitting at the fireplace.

"Ben! Have a seat," Trey said as he slapped a large stone in the hearth. "Not that it's cold outside, but it's certainly warm here."

Ben sat on the heated stone with his back to the fire. Arching his shoulders, he leaned back, feeling the warmth penetrate his tense muscles, relaxing his shoulders. He moaned, sat back up, and smiled. "Ah, that *is* good!" He almost felt as if he could ignore all the problems.

Eric smiled. "See, Robb *is* good for something."

"Robb? What did he do?" Ben asked.

"Not much," Robb said. "I merely helped get the fire going."

"The innkeeper said that he had a pile of freshly cut wood that wasn't dry enough to burn yet, but Robb decided to prove him wrong," Eric said.

Robb shrugged. "A waste of time to wait for it to fully season."

Ben smiled. "Well, it's nice that you can be of service to these folks here." He looked across the expectant faces staring up at him. "So, what have you guys been doing?" he asked.

"Well, with Doug up at the hospital, we don't have his dice," John said. "So we had to make do with what the locals do for gambling." He scooped up a handful of colored disks and let them fall on a set of circles carved into the top of the table.

"Yeah, I'd noticed those circles on the other tables as well." Ben said. "They use a bull's eye and a bunch of poker chips to gamble? How does that work?"

"We never quite figured it out," John said. "But Eric understood it. He'll explain it."

"Would you expect otherwise?" Ben asked. "Go ahead, Eric."

Eric sat up. "Well, it's obvious that they use a combination of the Monte Carlo method of deterministic calculations along with color combinations that are relevant in this culture."

Robb frowned. "It's obvious to who?"

Eric glared. "Obvious to *whom*."

"Is this an English lesson or a lecture on math…or colors?" Robb said.

Eric smiled. "Let's stick to the game here. Although the part color plays in the game still eludes me, thanks to Annie, we do know that color is relevant in the healing process. The red end of the spectrum is good, and the violet end not so good." He hesitated. "But how that applies here, I have yet to ascertain."

"And I'm certain you will," Ben said.

Eric continued, "On the other hand, the mathematics makes perfect sense, so let's focus there." He picked up a disc and put it carefully on the target shape. "You'll notice that the diameter of the discs is significantly less than the distance between the rings, right?" He waited for Ben to answer, then went on. "That corresponds directly with Buffon's needle but in a circular arrangement instead of parallel lines, and appropriately sized discs instead of needles, but the concept is the same. Like Buffon's needle, random throws are done, counting the number of times the discs intersects a line."

The room was filled with blank stares.

"Thank you, Eric," Ben said. "You have covered it quite well enough for us dummies here."

John laughed. "See, Ben? Eric can explain anything."

"Not quite *everything*, though. As I said the colors elude me." Eric frowned. "Though I *have* noticed that there is a positive correlation between the spectrum and the relative excitement of the native players."

Ben almost nodded off.

Eric picked up a couple discs, flipping them back and forth in his hand. "You'll notice how the color on opposite sides relates to the color wheel? Primary on one side and secondary on the other. I need to observe more, but I'm certain I'll be able to establish the relationship."

"You could ask Bear about the color," Ben suggested. "He may be able to explain how the colors work."

"Excellent idea, Ben. I may just do that."

"You go right ahead and talk to him about that, Eric," Ben said. "He's sitting right over there with Trey."

"Thanks, Ben." Eric started walking towards Trey and Bear

"I'm happy that you guys are keeping out of trouble." Ben paused then stopped Eric, staring. "Wait. This isn't a variation on Fizzbin, is it?"

"Oh, certainly not. The rules for Fizzbin are well codified. I should have brought a deck. I didn't know that we'd be spending so much time in such establishments." Eric said. "I'll check with Patrick, when he returns, to see whether the rules for *this* game are documented anywhere."

"Yeah, you do that. Meanwhile, try to not annoy the locals." Ben said as he walked away.

"Hey, Ben," Trey called out. "Do you realize it's been barely a week since we landed here?"

"It certainly feels a lot longer, to me," John said.

"Me, too," Robb added.

Ben stopped. "I was thinking the same thing. Do you think Tom's right about the time? I mean, wouldn't it be annoying to return and find that more time has passed back home than we thought?"

John laughed. "We're here a week and get back to find a month has passed. That would be hilarious. So how much does Tom charge for parking?"

"I was talking to Tom about the time difference," Trey said. "And he said that although the days here *feel* longer, it's limited to a feeling thing. The exact same number of days go by back home."

"Well, I know when we used to go on campouts with the scouts," Ben said, "sometimes it felt as if time passed slower." He smirked. "Mostly because there was nothing to do, and we were bored to tears."

"We sure don't have that problem now," John started, then considered their current situation. "Unless we're doing nothing but waiting."

"Yeah, waiting to get clobbered," Trey said.

"Time is relative," Ben said. "Five minutes sitting on a hot stove is much longer than five minutes with a pretty girl, right?"

They all laughed, but Eric piped up, "According to Einstein, time could in fact *be* slower here. That is if this planet were sufficiently close to a large gravitational field. For example, if there were a decent sized black hole nearby, it would affect the passage of time."

John poked Ben and whispered, "See? Explanations abound."

Eric continued, "We could use Tom's hour-glass to experiment. We'd have to calibrate it back home, then do a series of measurements here, tracking the sun's movement." He paused. "We'd also need a stellar observation device. I wonder if Tom's compatriots have done any tests in that direction already."

"It would have to be *you* to check that out," Ben said, "when we get back."

"*If* we get back," John added.

Ben frowned at him but noticed that Eric was so wrapped up in his little conundrum that he didn't even notice the negative comment.

Eric stood up and wandered back towards the kitchen, mumbling something about the technology available to Galileo: telescopes, pendulums, and an astrolabe.

John shrugged. "That should keep *him* busy for a while, but the rest of us—"

The door flew open, and Annie burst into the room. "Rudolph's moving again."

Everyone stood up and crowded near Annie. She held the compass on the flat of her hand. "I was between patients and decided to do a quick check, and that's when I saw Rudolph's point getting closer, and fast."

"So what's it show?" Ben asked.

Annie drew a finger across the compass. "Here's us right at the middle with Deezh, here's Melvin, and this one is Rudolph, the purple one. See how he's moving? He *was* heading in our direction, but now he's gaining on Melvin." She waited for a response. "The orange point. See it?"

Ben shook his head. "Still can't see anything on that thing. You'll have to tell us what's going on."

"Ah! Sorry," she said. "I've been up with Deezh and her helpers for a while. They all can see *something* on the compass, though none of them can see it quite as well as Deezh." She leaned over the compass and described what she saw. "Rudolph's army, I mean Rudolph when he was moving slowly, was heading mostly east, though a bit south, getting closer to *Roadranusis* every time I checked, but now that he's moving faster, he's heading more north of east, directly for Melvin. In fact, he's right at his location now. The points are so close that they're blending."

Bear smacked the hilt of his sword. "We go, we help. Melvin good."

Trey agreed. "We shouldn't wait if he needs help."

"Sit tight, Trey," Ben said. "Yes, Bear, Melvin *is* good, but even if we ran the whole way, we'd never get there in time. They have a head start and are hours away by now. Right, Annie?"

"They've been making constant progress," Annie said. "So by now I'm certain they are well into the forest above the falls," she stretched a finger and thumb across the top of the compass, "could be at the beach by now, I think, but I can't tell how close they are." She frowned. "This thing could use landmarks."

John leaned in to peer at the compass, though it did him no good. "So, what's happening now?"

"Same thing," Annie said. "The purple is so close to the orange that they are about to merge. Wait, not quite on top of each other. More like circling each other. Yes. The purple *is* circling the orange."

"Circling?" Ben asked.

"Yes. The purple point is going around and around, once, twice, now pulling away, heading back west."

"And Melvin is still there?" Ben asked.

"The orange point hasn't changed," she said. "So I would assume that Melvin's status is stable."

"That's good news, but I wonder what Rudolph was doing."

"Who cares, as long as he's gone now," Trey said.

John quit staring at the blank compass. "I'll bet he was doing a recon on his dragon."

"Probably saw Melvin leave town and wanted to know where he was heading," Ben said.

"And he didn't attack Melvin while he was there?" Trey asked.

Annie shrugged. "I didn't see any change in the orange point, so I wouldn't think so."

"Strange that he didn't," Trey said.

"Good point," John said. "He could have dropped in on that dragon of his and grabbed him."

"But is that what he wants to do?" Ben asked. "His goal isn't to suck the power out of Melvin anymore…it's to get home. If he attacked Melvin or snatched him again, he'd lose his ability to track us."

"That makes sense," Annie said, staring at the compass again. "The orange point is still heading north, slowly." She set the compass in her lap. "That means they aren't at the beach yet."

"That's good, right?" Ben said.

Annie shrugged.

Ben scowled. "It must be nice to be able to fly in, check things out, then fly away before sending in an army."

Annie put her hand on Ben's shoulder. "We'll be fine."

Trey spoke up. "Speaking of fine, Annie, as the medic here, how much longer before everyone in the hospital is ready to hit the road?"

"Unless you have a miracle up your sleeve, Shawn won't be on his feet for days, if not weeks. Some of the natives might be ready to head out in the morning…*after* they get a good night's rest, but the rest will still be under Deezh's care long after we're gone.

They will *all* need a good rest before tackling such a long hike." She frowned at Trey. "And I don't want anyone pushed too hard."

Trey reared back. "Yes, ma'am."

"So what can we do *now*?" John asked.

"Well, it's getting dark, almost too dark," Ben said. "But before it gets completely dark, why not go outside and do some sword practice. See if any of the *shmahseespe* want to help. We *may* not run out of ammo, but we are certainly going to run low, and it would be a nice to have a back-up plan."

"Well, while you're doing that, I'll head back up to the infirmary," Annie said.

"We'll send someone up in the morning to help you get going," Ben said. "Then we'll meet you, Doug, and any volunteers on the road at the fork. One more check on Rudolph's location, and we'll be on our way."

"Good. That way we won't have to backtrack through the village." She said. "See you then."

Ben stepped towards the group and pulled out the sword hanging from his belt. "Not bad, but kinda nicked up and rusty."

"Is that rust…or dried blood?" Robb asked, eyebrow raised.

John slapped his scabbard. "Mine's not bad, but it's heavy."

"Any chance of replacing them?" Ben asked.

Robb patted the sword he'd been carrying. "I'll stick with this one, if you don't mind. It's served me well."

Ben raised an eyebrow. "So we've seen." He asked the natives, "Is there an armory or something similar where we can get better swords? The ones we've picked up aren't exactly the best."

They talked quickly among themselves, then Bear spoke. "You need sword. We get, we give."

"Yes!" John shouted. "Now we're talking. I'm due for an upgrade, so I'm going with them."

"Everyone else, get what you need and meet out front as quickly as possible," Ben said. "As soon as it's too dark to continue, I want everyone back inside getting ready to go. Everything goes. This is our last night here, so if you leave anything, then it's his."

The innkeeper bowed slightly and smiled at Ben.

"After that," Ben continued, "dinner and bed. We want to be well rested for tomorrow." He glanced back towards the kitchen. "Oh, and somebody go find Eric."

"We'll get him," Trey said as he headed back to find the wandering prodigy, dragging Bear along.

Robb drew his sword, stepped back, and swung it through the air, the tip glowing at the apex of each swing. He headed for the door. "Yup, definitely need more room," he said.

Ben followed Robb out and found a group of *shmahseespe* already sparring in small groups, demonstrating different sword techniques to the crowd, which had materialized out of nowhere. Plenty of adults were watching and even more children in the crowd, mostly keeping out of the way of the swords, but getting close enough to stare at the participants, rubbernecking galore.

A bit later, John came up with a handful of swords. He offered them to Ben. "Here, pick one," he said. "There's plenty to choose from."

Ben picked through John's load and selected a nice, shiny one. "Not too heavy. I should be able to work with it." He pulled the old, rusty one he'd been carrying and held it up. "And this one?"

John let the rest of the swords slide out of his arms, making a loud clatter. "Drop your old one in the pile. They'll clean it up for the next guy that needs one after we're done practicing."

Ben deposited his old sword and hefted the new one. "Much lighter. I'll be able to use this one without tiring myself out."

Trey came out of the lodge with Eric in tow, Bear right behind them. "Found him. He was getting in the cook's way, sampling stuff being prepped for dinner."

"I was thinking, and I often get hungry when I think," Eric said.

"We'll eat later," Trey said, then led Eric to the pile of swords next to Ben. "Grab one. I'll show you how to use it."

Eric went to the pile and gingerly shoved it with the toe of his boot. Trying to find the right one, he shuffled the pile back and forth, making loud clattering noises.

"It doesn't make any difference which one. Just grab one," Trey said.

"I was hoping to find a good sabre. I usually prefer a curved blade. It has a better heft, a better appearance, but without horses and horsemen, the need never developed." Eric shrugged. "No cavalry, no sabers."

Trey stomped up and picked a sword at random. "Use this one. If it isn't to your liking, we can swap it out later."

Eric gingerly reached for the sword. When he finally gripped it, he waggled it about, then standing with his feet planted firmly, he held it high and said, "By the sword in my hand, I will conquer the land!"

Trey gawked at Eric, then reached out and batted the sword out of his grasp, sending it flying across the green. "Get a grip, will ya?"

"Hey! That hurt," Eric said, rubbing his hand.

"We don't have time for play, Eric. Stay focused. You may need to *use* that sword to defend yourself, so you'd best know how to use it right." Trey raised his sword. "Now go pick it up, and let's try that again."

Eric picked up his sword, then he and Trey sparred. Though everyone could see that Trey was holding back, giving Eric easy targets and blocking all of his attacks, the crowd didn't seem to mind. They were shouting encouragement to all the combatants.

Patrick showed up, drawn by all the noise, and handed out fairy lights to all the kids.

Ben leaned to John. "If he had balloons, he'd be twisting up a bunch of animals for the kiddies."

John laughed. "Yeah, but the extra light *is* making it easier to keep going."

"That's what we need: stadium lights to extend the session."

"Our last chance to get training, so why not?" John asked.

Ben agreed. "True. As long as his lights are bright enough. I don't want to add to the injured list."

"We'll call off the practice in a bit," John said. "Give everyone time to rest, then start packing for the trip out."

"John, I need to thank you," Ben said. "You're being more helpful than we thought you'd be. Nothing against you, but you do have…well, a reputation, you know."

John boasted, "A well-deserved reputation it is, but I don't need to toss my weight around here, and I certainly don't need any more attention. I have enough doing what needs to be done…like finding you."

"From what I hear, you put in quite a bit of effort, John. I'm impressed at how you handled that." Ben reached out and patted John on the arm. "Thanks again." He looked closely and could swear that John's cheeks were reddened.

John stepped out into the middle of the green, whooping and hollering to get everyone's attention. "It's too dark, in spite of Patrick's little fairy lights." He nodded to Patrick. "Thanks for helping. It let us get more time to train."

"My pleasure," Patrick said.

"So, did you learn anything interesting from the school teacher?" Ben asked.

"Yeah, you could say that," Patrick said." I'll tell you later." He leaned in closer. "When there aren't as many ears listening in."

"I'll wait for it," Ben said, thinking, *What's the new problem now?*

John wasn't paying any attention to them, instead standing next to the pile of swords. "If you aren't keeping it, drop it here, and if you are, sheathe it now. I don't want to see any bare blades in the lodge."

Ben raised an eyebrow. "Good job, John. I may need to promote you."

John merely smiled as he ushered half the crowd into the lodge.

Ben stepped to Bear. "Can you tell the other villagers that the party is over? We need to eat and get shuteye. They can come back in the morning if they want to, to see us off."

"Will tell," Bear said as he went to talk to the crowd.

Ben walked towards the lodge and spoke to no one in particular. "I wonder what's for dinner."

Ben walked into the lodge to find a festive atmosphere. Light conversation filled the room, mingled with the clatter of silverware and music. *Music? Where'd that come from?* Following the rhythmic noise to its source, he found a group of natives playing a bunch of outlandish instruments, and who was in the middle of the 'band'? None other than Eric! Joining the onlookers, Ben asked, "How did Eric get up there?"

Patrick put a hand on Ben's shoulder. "Yet another strange thing about Eric: He knows how to play those contraptions. How he knows that, I have no idea, but I'm certain he'll explain the whole thing when they take a break."

The music slowed for a moment, and the innkeeper, taking advantage of the pause, stepped up to the front. "You go tomorrow, you eat today!"

Bear pounded his chest. "Good eat!"

Patrick explained, "Due to our imminent departure, the innkeeper has decided to treat us to something special. And Bear is certainly happy that he gets to eat with the guests."

"How's that?" Ben asked.

"The innkeeper sent most of the natives home. The ones that stuck around were relegated to the tables in the back of the room."

Ben looked and saw a somewhat morose group of *shmahseespe* sitting at tables pushed off to one side of the room. "What's wrong with them?"

"Like I said, something special is for dinner, and they'd all like to enjoy it along with us, but the innkeeper is limiting it to the scouts," he indicated Bear, "and a few select natives."

"Wow. Different attitude than he had last night."

"I heard that Eric dropped a bit of coin," Patrick said. "And it changed the innkeeper's attitude towards all of us."

Ben laughed. "Leave it up to Eric to splurge like that."

"Well, what else was he to do with all those rings they use for money? He'll be gone tomorrow, so he may as well share the wealth today."

"Good point," Ben said. "Is that how he joined the band, too? With a bribe?"

"From what I could see," Patrick said, "as we were coming in, Eric noticed them tuning up and barged his way in."

Ben frowned. "And that didn't cause a problem?"

Patrick shrugged. "I saw him standing there watching them set up, then he picked up one of those…instruments?…and started playing."

"Eric knows how to play music here?" Ben stared at Eric jamming along with the rest of the band and shrugged. "Well, he must be doing a good enough job of it. The locals aren't complaining, so why should we?"

The innkeeper came by with another tray full of mugs, keeping everyone well lubricated as the band finished the set. Eric bowed and shook hands with all the other musicians, then joined Ben.

Ben swept his hand at the spot next to him. "Have a seat, Eric."

"Don't mind if I do." Eric sat. "Enjoyable music, isn't it?"

"Care to explain how you know the music here?" Ben asked.

"The brotherhood of musicians extends even to this world." He smiled, then became serious. "I didn't know their music before, but when I listened, I noticed that they were using something similar to a pentatonic minor 7th, reminiscent of the late Zhou dynasty, approximately 300 BC, based on the Wu Xing philosophy." He patted one of the various instruments on the stage. "I've never been much good with metal or fire, and I didn't see any earth or water instruments, so I picked up one based on wood and worked out the fingering for the various chords." He sat down. "String instruments are always easier than wind, and more fun, too. Polyphonic." He tapped a rhythm on the table. "Percussion is usually too boring to interest me, though I have seen some interesting drum bands in my time."

Everyone at the table had gone glassy-eyed when Eric had launched into his lecture, but when he finished, they all politely smiled in relief. Ben expressed everyone's thoughts when he said, "Interesting, Eric. We would have never known all that had you not shared."

Mercifully, everyone was spared an extended lecture by the well-timed arrival of dinner, and grateful comments were heard on that timing. The meal consisted of what appeared to be a standard stew, meat and veggies in a broth, served with more of that delicious, warm, brown bread.

Ben pulled off a large piece of bread and dipped it into the bowl in front of him, then, holding the dripping bread, he checked for Annie and grinned. "Not here." He slurped as he bit into it, as did most of the others. He suddenly sat up straight, choking. "Wow. This has quite a bite to it."

The others nodded, eyes watering. Patrick smiled. "I'd like to get a hold of *that* spice. Could be a fine addition to the menu."

"Add in that bread, and I'd be a regular," Ben said, then added, "Well, *more* of a regular."

"Speaking of Patrick's restaurant," Trey said, watching all the folks enjoying the meal, "any of the natives want to come visit *our* side?"

"That's a wonderful idea, Trey." Patrick said. "I'll host the meals!"

"Exactly what I had in mind," Trey said.

John spoke up. "Do you see any profit in starting trade from this side to the other?"

"If you are planning on getting something organized," Patrick said. "I'd be first in line."

"I may have to do that," John said. "Could be easy money. Both sides have something the other wants…and I could be the middle man." He smiled as he leaned back in contemplation of the quick cash.

Ben frowned. "I can see what they have to offer us, but what can we offer in exchange?"

"Protection." John patted the grip on his pistol. "And that's something I have…well…experience in."

"If that's all you have to offer," Robb said, "they'll need protection *from* you."

"Yeah," Patrick said. "I'll wait until you come up with something less controversial, then I'll be first in line."

"I'll work on it," John said. He leaned to Eric. "Hey, you might want to hold onto that money you've been collecting. May come in handy someday."

Eric replied around a mouthful, "Humph…yeah. If I need more, I can get more."

Ben raised an eyebrow. "Legally?"

"What's legal here?" John laughed. "Might makes right."

"That might not make the operators of the Door happy," Ben said.

John paused. "Oh, yeah. Might want to keep on the good side of those techies…until we buy them out." He laughed.

Patrick was sopping up the last of the juice in his bowl when he stopped. "Hey, John. I may have a product for you to import."

John raised an eyebrow. "You do?"

"Yeah, if you don't mind being known as a food monger."

"Well, we already talked about bread going in that direction, so what did you have in mind for coming this direction?"

Patrick leaned back and smiled. "Dessert."

John laughed. "Yeah, from what we've seen, something sweet at the end of a meal doesn't seem to be common here, except for in that dark valley." He craned his neck to stare the length of the table. "But we do have a special place in *their* hearts now, don't we, Eric?"

Startled, Eric managed a "Huh?"

Trey reached across the table and patted the dagger still strapped to Eric's chest. "Yeah, Prince of the Land People. That's what they're called, right?"

"Yes, the Land People, the *lahnpe*," Patrick said. "He's the *brahgarno* of the *lahnpe*."

"Yeah, that's it," John said. "We feel honored to be in your presence."

Eric tried to bow while sitting. "The honor is all mine." He picked up his bowl to slurp the last of the juice.

Ben stood up. "We're done here." He stared at everyone. "See you in the *morning*."

John slowly came to his feet to stand next to Ben. "Yes. *Early*, in the morning." He frowned. "With as many walking wounded as we have, we may need to hold our pace, so an early start would be helpful."

"Thanks," Ben said to John.

The innkeeper, noticing everyone getting ready to leave, came running up, jabbering. Patrick tried to get him to speak slower, then laughed. "Hey, Ben. Remember all that money Eric dropped on the innkeeper? Well, it covered the meal and then some." He grinned at the innkeeper. "He says that all the beds are ready for us…pre-warmed."

All the scouts stared as the meaning slowly settled in. Finally, Ben said, "Pre-warmed? Hmmm…" He made a big show of looking for Tom. "Everyone's had their shots, right?" He laughed. "As long as no one catches anything, we'll be good."

John poked Ben in the ribs. "Either that or there'll be a long line at the quickie-med back home."

Ben frowned. "If any of us brings home anything *new*…"

Eric piped up, "It could be similar to native Americans and smallpox, but in the other direction."

"Well, we wanted to be known for something, but I had trophies in mind, not diseases," Ben said. "Be careful, guys. You're on your own for this. I won't share the credit…or blame…for anything you bring back."

"But think of it," John said. "You'll be famous when they name the disease after you."

Everyone laughed as they all made their way to the rooms, quickly settling in to bed, though not necessarily dwelling on the early morning.

* * *

Annie had put her patients to bed much earlier and would have been in bed as well, but she had to do her middle-of-the-night rounds. Having a regular nursing staff would certainly help. Deezh's helpers weren't bad, but they didn't seem to understand everything. As she was finishing her second round of the ward, barely after sunup, there was a knock at the door.

"Ben sent us to see if you need any help," Robb said, standing on the porch next to John.

"We've already had breakfast, in case you were wondering," John said aloud, then whispered to Robb, "Anything other than that soup they serve up here."

"Well, I don't know if Doug is up yet. Last I saw, he was still sleeping soundly in a cot next to Shankaktos." Annie stepped back into the medic's hut and invited them in. "I'll show you the way." She headed through a back door of the hut and into the infirmary itself, both scouts following her, staring at everything.

They entered and walked quietly past rows of empty beds. "Shankaktos is in the last bed on the left." The cot next to his was empty. "Here's where Doug slept, but I don't know where he is now."

"Should we go look for him?" Robb asked.

"Go ahead," Annie said. "Check out back first. He may be taking care of business." She pointed. "That door leads out to an outhouse."

As John headed towards the door, it swung open, silhouetting Doug in the morning light for a moment, then he stepped inside, closing the door gently.

"Is it time to head out?" Doug asked.

"We're here to help get things moving," John said. "Ben and the others are already prepping. We're going to meet them at the fork."

Annie stepped towards the front room. "I'm going to check in with Deezh to see who she thinks she can send with us, then I'll be ready." She put her hand on his arm. "Doug, say your goodbyes. He won't be up and about until we're long gone."

Robb patted Doug on the shoulder. "It's good to see you're doing better. We'll go wait on the porch out front." He grabbed John's arm. "Come on." They walked through the room, past the front room, and outside. Before they sat, John walked to the edge of the woods and grabbed a short stick. He sat on the edge of the stairs, whittling, slowly turning it into little curled chips of wood.

Annie came out first, followed by a half-dozen *shmahseespe*. "Deezh says she has the rest covered." She held up a small cloth sack. "She also gave me medicine in case we need to do any emergency first aid."

Robb stood up and shouldered his backpack, delivering a kick to John's foot in the process.

"I'm moving," John said, slowly grabbing his bag and slinging it on his back. "We still need to wait for Doug."

"We need to be ready to go when he gets here," Robb said.

"I know," John was saying as the door flew open and Doug stumbled out. Both waiting scouts quickly headed out of town, neither one wanting to see the look on Doug's face, as he had to leave his friend behind.

Annie put her hand on Doug's shoulder. "He'll be fine. You can come back and visit later."

Doug sniffed, not replying. He straightened up and followed John and Robb, glancing back once to stare at the medic's hut.

The four of them trudged silently along the trail followed by Deezh's helpers who had volunteered to go with them, circling to the east past the fields, constantly moving towards the rendezvous with the rest of the troops. The sun was starting to warm the air before they cleared the fields, before they could see the main road, before they could even hear the river.

Approaching the road leading north through the forest, they slowed, hoping to catch sight of the main contingent, but no one was there.

Annie stood in the middle of the road, arms akimbo. "I'm certain he would have waited for us."

"Maybe he didn't leave town on time," John said.

"That's certainly possible," Annie said. "We'll wait here." She tried to find a comfortable spot, then pulled out a bag of trail mix and shared it.

"Thanks," Robb said.

"Mmmm…That's good stuff," John said. "What's in it?"

Annie shrugged. "It's a native concoction. Deezh says they use it all the time to keep up their energy."

Robb tipped his head towards John. "Well, don't tell *him*. He's liable to start importing it."

"Is that true?" Annie asked.

John's face reddened "I get hassled for suggesting ways to make easy money."

Robb laughed. "Awful lot of work for 'easy' money."

Annie smiled. "Well, I heard Eric saying something about importing bread, so why not this stuff, too?" She leaned to John. "You have a fine idea, John. Good luck, and may you succeed with it."

Doug sat up straight. "I hear something. It might be them." He stood up, searching the road back towards town. "Yes! I see them."

"In that case, let's get ready to head out," John said as he stepped to stand next to Doug.

Ben walked up, leading the group. He slowed as he approached, but John said, "Don't stop, unless you *have* to rest. We'll get any excuse about you being late as we're moving."

"Fine with me." Ben said. "Keep going!" he yelled. "But, John, we'll probably need to stop before too long, though."

"Not on my watch," John said. "We'll keep going until we make the bottom of the waterfall. We can stop for a *short* break there."

Annie cleared her throat. "Umm…John? Let's not push anyone too much." She stepped in between the two of them. "Last I heard, Ben was still in charge."

"Maybe he is," John said. "But I don't want to miss out on our trip home because of stragglers."

"I have an idea, John," Ben said as he put his hand on John's shoulder, "Can *you* keep those stragglers from getting separated from the group? If you keep them from falling behind, you can make certain we *all* make it, *and* you can hear all the juicy details of why we're late."

John shrugged. "That'll work."

"When you get back there, can you send Trey and Bear up? I'd like to have them up front," Ben said.

John slowed his pace, practically walking backwards.

"We'll fall back as well," Robb said as he pulled Doug's arm. "I want to catch up with what's been going on."

Annie watched the natives she'd brought fall behind as well, joining the mix of other natives. "So, Ben, what's the story with making us wait so long this morning?"

Ben harrumphed. "Eric. He wasn't ready to leave. In fact, he was considering staying here." Ben stared at Annie. "Something about being somewhere where he was appreciated, where his knowledge would be useful."

"Well, he does have a point," Annie said. "We always laugh at the tidbits of knowledge he's constantly sharing, but he *does* know more than most folks, not just here but back home, too. He could be useful."

"True, but I'm going to get him home first, *then* he can come back by himself if he wants to start an empire of his own. The only problem is that he already has competition—" Ben suddenly stopped in his tracks, and Annie ran right into him.

"What's wrong?" she asked.

"We forgot to check on Rudolph," he said. "We were going to check the compass as soon as we met up, so we'd know where he is and which way he's heading."

Annie stopped where she stood. They were deep in the forest. A slight breeze wafted through the dark green branches that closed overhead, filtering the sunlight, cooling the air. "It would be easier to get a reading if we weren't walking, so let's stop here. It's as good a place as any." She pulled off her pack and slid the compass out as Ben passed the word back along the line.

Ben came back with others who wanted to hear the news.

"So does the mystical, magical compass show we're in deep doo-doo?" Patrick asked.

Annie balanced the compass on the palm of her hand. "Based on Eric's suggestion, we can now see the village, the drop-off point, *and* Rudolph." She glanced sideways at Ben and whispered, "See, he *does* have good ideas."

"So his idea is helpful?" Ben asked.

"Absolutely," she said. "Rudolph is still definitely heading in *our* direction, in our general direction, much farther north than where Deezh is."

"Good. The town is safe…for now," Patrick said.

Annie stretched her fingers across the compass, measuring. "We still plan to stop at the beach overnight, right? So, assuming Rudolph doesn't keep going through the night, we might have a small advantage." She heard excitement move through the group as the news was passed along.

"Hang on, everyone," Ben said. "That isn't necessarily good news. Although we aren't behind, we'd like to have a *sizable* lead before getting to the drop-off point. We don't want to be standing there waiting for the Door to open when he shows up, so if we increase the pace, we can look forward to a nice, relaxing supper before bed tonight."

Annie frowned at him.

Ben clarified for the crowd. "Increase the pace only *slightly*." He paused. "You can do another reading when we get to the top of the falls to see if we've gained on him…to see *how much* we've gained on him. Then we'll know if we need to push it or not."

"That sounds fine," Annie said. "It'll have to do."

Ben yelled, "Move 'em out!" and the whole line groaned at the shortness of the break but was quickly moving again.

Rounding a corner, Ben heard someone shout, "Hey! There's the falls."

Annie smiled as they stepped out of the trees. "We're here. We made better time than I expected we would." She checked the group. "And no one is doing any worse than I'd feared."

"Does that mean we can maintain the pace when we get to the top?" Ben asked.

Annie patted the compass under her shirt. "That would depend on other things."

"True." As the end of the line caught up, Ben said, "Hey, John, thanks for keeping everyone moving." He smiled. "You were right about not stopping until the base of the falls." He called to everyone, "We break here, sit for a bit, get a drink." He dipped his canteen into the pool at the base of the waterfall. "Make certain you refill before heading out."

Trey stared at the pool. "I remember when we came past here the first time. Some of us wanted to go swimming, but Tom said we had to keep going. That was so long ago. What, a week?"

"A little over a week," Eric said. "We arrived on Thursday, and passed the falls on Friday, but today is Saturday, so, yes, about a week."

Trey plopped on a fallen log. "Thanks, Eric. That's unbelievable."

"As I was saying earlier," Eric continued. "Although the perception of time…the perception of the *passage* of time…can vary, the physical aspect of time may in reality be different in this world."

Trey blinked. "Not now, Eric. I'm too tired to listen."

Ben butted in. "Thanks for the lecture, Eric, but we still need to get up this hill." He stepped back to check the top of the falls. "Trey, why don't you and Bear hang back? I'll have a couple others lead." He spotted his victims. "Hey, John, grab Robb and Doug and bring them here."

When they arrived, Ben explained his plan. "The three of you head up first. Check it out, and let us know if there are any problems you can't handle. As soon as things are secured up there, let us know, and we'll send up the next bunch of folks."

"On the way," John said as he started the climb.

The three of them quickly scrambled up the cliff and vanished at the top. Moments later, John leaned out. "All's well. Send 'em up!"

Ben circled through the group, encouraging everyone, as he selected those to go next. When he found Trey and Bear, he said, "Can you two cover the rear?"

"We'll wait until everyone has made it up the cliff, then follow," Trey said.

"Perfect. Thanks." He went to Annie and Patrick, near the base of the cliff.

Annie watched everyone struggle their way along the twisting path, then asked Ben. "Any chance of making this easier?"

"Why not?" Ben asked. "Would you prefer stairs or an elevator?"

Patrick laughed. "Hey, Annie, go for the elevator."

She ignored his comment and said, "Maybe ropes tied off at the top, with knots every foot or so. That way we'd have grips to help us up."

Ben leaned back and considered the slope of the hillside. "That wouldn't be too tough." He stepped back. "Patrick, remind me to bring a bunch of extra rope next time we come here…and some spikes."

She stared at him. "Next time? You planning on coming back?"

Patrick blinked. "When else would we be able to build your elevator?"

"Why not?" Ben asked. "We could have an event, like a family reunion but with scouts instead."

"We could even make it an annual thing," Patrick said.

"If you plan it well enough, I'll bet Tom would give you a discount. Think of all the extra business he'd get."

"How much business does he want? Can you see an entire district showing up? This would make a great super activity."

Annie laughed. "You and your big plans. Have you talked to John recently? I hear he has ideas, too."

"I'll have to do that." Ben paused. "Going into business with John. That's something I never thought would happen, but think. If John gets a lot of business, Tom could be famous!"

Annie sighed at the mention of his name.

"I know, I know. I shouldn't have brought him up," Ben said. "We'll get there as soon as we can."

"That's fine," Annie said. "I know we'll catch up with him soon."

"We'll catch up with *them* soon." Ben watched the last group head up the hill. "You're next, Annie. I'll get Trey and bring up the rear." He found Trey and Bear still keeping an eye behind them.

"We're the last ones left. Time to get up the hill."

The three of them made it to the top, and Ben went right to Annie. "I'm liking your idea of ropes. That climb is a real pain."

Annie smiled.

"So, what's the story with Rudolph now?"

She pulled out the compass. "Pretty much the same, but we may have more of a lead." She tried to measure across the top of the compass. "Ben, when you bring that extra rope, bring along a ruler, too. It would make this much easier."

"I'll put it on the shopping list," Ben said grinning.

"So, although we're getting closer to Melvin, so is Rudolph. And I'm not certain, but I think Melvin is more east than he was earlier," Annie said.

"That makes sense. If they made it to the beach before they stopped, then they should be heading straight to the pick-up point by now."

"That works, but Rudolph is now taking a more direct path to Melvin, slowly, so he must be back to marching." She traced across the compass. "We still need to veer east to catch up with Melvin."

"We'll head that way when we leave tomorrow morning," Ben said.

"Good," she said as she tucked the compass into its sack and dropped it back into her shirt. "We'll be able to maintain the lead…unless we're slow in the morning."

"We may need to skip breakfast," Ben said. "How much of that trail mix do you have?"

"Not enough for breakfast, but I'll share what I have, so no one will have to march on an empty stomach…today. Tomorrow's a different day."

"Thanks." Ben called to John. "Hey, can you continue running point, along with Robb and Doug?"

"Yeah, as long as they can keep up," John said.

"Don't rush it too much," Ben said. "Keep it slow and steady, and we'll be at the beach in no time."

"No problem," John said as the three of them headed out.

"Trey, can you and Bear cover the rear again?" Ben asked.

"Yeah," Trey said, then took another swig from his canteen.

"Everyone ready?" Ben asked. "Time to move out."

This time there was no groaning, as the break had been long enough for everyone to get well rested, and the mention of the beach spurred them on. The throng moved quickly, heading north.

Hours later, in the late afternoon, the sun was well past half way to setting, making shadows longer, and Ben noticed that he had to keep slowing to avoid passing the slower folks. "Hey, Patrick, can you see anyone in front of you?"

"Yeah, but they're way ahead. We're going too slowly. The line is getting spread out."

"I thought putting John in front would work…as long as Robb or Doug could keep him from running," Ben said. "but even they can't keep him from going too fast. We need to slow him more."

"Do you want me to run ahead?" Patrick asked.

"No. That would cause more problems. John is…well…stubborn. I'll go talk to him," Ben said as he trotted off.

Ben passed folks scattered along the trail, and when he caught up to the front, he shouted, "John! Wait up."

"What's up?" John asked as he kept walking. "Can't keep up the pace again?"

"It's not me. There are a bunch of others who can't. We need to cut the speed, or stop and wait for them to catch up."

Robb frowned. "I've been telling him that for the last hour or so, but he won't listen."

"Hey, John, whether I say it or someone else says it, you have to listen." Ben noticed a wide spot in the trail ahead. "We'll stop there and wait for the others."

John frowned. "We'll never get there if we keep stopping."

"We'll get there eventually," Ben said. "We don't need to hurry now, but we may need to push it in the morning." He asked, "Can you hold off until then?"

John slowed to a stop. "Yeah, I can." He led his group to the side. "Stopping here!" He scowled. "…waiting for the slowpokes to catch up."

They all found places to sit, glad to catch their breath, waiting for the end of the line. When Trey and Bear came into sight, Ben jumped up. "Here they are."

John stood. "Hey, how's the back end doing?"

Trey frowned and stepped up right in front of John. "We're not doing bad, but you might want to watch out for the others."

John leaned in to Trey and sneered. "They'll make it."

"Cool it," Ben said, stepping between the two of them. He waited a moment, then said, "Annie, still a ways to go, right?"

"Oh! I should check," she said, pulling out the compass. Levelling it in her palm, she stared at it. "Yes, still a ways to go to catch up with Melvin." She frowned. "But we're right in line with both of them."

"Is Rudolph getting closer?" Ben asked.

"Yes, but not just closer," Annie said. "We're lined up in a straight line." She held her arms out in a T. "He's to the west, and…Melvin is to the east. We're almost half way between."

John peered at the blank-to-him compass. "If we're right between them, then should we be pretty close to the beach."

"That would make sense," Ben said. "Trey! Can you run ahead and do a quick recon? See how far we are from the beach."

"I'll be back in a sec," Trey said as he dropped his pack and trotted off. "Come on, Bear!"

The two ran off up the road, and Ben convinced John to sit and wait.

Sitting in silence for a while, John finally burst out with, "Feels like we're always waiting."

Annie laughed. "You sound like Joe. He says in the military, they like to hurry up so they can wait."

"Sounds typical, but we're not in the army," John said.

"Not exactly in scouts either, but here we are," Ben said.

John was about to respond when Trey and Bear ran into sight.

Everyone stood up to get the news, but Trey sat down when they arrived, and calmly caught his breath.

"Well?" John asked. "What'd you find?"

Trey slowly gazed up at him with a glint in his eye. "We found the beach."

"At last!" John said. "See, Ben, we didn't need to stop here. We could have kept going, and we'd be there by now."

Trey stared at John. "If you were there now, you wouldn't be going home tomorrow."

John's head snapped back to Trey. "Huh? How's that?"

"I mean," Trey responded slowly and deliberately, "Rudolph must have been flying back and forth between here and his main army, carrying his troops back and forth." He glared at John. "There's an entire army at the beach, and they're sitting there waiting for us."

John gulped. "Oh."

Ben frowned. "The compass didn't show Rudolph moving like that."

Trey shrugged. "Maybe we weren't looking at the right time."

"Well, thank you for the info, Trey." Ben stepped back to address the group. "Everyone sit tight. We're going to scout ahead." He dropped his pack. "John, you can sit tight with everyone else, right? And keep an eye on things here?"

John nodded silently.

"Good. I'll head up there to see what we need to do," Ben said. "We need our best team to go check it out, but with Joe already at the pickup site, we'll have to do with what we have." He called out, "Someone fetch Doug and Robb," he paused, "and Patrick. He could be useful. Oh, and Trey, you and Bear are with us, too." He ditched his pack next to the others, grabbed his rifle, and glanced towards the afternoon sun. "We'd better hurry."

The small group quickly trotted off. Trey led, slowing to stop as they approached the campsite near the beach. They ducked behind bushes and looked ahead.

"Wish Carl were here," Ben whispered. "He has that eagle-eye. Can you see anything, Patrick?"

"All I see is a couple guys sitting by a campfire," Patrick said.

"A couple guys?" Ben said leaning forward to squint through the bushes. "Yeah, I see three. That's it." He frowned. "So where's this army you told us about, Trey?"

"Well, I may have fudged the quantity," Trey grinned. "But John needed to be put in his place. He's been getting mouthy lately."

"Good point." Ben laughed. "Thanks."

"You're welcome, any time."

"So we take these guys out?" Patrick asked.

"Yeah," Robb said, "You brought us out here for a reason, right?" He patted the hilt of his sword.

"Of course." He grinned his fellow conspirators. "Patrick? You have the honor of blowing up the campfire, but give us a moment to spread out."

"Keep sitting there staring at the flames," Trey mumbled at the soldiers.

They split up, Trey and Bear circling to the right, Ben and Doug taking the river side, planning to catch the soldiers in a crossfire.

Ben kept an eye on the soldiers at the campfire as he crept towards the river with Doug, freezing as a loud splash startled him. They dropped behind the trunk of a fallen tree and peered through the bushes to see three more soldiers sitting by the river, chatting and tossing pebbles into the water.

Ben looked at Doug, then waggled his head towards the three soldiers by the river, thinking, *These three are mine.*

Doug dipped his head, then faced the campfire.

Ben looked past Doug to see Trey already sighting in, ready to start shooting anyone who survived the blast. Bear crouched next to him, sword out, ready to charge.

He braced his rifle across the top of the tree trunk and sighted on the three, aiming for the one in the middle, hoping that the gunshot would surprise the other two, giving him more time to re-aim.

Suddenly the campfire exploded, and Ben flinched, inadvertently jerking the trigger, missing his target completely.

Two of the soldiers ran towards the fire, swords drawn, but the last one headed straight for Ben. He shot again, this time taking better aim. *Got him! One down. Two to go.* He was going to aim at the other two, but they were out of sight, running towards the campfire. He had heard two other shots, Trey and Doug, so now it was time for hand to hand. He slung his rifle, drew his sword, and ran up the slight rise from the beach towards the campfire.

The two soldiers from the beach had run right into a fireball—one dropped immediately, but not the other. Ben swung at the one still standing. The soldier must have heard Ben running up because he suddenly spun, his sword high, swinging at Ben's head. Ben stepped back, managing to get his sword up to block, but just barely deflecting the other one enough.

The soldier glanced back at Robb and, seeing him busy with other targets, advanced towards Ben, his sword in Ben's face. The look on the soldier's face alarmed Ben. This guy wanted to do serious damage.

Ben backed away slowly, keeping the soldier's attention, hoping the others would see his predicament and help out—no one did. Ben was on his own. He held his sword up, aiming at the soldier's face, but that didn't seem to bother the soldier.

The soldier lunged, then laughed out loud as Ben flinched and pulled back, heading down the slope towards the river, giving the soldier the upper hand…literally.

Ben quickly looked left and right, but there was nowhere to go. He could hear the water rushing past his feet. One more step and he'd be in the river.

The soldier slowly raised his sword for one more chop at Ben's head.

Ben stepped back, feeling the cold, wet torrent washing over his boots. He didn't dare look to see where he was putting his feet.

The soldier's face twisted into a grimace, and he started his swing.

Ben heard Patrick yell, "Drop!" and he plunged into the water without thinking, the soldier flying past, sword loose in the air.

Trey ran up. "Are you hurt?"

Ben sat there in the rushing flow, trying to catch his breath. "I don't think so." Bear ran up, and Ben asked, "What took you guys so long?"

Trey laughed. "We had our own to deal with."

Bear lifted Ben out of the water. "You do good."

Ben stood there dripping wet. "I did?"

"You did," Trey said. "You kept him occupied, so Patrick could blast him from behind."

Ben sloshed up the hill back to the campfire, sat on the first log he found, and unlaced his boots. "So, what was the body count altogether?"

"Three by the fire," Doug said, "…and the three you tried to take on all by yourself. You could have let me help with that."

"Next time, I'll let you. You can count on that," Ben said, starting to shiver.

"You look cold, Ben. Come closer to the fire," Trey said. "We can haul these guys out of here later."

"Thanks," Ben said, shifting along the log. He thought about how much work it was to bury the three *nimre* nearby. "Let's just leave those bodies where they lie for now. Once everyone else gets here, we can dump them in the river to get rid of them."

Bear frowned. "River go to *Roadranusis*. We not send there."

"Ah, you're right, Bear," Ben said. "Any other ideas?"

"We bury there." Bear proposed a spot well inland from the river, much farther than where they had hastily buried the *nimre*.

"Good thinking," Ben said. "I'm not good with disposing of dead bodies." He shrugged. "Not much experience."

"And that's a good thing," Patrick said.

"Trey, can you head back and bring everyone else up?" Ben asked. "And see if you can find anything to dig with. We'll need to do something with those bodies."

"I'll see what I can find," Trey said. "Doug, wanna help?"

"Be glad to," Doug said and headed back.

"Hey, Trey," Ben called after them, "Do you need help carrying all our packs?"

Trey counted. "Mine and four more?" He snorted. "Not a problem. See you in a bit." He ran back down the road at a full sprint.

Ben squeezed out his socks behind the log, then wafted them at the fire. "Well, we better get at it." He stood slowly and checked with Bear. "Is that good?"

"Is good," Bear said.

Patrick butted in. "Ben, why don't you stay here by the fire and let Bear and me do the dirty work?" he asked.

"Thanks. That'd be fine," Ben said, sitting back down, still trying to get warm.

Robb leaned in towards the fire and gave it boost. "That should help."

"Thanks," he said.

Patrick followed Bear deep into the forest. Once they were far enough out, Bear stopped. "Here good. Trees good here." He smiled at the branches closing overhead.

"Yes," Patrick said. "This is a nice place." He scraped the forest floor, moving debris, leaves, branches, and small bushes, leveling them as best he could with his sword, opening up a large enough area.

It was getting dark when Doug showed up with a couple shovels. "Not very big, but that's all we have. Joe has all the good ones with him."

"We'll make do with them," Patrick said.

Bear grabbed one of the shovels and started breaking ground.

"Thanks, Doug," Patrick said as he grabbed the other one, digging in. "We'll get these ready, and you guys bring the bodies when you get a chance. I imagine that Annie is getting things set up back there."

Doug laughed. "Yeah, you should see it. John is kowtowing all over the place. I don't know what happened, but he's eating humble pie."

"Ask Trey later. He'll have a story to tell."

"Sounds good," Doug said as he ran off.

As they dug, Patrick said, "Be certain to return these, Bear. We don't want anyone to think we forgot to return borrowed equipment."

"*aa-eh*," Bear said, continuing to dig. After an hour or so of virtual silence, the bodies had been delivered and were now well covered, though, not six feet deep as was tradition, but Bear was satisfied, and so Patrick let it go at that.

Back at camp, they found that Annie did indeed have things well up and running. Most of the tents were set up, Robb had the main campfire roaring with a small cook fire on the side, and Annie even had a wash station set up at the river's edge.

Ben stood by the fire and looked across the site. A golden glow in the west lit the entire scene, and he smiled. Everything was as it should be, and everyone was happy, but that wasn't to last.

As they were rejoicing in the peacefulness of nature, the sky darkened, and everyone froze—Rudolph's dragon circled overhead.

Ben ran to grab his rifle, Patrick lifted his arms, and Robb drew his sword, but before anyone could open fire, the dragon made one last, low pass above the camp, then turned west and disappeared into the dim glow—one last reminder of what awaited them in the morning.

"This waiting is going to kill me," Joe said sitting by the small campfire, cooking some breakfast. "I know that in the military everything is hurry up and wait, but I've never had to wait *this* long before."

"What else would you suggest?" Tom asked. "There's nothing left for us to do." He strode around their makeshift campsite. "We have all the booby traps set, the deer stand is ready to be occupied, and our camp is as ready as it needs to be."

"True, we're almost ready," Joe said. "But there's still things we can do today." He stood up, then glanced at Carl. "Can you help me explain trip lines?"

"If I knew what they were, I could."

"I'll tell you what to do, and you make certain the locals understand."

"Hey, I may be dressed like a native," Carl complained, "But that doesn't mean I speak the lingo. If you want a translator, go find Patrick."

Joe laughed. "That may be true, but you certainly *look* the part." He kicked at Carl's foot, still clad in a standard hiking boot.

Carl frowned. "If it were *you* in this situation, I wouldn't make fun of you."

"Yeah, right," Joe said. "You certainly would." He strode away.

Carl climbed to his feet and shrugged at Tom. "I can *try* to help." He asked Fredekas, "Do you know about trip lines?"

"Not know trip lines, but will do if told," Fredekas said.

"Yeah, I can follow instructions, too. Let's go."

Tom followed, to watch the action.

Melvin glared at the departing backs and yelled out, "If there's nothing else to do, I'll just sit here and be a target. Mr. Sitting Duck. Is that what you want?"

Carl laughed. "Better you than me."

Joe headed back, well beyond the deer stand, then stepped into the bushes on the side. "In case they don't stay on the main trail, which they shouldn't, we want to know when they get here. We don't have any grenades or claymore mines, so we're going to set up trip lines…or even better, snares."

"Are we planning on catching rabbits?" Tom asked.

"Are there rabbits here?" Carl asked. "Patrick may want to cook one up."

"Not actual rabbits," Tom said, "but something similar."

Joe interrupted the conversation. "No, not rabbits. We're going after bigger game. Remember the old Tarzan movies? Where the explorers inevitably get pulled up into the trees in nets?" He snickered. "We're going to try for something like that."

"Did you guys bring nets?" Tom asked staring at the scouts.

Carl stared at Joe. "Did we? Or could we make some? Or should we just use a noose, like a lasso?"

"If we had enough rope. Did we get any from Shess?" Tom checked the supplies Joe had brought from town.

Joe shook his head. "Doesn't look like we'll be able to use either nets or regular rope lassos," he said, "but we can build something. Get me that ivy-looking stuff crawling up those trees." He pulled out his knife. "We'll strip off the leaves and use the individual strands as our trip wire. The fact that it belongs here will help it blend in with the bushes."

"Pretty ingenious," Tom said.

"If Eric were here, he'd be giving us a lesson on biology and natural camouflage." Carl snickered.

Joe put most of his troops to work pulling and stripping the vines. "Once we get enough, we'll braid them into a rope to hold the tension on the snares."

"And we'll use the ivy rope to make lassos?" Carl asked.

"That would be good, but I don't think we'll be able to pull it off. If we could knock some out of action early, we won't have to fight them later, but as a quick fix, making noise will have to do." He showed them how to bend a young, green tree, tie it off to a stake, and run a trip wire through any gaps in the underbrush. "They'll be busy pushing their way through branches, so they won't even see the vine under their feet."

"So a bunch of trees spring up. I assume that's supposed to be helpful, right?" Carl asked.

"First thing we'll do," Joe said, "is make baskets—"

Carl interrupted, "Wait, we're going to do basket weaving?"

Joe shook his head. "No, this isn't scout camp. We're just going to make containers to hold a bunch of rocks and dirt. We'll use the wide, flat branches of those pine-like trees. When they hit the trip wires, the bent trees will be released, and we'll know where they are."

Tom leaned back and smiled. "Rocks flying through the air will certainly make *some* noise, but I'll bet the startled people will make more."

"Exactly," Joe said. "So who needs a doorbell?"

They spent the rest of the afternoon building Joe's field-expedient alarms, even getting help from Melvin who had tired of doing nothing.

After supper, they bedded down quickly, anticipating an early morning—the morning of their departure.

When the first blush of light hit the morning sky, Joe was on his feet. He checked the whole area, searching for anything awry. "Didn't set a watch. What kind of fools are we?" he mumbled. Finding nothing amiss, he concluded, "Fortunate fools is all I can say." Satisfied that all was well, he stoked the fire, added more wood, and set a pot of water in the coals, heating it for their breakfast.

Soon everyone else was up and casually sitting by the fire.

"Now *this* feels like a real campout," Carl said. "It took long enough, but things are finally starting to feel normal."

Tom stretched out his legs, warming his feet by the fire. "First chance we've had to relax."

Joe made a couple circuits around the fire, watching off into the distance. "No one's chasing us, not that I can see, so I'm going to sit right here and relax." He kicked a large branch from their woodpile, rolling it towards the fire, and sat on it.

No sooner had his butt hit the log than he jumped back to his feet. "What's that?" he asked, staring south.

Tom spun and looked. "Close to the treetops, something big, flying, heading east." He watched the object as it disappeared into the rising sun. "Can't see it now." He shaded his eyes. "Did anyone else see it?"

Carl had his rifle up, swinging around. "Was tracking it, but lost it in the glare."

Melvin, still sitting at the fire, said, "Had to have been Rudolph's dragon, and he's tracking us… more accurately, he's tracking *me*."

"Well, he's staying far enough away," Joe said. "But all that means is that we can't let our guard down…even for a moment."

Melvin looked west. "I hope Ben wasn't delayed."

* * *

Ben was up early, roused by John, the last person on watch.

"So why did you want to get up so early?" John asked as he leaned to look into Ben's tent.

"I want to keep an eye on things," Ben said, crawling out to put on his boots. "I sorta feel responsible for everyone here, so I want to make certain it all goes according to plan."

"According to plan?" John laughed. "When did that become relevant? And when did we have a plan?"

Ben shrugged as John wandered off to walk his patrol around the camp one more time. Ben headed towards the bright orange tent. *I wouldn't mind having such a stand-out tent if we were hunting animals, but with people after us, it stands out too much*, he thought. *A camo tent might be better next time. I'll have to check with Joe about getting a surplus one.* He reached out and rattled the side of the tent. "Hey, Annie," he said. "Can you help Patrick get going on breakfast? I'm heading to wake Robb." He heard mumblings in response and assumed she'd be out shortly. Stopping by the next tent, Ben whispered loudly, "Robb? You there?"

Soft noises emanated from the depths.

"We need to get the fire going for breakfast," Ben said. "We don't want to delay our exodus, and Annie is getting things ready."

A head popped out. "Annie's making breakfast?" Robb asked.

"She and Patrick are working on it together…or are going to be."

"Close enough. I'll get the fire rip-roaring. Let me get dressed." As he pulled his head back into the tent, shuffling sounds could be heard.

Ben headed back to roll his bag and drop his tent, encouraging everyone to eat quickly. "We need to head out as soon as possible."

In the middle of breakfast, John came running up. "Hey, Ben. We have a problem across the river."

Ben joined John, and the two of them went back to the river, followed by other curious folks. Before they were even close to the river's edge, it was evident what John meant. Directly across from the small beach, on top of the bluffs, a mob of soldiers were hopping and shouting, and Ben could hear them in spite of the noise of the river.

"Whoa," Ben shouted. "They're here." He paused, remembering that they hadn't been able to cross the river here. "They can't get to us right now, with the river in the way, but we need to get to the drop-off point," he frowned at the soldiers, "and as far from this river as possible."

John looked downstream. "Did anyone notice if our bridge was still up?"

Trey raised his hand. "Uh, Ben. When we were at the top of the cliff, and you were checking with Annie, Bear and I wandered by to look."

"And?" Ben raised his eyebrows. "Is it still there?"

"Mostly, but the middle is missing, knocked out when those logs bashed into it. If the soldiers used it to get across, they must have rebuilt it." Trey shrugged, then added, "But it was completely unstable."

"If they could use it, stable or not, we need to get going." Ben called to the group. "Grab your gear and head out. We don't have any time to waste."

Everyone hotfooted it back to camp and packed the remaining items.

"Doug, can you head out first with Annie?" Ben asked. "I want as much distance between her and Rudolph as possible."

"Yeah, not a problem," Doug said. "Which way?"

"We could have taken a reading earlier to be certain," Ben said, "but we know we have to get away from those soldiers, so that would be east."

"Where do we go after that?" Annie asked.

"If they put a blaze on *this* tree," Ben said. "There should be more to follow as we go."

Doug stood over a small pile of rocks. "The ducks confirm that," he said, "right towards the rising sun."

"The sun will be right in our eyes," Annie said.

"It might make it difficult to see where we're going," Doug said, "but it also means the soldiers won't be able to see us as they follow."

"Keep your hat brim low. Shade your eyes. Watch for more ducks." Ben paused. "By the time they catch up, the sun will be high enough that it won't bother them, then again, by the time they catch up, I hope we'll be out of here."

"If we keep moving, we'll stay far enough ahead that they won't catch up at all," Doug said as he stepped towards Annie. He dropped his gear next to her and said, "Give me a sec to put out the fire, and we'll be on our way." He headed towards the fire, but Ben stopped him.

"We'll handle the fire," Ben said. "You get moving."

"All right," Doug said as he shouldered his pack. He escorted Annie and those who were ready out of camp and off towards the rising sun.

Ben ran through the site, helping the slowpokes get packed and out, ignoring the campfire completely. *If there's ever a time to stop and put out a campfire, this isn't it.* An interesting trip, this one turned out to be, but now their focus was to get home.

He was ready to leave when he noticed Robb and Patrick standing shoulder to shoulder facing the river. "What are you guys doing? Let's get going."

"We figured we'd try to delay the soldiers like we did at Rudolph's city," Robb said. "Slash and burn, right? Isn't that what Joe says?"

"Yeah." Patrick grinned.

Ben hesitated. "Do you think that's wise? The fire we started before was in a narrow, rocky mountain pass. No place for it to spread." He gazed at the forest surrounding them. "If you were to start a fire here, it could burn everything from here all the way to *Roadranusis.* I don't remember seeing anything to fight fires in town, so if it gets there, it could be bad." He paused. "Do you think Shess would be happy if we did that?"

Robb frowned and tossed a small fireball into a bush at the side of the path. "Yeah, it would be better to avoid burning any bridges…or forests."

Ben watched a trail of smoke coming up from the smoldering bush. He raised his eyebrows. "Really, Robb?" He signaled Patrick. "Can you take care of that?"

Patrick launched a small pop at the bush, blowing out the flame. The plant shook in the shockwave, as much as it would in a stiff wind.

"Thanks. Let's get going." Ben started walking, then stopped. "If you guys want to do something destructive, why don't you wipe out any ducks you see as we pass them. I don't know if these guys would know what they mean, but we don't want to give them any clue where we're heading.

Patrick blasted the ducks in the camp, sending them flying.

Robb frowned. "I'm getting the next ones."

"Keep moving," Ben said. "We need everyone bunched together, not spread out all across the countryside."

As they were coming out of the deepest part of the woods, Ben didn't see but rather felt a shadow pass by them. Rudolph's dragon flew directly over them, swooping off to one side, then circling back behind them.

Robb readied a fireball, but the target dove out of sight before he could fire it. "What's he up to now?"

Patrick shrugged.

"Don't know, but we'd better be ready for anything," Ben said, "in case he comes back."

Patrick spun to the other side. "He's that way now."

By the time Ben and Robb reacted, the dragon had dropped below the trees. "I saw him, for an instant," Ben said.

"Yeah, me, too." Robb tossed a small fireball back and forth, hand to hand. "I'm going to be ready if he gets close enough."

"Keep at the ready. Whatever he has in mind, it isn't going to be good," Ben said.

They headed out at a quick pace, watching to both sides, occasionally spotting the dragon flying low, barely above the trees.

"I wish he'd get close…even for a moment," Robb complained.

Ben spun at the sound of someone crashing through the trees behind them. "I thought *we* were bringing up the rear. Who's behind us?"

The three of them waited, listening to someone bashing their way through the undergrowth. Robb held up a fireball, the size of a softball, and bounced it in his hand. The noise kept moving, then suddenly, from the side of the path, a soldier popped out. He stopped for a moment, spun, then charged right at them. Robb threw his fireball, hitting the soldier full in the chest.

Ben could feel the heat as the fireball exploded. "Yow! Watch it, Robb. He was too close for that."

Robb hefted another fireball. "I'll aim farther next time."

Ben looked west, towards the river. "They must have gotten across. We need to run."

Another soldier darted out of the bushes right next to Patrick, so he sent a blast, knocking him flying back into the bushes.

Without sighting any more soldiers, they ran ahead until they caught up with the tail of the group.

Ben yelled to the others, "Run, and keep running. We'll guard the back." He drew his sword and crouched in the middle of the path. "Hey, Patrick, Robb, spread out and get ready."

Patrick jumped into the bushes on one side and Robb dove into the other. They waited for a while, but no one showed up. "Is that it? Only those two?" Ben finally asked.

Patrick stuck his head out of a bush. "I don't know. Those two made it across the river, so the rest should be here, too."

"Only two made it, why?" Robb asked from inside his bush.

Ben stood up straight and tapped his toe. "I'm getting tired of waiting for them." He noticed the other scouts were out of sight. "Let's get going. We can watch back here, but we don't want to get too far behind."

Robb was climbing out of the bushes when a gunshot rang out up ahead.

Ben spun and stared in the direction of the rest of the group. "The soldiers are past us?"

Patrick sprinted by as Ben glanced towards the river. They ran ahead and overtook the tail end of the group, catching up to find John standing over the body of a soldier.

"What happened?" Ben asked.

John shrugged. "This guy jumped out of the bushes," he kicked the body, "and tried to slash Eric, but I shot him before anyone could get hurt."

"Good. Keep an eye out for any more," Ben said. "So far we've only seen a couple, but if they've made it across the river, there should be a lot more of them." He frowned towards the river.

"Dragon!" Patrick shouted, dodging to one side.

Robb pulled back and let a fireball fly. The fireball exploded as it faded from view. "Missed. Not close enough. We need to get clear of these trees. I can't see through all the branches."

Everyone squinted through the treetops, waiting for movement, but nothing appeared.

"Get going," Ben finally said. "We can deal with the dragon later." He yelled to the rest of the group. "You guys head out. We'll catch up."

"Keeping an eye on the rear?" John asked.

"Yeah. We'll move on when it's safe."

John faced the river. "Let those soldiers try to get past me." He stood ready for anything.

Ben stood next to John. "You guys cover the sides like before. We'll make a wall for them."

Patrick and Robb extended the wall, waiting a while, watching, yet no one arrived. Then, a noise behind them caught Ben's ear, and he silently swiveled to see one of Rudolph's soldiers sneaking away, unaware they were there—his back to them. "Behind!" Ben shouted as he darted towards the soldier, sword in hand.

The soldier twirled to meet Ben's attack, blocking the first swing, just about knocking Ben's sword from his hand. Ben stumbled, regripped his sword, and stood to face the soldier as a fireball zoomed by. The soldier stared at the fireball, watching it hit a tree and burst into flame. Ben used the soldier's distraction to smack him with the flat of his sword, dropping him on the spot.

Robb ran up. "Oops. Didn't mean to get so close…again."

Ben's sword slid from his hand, and he stooped, hands on knees, staring at the soldier. "I don't know about this." He gasped for air, then stood up. "John, I don't know if I'm cut out for this. You're so much better in a fight."

John laughed. "You need more practice. That's all. Once you've been in as many fights as I have, it's second nature." He put his hand on Ben's shoulder. "You did the right thing. It was you or him…just one thing."

"What?" Ben asked.

"Next time you want to tackle a big guy like that, use your gun first."

Ben stared. "That slipped by me completely. I'm so used to swinging a sword that I forgot. It didn't even occur to me to shoot."

Robb walked up. "Not a bad thing."

"Yeah, shooting first isn't a habit you want to get into," Patrick said. "It might not work real well when we get back home."

"For that matter, neither is swinging a sword."

John bent to examine the soldier. "Well, if it makes you feel any better, Ben, this one is still alive."

Patrick picked up Ben's sword. "Here, you might want this."

"Thanks." Ben sheathed his sword. "We need to keep up with the others," he said stepping over the unconscious soldier. "A solitary soldier, again. Why are they doing that?"

John stopped to give the soldier one last kick before following Ben. "One from up here, one from back there," he said. "But you said you had a couple of them attack?"

"We had two, but they attacked separately. One from one side of the path, and a moment later one from the other side, the same as here."

"Not even at the same time? That might've worked better," Robb said.

"Yeah, they had no coordination at all," Ben said.

"So, *some* of them made it across the river, but why didn't more of them make it across?" Patrick asked.

"Robb was asking the same thing," Ben said. "The only thing I can figure is they spread out after crossing the river," he said. "They don't know exactly where we've gone, so they need to cover a lot of territory to find us."

"That *could* make sense," John frowned, "but I don't need to have Joe's training to know that it's not a smart move to go up against anyone alone. You always bring friends to a fight." He reached out and patted Robb's shoulder, smiling at Patrick.

Ben smiled. "Thanks for considering us your friends."

"Who else would I want to have at my back when we're in a bind?"

Ben started to answer, but Patrick froze. "Was that the dragon again?"

Patrick stood there, his arm extended. They all followed his gaze.

"Yeah, I see something big moving out there," Robb said. "Too far away. I can only hit as far as I can throw." He faced them. "I wish I could hit farther away, like you do, Patrick."

"I wish I could make fireballs like you do," Patrick said. "It would really impress the chicks."

Ben laughed. "You two are pretty funny sometimes. Each of you can do some pretty extraordinary things…and you want the other." He shook his head.

The mood lightened as they continued walking, constantly checking the trees behind and to the sides.

John continued analyzing. "Let me get this right," he said. "Neither of the ones that attacked you were *on* the path."

"Right," Ben said.

"This last one was," Robb said.

"But they *must* have been coming from the river, right?" John asked.

Ben shrugged. "Where else could they be coming from?"

"Well, you said one came from one side, and one from the other. Could they have been trying to circle ahead of us?" John frowned. "Yet still they attacked alone, not waiting for anyone else to join them."

"Yeah, doesn't make much sense, does it?"

"That's the biggest question. Why one at a time?" Patrick said.

"It would make more sense to gang up on us," John thought about it, "hit us with a big group all at once. They'd have better defense that way."

Robb shrugged. "No clue, but as long as they keep coming at us singly, we'll keep taking them out that way." He flipped a small fireball from one hand to the other. "Wanna see me juggle?"

Ben noticed dry leaves underfoot. "Better wait until we get to solid ground." He kicked at the dirt. "Or better yet, near water."

"So the other question is where are they crossing the river? I still don't understand that," John said.

"Yeah," Patrick said. "Think about this last guy. He was past us *and* was right on the path, without us seeing, or even hearing, him."

"Well he had to have come from the river. We know that much," John said. "And if he circled wide to get in front of us, he'd have much farther to go, so even if he'd run the whole way, he'd still be way behind us, right?"

"But if he ran the whole way," Ben said. "Wouldn't he have been out of breath? I didn't notice that."

"I don't think you noticed much of anything," John mumbled.

Patrick and Robb snickered as Ben's face reddened. "Yeah, I *was* in a hurry."

"What if there's another bridge that we don't know about," John said. "Upstream more, where we haven't been yet?"

"That's a possibility, but wouldn't that put him even farther away?" Ben asked.

"Yeah, and we don't need to have Eric give us a lesson on distances." John laughed. "So unless these guys have other means of transportation, I don't understand it."

All four of them paused for a moment when they heard shouting and the sounds of a scuffle, ahead of them through the trees. They sprinted up to find Trey and Bear shoving a soldier back and forth. He had already dropped his sword and was trying to give up, but they wouldn't let him stand still, tossing him like a doll.

"Hey, where'd you get him?" Ben shouted.

Trey grabbed the soldier and wrapped one arm around the guy's neck, strangling the soldier under his armpit. "Oh? This guy?" He shrugged. "We found him sneaking through the undergrowth." He shook the soldier at the side of their path. "Eric just about tripped over him, but Bear snagged him when he tried to run off."

"He not quiet. Catch easy," Bear explained.

"Well, don't hurt him," John said. "We want to know how he got up this far."

Trey twisted the soldier to face Patrick. "Go ahead. Ask away."

Patrick stepped up and spoke to the soldier, but the soldier merely gurgled, eyes bulging. "Um, Trey, can you loosen your hold a little. He can't breathe."

"Oh, you want him to be able to answer?" Trey asked. "Let me see what he has to say." He flexed his bicep, throttling the soldier even more, then relaxed his grip and waited. "No funny stuff. Understand?"

The soldier craned his head up at Trey, trying to show he understood the situation.

Patrick tried again, and the soldier lifted a finger skyward, answering with one word they all understood: "Rudolph."

"We know him. What's he doing?" Robb asked, flipping a small fireball back and forth in the soldier's face.

The soldier let loose with a whole confession, singing like a canary, as Eric would say. Patrick listened, finally stepping back, and translating: "They're being transported by Rudolph's dragon."

"So they *are* being airdropped," John said. "Wait until I tell Joe he was right."

"Well, that explains how they're getting in front of us," Ben said.

"And I'd surmise that they are arriving singly because the dragon carries one in each claw," Eric said.

"He'd still be better off dropping them together instead of one here, one there," John said. "He could use lessons from Joe."

"Let's not give too much advice to the enemy."

Patrick continued. "He says that they're being dropped off to slow us down, to hinder us, to give Rudolph time to get the rest of his army across the river."

"I can see dropping them up here one at a time, but if he's ferrying them across the river on his dragon, we have plenty of time," Ben said.

"Not necessarily," Patrick said. "This one says that Rudolph had a group of soldiers building a bridge…but it was not quite done when he was picked up."

"Bridge? I wonder if they rebuilt *our* bridge," John said.

Patrick shrugged. "That's a possibility. We'll have to check, but not *this* time through the Door."

"Right now, it's not bridges," Ben said. "It's soldiers that we need to focus on."

"Yeah," John said. "If they're across the river, then they'll be right at our backs any moment now. We'd better get moving."

"Trey, will you and Bear join the others in keeping our tail clean?"

"We'd be glad to," Trey said. He thumped Bear on the shoulder, and Bear hunched over, growling. Trey grinned. "I taught him that."

Ben stared. Not the best impression we're leaving with these folks.

"And this guy?" Trey jiggled the soldier, still dangling in his grip.

"Tie him up and drop him in the bushes somewhere," John said. "He'll either get loose on his own or someone will come along and rescue him, either way, hopefully after we're long gone."

"That works," Ben said. "When you're done with him, keep an eye out for any activity behind us but keep moving, don't let us get too far ahead."

"I'll tie him up real good." Trey gave the soldier one more shake.

"I'm going to check with Annie on our direction. I want to see if we're still on course…in case someone panics when the soldiers show up." He glanced towards Eric. "I don't want anyone running off and getting lost, certainly not when we're this close."

Ben jogged up the line, encouraging the folks he passed to keep hurrying, finally catching up to the lead where Doug and Annie were striding along. They both slowed as he approached.

"What's up?" Doug asked. "Any news from the back?"

"Keep going. I'll update you on the fly," Ben said as he continued walking past them. "They've crossed the river, on a bridge, either ours rebuilt or their own. Either way we expect to see them come storming up any minute now."

"Oh!" Annie said as Doug hurried to keep up with Ben, keeping an eye on the path behind them.

"Can you see if we're still on the right path?"

Annie smiled. "I've been doing that as we walk." She held out her hand, showing the compass. "We're heading right towards Melvin." She checked the compass. "I've also been watching Rudolph circle us."

"Circle us? Where's he been?" Ben asked.

"Here, there, everywhere. He circles up, loops the Melvin dot, then heads back, probably all the way to the river. He's been doing that all morning, going back and forth with loops, stopping for a longer bit when he's at the river. I imagine that dragon of his is getting pretty tired."

"That's good." Ben smiled. "When he goes by, can you *see* him?"

"No," Annie said. "He swings wide to the south on his way out, and to the north on his way back."

Doug frowned. "If he flew closer, we could've taken some easy shots in spite of the trees. He's being so predictable you could set your watch by him," he paused, "if you had a watch, that is."

"And you haven't seen any soldiers up here?"

"Up here? No way. How could any of them have gotten past all you guys?" Doug asked.

"When he does those loops," Ben said, "he's been dropping off soldiers along both sides, to hassle us."

"He's trying to spread out our line to make easier targets," Doug said.

Ben leaned in to squint at the compass. "So what's it show distance-wise?"

Annie measured the invisible distances. "We're definitely getting closer to Melvin, and if the farthest back Rudolph goes is the river, then," she measured again, "based on how far we've gone," she smiled at Ben, "we should get there in less than an hour."

"Good." Ben checked behind them. "Hopefully, we'll be ahead of the soldiers." He checked the sun's position. "And it'll definitely be well before noon."

"Arriving before noon is good, right?" Doug asked.

"Well, it could be," Ben said. "Tom said that's when they open the Door, so assuming they are on time, we'll only have to stand around a bit waiting it to open…with Rudolph right on our backside."

"As long as we don't wait long, it won't be a problem," Annie said.

Ben shrugged. "When we catch up to Tom, we can ask him how long he thinks it'll be."

Annie looked ahead eagerly.

"Sorry."

All of a sudden, a loud boom came echoing up from behind, and Ben spun to see a fireball blossoming above the trees in the distance. Everyone in the line stopped to stare, but Ben yelled, "Move it!"

More explosions went off in the distance, and gunfire echoed across the forest.

Ben spun and yelled, "Run!" A sudden commotion at the back of the line caught his attention. He could see Eric running up, yelling and screaming, his arms and legs flailing wildly. When he was close enough, Ben asked, "What is it, Eric?"

"They're here," Eric panted. "The soldiers are here. Hundreds of them." He stopped to catch his breath. "Trey sent me up here to let you know."

"Thanks, Eric. We could hear something going on," Ben said, pushing Annie towards Doug. "Get her out of here."

Doug grabbed Annie's arm and dragged her forward, yelling back, "She'll be safe with me."

"Eric, try to keep up with Doug." Ben started to point, then stiffened and screamed, "Doug, freeze!"

Doug slammed to a halt, bringing Annie to a stop with a jerk.

She screeched, "Ow!" and rubbed her arm.

"Oops, Annie. You all right?" He stared at Ben. "What is it?"

"Triple duck," Ben said.

Doug slowly searched the ground. "Good catch. My foot was right next to that one, and there's more." He looked along the path ahead.

"What's a triple duck?" Annie asked.

"A warning," Ben said. "We used them in scouts to mark places to avoid."

"Another one right there," Doug said, sidestepping back to the middle of the path, pulling Annie with him. "Well, we've caught up with the advance group."

Ben trotted up carefully, watching the ground as he walked. "Yeah, but where do we go from here?"

A voice came floating out of the trees. "Keep going straight, but stick to the middle of the path."

Ben spun, hunting for the voice in the branches overhead. "Carl?"

"Yeah, it's me." The branches above Doug's head shook, then a hand popped out. "The rest are ahead, but stay on the marked path."

"Uh, thanks, Carl."

The group behind Ben was approaching, and Eric squinted up into the trees. "Carl's up there? Where?"

The hand wiggled around again. "Right here."

"I see your hand, but why are you up there?" Eric asked still staring.

"Waiting for Rudolph's troops." Carl pulled back the bolt on his rifle and slammed a round into the chamber.

"Finally doing that?" Ben asked.

"Range safety," Carl said. "Waiting until all of you were past."

Ben blinked. "Ah, some of that training stuck?"

"Yeah, seems like it." Carl laughed.

"Well, there are still a couple more out there, but you won't need to wait long," Ben said. "I can hear both Patrick and Robb blasting away."

"Yeah, I heard it, too, but you'd better get going, so you don't give away my location. I want to see how well the element of surprise works for catching those soldiers in the traps."

"Traps? Where?" Eric asked in a panic.

The hand twisted back and forth. "Some here, some there, but mostly off to the side. You shouldn't have any problems…as long as you keep your eyes open."

Doug leaned to Eric. "Don't worry, Eric, just stick close to us."

"Stick close to *me*, Eric," Ben said. "Doug, can *you* hold back to warn the others in case they don't see the ducks?"

"But don't give me away," the voice from overhead added.

"Yeah," Doug said. "I'll wait back here," he said as he cautiously stepped past the trunk of Carl's tree. He gazed up into the tree. "Hey, Carl, let me know when they get here."

"Gotcha!"

Ben called back to the rest of the group holding back. "Everyone listen up, on me," he said. "Single file, no wandering."

The group formed up behind Ben, Annie first, Eric next, followed by the rest, and they moved out at a slow deliberate march, continuing along the path. Ben kept an eye on the ground as he walked, guiding the line right, then left, weaving back and forth. He'd call out to the group and point whenever he had to make a quick turn. Almost fifteen tense minutes later, he paused, telling everyone to stop.

Right there in front of them was Melvin, sitting with his back to them, not moving, in front of a small campfire. Ben was getting ready to draw his pistol when he heard a voice coming from bushes on the far side of the campfire: "Hey, Melvin. Ben is here."

Melvin swiveled to face Ben. "Ah, there you guys are. We were wondering if you'd make it."

Ben stared at the bush. "Talking trees, now talking bushes. What's next?" He stepped to Melvin. "Is that Tom…in that bush?" he asked.

Annie's head snapped to look. "Tom?" she asked as she pushed past Ben.

Ben laughed at Annie saying, "What can you do?" shrugging.

Melvin watched Annie disappear behind the bush. "And Joe's in the other one. We were waiting in case Rudolph made it before you guys."

"Well, you don't need to wait any more. He's right behind us."

Melvin sat up. "He is? Where?" He leaned back and forth, trying to see past Ben.

"Back there," Ben said. "We had run-ins with his soldiers. Some of them have made it across the river, and they're right on our tail. They'd be here already except we left some behind to delay them."

"Left behind?" came a voice from the other bush. "Who did you abandon?"

Ben spoke to the second bush. "Not abandoned. They stayed behind to cover our backside. It was Robb and Patrick. Oh, and John, Trey, and Bear. They can handle it."

"Yeah, they're good guys." Joe agreed.

"Doug stayed behind to warn them of the ducks," Ben said. "Thanks for marking your traps like that."

"Carl did most of the work," Joe said, "so if any of you get caught in a trap, you can blame him."

"No blame needed. They are well marked," Ben said.

"So they're close now?" Melvin asked.

"Very," Ben said.

"Then I don't need to sit out here in the open any longer. They know where to go." Melvin stood up and grabbed his rifle. "Where do you guys want me?" he asked the bushes.

"Out of my kill zone," came Joe's sarcastic voice.

Ben raised his eyebrows. "Then *we* need to get out of the way, too." He signaled to the rest of the group. "This way! Get moving."

They followed Ben's lead as he and Melvin headed past the campfire and up the slope. As they passed the occupied bushes, Ben glanced to both sides, seeing Joe prone, his eye to his scope, and Tom lying behind the other bush. Annie was kneeling next to him, chatting. They were deep in conversation, so Ben didn't interrupt, but Tom called out, "How much farther back are they, Ben?"

Ben motioned for the group to continue as he stopped to talk with Tom. "Quite a ways, I'd say. We could hear shots and see Robb's fireballs when the soldiers first ran into our rear guard and could still hear activity when we ran across Carl. Haven't heard or seen anything since then."

The bush behind him shook as Joe spoke. "Ha! I told you I heard gunfire."

Tom shrugged. "So you have good ears, Joe. Do your ears tell you anything about Rudolph now?"

"My ears? No, but my eyes. That's a different matter." Joe leaned out from behind the bush and flapped his hands, watching the sky. Off in the distance, they could see Rudolph's dragon circling. "Not quite past Carl, I'd say, but close."

"Annie, I don't want you too close to the combat," Tom said. "So head out with Ben, and keep back a ways. If you need to hide somewhere, our packs and stuff are stashed there." He motioned to a copse of trees near the creek.

Annie put her hands on her hips and stood face to face with Tom. "You want me to sit it out? Ha! That isn't going to happen. Though I *will* try to keep out of the *middle* of things." She frowned at Tom. "But I don't need to go *hide* anywhere."

Ben laughed at Annie's antics. "You'll learn…some day, Tom."

Tom threw his hands up in mock resignation. "All right. All right, already. Go ahead." Slowly smiling at Annie, he said, "Be careful." He glanced at Ben. "And you, keep her safe, will ya?"

Ben shrugged back. "I'll do what I can, but I won't even *try* to stop her from doing what *she* wants to do."

Tom smiled at Annie. "That's all I can ask. Thanks, Ben."

Ben was reaching for Annie when he paused. A shadow darkened the sky as the dragon soared down, swooping right at them.

Ben dropped, pulling Annie with him. "Don't move. He may not see us."

A couple shots rang out from the next bush. "Missed," Joe said. "He flew by before I had a chance to aim."

"Well, he knows where we are now," Ben said. He grabbed Annie's arm. "Come on. Let's get out of here." They ran for the cover of the trees nearby, running past Eric who appeared lost, standing out in the open. Suddenly Ben had an idea. He leaned to Annie. "Can you help keep Eric out of harm's way?"

"As long as he doesn't get in *my* way," she said.

"It should be easy enough to keep him close, but not too close," Ben said, then yelled, "Hey, Eric! Can you help out by keeping an eye on Annie?"

Eric spun. "Me? Be a look out for her? Yeah." He walked up, and Ben escorted him to where Annie was standing under the trees.

"Stay near her," Ben said, "but not too close. Give her enough room to do what she needs to do…medically that is, and help her if she needs it."

Eric smiled. "I'd be honored to stand by her," he smiled at Annie, "and assist in whatever way she desires."

Ben crouched, running towards Tom. He squatted behind the bush and peered through. "Can't see much from here."

"Don't need to see much, as long as we can see enough," Tom said. "The plan is to wait until they get into that open area by the campfire, then we wipe them out. That's all we need to be able to see."

"Well, I can see the campfire out there in the middle," Ben said. "But what about the soldiers farther out?"

"That's for Carl to handle."

Tom jumped as gunfire broke out in the distance.

Joe yelled, "And that would be Carl now. Get ready for an influx of frantic soldiers."

Ben stood up and looked across the open area. "I see Trey and Bear out there, but no one else." He circled the bush and headed towards the campfire. "You guys hold your fire until we all make it past."

Joe mumbled loudly from behind his bush, "That's not how a kill zone is supposed to work."

Ben ignored him as he rushed up to join Trey and Bear, both slowly backing up the trail as they fought off groups of soldiers. "Where's the others?" Ben asked as an explosion went off in the trees ahead.

Bear grunted. "They there."

"Yeah, so I see." Ben ran forward, shouting back, "Watch for the ducks."

"Yeah, Doug told us," Trey answered back, between swings of his huge sword.

Ben dodged through the trees, heading towards the sound of battle, slowing a couple times to handle soldiers who'd managed to sneak past the defenders. Once, he barely missed tripping into a well-concealed hole. Starting to cuss at Joe and his buddies, he finally noticed the triple duck…on the *far* side of the hole. "Duh!" he said, slapping himself on the forehead. "They're marked to notify people coming from *that* direction, so I need to be extra careful going *this* direction," he said aloud.

He approached the loudest part of the conflict and found John dancing with a dozen soldiers surrounding him—trying to face them all. "Need help?" Ben shouted as he sliced through the armor on the backs of two of the soldiers.

John spun, swinging his sword wildly, keeping the other soldiers at bay. "Nah, why would I need help?" he shouted, grinning madly. "This is the most fun we've ever had on a campout."

A couple of the soldiers switched from John to face Ben, exposing their backs to the whirling dervish. Ben kept them busy as John dispatched them one at a time.

John paused to catch his breath. "Wow, that's a workout."

"As soon as you're ready, head on," Ben said. "Past the campfire, and between two talking bushes. Everyone else is up there waiting for you."

"You have this?" John asked.

"Yeah. I'm just collecting folks. You get to the high ground."

"See ya there!" John tossed a sloppy salute and ran.

"One found, more to go," Ben mumbled to himself, realizing he could smell smoke. "Robb?" He swiveled to catch the scent but couldn't tell where it was coming from.

Focused on his search, he didn't see a soldier sneaking up on him, but when he heard the snap of a twig, he spun, sword out, barely missing the soldier. The soldier jumped back and raised his sword, ready to slice through Ben when a loud bang startled them both. Ben watched the soldier's eyes roll back in his head as he slowly toppled, landing right at Ben's feet. He was about to panic when he saw Patrick peering out from behind a tree.

"I've perfected the back-of-head blast," he said, walking to Ben, glancing at the body as he stepped past. "He may not be out for hours, but it'll be long enough for us to be long gone…and when he *does* wake up, he'll have one heck of a headache."

"I'm amazed at what you've learned to do with that. The first time you did it, all you did was spill ale."

"Like Zhahmonichas said, keep practicing and it'll get easier. I'm even getting so I can hit where I can't see, like the back of someone's head, even if he's charging at me."

"Well, keep hitting, but keep moving, too." Ben frowned. "Any idea where the others are?"

"Robb and I split up a ways back. We kept getting in each other's way, going after the same targets."

"I should be able to tell where Robb is," Ben said as he checked the skyline for smoke, "but I'm still missing Doug."

"Last time I saw Doug, he was hiding behind a tree right along the path. That's when he warned us about the triple ducks."

"That was probably Carl's tree. Did you see him at all?"

"Carl?" Patrick blinked. "Nope, not anywhere. Is he out here, too?"

"Yeah, up in a tree. He's so well camouflaged that I didn't know he was there…even when I was standing right under him."

"Must still be there." Patrick paused. "Doug told us about the ducks then told us to keep going. He stayed there in spite of us being the last to come through. No one behind us but soldiers, oh, and Rudolph."

"Oh, yeah. Can't forget him," Ben said. "Where was the last place you saw him?"

"We saw him fly by a couple times, up front for a while, but then he circled back near the river, looping up and back, again and again." Patrick paused. "He didn't seem to be doing much in the way of battle, mostly observing."

"Directing the battle from the air?"

"Yeah, that could be what he was doing." Patrick leaned around, looking past Ben, then opened his hand in that direction. There was a small bang and leaves from the tree overhead fell on them.

Ben twisted around to see a soldier lying sprawled on the ground. "Good shot, or whatever you call it. At least you won't run out of ammo."

"Yeah, no ammo here, but it's not as easy as it looks. After doing big blasts, it hurts to do more. That's why I developed the small back-of-head hit. Not as much force needed."

"Oh? It hurts? Interesting, but don't burn yourself out. We don't want you to exhaust yourself," Ben said. "I sent John back to join the others. You head that way, too, and I'll try to get the rest out of here before Joe opens up on his blast area or whatever he calls it."

A low boom echoed across the forest, and Patrick pointed at a small trail of smoke drifting up through the trees behind them. "That would be Robb. He's up that way already. I'll join him and head on to the meet spot," he said as he headed out.

"Thanks," Ben called out, then continued his search for Doug…and Carl.

As he was tromping through the trees, Ben heard talking and didn't recognize the voices. Dropping to hide in the bushes at the base of a tree, he peeked out through the leaves and saw a group of soldiers walking along the path in a somewhat casual manner.

Ben noticed that although they were talking calmly as they walked, they kept glancing up at the sky. Then he realized why: these were the officers, the ones in charge, and they were watching for Rudolph to fly by, to give them intel on the situation ahead.

Ben smiled. *Ha! The trees are too close together for him to land, so he can't give them any info.* As if on cue, Rudolph circled by. Ben held his position, waiting. One of the officers, dressed in a bright red coat with black cording and wearing a red feathered hat, stepped out into a shaft of sunlight and stopped, his hands overhead. He waited there for a moment, then reached out and caught something that came drifting in…on a small parachute: a dropped message. Ben frowned as the officer called to the others. They chatted for a moment or two, then started out.

Suddenly a shot rang out and the officer with the message still in hand flew backwards. The others spun, drawing their swords and backing away. Ben heard another round being chambered, and a piece of hot brass bounced off his shoulder, landing right next to his foot. Another shot and another officer dropped. The rest ran for cover on the other side of the path. As they ran, one or two of them abruptly fell, crying in pain. He heard a laugh come from the tree overhead.

"Carl? Is that you?" he whispered loudly.

"Yeah, Ben. It's me, and you can let Joe know that his troodle-de-do traps worked perfectly." Another shot rang out. "Give me a minute and I'll have *all* of them out of the battle. That'll make Joe happy. Get rid of the leaders and see what happens to the little guys." More brass rained from the tree as Carl shot more of the officers, the rest diving for cover, landing in, on, and near the spiked pits. After a moment, Carl broke the silence. "We're done here. Now to back off and join the others."

"We're not done here," Ben said. "I haven't come across Doug yet. How long since you've seen him?"

"You want to know where Doug is?" Carl asked. "Ask him yourself."

Ben was starting to ask what he meant when Doug spoke up. "Pretty good camo, isn't it?"

Ben rolled to stare at the bush next to him. "Doug?"

"None other." Doug laughed as he sat up. "I had a tough time keeping quiet when you landed practically on top of me."

The tree overhead rattled and shook as Carl shifted finally swinging from the branches, dropping to the ground in front of them. He laughed at the wounded officers. "Let's get out of here before they get the nerve to follow."

A shadow crossed their position, and Ben swore he could hear cussing and screaming coming from overhead.

Carl casually swung his rifle up, taking a couple potshots through the tree branches. "I don't know if he has that shield of his going or if that dragon is bulletproof, but nothing seems to slow him down."

"Well, we need to move." Ben grinned. "I think someone is upset."

The three jogged off, coming up on groups of disorganized soldiers, mostly nursing injuries caused by falling into more of Joe's stick traps. The three attacked the groups of soldiers from the back and ran through before the soldiers even knew what hit them.

Ben glanced up every now and then, watching Rudolph monitor their progress. "Keep to the thick trees," he said.

They kept running and evading until they burst through into the open area with the campfire, suddenly having to jump and dodge past multiple bodies.

Carl stumbled past the sprawled bodies. "Yow! Joe's ambush worked as well as the one we had set up out there."

As soon as they stepped into the open, the overhead shadow swooped at them, and all three hit the dirt, Doug rolling to his back to shoot straight up. As the dragon swerved to the side, a ball of flame burst out of the trees ahead.

Ben jumped to his feet. "Robb made it," he said. "Where are the others?"

Tom yelled out. "All are here now. You guys were the last."

"Out of my kill zone!" Joe bellowed. "More behind you."

Ben grabbed at Carl and ran for the gap between the two snipers, Doug right behind. The dragon continued to circle overhead. More fireballs flew up, and the dragon headed towards the far end of the open field and made a big show of landing.

Ben rushed between Tom and Joe, stopping when he passed them. "You see that?" He stared across the field. "Rudolph is on the ground."

Joe shot at the dragon flying past, then popped out of his bush. "Not on his dragon? Where? By himself?"

"Yeah, that dragon of his flew off without him," Ben said.

"Then we have him." Joe jumped up. "Come on, Tom!"

Ben yelled back to Doug and Carl, "You're in charge here." Then he yelled at everyone else. "We're going after Rudolph. Watch for more soldiers."

The group split up, making a wide gap for Rudolph's soldiers to run into, ready to engage them from both sides when they made it past the bushes and up the slope.

Ben ran to catch up with Joe and Tom, running across the field.

Tom frowned at the impending melee. "As long as they don't trample the marker. I know we're close, but it would be better if we knew exactly where the Door had opened before."

"Can't control that now," Joe said. "We have more pressing needs." He lifted his pistol and aimed at Rudolph. "More pressing even than getting home!"

Ben and Tom joined him, firing across the open field at Rudolph, but he must have been using his shield because nothing connected. As the threesome approached, they stopped firing…for a moment…but Rudolph was waiting for the opportunity.

He raised his staff and shook it at them, sending a blast across the field. The shockwave hit them, stopping Ben in his tracks. He stumbled backwards and fell to the ground. Tom went flying to the side, rolling in the dirt, but Joe bent forward, leaning into the explosion, pushing his shoulders into it, lurching onward, keeping on his feet, opening fire again.

Ben rolled to prone and fired a couple shots at Rudolph. That's when he noticed how far off Joe's aim was. He was hitting the ground well in front of Rudolph. He was amazed that in spite of his skill, Joe was unable to accurately aim in the face of the blasts.

Ben fired again, but he suddenly noticed something weird about the dust clouds Joe's shots were kicking up—they were being pushed by an invisible, round area in front of Rudolph. Joe didn't have a bad aim…he had figured out how to make the shield visible.

He kept an eye on that sharp edge, and when it abruptly shifted, letting the dust clouds drift past Rudolph, he yelled, "His shield is off. Hit him now."

Joe dropped to one knee, aimed carefully, then fired.

Rudolph spun as the round hit him, toppling him to the ground. He inched to his knees, then glared at Joe, holding his staff for support.

The dust billowed up against the invisible shield again, and Ben yelled, "Shield's back up. Hold your fire."

"Thanks," Joe yelled, then frowned as Rudolph stood up. "He's still going. I must have missed."

"You didn't miss," Ben said. "But it wasn't as good as before. His shoulder is bleeding."

"His shield must have deflected the shot," Joe said.

"Yeah, that's why you missed," Ben said, grinning.

"Not good enough, but it should slow him," Joe said. "Watch that staff. When he waves it, he's about to blast, but he needs to drop his shield before he blasts…for a second."

"So I figured…the dust."

"Yeah," Joe said. "I noticed that, too." He fired a couple more times. "Gotta keep him trapped behind that shield, so he can't hit us."

"He called it a two way shield, so he can't attack from behind it. Still, be careful, and think about ammo. Make every shot count."

Joe patted a pouch on his belt. "One more full clip, last resort."

Ben glanced back quickly and saw Tom, on his back, unmoving. "Can you keep Rudolph busy? Tom's down." He ran to Tom, trying to spot Annie through all the fighting. "I need to get him first aid."

"I can keep him occupied…as long as he keeps his distance, but if he gets too close, I risk a ricochet."

"Yeah, that and watch that staff."

"Be quick," Joe said as he popped off a couple more shots.

Ben ran into the middle of the fray, drawing his sword and slicing through any resistance. Coming out the other side, he stopped right where Tom and Joe had overlooked the kill zone. A circle of scouts, all facing out, was surrounding some action on the ground. He ran up to find Annie caring for someone. "Annie! We need you," he stressed, "out there."

She dismissed him without taking her eyes off her patient.

Robb was on the ground in the middle of the circle.

Annie finally glanced up and said, "They ganged up on him." She went back to her ministrations, talking over her shoulder. "They were all going after him."

"That makes sense. Those fireballs of his are good for a bunch at a time, but we need your ability, we need *you*," Ben insisted.

She leaned back. "Let me finish up here."

Ben hesitated, then said, "It's Tom."

Annie's head snapped up. "Tom? Where?" She stood up, stepping towards Ben. "Lead the way."

"Wait," Ben said. "How's Robb? Can you leave him now?"

She glanced back at Robb, evaluating him once more. "He's fine enough." She nodded to Trey and Eric. "You can move him now, but be gentle. Get him out of the battle and let him rest a minute or two," she frowned, "before he gets back to taking on the entire force." She pointed. "Find a safe spot back there, towards the river, past Joe's kill zone."

"It might be better to keep him closer. We don't want everyone to get too spread out." Ben said. "That spot in the trees by the creek might be good. Pretty easy to defend there."

"What? Where Tom wanted me to hide?" She snorted. "Yeah that's a good enough spot. Keep him hidden there as much as you can, Trey." She spun. "He's taken care of, so lead on."

As Ben headed back through all the skirmishes, Trey hefted Robb onto his shoulders. "I have him, Eric. Stay with Annie. She needs protecting."

"That's my job!" Eric said as he rushed to catch up, jumping through, dodging between, and generally trying to avoid all the clusters of fighting, though as he ran through clutching his sword loosely, he did manage to smack one of Rudolph's soldiers on the back of the head.

John smiled. "Thanks, Eric." Then he spun to face another soldier.

Eric shrugged and ran up to Annie, sitting next to Tom.

Ben was asking, "So, how is he?"

"I can't see anything specific wrong with him," she said as Tom moved slightly, moaning.

Eric stood over them. "At least he's not dead."

Annie frowned at Eric. "Not dead? What a thing to say."

Tom's eyes fluttered open, and he tried to sit up.

Annie put her hand on his chest. "Wait there. You were out for a moment."

Tom coughed. "Had the wind knocked out of me. That's all," he insisted. "I'm fine. Really I am."

"Sit tight anyway. At least for a moment. No need to rush things."

Joe yelled, "How is he?"

Ben saw Joe still trying to keep Rudolph at bay. "He's fine. How're you doing?"

"He's still advancing," Joe said. "Keeps moving between shots." He dropped an empty magazine as he grabbed for another. "Almost out."

"Annie, if you have things under control here," Ben said, "I need to go help Joe with Rudolph."

Eric jumped up excitedly. "Do you want me here with Annie? Or should I come help with Rudolph?"

Noticing how close Rudolph was, Ben said, "Better stay here in case Rudolph gets past us. If he does, get Annie and Tom back to safety, back with Robb. Trey will help." He glanced down at Tom. "I don't want anyone interfering with Annie." He glared in Rudolph's direction. "I think Joe and I can handle together, but we need to keep him out of the main fight. He does a lot of damage with that staff of his, and he doesn't seem to care if it's us or his own men he's hitting."

"If that's what you want," Eric said. "But I'll keep an ear out, so you can let me know when you need me."

Ben ran, dropped to the ground next to Joe, aimed, and fired. He could see a flash where he hit Rudolph's shield. "Still can't get him, can we?"

"Keep him hopping, and he won't be able to do any of that blasted blasting of his." Joe fired again, but his slide locked back. "Augh! I'm out. Any ammo left, Ben?"

"Not much. I was planning on a little hunting. Not a full-on war."

"Yeah, well, I figured that if some is good, more is better, so I brought extra, and it paid off, but I still could have used more." Joe spun to check his target. "He's moving again, to the side. See if you can cut him off."

Ben fired, trying to stop Rudolph's progress, but Rudolph maintained his pace, keeping an eye on Ben and Joe, but sidestepping, circling the edge of the field. "I can hit him head on, but he's going sideways. We need to flank him to keep him from getting past us."

Joe holstered his pistol, jumped to his feet, and vaulted Ben, running to cut off Rudolph, trying to block his movement and keep him isolated.

Ben shot once more, and his slide locked back as well—he was out of ammo, too. He crammed his pistol into his holster and climbed to his knees, seeing the dust shift. "He dropped his shield!" he yelled at Joe. "Hang on for a blast."

Rudolph was raising his staff when a shot rang out right over Ben's head, and Ben watched Rudolph convulse, losing his grip on his staff. Ben smiled, but only for a moment.

Rudolph fumbled for his staff finally getting a solid grip, then grimaced as he grabbed at his other shoulder, his shield popping back up.

Ben checked Joe's position, still running at Rudolph, then glanced behind. Eric stood there, pistol still levelled at Rudolph. "Good timing, Eric! Thanks." He jumped to his feet and joined Joe running across the open space, trying to get to Rudolph before he could send another blast at them. He sprinted, getting there as Joe dove to tackle Rudolph.

Joe bounced off the invisible shield, a full meter away from Rudolph.

Ben frowned. "His shield is bigger than when we were getting Melvin. Can't even get close now."

Rudolph paid no attention to Ben as he continued towards the fracas. "Once in the middle of the battle, I can drop everyone." He hefted his staff. "Then we'll see how well your army fights…lying on their backs."

"Not if I can help it," Joe said as he drew his sword.

Rudolph glanced at Joe sideways, then sneered. "Go ahead. Do your worst. This is a battle shield, not the personal one I usually use."

Joe settled into a combat stance, circled his sword high above his shoulders, then swung hard, right at Rudolph's head. When the sword hit the shield, it slowed but kept moving, leaving a trail of light, like chopping through invisible jello. When it was a mere hand's breadth from Rudolph's head, it came to complete stop.

Rudolph paused casually and slowly tipped his head back, scowling at the blade hovering barely above his eyebrows. He stopped and planted his staff on the ground, then with his free hand, he reached up and put a finger on the edge of Joe's sword, still frozen in the air. Rudolph glanced at Joe and leered.

Joe held his stance for a second or two, then, his face spasming in pain, he let go of the sword and fell back. The sword hung in the air for a second, then slowly tumbled to the ground, glowing white hot. The grass it landed on immediately burst into flame— even the dirt itself was burnt.

Rudolph glanced at the sword and laughed. "Ha! See what happens when metal contacts the shield?"

Joe cradled his burnt hand as Rudolph resumed his advance.

Ben circled to stand in front of Rudolph, staring him in the eyes, and held his arms out wide, trying to block his progress. He felt Rudolph's shield press up against his chest, then arms, then legs. Rudolph paused for a moment, staring back at Ben, then slowly shoved his way forward.

Ben planted his feet, trying to hold his position, but Rudolph kept driving onward. Ben's feet slid in the dirt, gouging a pair of wide furrows.

Continuing to struggle, Ben noticed that they had moved into the middle of the melee, now surrounded by other struggles. He scoured the crowd, trying to spot someone to help, but everyone was busy with their own fight.

Annie was still tending to Tom, though by now he was half sitting up, staring back.

Suddenly a shot rang out from right behind him, and Ben felt the shield quiver and shrink a bit. He snapped his head around to see Eric standing by himself in the middle of all the action, pistol held out in one hand, still aimed at Rudolph. "Not bad, Eric. It seemed to do something to his shield, but watch where you're aiming."

Eric shrugged. "It helped last time, so I figured I'd try again."

Ben grunted as he tried to slow Rudolph's progress. "Can you come help with—?"

A high-pitched whistle pierced through the noise of battle. Ben jumped. Rudolph paused. Eric stared. The closer battles slowed as the noise caught their attention, but the rest of the fighting kept going, unabated.

Ben spun, trying to locate the source of the sound, and even Rudolph stopped pushing. They both searched the area, and Ben finally noticed a large dot floating in the air…directly above Eric.

The dot grew, starting off as a white ball, as before, but this time no flames, instead white clouds slowly spun…appearing to be swallowed up inside the ball instead of spreading out. Ben felt as though he were watching water swirling down the drain of a tub, except that this drain was in the air, and the clouds were swirling *up* into it.

A voice in the crowd yelled, "It's the Door!"

Eric stood there, petrified, staring straight up at the hole.

Trey burst out of the masses and tackled Eric, pulling him away, so he wouldn't get sucked in along with the clouds. Trey's motion carried them away from one danger but headed them right towards another: Ben and Rudolph.

Ben glanced at Rudolph to see him gawking at the Door, slack jawed. He noticed that the nearby fights had stopped as the combatants were also riveted by the still growing Door, though the closest ones were quickly backing up more and more, giving the Door plenty of leeway as it grew.

"That's it?" Rudolph asked, his arms hanging limply at his sides. "That's the gateway?"

Tom shuffled up, supported by Annie. "Yes, that's it. We call it a Door."

The Door floated there in the air, slowly expanding. By the time it had grown to the size of a basketball, the whistling noise had stopped, and Ben was glad to see the dark hole.

It continued to swell, finally getting big enough to go through it.

Rudolph stepped towards it hesitantly, but Tom warned, "Wait! Let it settle. It's not safe to go through before it's stabilized."

"But you just step through?" Rudolph asked slowly. "That's all?"

"That's all," Tom said.

They all stood there a moment, and when it appeared to stop growing, Ben asked, "Is it ready?"

Tom watched the Door go through one last growth spurt, the edges bouncing out and back in, then it sank to the ground, the bottom part flattening out. "It's stable now. Can you see any of the techs inside?"

Ben stepped forward and stared into the darkness, a shaft of sunlight catching a white lab coat fluttering as one of the techies ran past. "I see movement," he said. "Yup. They're in there." He stepped back to join Tom, then frowned at the combatants across the field. "We need to stop the fighting. It's over. We're going home."

Tom spun around, considering all the fighting still going on. "How?"

Suddenly Rudolph jumped forward and grabbed Eric by the throat. He hauled him towards the Door. "If any of you get in my way, this peon suffers."

"Stop," Ben said, but Rudolph didn't even slow for a moment, Eric now choking. Ben yelled, "I said stop!"

Rudolph glanced up, one foot in the Door. "Why should I?"

Ben paused as he noticed a sudden quietness behind him, utter quiet. He slowly twisted around, to discover half the combatants across the battlefield standing still, not moving, petrified mid-stride, mid-swing, mid-shout. The farther off struggles were still in progress, but many of the close by ones had stopped dead in their tracks.

Rudolph followed Ben's gaze. "Impressive, but it won't do you any good." He tightened his grip on Eric, now turning decidedly blue, his eyes bulging in panic, his mouth opening and closing like a fish out of water.

Ben stared at the stopped fighters, then paused as a thought came to him. He scrutinized the nearest opponents, finally spotting Melvin, off to one side, eyes glazed as he stood transfixed like all the rest. Keeping his eyes on Rudolph, Ben slowly backed away, heading for the power source.

"Giving up now, hmm?" Rudolph taunted. "Letting me go without trying to do anything?"

Ben's slow pace had carried him close enough to Melvin that he was able to reach out and grab his arm.

Melvin's eyes fluttered as they slowly refocused. "Huh? What's going on?" he asked.

"Come with me," was Ben's terse reply. Holding Melvin by the arm, he strode back. He spoke directly to Rudolph. "I said stop, and they did." He perused the battlefield. "Now you will, too."

Rudolph leaned his head back and laughed as Ben gripped Melvin's arm harder and shouted, "Stop!"

Melvin gasped, then froze as an abrupt silence echoed across the field. Faint shouts from distant melees faded away, the wildlife stopped, birds landed, crickets went silent, even the leaves on the trees became motionless. Rudolph had stiffened mid laugh, his head still tipped back, mouth open in a twisted grin.

Ben's voice carried across the silent field, "We shall no longer fight."

Rudolph's arms drooped to his sides. He stood there mesmerized.

Ben faced the battlefield and said, all but reverently, "Stand."

All the combatants, some already standing, some partially crouched, some in mid roll on the ground, unhurriedly stood straight up.

"Drop your weapons."

Weapons right and left clattered to the ground—in front and behind, all hands were empty.

Ben noticed Melvin breathing heavily. "How you doing?"

"Fair enough," Melvin said. "I can handle it. Keep going. You have them." His eyes slid across the scene.

Ben gazed at everyone. All the scouts, and *shmahseespe*, and soldiers near him—everyone was standing still, totally unarmed.

He lifted his hand off Melvin's shoulder and said, "Sit."

The people nearest him swiveled to look. A couple gently sat. One asked, "What's up, Ben?"

Ben put his hand back on Melvin's arm and again said, "Sit."

There was a sharp rustle as everyone across the field sank to the ground. Ben glanced at Rudolph, who was also now sitting. He checked the area…everyone was sitting, facing him—the entire fighting force on both sides were all quietly waiting for his next command, a class of children patiently anticipating instruction from their teacher.

Ben pulled his hand back from Melvin. "Did you see that?"

"Yeah," Melvin said. "They did everything you said. You gave an order, and they did it."

Ben checked on Eric. He was sitting next to Rudolph as if they were schoolyard pals. He called out, "Hey, Eric."

Eric blinked, his eyes slowly focusing on Ben, then his head pivoted to consider those nearby. Seeing Rudolph sitting right next to him, he jumped and scrambled on all fours, straight to Ben.

"So, how's your throat?" Ben asked.

Eric rubbed his neck and coughed. "Good enough." Slowly rising to his feet, he revolved again and again. "What's going on?"

"Ben did it," Melvin said. "He told them to stop, to sit, and they did."

Eric stared at Ben. "You did this? You told them to stop?" He looked across the battlefield. "And they did? You can control them, all of them?" he said with awe.

Ben shrugged. "Yeah, it appears I can."

"He can even control Rudolph," Melvin said in amazement.

Eric spun to stare at Rudolph, still sitting cross-legged, right on the edge of the Door, unmoving. Eric jumped behind Ben.

Ben gazed at their former adversary, now sitting motionless in the middle of the stillness. "See?"

Eric leaned up, holding Ben's shoulder and stared. "Tell him that these are not the droids he's looking for."

Ben stared at Eric. "What?"

"Tell him that these aren't the droids he's looking for, then make him repeat it."

"Eric, sometimes I wonder about you." He faced Rudolph. "Stand."

Rudolph stood cautiously, shaking his head as his eyes came back into focus. He reached for his staff lying nearby. Standing with it in hand, he stared at all the fighters sitting on the ground. "What have you done?" he shouted.

Ben yelled to him. "Stop."

"Stop? Stop! You dare to tell me to stop?" Rudolph raised his staff and shook it at Ben.

A shockwave hit Ben knocking him to the ground.

Melvin reached out to him, and Ben, panic stricken, grabbed at Melvin's hand, but he couldn't reach it—too far. Melvin stuck out his arm and grabbed Ben's fingers. Ben gripped tightly, then they moved closer to each other.

Still holding onto Melvin, Ben slowly rose to his knees, faced Rudolph, and said, "Drop that staff."

Rudolph's face contorted in anger as his hand opened, the staff bouncing off the helmet of one of his soldiers.

The soldier picked up the staff and smiled. "You dropped this," he said offering it to Rudolph.

Rudolph's arm refused to reach for it, and the soldier shrugged and set it on the ground, then waited for Ben.

"What have you done?" Rudolph repeated, his arm still out straight, his hand grasping at empty air.

"I stopped the battle. No one need fight. You are no longer a threat." Ben stood and reached to help Melvin to his feet, whispering, "Stick close for a while, will ya?"

"No problem," Melvin said, following Ben as he walked right up to Rudolph.

"You have no power," Ben said softly.

"I don't need my staff to crush a piddling like you." He scrunched up his face as he tried to strike at Ben, but nothing happened.

"I said, 'You have no power' and that's what I meant. You are powerless. You have no 'magic' or whatever to use on us."

Rudolph continued to struggle but to no avail.

Ben located Tom in the crowd, calling out, "Hey, Tom!"

Tom's head rotated to face Ben. "Yes?"

"On your feet! Snap out of it!"

Tom put his hands on the ground and started to stand, but froze halfway up, noticing the quiet. "Uh, what's going on?" He stared at all the combatants still sitting. "Did I miss something?"

"Yeah," Eric said, grinning. "Ben has the force. He's controlling everyone, even Rudolph."

"Whatever," Tom said, stepping towards the Door. "We need to get in there." He suddenly noticed Rudolph writhing unsuccessfully. "What's *his* problem?"

"No power," Eric said. "Ben told him he has no power, so now poof—he has no power."

"Ben told him?" Tom frowned. "What's going on?" He walked to Ben, staring at all the sitting troops.

"Later, Tom. When we're back home," Ben said. "Right now, can you round up the scouts? We need everyone through the Door." He pulled Melvin. "We're running out of time. I can hear the techies yelling."

Tom glanced at the Door, suddenly aware of all the shouting coming from the other side. "Oh! Gotcha." He jumped and dodged through the seated crowd, smacking each scout on the head. "Grab your gear and get through the Door."

The scouts dashed to the pile of backpacks, grabbed what they could, then ran for the cool darkness of the Door.

When he came to Annie though, he changed his technique. He squatted, put his hands on her shoulders, and gently brought her back out of the trance.

As the light came back into her eyes, she smiled at Tom, then snapped her head around to stare. "What's going on?"

He shrugged. "I'd explain, but I don't exactly know," he said to her. "But we need to get to the Door."

He helped her to her feet, and they joined the rest of the scouts running to escape.

Once all the scouts were roused and moving, Ben said, "I suppose I should let all those soldiers go, now that we're about to leave."

Tom laughed. "Yeah, better not leave them stuck sitting there."

Ben looked across the field and said, "Wake up." When hardly anyone moved, Ben shrugged. "It was worth a try." He put his hand on Melvin's shoulder and tried again. "Wake up."

There was a general stirring across the field, but when the soldiers stood, they instinctively grabbed their weapons, taking defensive positions.

Ben realized what could happen, so he commanded, "Stop. Stand still. You are all friends now." Despite the language barrier, Ben's command carried across the field.

The soldiers and *shmahseespe* little by little faced each other and stared. Slowly, they began chatting, the sound of casual conversation filling the air.

Ben was satisfied, but Rudolph asked, "Will that still be in effect when you leave? Or will you return to find a field of bones?"

"Good question," Tom said. "We'll find out, as you said, when we return."

Ben noticed Rudolph staring into the darkness of the Door. He could see that even though Rudolph had kidnapped Melvin, tried to kill them, and basically made war on them, he was now powerless, no longer a threat. He put his hand on Rudolph's arm. "Do you want to come back with us?"

Rudolph stared at Ben. "You'll let me?"

"It's all you wanted," Ben said.

Rudolph smiled slowly. "It's all I ever wanted from the first day here, and now it's right there, right in front of me."

Ben smiled. "You've been away too long. It's time you went home."

Rudolph slumped. "Home? What home? Everyone I know…I knew will be gone, gone or moved on. There is no home for me there."

Ben glanced at Tom. "Then we'll have to make a home *for* you. We'll help you adjust to the way things are now."

"You think I could make it?" Rudolph asked.

"Yes, it wouldn't be a problem at all." He put his hand on Rudolph's elbow and felt it quiver. He glanced at the scene one last time. "Let's get out of here." He pulled Rudolph, guiding him through the Door. They followed the other scouts into the cool darkness, leaving the other world behind.

Ben watched as the Door started closing. From the other side, bright light flooded into the room, and he could still see trees and grass, and farther off, the mountain range that had earlier attracted Trey's attention. "Someday we should go visit there," he said to no one in particular.

Tom pushed everyone to the side of the room to stand behind a small circular railing. "Wait here until they close it."

Ben pulled Rudolph along to join the rest. The techies bustled about, going from console to console, making notations on clipboards, flipping switches, and spinning dials. The Door slowly crept in on itself. Ben dropped his pack and leaned on the railing, watching all the activity. The techies were frantic as the Door became smaller and smaller. As it was closing, the last beam of light from the other side still lit up the room, and Ben marveled at how it made everything glow, but then the Door finally shrank to nothingness, leaving the room dark, except for dozens of lights blinking on all the various consoles. He squinted in the darkness until the ceiling lights in the room flickered on.

Ben quickly counted the scouts, glad that they had all made it back, mostly unscathed. He tried to talk to Tom, but there was too much noise, so he waited for the platform to finish spinning, sounding like a jet engine winding down.

When everything finally quieted enough to be heard, he leaned to Tom. "Well, the marketing folks certainly had it right. It was all they said it would be. No false advertising there." He grabbed his pack. "Can't fault them there, but you might want to put in a warning or two."

"Yeah," Tom said. "This trip has been unique in a variety of ways." He grinned at Rudolph. "We've never come back with more than we left with before." He tapped his fingers on the railing, frowning at the techies to hurry up and finish. "This part is tough, waiting for the shutdown."

"How long?" Ben asked.

"Not too long, but coming off the adrenaline rush always makes it seem longer, you know. As soon as they're ready, we'll gather in the briefing room."

"And I suppose you'll want the engineers to talk to Rudolph, too, right?" Ben asked.

"Yeah," Tom said. "The report this time is going to be interesting, and I can't wait to see the reactions of the engineers when they meet him."

The techies finally finished bringing all the equipment to a stop, and Tom led the group to the exit. They waited as the exit hissed, letting the air pressure equalize. Tom plugged his nose to clear his ears, then walked towards the silvered window. "Everyone sit. Shouldn't be long to let them know the situation." He paused as he went through the mysterious door and said, in an Austrian accent, "I'll be back."

Ben leaned to the group as they all sat. "So, I wonder what's behind that window. It's a one-way mirror, I'm certain."

"Obviously," Eric said, glancing up. "You can see the silhouettes of the people inside when the door opens and light reflects on them."

"Leave it to Eric to notice something like that," Ben said.

Tom came right back leading an engineer to the group. "We don't usually include the top staff in the debriefing, but this time we have more interesting things to share."

The engineer had on a short-sleeved white shirt, boring tie, and dark slacks, and his shirt pocket was full of different colored pens and pencils.

Eric stood up. "Hey, Uncle Eugene. How's it going?"

"Eric, you *have* to do something about that shirt. It's filthy," Eugene said. "And your sister…do something about her will you?"

"Liz? What's wrong with her?" Eric asked.

"We were trying to keep a lid on things about the trip here, but she's been blabbing all over town about not being able to go camping with her brother to a distant planet." He frowned. "We don't know how distant the planet is. She's making assumptions. That planet could be right here in the Orion arm."

Ben sat up. "She knows about this? And has been telling everyone?"

"Yes. I've been getting calls from all your parents about your safety," Eugene said. "All I could tell them was to wait until you returned." He smiled. "And now you have…all safe and sound." He looked across the group, pausing when he came to Carl and Rudolph. "What's this? You brought back natives?" He frowned at Tom. "I'd like to hear your reasoning for doing that."

Tom laughed and grabbed Carl's shoulder. "He's one of the scouts. He needed a change of clothes, and that's all they had to offer." He moved his attention to Rudolph. "Now this one is different. He's not a native either, but exactly what he is, I'm not certain."

Rudolph stood to look Eugene in the eyes. "Rudolph Valentino Ivanoff, at your service." He bowed slightly.

Eugene stared. "Where'd you come from?" He gasped. "We didn't leave any behind, did we?"

Tom stepped up to Rudolph. "He's been living there…for quite a while."

"Living there? Where? For *how* long? What have you been doing there?" Eugene sputtered out his questions. "Wait, how'd you get there?" He glanced back at the silvered window. "Has someone been running unauthorized experiments?"

"This may be more involved than that," Tom said. "Should we sit?"

"Yeah, sit," Eugene said absentmindedly. He pulled one of the chairs to face the others, then plopped. "So, tell me your story, Mr. Ivanoff."

"You may call me Rudolph." He paused. "I'm not certain how much I should tell, then again, it has been so long, it may all be public knowledge by now." He shrugged. "We, the group I was working with, were doing experiments with magnetism." He frowned. "Though I'm not certain it was all original research as several of the pieces of equipment we were given appeared to be labelled in a language I didn't recognize."

Eugene leaned forward with interest. "Sounds familiar," he said. "We *know* where Frank acquired the equipment *we've* been using." He glanced sideways at the scouts. "But we can't say." He winked at Eric.

"So, once we figured out how to open the gateway, we sent a small unit through to check it out, and it drew the interest of those in charge, so they decided to send out an entire team to do more a detailed exploration."

"How many did you send out in that first foray?"

"The military sent along a half-dozen soldiers to accompany the scientists and technicians. We had loaded all the equipment we'd need into the lorry and were ready to head out before they opened the gateway."

Eugene held up a hand. "Uh, wait. A lorry? That's a big truck isn't it?"

Rudolph frowned. "Yes, that's what it is. Why do you ask?"

"You didn't just *walk* through?"

"Well, some of us did. Those of us that walked went on ahead before the lorry moved out. We couldn't all fit in, with it being full of supplies."

"But," Eugene stuttered, "what kind of vehicle did you use?" he asked. "Nothing that uses electricity would work. Any kind of vehicle driven through from this side would stop as soon as it crossed the border of the Door." He paused. "Unless you somehow managed to have it going fast enough, but then it wouldn't coast far before it stopped. What if it became stuck right in the middle?"

"That's exactly what happened!" Rudolph shouted as he stood up. "The gateway lost power with the lorry half in, half out."

Eric winced at Rudolph's shouting.

"Trying to move *that* much mass through the Door would have caused a major drain on the power," Eric said. "Wouldn't it, Uncle Eugene?"

"Yes, Eric," Eugene said slowly. "We, Frank and I, spent many years trying to figure out how to avoid the power consumption caused by magnetic mass." He leaned back. "We never did. That's why we always check what's going through. We have to contain the magnetic fields."

"I remember the tech saying something like that," Ben said. "I didn't realize that it would cause a problem other than an extra drain on the power or something."

"Not just an *extra* drain, but a *substantial* drain," Eugene said. "We save up as much power as we can, but that's barely enough to keep the Door open for the short while we can. The more magnetic mass that goes through, the faster it drains the stored charge." He stared at Rudolph. "And if we would have tried bringing something as large as a vehicle through, it would have snapped the Door shut so fast…" He shuddered. "I can't imagine what a backlash in the electrical systems like that would do to the electrical grid."

"So you understand the situation," Rudolph said slowly.

Eugene spoke to the person next to him, Ben, and asked "Can you imagine the repercussion of an electrical wave going back through the power supply?"

Ben shrugged, wide eyed. "I don't understand how *any* of it works."

"We don't understand *all* of it." Eugene looked embarrassed. "But we do know how much power is needed to hold it open. That's why we wait so long between openings, charging up a bank of capacitors."

Eric spoke up, "I wanted to call them flux capacitors, but Uncle Eugene's partner, Frank, didn't get the joke."

Ben smiled. "Oh? Imagine that."

Eugene continued. "With the system we have now, we manage to open the Door once every ten days, after a long charge-up." He leaned closer to Rudolph. "We're not hooked up to an unlimited power supply."

"Well, we *thought* we were, but apparently that wasn't enough."

Eugene perked up. "You were? Hmm…We might want to spend more time discussing this with Frank. You may have answers to some of the remaining problems. How successful were you in controlling drift?"

"Drift?" Rudolph asked.

"The aim," Eugene said. "Reproducing the location on the other side."

"Aim? We didn't have any way to aim it. We would open the gateway and go through."

"No aim?" Eugene was astonished. "How did you do repeat excursions?"

"We didn't," Rudolph said. "When we first opened the gateway, we sent only one or two men through to see what we could, and when we opened it later, we expected that they would still be there waiting for us." He shrugged. "When we didn't see them, we assumed they had wandered away." He frowned. "We didn't understand why they'd do that." He paused. "It was quite a bit later when someone finally noticed that the landscape changed, that it was different each time."

"The drift. I understand," Eugene said.

"That's when we realized that it wasn't that the men weren't there, rather we weren't opening where the men *were*. Couldn't even tell if it was the same world. By the time we discovered that, there wasn't anything we could do for all the men we'd already sent through." He shrugged. "I would suppose that they are still there, somewhere." He paused. "They or their progeny."

"We had the same problem," Eugene said. "That is, we can't aim it as accurately as we'd like. It tends to open *near* where it had previously opened, but not always exactly the same place."

"So you didn't even know if the gateway would open right where you were heading?" Rudolph asked.

"We knew it would be close," Tom said. "Close to the marker. That's why we put it there, so we'd know where the Door dropped us off." He stopped. "It's always close…we weren't going to get stuck over there."

"With a standard ten-day trip, it's always fairly close to the same spot," Eugene said. "That's why we try to keep the trips as short as possible. Longer trips have more drift."

"Interesting," Rudolph said. "We never tried to track that aspect. I wonder what causes it."

"We're not certain if it's related to time or position…*our* position."

"Your position? But you're always here," Ben said. "Aren't you?"

Eugene smiled. "Ah, when I say *our* position, I'm referring to the position of the planets. We do know that wherever it connects to, it's not close to here, maybe not even in the Milky Way, so the location of even the most distant stars could be relevant."

"If you guys don't mind continuing your chat later," Tom said. "The scouts have something they'd like to share as well, and then we could let them get back to their own lives."

Eugene dragged his attention from Rudolph. "Oh, yes. Tom says that you have something to show me, something you learned while on the other side?"

Ben stood up. "The best example would be either Patrick or Robb."

"Good choice," Tom said.

"What did Patrick learn?" Eugene asked.

Ben called to Patrick, "Show him."

Patrick strode up and smiled. "This is going to be good," he said to Ben. "Which should I do first?"

"Do the fairy light," Tom suggested. "You can show him the pop thing later."

Patrick smiled as he held his hands up to his mouth and mumbled into them. Then he opened them ceremoniously. "Voilà!"

Nothing was there.

He frowned and tried again, this time speaking aloud.

Again, nothing.

"Well, I must say I'm impressed with your grasp of the native language," Eugene said. "We've had a couple of linguists on staff here that have been working on that for months now, and they can't speak it anywhere as smoothly as you, but I fail to see what the hands have to do with it."

"Wait, there's more," Tom said. "Give him a moment to concentrate." He put his hand on Patrick's shoulder. "Try again."

Patrick looked intently at the floor and spoke again, but nothing appeared.

"Try the pop," Tom suggested.

"I did," he replied. "But it didn't work either. Neither of them work."

"Hey, Robb!" Ben called. "Show him *your* trick."

Robb held up his hand and snapped his fingers.

Nothing happened.

He frowned and tried again.

Still nothing.

Eugene stared. "Not impressed so far," he said. "What was supposed to happen?"

"Fire," Tom said. "He can make fire."

Eugene leaned back and frowned. "Oh? He can, can he? Well, that sounds interesting enough. Let's see it."

"I'm trying, but it isn't working," Robb said.

"Melvin, come here," Ben said. "See if you can boost them."

Melvin trotted up and put a hand on each of their arms. "Try again."

Both tried—still nothing.

Eugene sighed. "Tom, what are you trying to pull?"

"It's not me." Tom backed up, his hands in the air. "Ben?"

"Something's wrong," Ben said. "Is everyone affected? Carl?"

"Never mind him," Tom said. "Annie, can you see colors?"

"Colors?" Eugene asked.

Annie gasped as she spun, checking everyone in the room. "In the excitement I hadn't noticed, but all the colors are gone."

"So everyone *is* affected?" Ben leaned back in his chair. "Welcome back to the normal world," he hesitated, "and *being* normal."

"Interesting," Tom said slowly. "What worked there, doesn't work here." He stared at Eugene. "The same as a flashlight…but reversed."

Eugene stood up straight. "Yes, electricity doesn't function the same on that side of the Door. We've known that for a while, but what is this other power?"

"We'd have to go back there to show you," Ben said.

"So it won't work here," Tom said considering the implications. "Just like electricity, but backwards," he repeated, slowly.

"That could be true," Eugene said. "Whatever you could do there must be connected to the basic differences between the two worlds. We've hypothesized a change in the laws of physics, based on disparities with the elementary particles, but have been unable to isolate exactly what has changed."

Rudolph gasped. "So that means I've lost my power, too?"

"I would assume so," Ben said. "Which means I can't even release you from the hold I put on you, for all the good it would do now anyway."

"But how can I live without my abilities?" Rudolph asked.

"You won't need any special abilities here," Ben said. "No one else has any, so we'll all be normal." Ben plopped back into his chair. "Normal and boring," he added.

Eric piped up, "Not so boring. There have been many changes since you left back in 1986, and I think you'll be amazed at them," he said to Rudolph.

"Changes?" Rudolph stared at Eric. "I can't even imagine the changes that have taken place out there." He moaned. "For me, everything has changed. All that I had before is gone. Even if any of my family is alive, they won't know me. I'm dead to them." He sagged, his face in his hands.

Ben put his hand on Rudolph's shoulder. "We'll help you adapt."

Rudolph's head snapped up. "Adapt? I can't even imagine what that would entail."

Eric tried to be helpful. "Wait until you get your first smart phone. You'll find the Internet interesting, too."

"No. I can't." Rudolph looked away from Eric and stared at Ben. "Even just hearing about all the changes…It's too much, just too much."

"You can't just hide from the whole world," Eugene said.

"Ten days. That's what you said, right? I can go back in ten days," Rudolph pleaded with Eugene.

"Yes, that's right. We can reopen the Door in about that long."

"Then I'll stay here with you for the next ten days and share what I know of the gateway." He begged Eugene. "That is, if you'll have me."

"I'm certain we can arrange that," Eugene said.

Rudolph stared towards the Door. "And I was able to accomplish all that with limited resources. What I could have done if I'd had more." He leaned back. "And you can arrange that, can't you?"

Ben thought about Eric and his bread. "Well, we *had* talked about starting trade routes to the other side," he waited for a response from Eugene, "so I don't see why we couldn't include any equipment you'd need in that, too."

Eugene paused a moment, then said, "Trade routes? Interesting. We hadn't considered that, but, yes, I think it's doable." He asked Tom, "Will we have the proper support for it?"

"I'm willing," Tom said. He waggled his head towards Annie, then at the scouts. "As long as I have enough *staff* to come along and assist me."

Eugene raised an eyebrow. "Oh? Hmm…Yes, considering what all of you have managed to achieve, I think we could allow open access to the Door for any of your friends." He put his hand on Eric's shoulder.

Rudolph smiled. "In that case, I'm willing to stay here and help, that is, until the next opening of the gateway. I have a life there, and it may not have been the best, but I did well…didn't I?"

"Yes, you did," Ben said. "We were impressed with what you'd managed to accomplish."

"Then it's settled," Rudolph said, smiling at Eugene. He put his hand on Ben's shoulder. "We may meet again…I wish you well."

"Yes, Rudolph, we may meet again," Ben said to the man, once his enemy. "This is an adventure I wouldn't want to do just once."

About the Author

Westley used to read to escape reality, but once he started transcribing the bedtime stories he told his children, he found a new way to ignore the trials and tribulations of the world.

Having been raised by two school teachers (his mother teaching English and his father music), his education took him far and wide. Initially completing a series of degrees in computers and electronics, he later returned to the same university where his mother had taught as he worked towards a teaching position himself.

On the way to his goal, he discovered that more than just his children wanted to hear the stories in his head, and so he entered into creative writing, joining with other writers in the area, piecing together various narratives with his children, thus Ex-Terra Expeditions was born, incorporating many experiences and desires from his own youth.

He currently resides in the Sierra foothills near Sacramento, California, with his wife, two dogs, and a cat.